The Lazarus Pit

The Lazarus Pit

by

James Patterson

authorHOUSE™

1663 LIBERTY DRIVE, SUITE 200
BLOOMINGTON, INDIANA 47403
(800) 839-8640
WWW.AUTHORHOUSE.COM

© *2005 James Patterson. All Rights Reserved.*

No part of this book may be reproduced, stored in a retrieval system, or transmitted by any means without the written permission of the author.

First published by AuthorHouse 02/01/05

ISBN: 1-4208-1679-9 (sc)

Library of Congress Control Number: 2004099401

Printed in the United States of America
Bloomington, Indiana

This book is printed on acid-free paper.

Previous books by James Patterson:
The Thirteen
Sphinxes

— Acknowledgements —

Preparing Jim's manuscript for publication involved the efforts, contributions, and skills of many persons. It is a testament to the strengths of the relationships he forged throughout his life that all were so willingly offered.

Special thanks to the friends who read and edited the manuscript, Shirley and Don Rank and Jo Anne and Norm Haddad. And very special thanks to Richard Theriault, who spent many hours on the final and major edit. Jim would be pleased with the results!

Very special thanks also to Scott Kelby, Jim Workman, and particularly Felix Nelson, for translating Jim's designs and images into electronic files; and to and everyone at KW Media Group, Jim's fond associates through his many years of writing on photography and technology.

We all hope we can work together and eventually publish *Belle Prairie*, an almost-completed fourth novel about Five's ancestors as they settle the Ohio Valley in the late 1700s.

—Betty Patterson

— Foreword —

Jim Patterson was a writer, journalist, graphic designer, traveler, and—perhaps above all—a photographer. His skill at creating beauty through his cameras was an inspiration to many. His knowledge of the photographic arts and of both film and digital equipment made him a source of advice and guidance to thousands through his columns in various publications.

Jim's life defined versatility, and nothing slowed him down. He had multiple careers, often several at once. His first, as an Army Counterintelligence agent, developed the powers of observation, alertness, and accuracy that made him a successful journalist and travel writer. His design skills blossomed in his graphic arts and design business, from which he eventually retired—only to decide it was time to write some novels. Not the sort of new venture the faint of heart would undertake late in life.

The thread that ran through everything was Jim's love of and skill in photography. He saw and captured marvelous images where others saw nothing special—and he lovingly worked with those images to create photographic art, not mere pictures. One of his long-standing desires was to photograph Monet's gardens at Giverny, France; and he fulfilled that desire as the last in a lifelong parade of accomplishments. Jim passed away in the midst of those glorious gardens—with his camera in his hand.

Shortly before leaving for France, Jim completed the manuscript of this novel, planning to prepare it for publication on his return. Finishing the job for him has been a labor of love by his family and friends, who all considered it a privilege.

— Richard Theriault

— Prologue —

I'm Thomsen Lowrey, V. That's 'Lo-ree,' and nearly everyone calls me Five. This is my third novel—I've discovered I really enjoy writing them. In the first one, I covered nearly three years of my undergraduate days at Ohio State University, fraternity hazing, and a sadistic fraternity brother who ended up a murderer.[1]

Acquaintances from those years became lifelong friends and shapers of events—like Culden Ellis and Dick West, Josefus "Benjo" Kostic, and Denzel "Bear" Duerhoff. Others, like my sometime college "flame" Darcy Robinette, surfaced from time to time as remembrances of times past and with varying effects upon the present.

My second book spanned only a year and a half: my post-graduation enlistment in the Army Counterintelligence Corps; my training at Baltimore's Ft. Holabird; and my first big case, which eventually took me to the south of France—with an ending more thrilling than I'd ever expected.[2]

---

[1] *The Thirteen*, by James Patterson: www.authorhouse.com
[2] *Sphinxes*, by James Patterson: www.authorhouse.com

I should probably account for the four years that followed, but instead of doing that here, I'll let an employment interview do the job later in this story. They were interesting years.

— 1 —

A Brush with the Past
Begins My Future

Ohio University's Chairman of Fine Arts was Doctor Gordon Logan. His secretary, Glenda, appeared in my tiny graduate student office one morning and beckoned with a finger. I followed her down the hall and into the Chairman's smoky office.

There, Gordon Logan sat with Richard Thomsen Ellis in his lap, blowing puffs of pipe smoke for the baby's enjoyment. Culden looked up from a visitor chair with a big grin.

"Well, it's been a long time as you can see from the size of your godson. Do I get a kiss?" Culden beamed at me.

"Culden, Culden! Why didn't you tell me you were coming?" I hugged her and ran my hand through her unruly hair. "You've cut your hair again."

"I had to," she answered. "Either cut it or let Jackson pull it out strand by strand."

"Jackson?"

"Oh, little Dicky Reb. I started calling him Jackson when he began walking. He'd strut around without a diaper and

1

make the cutest little drip paintings on my white rug," she laughed. "Thank God, he's over that now."

"Fi! Fi!" little Dicky Reb shouted at me from Logan's lap. "Gampa!" he said, grabbing for Logan's pipe.

"I've showed him your picture and taught him to say your name, sort of," Culden said. "And he recognizes Doctor Logan as a genuine grandpa."

"Five," Doctor Logan said, "I'm going to take this fine boy for an ice cream cone and let you two visit in private." With that, he hoisted the baby and left the office trailing a plume of Prince Albert.

Culden gave me another hug as I sat in the other visitor chair. "Why didn't you let me know you were coming? Are you in Zanesville with your folks?" I asked.

"Doctor Logan knew but I asked him not to say anything about my visit," she said mysteriously. "It's not exactly a social call. I'm working."

"Working? At what?"

"Oh Five, it's so exciting. I've been hired as Chairman of the Visual Arts Department at Seneca University."

"Seneca? You mean Seneca College. Up near the West Virginia panhandle?"

"Yep! It's been Seneca U. since 1952 and it's growing like Queen Anne's Lace. The Dean of Fine Arts hired me and gave me a clean palette to establish a Visual Arts curriculum. That's why I'm here.

"I had one person in mind but decided it would be wise to talk to Doctor Logan. He and the other faculty are convinced that my candidate would be a great teacher in the right academic program. Doctor Logan recommended that I talk to you and here I am. Five, I want to hire you as an assistant professor at Seneca."

"My God, Culden. If it pays anywhere near Western Hills High School and I don't have to monitor study hall, I'm yours!" I responded with a big hug.

"Well," she said with a grin. "I have a first year budget for an assistant professor, two instructors, and a secretary. And of course, you'll have to come up for an interview."

I nodded enthusiastically.

"Are you still driving that goofy French pup tent car?" she asked. "I'm not sure it'll make it over the mountains."

"It did once," I replied. "I'll try it again.

— 2 —

Country Roads

Driving to Seneca, West Virginia, meant 175 miles east on U.S. Route 50, then twenty miles south to Petersburg and finally five miles west to the tiny valley town. My Citroën 2CV, purchased used in France, huffed and puffed with stops for fresh water about every forty miles. But I made it.

I called Culden from Petersburg and she said she'd meet me at the Seneca town limits. "You can't miss me," she said, "I'm driving a Dodge woodie. And when I see the pup tent coming, I'll blink my lights."

Driving into a steep valley, I rounded a curve and found Seneca perched on and between two mountainsides. Culden's headlights blinked and I pulled the 2CV up beside her bright red station wagon with fake wood trim.

"Welcome to the 'holler,'" she said as we embraced.

"Fi! Fi! Hi," cried little Dicky Reb from the window of the Dodge. I gave him a big hug as well.

"Follow me and we'll go to my place first," Culden directed. "You can freshen up. I know that's a bitch of a drive. You ought to try it with the monster here."

"Me no monster," the monster protested.

• • •

Entering Seneca, I saw the college campus perched on a steep hill to my right and other newer buildings at the bottom of the hill. To the left of the highway, a variety of academic buildings and frame, brick, and stone houses rose up a lesser grade and it was into this part of town that Culden turned.

Her two-bedroom house was bright and cheerful, a mini-Victorian with a broad porch and stained glass door.

"We'll check you in at the Smoke Hole Lodge later," she told me. "Naturally, you could stay here but the gossips in this town would have us screwin' our brains out by morning."

Culden glanced through the open front door, "And here comes gossip central right now." A chubby young woman with a baby about the size of Dicky Reb in tow came up the front walk. "Hey Culden! Am I late?" she called.

"Hi, Maddy. No, we just got here." To me, "Five, this is Madeline Bristo and this guy is Hez. Maddy, this is Five Lowrey, the man I told you about."

"Pleased to meet you, Five," she smiled broadly.

"Maddy and Hez take care of Dicky Reb for me," Culden told me. "The Bristos are pioneers in the Seneca Valley. Anything you want to know, ask Maddy." Then to Maddy, "I'm going to give Five a tour of the campus, then we'll come back here and pick up his car to check into the Smoke Hole Lodge." She paused for a second, "Oh, and can you watch him tonight until about nine? We'll be going to dinner at the Faculty Club with Livinda Ferris."

• • •

Culden wheeled her big Dodge woodie with one hand and waved at various landmarks with the other. "Seneca Institute was founded by the Congregationalists in 1852. In

1902, it became Seneca College and had about 900 students until World War II. That building on the top of the hill is Old Main, of course, and the two buildings flanking it are part of the original campus. The one on the left is our building and the studios have north light."

As we drove past Old Main, I could see a very steep set of steps climbing about 200 feet to the building. A serpentine walkway took a gentler path and crossed the steps three times.

"In the old days, all students lived down here and had to climb the steps. The bike path is a recent addition," Culden said. She turned left onto a major drive and we started up the steep hill. "Vets coming back from World War II swelled the enrollment to about 1300 and students were living anywhere… no shit, even in chicken coops."

Behind Old Main larger, more modern buildings stretched down a gentle slope to a moderate-sized stadium. Culden continued on the drive along the hillside.

"The big house is President Skinner's and the next two are housing for the Provost and Dean of Students. Seneca still adheres to the dean system for everything academic."

When we hit a turnaround circle, Culden pulled over and we got out. Below us were spread six big buildings and an obvious Greek row. "Dormitories and cafeterias. And we've got five sororities and four fraternities," she paused, "including your old ACE buddies. You're not still involved with them are you?"

I assured her my fraternity days were behind me.

"Then you can see downtown Seneca, such as it is. What we can't see is the Underhill Campus with giant buildings for Arts and Sciences and Engineering."

I detected a slight tone of disapproval in her voice and asked, "How did it get to be so big, so fast? It's an amazing campus."

Culden shrugged, "In 1952, the Congregational Church dissolved its relationship with the college. Busby Ferris, a millionaire who made his fortune in mine construction, then invented the adjustable roof bolt, was invited onto the Board of Trustees. He brought along with him Oliver Monckton, another millionaire who got rich by inventing the mechanical wall machine, pretty much eliminating blasting from mines."

"Together they contributed... are you ready for this?... ten million dollars to the college and another twenty million to the endowment fund. Their only proviso was the establishment of Colleges of Arts and Sciences and Engineering to make Seneca a full-fledged university," she smiled. "And this is the result."

We drove around the big green plaza Culden called 'Eden Fields' and parked in a faculty spot by the Fine Arts wing. "A perk of membership in the club," she grinned. "A faculty parking sticker."

The two-story Fine Arts Building was constructed of brick and stone and matched the Georgian architecture of Old Main. It was attached by a covered walkway to the larger building. Later, I would find that the matching Liberal Arts wing was on the other side of Old Main.

"The basement will eventually house three-dimensional studies... sculpture and ceramics. Eventually, the ground floor will have an arts library and small supply store, plus some classrooms and studios," Culden pointed out. We climbed a set of stairs and arrived at a long hall. "Offices on the left, five classrooms on the right, and two teaching studios at the end, facing north," she said with pride.

We walked the length of the hall and Culden threw open one of the doors. Spectacular light washed the huge room and a new skylight with an adjustable shutter covered half the ceiling.

Directly below was the Underhill Science Campus with its huge buildings and beyond, the magnificent tiers of mountains stretching west. Looking at that scene, I decided to take whatever Seneca offered or even work for free.

— 3 —

Meeting Livinda Ferris

Class bells rang and the campus took on life as students poured from buildings after their last class of the day. Standing at the window of her office, Culden watched as streams of students rode their bikes down the steep hillside.

"Having that bike path is another of the perks of this job," she laughed. "The kids look so grim pumping up the hill in the mornings... and so joyful going home. I haven't been here in the snow but I would guess everyone has to climb those steps."

I noticed the students had a slightly different appearance than their counterparts at Ohio U. These kids wore more jeans and sweatshirts. There didn't seem to be as many people in hippie costumes. I mentioned this to Culden.

"This *is* West Virginia, Five. Lots of these kids come from rural homes and they're just not as *with it* as they were at Hood and OU. And I'm just seeing the beginning of headbands, granny glasses and the counterculture thing. I'm sure it'll get here sooner or later. And we may get a different, more creative type of student when we open the Fine Arts Department next fall."

We smoked and kicked back in her office while she continued on the history of Seneca U. Ferris and Monckton's gifts paid off. Enrollment kept climbing. But their idea of a complete university was the Underhill Campus, new dorms and more competitive athletic teams.

"So we got Piper Stadium, which holds 30,000, and a gym with seating for 7,000 fans. The Stadium is named for Lester Piper, a World War II hero.

"The best thing to happen was in '58 when Livinda Ferris earned her Ph.D. at Pitt and came back to campus. She's Busby's daughter and they voted her onto the board, also hired her as a full professor. In a year, she was promoted to provost."

"Pretty fast career," I commented.

"Rich, connected, and... verrry smart," Culden responded. "I think you'll like her. Anyway, Livinda kicked her old man's ass in some trustee meetings and got the OK for expanded Humanities, Liberal Arts and, last year, Fine Arts programs. And... of course... I think she's great 'cause she hired me."

• • •

Back at Culden's house, I picked up my car and followed her downtown to the Smoke Hole Lodge. It was a nice motel, named for the huge cavern located just outside of town. I took a quick nap, showered, and put on a tie and tweed jacket. I was in the lobby when I saw Culden's red wagon pull up.

"I would've had you meet me in the bar but all you can get is 3.2 beer," she said. "The Faculty Club and a couple of veterans' clubs are the only places in town where you can get a real drink."

Once more we parked in Culden's reserved faculty slot. With envy I eyed another empty faculty space with no name on its sign. We walked across one end of Eden Fields beneath huge oak and maple trees and entered the only modern building on the Hilltop Campus.

The Seneca Student Center occupied the ground floor of the building. The second floor featured a huge gallery, devoid of art except for some black-and-white prints from last football season. An outdoor deck covered the roof of the Student Center below.

Another stairway took us to the Faculty Club, perched on the third floor with broad windows overlooking the mountains and peering into the stadium below. Culden spotted Livinda and waved as we made our way through an elegant candlelit dining room.

She was certainly not what I'd expected in a provost. Instead of a middle-aged academic in tweeds and sensible shoes, this provost had honey-colored hair, and a trim figure under a sweater set and knee-length skirt. In short, she was close to my age and gorgeous.

"Hello, I'm Livinda Ferris," the provost announced, extending her hand. "I'm so glad we could get together." She was almost as tall as I, and her smile sparkled. I was smitten.

"Thomsen Lowrey V, Doctor Ferris," I stuttered.

"Oh, wow!" Culden exclaimed. "His name is Five and forget all that Thomsen and Fifth stuff, Livinda."

"Welcome to Seneca, Five," Livinda smiled. "Now, let's all have a drink."

The martinis were chilled and delicious. Actually I had ordered a vodka Gibson but was disappointed when the student waitress arrived with a nasty-tasting Gimlet. "Darling," Livinda instructed her, "a vodka Gibson is just a martini made with vodka instead of gin, and onions instead of olives. Please go inform the bartender."

To us, "God, I'm the provost *and* social guardian of so many of these kids. Our waitress is bound for graduate school in the classics yet she can't remember drink orders. The bartender will also be in grad school somewhere in engineering but the only drink he'd ever had before he got here came from a quart screwtop jar."

Salads arrived. Two quarters of iceberg lettuce covered with orange dressing. But small loaves of bread were hot out of the oven and a big dish of butter patties accompanied them.

"Five, I took the liberty of showing Liv your portfolio," Culden said.

"It's an excellent assemblage of work," Livinda commented. "I spent every weekend in Pittsburgh at the Mellon Gallery and some of your work could easily hang there." She paused. "Haven't I seen you in Pittsburgh?"

"Well, I'm flattered," I sputtered. "And I have spent a few weeks in Pittsburgh, mostly at Carnegie Tech. But a lot of the work I sent to Culden was grad school experimentation... just to show I could do it... and teach it."

"Well, I certainly hope you and the dean can work something out," she told Culden.

"And I know where I've seen you." She grinned. "You were at a meeting of Students Against Warfare. I was there with a date that never got off the ground."

I smiled, didn't acknowledge her comment, and let the identification pass.

— 4 —

My Return to Academia

Dean of Fine Arts Jorge Cruz-Garcia was configured like a thin question mark. Bushy black eyebrows shaded deep-set black eyes. He sported a marvelous Mexican *bandito* moustache, beneath which jutted a very long cheroot. His smoky office walls were covered with vivid paintings which Culden had told me were the product of his days in Mexico. They were faintly reminiscent of the work of Diego Rivera. I was pleased to see several explicit nudes among them.

Fat, bald, and bespectacled in a gray sweater pitted with burn holes, Wayman Minteer, the Dean of Academic Affairs, seemed poured into his chair in Cruz-Garcia's office. Culden Ellis made the third party of the interview team. Since it was a Saturday morning, Culden was also dressed casually in a bulky fisherman's sweater and jeans.

I was the only one wearing a coat and tie, which was as it should be, for it was my employment interview.

"I've talked with Gordon Logan at Ohio University. His opinion of you is as high as that of Professor Ellis here," Cruz-Garcia said. "But I have trouble dealing with the gap between your baccalaureate degree and the present. Tell us a little about how you spent those years."

"As Professor Ellis has probably told you," I started, "I spent nearly four years in the U.S. Army... in the Counterintelligence Corps... as a special agent. My training was at Fort Holabird in Baltimore, and that's where I became reacquainted with Professor Ellis while she was teaching at Hood."

Minteer interrupted my narrative. "We understand that you are represented by a gallery in Paris. How did that come about?"

"Well, I can't go into classified details but I was assigned to a special unit in Baltimore. My first case took me to France, where I helped recover a kidnapped CIC agent. His daughter, Gigi Marchant, started a gallery in Paris and that's where I'm represented."

I continued, "During my three-year enlistment—CIC agents are all enlisted college graduates—I was sent on TDY—er, temporary duty in military lingo—to dozens of college campuses and a number of overseas postings."

Cruz-Garcia asked, "Did you serve in Vietnam?"

"Not exactly serve, sir," I responded. "My TDY in Vietnam was supposed to be about a week but I was hospitalized after two days and evacuated from Saigon to Tripler Army Hospital in Hawaii. That's as near to Vietnam as I care to get ever again."

Minteer added, "You mentioned a three-year enlistment. But your *curriculum vitae* states you served 44 months in the Army. Can you explain that?"

"Yes, Dean Minteer. The Cuban Missile Crisis occurred just before I was due to be discharged. The Navy and Air Force extended their enlistments. My circumstances were such that I could've been transferred to a combat unit. So

I voluntarily reenlisted for a year to stay with the CIC. I've also served on active reserve and am currently on inactive reserve."

"What else can you tell us about your military service?" Cruz-Garcia continued. "What are the chances of your getting called back?"

"Well... without revealing classified information, I can tell you I was assigned to about twenty college and university campuses in the past two years."

"Doing what?" Minteer interjected.

"I can't go into details but I was investigating student radical organizations."

Both deans gave me a long stare and then nodded to each other.

"What is your opinion of these organizations?" Minteer went on.

"Since President Kennedy's death," I said, "the young people of our nation have undergone a transformation from our generation of carefree students in the Fifties. They believe they can honestly make changes for the good of society, and most of them want to solve the problems that we face. Things such as voting rights, freedom of speech, women's rights, even *in loco parentis* on campus, as I'm sure you're aware."

Culden remained quiet but nodded in agreement.

"At the same time," I continued, "many are disillusioned with our government and the constant escalation of combat in Vietnam. I believe the protests against the war will continue. Just because the military doesn't approve of protest doesn't mean the military is right.

"I've found many of the so-called 'radical organizations' are honest in their beliefs and goals. But they're also excellent vehicles for hiding the activities of real *political radicals* with more sinister goals. Thanks to the hippie movement, the college kids and the professional agitators look alike. And... it's very hard to identify them until something is blown up or some campus office is trashed."

"I tend to agree with you, Mr. Lowrey," Cruz-Garcia said. "We've seen a beginning of change in our own student body. I feel we must be vigilant."

"Who is this Richard Ellis that you give as a personal reference?" Cruz-Garcia asked.

"He's a long-term friend, a fraternity brother actually, and a photographer for *Look* magazine," I answered.

"He's also the father of my baby," Culden inserted. "And Mr. Lowrey is the godfather."

Culden and Dicky "Reb" West had conceived Richard Thomsen Ellis two years before at a hippie love-in in the Allegheny Mountains. Both deans looked a little uncomfortable. Surely the university hadn't hired Culden without knowledge of her child?

"What fraternity?" Minteer asked.

"Alpha Chi Epsilon, sir. ACE." I replied.

"We have a chapter here," Minteer stated. "If you were hired, do you think you would participate in their activities?"

This was a sharp-edged question. I knew my answer immediately, but pretended to ponder the question for a few seconds.

"Actually, Dean Minteer, I rather doubt it," I said. "My fraternity experience was a mixed bag of joy and anguish. I'm afraid my Greek days are behind me."

Culden again interjected, "Dean Minteer, Mr. Lowrey was responsible for apprehending a fraternity brother who was both a murderer and a rapist. He was responsible for saving my life in the situation."

"Well, a shame, perhaps," Minteer grunted. "The ACE house here could use a little guidance."

I sat quietly while the two deans opened and pored through my portfolio of photos. Culden stood over their shoulders and occasionally made a quiet comment.

"God," Cruz-Garcia gasped, "who are these two creatures?" He turned the book so I could see my painting of Gigi and Anna asleep in their Paris bed.

"I don't usually discuss my models," I began, "but in this case, they are the two owners of *Galeries Stansbury-Marchant*. My gallery in Paris."

"Are they? Are they...?" Dean Minteer stuttered.

"Lesbians?" Culden asked. "I hardly think that matters."

"All right, Mr. Lowrey," Dean Cruz-Garcia said. "I'm quite satisfied with your skills. Tell us a little about your graduate work."

"Yes," Minteer chimed in, "your undergraduate GPA was hardly a sterling example of academic achievement. How did you get accepted to Ohio University?"

Culden beat me to the punch. "To begin with, I wrote a strong letter of endorsement. I've seen the work Mr. Lowrey has accomplished as an undergraduate and since. As his former studio partner, I've never had doubts about his talents."

"Doctor Logan was not only my mentor," I said, "but also a close personal friend. Almost like family. Once I was able to convince him of my desire to teach, and thanks to the recommendations I received, he recommended my admission with some reservation."

"With all that talent, what was your problem as an undergraduate?" Dean Cruz-Garcia asked.

"Personal problems," I answered. "Fraternity life. Abandoned romances. The repetition of college life. I just coasted my last two years. I'm sure you see it here at Seneca among some students. Joining the Army just seemed like a good idea. And it was a good experience to help me mature," I continued, hopeful that this would suffice.

"And why do you want to teach here at Seneca University?" Dean Minteer asked.

"Frankly, gentlemen, my other teaching offers were from high schools with depressingly low-pay, low-interest jobs— including one where I would also drive a school bus. Art doesn't seem to have a very high priority in Ohio secondary education. I'm afraid I didn't have a lot of enthusiasm for my future. Until Culden Ellis came back into my life."

• • •

The interview went on for more than an hour, covering everything from my graduate work, to my representation in a Paris gallery, to a quest for details of my Army career, which I tap-danced around. Of particular interest to the two deans were my experiences on college campuses and my opinions of the 'counterculture movement,' as they put it.

After a lot more questions and discussion, I was asked to leave the room. As I left them, all three were lighting cigarettes. In the hall, I did the same. Dean Jorge Cruz-Garcia's office was in the Humanities building next to Fine Arts and I strolled its hallway, thinking it would be a perfect setting for student paintings. Three Pall Malls later, Culden opened the door and joined me in the hall. Her expression was serious.

"Well Five, you certainly did it by including the Paris nudes," she said in a low voice.

"You mean I screwed the moose?"

"Not at all," she grinned. "They loved your work and those two horny old toads can't wait to hire the guy who painted those French tarts. Then we called the Provost and she cinched the deal. Come into this lounge."

We settled into a small lounge. I felt sort of like I had on rush night at the ACE house.

"Here's the deal. If you want, we can go back in and negotiate but here's what I'm authorized to offer you." Culden paused, then pulled a small note pad from her jeans. "Assistant professorship. Full title. It'll be up to you and me to work out your teaching load. No tenure guarantee. Cruz-Garcia will speak to you about that. Two months off in the summer and of course, holidays. And…" Culden halted as if there were something she couldn't remember, "… sixteen thousand, five hundred a year. And… a reserved faculty parking place." Her grin triggered one of my own.

"Oh, yes, and a three-thousand annual expense budget for materials, travel, and the like." Another pause. "Do you want to negotiate?"

"Nah," I responded cavalierly, "I want to go to work."

• • •

Jorge Cruz-Garcia, Wayman Minteer, and Culden stood in the dean's office beaming at me. I beamed back. The door opened and President Frank Skinner joined us with a pair of sweating champagne bottles..

Cruz-Garcia shook my hand, as did the others in turn. "Congratulations Professor Lowrey," he said. "I believe you're the kind of teacher we want here at Seneca University. As Culden mentioned, we can't establish a tenure track because we can't yet offer graduate degrees."

The provost took over, "But I have told Doctor Cruz-Garcia that I think a five-year track based upon your artistic production, and evaluation of your teaching skills, is reasonable for you to pursue a Ph.D. from a reputable institution… I'm partial to Pitt but there's also West Virginia, even UVA isn't too far away."

Minteer burst in, "Seneca will pay your tuition and expenses."

Once more I grinned at the four of them. *Me, Five Lowrey with his 2.7 GPA, chasing after a sponsored Ph.D.?* "There's just one thing. It'll take awhile for me to get used to this Professor title and very few people call me by my given name. My friends call me Five."

— 5 —

From the Smoke Hole
to the Forest

Culden had her feet up on her desk and poured me a refill from a bottle of champagne. "You know what really blew them away?" she asked then, without waiting for my answer, "when they asked about your military experience."

"I'm afraid I couldn't tell them very much. It's all classified."

"That's just it," she chortled. "They were drooling to know more. And I'm the one that knows more. Boffing that pretty Peggy. And maybe that blonde WAC. And Gigi. And I suspect, that Anna French girl too!" Her laughter echoed through the office. "Five, Cruz-Garcia and Minteer are two of the horniest toads in the swamp. You're going to be just great here at Seneca."

• • •

That afternoon, we stopped by Seneca's Bristo Realty, Seneca's only real estate office where Daniel Bristo, Maddy's brother, held the desk. I looked through an album of available rental houses and at several that were for sale.

Danny made some notes and the three of us piled into his Cadillac. None of the houses in town excited me, especially the rentals.

At a little cottage that might've been converted from a chicken coop, Culden whispered, "Ask him about houses for sale. You wouldn't believe what I paid for mine, and you'll certainly be able to afford it."

"Do you have to live in town, Five?" Danny asked. "Do you want to walk to work?"

Thinking of the Old Main hill and its steps, I responded, "Lord no. I don't want to live, say in Petersburg—but in town? Not necessarily."

"And would you like a place to paint at home? A studio?" he continued.

Culden and I looked at each other. "Do you have something in mind?" I asked.

He nodded. "Let's go see."

We rode past the Underhill Campus and across a little river for about three miles. Danny then turned left onto a small paved road that wound up a narrow valley. After a mile, the paving stopped at a small creek.

"Gerwig Run," he said, nodding at the ten-foot-wide stream. "She rarely gets out of her banks but... well, you'll see." With that, he drove the Cadillac into the stream and across the invisible ford. The road on the other side turned to gravel and dirt and wound through a dense thicket before emerging in a clearing. There, on the hillside was an authentic West Virginia mountain cabin. A pitched wood-shingle roof, covered rough-hewn siding with a broad front porch overlooking the creek and its small cascade. The house wasn't painted but had the natural brown-gray of weathered raw wood.

"The place has been empty for about seven months," Danny said. "But it was well-built and has been looked after. It originally belonged to a man named Sibley who was an artist of a sort."

We walked up the wooden steps to the porch. All seemed solid. The front wall held a door and two tall windows. Danny worked the key and the door opened without a squeak. On the right was a large dining area that led back to the kitchen. To the left was a living area by a stone fireplace. We followed him through a door beneath a set of steps leading to a second level.

"And indoor plumbing. The original place had an outhouse but the last people who lived here put in a septic tank about 200 yards down the hill and away from the creek. Fresh water comes from a spring house about a quarter mile up the mountain. It's been tested yearly. The property's got five acres along the creek, three on this side."

Up the stairs, a pair of large dormer windows lit the bedroom from the rear and two smaller dormers looked over the front. A doorway was set into the side wall.

"Here's the part I like," Danny said. "Mr. Sibley was a woodcarver and he built this little building he called a studio." He opened the door and then held his arm across the opening. "This is the only part that's not in good shape."

What had been a small footbridge leading across a little ravine to a second building was smashed by a fallen tree. Anyone walking through the door would have tumbled fifteen feet. Danny closed the door and we trooped back down the stairs.

"I'll bet we can get up there by going through the woods," Culden broke her envious silence. "But I just know I'm going to *hate* what I see."

The building perched on a large rock jutting out toward the creek. I glanced up at the sky. "Faces north," I muttered. Culden growled. We climbed up the short side of the remaining footbridge and Danny unlocked the door.

Musty and cobwebbed, the interior sported an old-fashioned potbelly stove and a huge window looking over the creek. I looked at Danny. "How much?"

"Well, the estate wants nine thousand to rent but they'd like to get rid of it. That's 750 a month. But I'll bet you can buy it for less. I would offer six thousand and relieve them of the worries of renting."

Back at Culden's. "I hate you, Five Lowrey. *Really* hate you," she grinned wryly at me.

"Culden, it was for rent! You wanted to buy a place for you and the baby."

"But I paid nearly as much for this little house *in town* and it doesn't have a studio," she moaned. "Ah Five, you know I'm just kidding." She paused and rolled her eyes toward the ceiling. "Perhaps I'll offer fifteen thousand Monday morning. You'd better not give me as a loan reference."

• • •

On Saturday night, we drove into Petersburg and had a nice dinner of chicken and dumplings. Richard Thomsen was enamored of dumplings, both for eating and playing. Then we finished our wild night by seeing *The Sound of Music* and munching hot buttered popcorn in double paper bags.

Sunday, we rolled the top back on the *deux cheveaux* and drove down the valley to Smoke Hole Caverns. "Little Dicky loves this place," Culden said as we paid the admission. In the cave, artfully lighted rooms showed marvelous collections of stalactites and stalagmites. The baby oohed and gurgled as we went from room to room. "This is the only commercial cave in the area," she continued, "but there are hundreds of what they call *wild caves.* Caving or spelunking is one of the big activities on campus. There's even a grotto, or chapter, of the National Speliology Society."

We emerged into the daylight and Culden drove on down the valley. Then she turned onto a secondary road and we drove into an ever narrowing, steep valley. "This is what I call a *holler road.* The locals call these valleys 'hollers' and someone usually lives at the end of each one."

She honked and waved at some kids playing in the yard of a cabin much like the one I was buying. A swinging footbridge crossed *their* creek. We continued on the road and began to climb a grade with switchbacks.

In my lap, Little Dicky laughed aloud as the road continued upward and plunged into a thick forest. Branches rattled against the side of the car. Suddenly, Culden hit the brakes. "You might want to close your eyes," she laughed. "This is the tricky part." She steered the woodie into a narrow gap between two steep rocks. "I don't know who built this road," she said as she judged the distance on each side of the wagon, "but it's one of the few that jump over to the other valley."

"Moonshiners?" I questioned.

"Could be, but whoever, they did *just enough* to get through."

We got through the gap without scraping the paint. The road now pointed downward on a steep long grade through a tunnel of trees. Gravel and rocks banged against the underside of the car as Culden eased us down the grade.

After a few curves, we hit a paved road in another holler. I wasn't prepared for my first sight of Seneca Rocks, sheer pinnacles of limestone rising nearly a thousand feet above the North Fork River.

"Oh, hey, this is magnificent. Look at that one that's leaning."

"Yeah," she responded, "they're all pretty phallic but I know that skinny one is called The Gendarme. The Rocks are appealing to more climbers every year and they give the peaks names. That's another of the activities at Seneca U., a climbing club."

"Who owns the Rocks?" I asked. "Do they charge to climb them?"

"Private owners right now, but there's talk of the Feds, the Forest Service, buying them."

My thoughts were of Gigi Marchant and how much she would enjoy finding a way up one of these pinnacles.

• • •

We spent the rest of the afternoon eating our peanut butter and jelly sandwiches, splashing in the shallow creeks that poured into the North Fork, and hiking wooded trails through the hillsides. We returned to Seneca by way of Highway 33, the same U.S. route that runs through Athens. "I'd like to take 33 back to Athens sometime," I commented.

"God, I came over that way. It's a winding bitch of a road," Culden exclaimed.

"Bit, bitch," Little Dicky chortled. Culden and I exchanged glances.

Driving across a ridge of Alleghany Mountain, we got our first glimpse of Seneca with the late afternoon sun glinting off the windows of Old Main and downtown already creeping into the shadow of the mountain. Culden left the highway and drove through downtown.

"We'll leave the baby at Maddy's," she announced, "then come back for the Saturday night special at the Linger Longer."

"Skettios! Ghettios!" the baby chanted.

"Guess what the Saturday night special is at Maddy's?"

— 6 —

Seneca Saturday Night Special

The Linger Longer seemed to be Seneca's number one dining place but we managed to find a booth in the rear. A round middle-aged waitress greeted Culden by name and gave me a visual once-over.

"Hey, Delores," Culden returned. "This is our newest faculty member, Five Lowrey. What's the special tonight?"

"Same as every other Saturday night. Ground steak, mushroom gravy, salad, coffee, and dessert."

"That's what I'm having," Culden laughed. "And you too, Five, if you know what's good for you."

"Y'all want a drink before dinner?" Delores asked.

"Yep," I said. "Two martinis on the rocks."

Delores broke up. "Got it. You want Iron City or Rolling Rock martinis?"

As we sipped our beers, a familiar-looking man walked through the Linger Longer scanning the booths. "Here comes Danny Bristo," I said, "but he looks a little different."

Culden turned and looked. "That's a Bristo all right, but it's Bubby, Danny and Maddy's brother."

28

Bubby came right to our booth. "Hi, Miss Culden. Hope I'm not botherin' you."

"Not at all, Bubby. This is Five Lowrey and I'm sure you know he's going to be our newest faculty member."

Bubby shrugged under his plaid shirt. "Yes'm. Both Maddy and Danny called me."

Culden explained to me. "Bubby's Seneca's most talented man. He's a carpenter and contractor and can do just about anything."

"Danny said you're going to buy the old Sibley Shack," Bubby said to me. "That little bridge has got to be fixed and there are some other things need to be done. And this winter, you'll need the road plowed."

I stared, dumbfounded. *The old Sibley Shack?* Bubby continued, "Lucky for you, we're neighbors. I live next holler up on Dunfy Run. I won't bother y'all any more but I'm free tomorrow after church if you want to give me a call."

He shook hands with each of us and departed as quickly as he'd come.

Over our iceberg lettuce wedges with orange-colored dressing—the Linger Longer added a tomato slice—I asked, "Gosh, how many Bristos are there?"

"Oh, dozens, I'm sure," she answered. "But Danny, Bubby, Maddy, and Glendora, she's the town beauty operator, are all brothers and sisters. If you want something done, give one of 'em a call and a Bristo relative will be on your doorstep *toot sweet.*"

Our dinners were wonderful. Huge chopped steaks, medium rare and smothered in rich mushroom-onion gravy. Mashed potatoes. Green beans. A side of applesauce. White bread and butter.

I was mopping up the plate with a slice of bread when Delores appeared with coffee. "Dessert tonight's either ice cream sundae, apple pie, or strawberry shortcake." I settled for pie and Culden ordered the shortcake.

"Other than the salad, this was a terrific dinner. Who writes the salad recipes in this town?" I asked.

"That's Livinda's biggest gripe right now," Culden answered. "She's working on the Faculty Club chef to come up with something better than iceberg lettuce, but... this *is* West Virginia."

Delores returned, refilled our coffees and tore the check off her pad. Culden made a grab for it but I snatched it first, then went into shock. "Culden, this can't be right. $4.30 for two dinners?"

Her smile was huge. "Don't forget the tip, Five. I guess you can afford dinner tonight. So what do you think of Seneca so far? Can you afford to live here? Don't forget, this *is* West Virginia!"

A nearly full moon was high in the sky when we left the Linger Longer. "Let's drive out and take a look at your house by moonlight," Culden suggested.

Culden missed the turnoff the first time. "You'll need a sign or some good directions," she muttered. When we got to the curve that led down to the ford, she paused. "Looks like a gravel road keeps going straight," she observed. "Want to try it?"

"Sure!"

The gravel road was little used and paralleled the creek opposite my house. It climbed a slight grade and then the brushy sides gave way to a wide clearing. We got out and walked to the bushes at the edge of the clearing.

"There's the studio, just over there," I pointed. "But what's this?" I pulled a bush back, revealing a large timber frame holding some cables.

"It's a footbridge, Five," Culden exclaimed, "an old swinging footbridge." She gave the structure a push and it didn't wobble. "We'll have to ask Bubby about it tomorrow."

We cleared some small bushes and sat on a flat rock. The cascade below made a cheerful noise and we stared quietly at the cabin and studio on the far bank. I lit a pair of Pall Malls and the smoke drifted silver in the moonlight.

"If the creek does get high, I could park on this side and walk over the bridge," I observed.

"If this is part of your land, you sure could." Culden squeezed my arm. "I'm so glad I could hire you, Five. We're going to have a great time and make a terrific faculty." She put her arm around my shoulder and pulled me to her. "I only wish Dicky Reb were here but since he's not..." and Culden kissed me on the cheek.

— 7 —

Day of Rest at Gerwig Run

I slept late on Sunday morning but was delighted to discover the Smoke Hole Lodge served breakfast until noon. A copy of the *Charleston Gazette* told me nothing important had happened in the world while I was gone.

Cleaned up and ready to go, I drove to Culden's. She was spooning something nasty-looking into Richard Thomsen's mouth and he wasn't really buying it. As he flung up both arms, the food went flying and the baby chortled, "Fi, Fi. Hi Daddy."

"No, no, Dumbo. It's Five but he's not your daddy." She grinned. "He's your godfather."

"Fi, Fi. Gaw-fa," my godson said.

• • •

We took the 2CV with the top rolled back, much to the delight of the kid. "Gaw-fa, gaw-fa," he chanted.

"I called Bubby early this morning. He said he'd meet us about one o'clock," Culden said. "The Bristos are all staunch church-goers. Pentecostal Word of the Truth. We'll have to go sometime," she laughed.

I slowed down to try to spot the turnoff. "Look! I could put a couple of reflectors on the trunk of that tree there," I pointed to a large tree just beyond the road. "I don't want a sign or anything but a couple of reflectors would be enough for directions to make sense."

The cabin looked brighter this morning, perhaps because it would soon be mine. Below the ford, a shallow pool stretched for maybe twenty yards. I parked the Citroën and we walked back down to the creek. Culden peeled off Little Dicky's clothes and let him wade into the pool, which barely came to his shins.

"My god, a swimming pool and everything," she exclaimed. The baby squealed when he grabbed a crawdad. "Even freshwater lobster."

"Don't mock," I returned. "They eat them with butter and garlic in France."

We walked around the outside of the cabin. At the rear, it sat on a foundation of rock, carved away from the hillside to accommodate a back door. As the hill sloped away, stone foundation pillars supported the building toward the front. The front porch was about seven feet above the ground with wide steps leading down.

Engine noises grew louder announcing Bubby's arrival. His rusty GMC pickup hit the ford and threw up a huge wave. The radiator steamed beneath the hood where the cold creek water had hit it.

"Hey, y'all," Bubby yelled as he climbed from the cab. "I'm a little late but I didn't want to come in my church clothes." I said it was OK. Bubby wore bib overalls over a gray T-shirt.

But Culden chimed in. "'Fraid you might still have a rattler in one of your pockets?"

"Now Miss Culden, I know you're funnin' me but it ain't nice to poke at other folks beliefs." He grinned, "and your invitation to come to church stands anytime."

We walked around the cabin again, then to the far side where the big tree had crushed the bridge to the studio. Its leaves were brown and just a few remained on the branches.

"Pin oak," Bubby observed. "Gonna be mighty fine firewood. I'll cut it up and split it for you, Mr. Five, on shares. Two cords for you, one and a half for me." Culden nodded yes imperceptibly.

"You've got a deal Bubby," I responded. He put out his big snake-handling paw and we shook.

Bubby climbed under the tree and looked up at the bridge. "She only knocked out one set of supports, which shouldn'a been in the creek anyway. And some boards on the walkway." He poked at the remaining upright supports with a long branch. "They're sturdy. I'll draw up an arch for the center span and we won't need to rebuild that support."

Bubby produced a small notebook and made detailed notes with a pencil stub, licking its point from time to time. He poked the exterior siding with his stick and pushed on the window frames. As the afternoon wore on, he dropped straps and skinned out of the T-shirt.

"The floorboards on the bridge are in pretty good shape," he observed, "but I think we should replace 'em all."

We made our way to the studio. I discovered a back door I hadn't seen before but it dropped about four feet without steps. "New steps there," Bubby muttered. Finally, I climbed down and walked up a path by the creek's edge to discover the second support for the swinging bridge.

"Yowee!" Bubby exclaimed. "I haven't hunted coon up here for three, four years but I remember that bridge. Mr.

Sibley built it to get across when the creek was high." He shoved on the pier, then walked the cable back to where it was anchored around a pair of sturdy trees. "Looks in pretty good shape, the cable does."

"I wonder—what happened to the bridge?" Culden asked aloud. "Where are the boards?"

"Don't know," Bubby grunted as he jumped and grabbed the support cable and then hand-over-handed himself out over the creek. Toward the middle, he could put his feet on the cable that had held the bridge deck. "She seems strong, though," he wheezed, pausing in the center. "Some new tie-bolts and cables, new deck and steps on each end, she'll be good as new." Pause. "If you want to do her, Mr. Five?"

With the baby sleeping in the 2CV, the three of us sat on the bed of Bubby's pickup truck as he itemized his To Do list. He would study an item for a few minutes, then mutter and barely move his lips.

Culden and I exchanged glances and eyebrow raises.

"All told, with materials and hardware and all, I can do the cabin, footbridge, and studio for no more than 800 dollars." I gasped. "And I'll put a shed roof on the back and widen the parking area for that little car if you're plannin' to keep her. It'll be snowing pretty hard this winter. That'll be another 150 bucks.

"We'll save the floorboards from the studio bridge and any other good lumber for when you're ready to fix the footbridge. That'll be expensive… about 250 dollars I would guess."

"Bubby," I exclaimed, "that's crazy! I couldn't get all that done for three thousand in Ohio."

"Yeah, but this ain't Ohio. It's honest labor, honest price here in West-By-God… and… you're goin' shares with me on the firewood and… you'll be wantin' me to plow fer ya this winter. Hit's fair, Mr. Five." He spat in his hand and extended it. I did the same and we shook.

"Good deal, Bubby," I said. Culden didn't spit but placed her hand on top of ours. "But one more thing. I'm Five, so quit callin' me Mister."

That night, I pulled out my checkbook and sketchpad and doodled the financial possibilities of buying a house.

— 8 —

Becoming a Hillbilly

Culden joined me for breakfast at the Smoke Hole and as we were finishing, Danny Bristo appeared with my contract in hand.

"Here she is, Five," he smiled. "I only had to contact the estate's one power of attorney and she *loved* the idea of selling the place. I drove up to Elkins yesterday afternoon to get her to sign." Indeed, the contract offered six thousand dollars and was accepted and signed by Lureline Sibley.

"What's the next step?" I asked.

"Well, I took the liberty of calling Champ Norris last night. He's the president of Seneca Bank and Trust and we've got an appointment with him at 9:30." He glanced at his wristwatch. "Guess I'll have a cup of coffee since we've got about twenty minutes."

• • •

Champ Norris was gray all over. Curly gray hair. A curly gray moustache. A tweedy suit, too heavy for spring, only a shade darker than his hair. Danny made introductions and told Champ about the offer on the Sibley cabin.

"Mr. Lowrey's got to get back to Ohio tomorrow at the latest, so we'd like to establish some financials and set up a closing date," Danny explained.

"So, you wish to apply for a loan, Mr. Lowrey?" Norris' tone was unctuous and smarmy. I took an instant dislike to him. I nodded to Danny. "Can I have a minute with Mr. Bristo?" We went outside and conferred.

Back in Norris' office, I stated, "Actually, what I wish to do is open an account and put a down payment in escrow on this contract. I can do that with a check from my account in the Bank of Athens or I can write the down payment from my new account here."

Norris' eyebrows popped up and he swallowed visibly.

"I've decided I'll pay cash for the property," I said calmly, "unless you can convince me that it would be in my best interest to take a mortgage."

Norris could not. So I wrote a check for four thousand dollars to cover the down payment, and opened an account in Norris' bank for another two thousand.

"God, Five," Danny exclaimed, "ten or twelve percent is a customary down payment. Cash?"

"I can see right now I offered you too much money." Friendly sarcasm rang through Culden's statement.

• • •

Back at the Smoke Hole, Danny made notes. "We'll set the closing for a week from Friday," he said. "That'll give you time to graduate and get packed. With this kind of down payment, I'm sure I can get the estate to OK Bubby's going to work before the closing.

"That'll also give me time to get a good title search," he added. I looked puzzled. "Just verify that no one else has a claim on the property. If the Feds are going to be buying land in the forest, you'll want a clear and strong title."

Just after lunch, I steered my *deux chevaux* back down the valley and set out for Athens on Route 33.

— 9 —

Pomp and Circumstance

Mom couldn't quit grinning and getting up to pat me… on the head… on the shoulders. "Five, I can't believe it. A job and a new house all in one weekend? Unbelievable!"

I think she could see me living out my life in a rental apartment with used furniture.

"Well, it's not exactly a house… kind of. Here are some sketches I made," I said apologetically. "It's gonna take some work."

"What color is it painted?" she asked.

"Ahh… it's not exactly… er, painted. The shingles are oak. And the siding's wood called heart of pine. I guess the door and window frames were painted but I can't remember what color."

"Well, we'll just have to get to work on it. I'm glad I have a lot of vacation. The Captain and I were planning on two weeks at Virginia Beach at the end of June. Now we'll just make it West Virginia."

"But Mom, I've got a man who's already doing a lot of the work," I protested.

"And we'll rent a truck to move your furniture up there," she rambled on.

• • •

The week flew by in Athens. I presented my thesis rationale for the painting *11/23/63* and it was accepted by Doctor Logan and Trish in an afternoon's read. I was ready to graduate.

Sissie Eileen (my sister kept wanting us to use 'Eileen' instead of 'Sissie' as we'd called her all her life, but the switch wasn't easy) arrived from Oxford, Ohio, on Friday afternoon. Mom and the Captain pulled up a half hour later. We had cocktails at the Logans', then went to the Tavern for one last student pizza. Everyone asked about Culden and the baby. I passed around my sketches of the Gerwig Run cabin.

"A real studio, Five?" Trish Trevayne asked. "And they'll encourage you to paint privately?" She seemed impressed.

"Five, are you sure you don't want to get a mortgage on the property?" Mom asked again. "It would make you seem more respectable in the community."

"I think you should paint the house yellow," Sissie—ah—Eileen chimed in.

— § —

One last smoke before the procession begins under the elms. A few stragglers are hurrying to find their seats as the marshals are forming up the undergrads. Finally, the strains of Elgar's *Pomp and Circumstance* drift across the lawn and I go to join my marching partner. I'm the only one of the Master's candidates to wear the brown hood and tassel of the College of Fine Arts. *Brown? Burnt Umber? God!*

From the far side of the lawn comes the beginning of the Academic Procession, led by the Mace Bearer, preceding the faculty in their variety of colorful robes and gowns. As the last faculty member passes, we graduate candidates fall into line and are shown to our chairs by marshals. Finally, 900 Bachelor candidates march onto the lawn.

The crowd is loud and raucous as each candidate walks across the stage to receive his degree. Finally, I'm at the steps to the platform and hand my card to the reader.

"Thomsen Lowrey the Fifth," she announces, "Master of Fine Arts."

Doctor Logan rises and shakes my hand, then leads me to President Alden who also shakes my hand and mutters congratulations.

And it is done.

— 10 —

To the Place I Belong

Hairpin curves and hills, tiny towns with colorful place names: Cox's Mills, Burnt House, Alum Bridge, Job, Onego. As I steer my little French car along Route 33, I find myself wondering if someday a song will be written about these quaint and narrow roads.

The towns are tiny and many seem pathetically empty of life and activity. I study the architecture of swinging footbridges, for they're numerous whenever the road parallels a creek. Even an hour away from Seneca, I'm behind the Route 50 driving time by a couple of hours.

As I head into the state, I notice that about three out of five cars coming at me wear Ohio license plates. I'd heard talk of employment in West Virginia being so scarce that many of the state's workers were fleeing to Akron and the tire factories.

Finally, I turn onto 55 and head up the valley beside North Fork Mountain. Once again, Seneca presents itself and I feel I'm home. To the place I belong.

— § —

I drove straight up to the Hilltop campus and parked in the as-yet-unmarked faculty slot beside Culden's red wagon. The rest of the campus was quiet, with graduation over and no summer session. The door to the faculty office anteroom was open and I entered.

A cute young woman with a Shirley Temple mop of coal-black curls and a too-tight knit top sat behind the secretary's desk. "Hi," she chirped. "What can I do for you?"

"I'm Five Lowrey," I responded. Her smile was huge.

"Professor Lowrey! I'm Cyndy Byrd, the new secretary, and this is my first day."

"Mine too. Is Professor Ellis in?"

"Sure is. I'll let her know you're here. She was hoping you'd get here." Cindy pushed several buttons on her phone set, then shrugged and walked to Culden's office. Her butt wiggled alluringly in a too-tight pair of jeans.

Culden burst out of her office. "Five, you made it. Great! You didn't check in at the Smoke Hole, did you?" I shook my head no.

"Dan was here this morning. You can close this afternoon if you're still paying cash. The title's clear as gin and the place is practically yours. Come on in."

I went into the office and Culden pulled the door closed. "What do you think of our new secretary?"

"Well... she's ah... well packaged," I started. "Where did she come from?"

"She's a good kid," Culden answered. "Couple of years of college. Married to an artist. Knows the jargon and needs the work."

"A starving artist?"

"Well, sort of. He's a potter and they're living in a yurt out in the forest. Built himself a little kiln and is throwing pots from natural clay."

44

"I think Cyndy will lend just the right touch to our new department."

Culden laughed. "Fuckin' A."

I changed the subject. "If I close this afternoon, can I sleep at the cabin tonight?"

"It's your house, why not? Are you still paying cash?"

I nodded. "Culden, I want you to keep this between us, but I can afford it. I've got back Army pay and savings from my gallery sales… nearly eleven thousand dollars. But I really don't want it spread around that you hired a rich guy." I grinned, "They'll want me to join the board and contribute to the endowment fund."

"Gotcha. So, should I call Danny?"

• • •

The closing was uneventful. Champ Norris reported that my deposit had cleared and I was now a certified account holder at Seneca Bank and Trust. I gave him a check for another three thousand dollars for deposit. Danny produced my four thousand down payment check and an itemized list for the final payment. With tax stamps, fees, and a small percentage for Danny, I closed with a check for two thousand, four hundred. Danny handed me a set of keys and a big envelope.

Culden told Cyndy where we'd be and then followed me as I drove to my new home. We forded the creek and drove through the thicket on a newly widened lane. The clearing revealed Bubby's pickup and a hydraulic log splitter. We got out and walked slowly up to the house. "I've got a name for your estate, Five," Culden informed me. "Since it's five acres, I thought *Five's Five* might be appropriate."

I looked up at the gray-brown cabin and wondered if it were imposing enough to have a name. *Why not?* "I like it. *Five's Five* it is." I gave Culden a squeeze.

The front steps showed signs of repair, two new floorboards contrasting with the weathered older ones. A brand-new swing hung from chains at one end of the porch. "My housewarming present," Culden said.

I tried to unlock the front door, but it swung open. Bubby stood in the kitchen, hanging the last of a new set of cabinets. "Your housewarming present," Culden announced. "Bubby put a jar of shine on that old shelf over the sink and the whole damn thing fell down. Ruined a perfectly good quart of whisky."

"Hey, Mr. Five, welcome home." Bubby shouted. "I'd hoped to have her finished but Miss Culden keeps adding stuff to my list. Come see everything."

From the back door, I inspected the new small porch platform that gave onto a wider area. "I cleaned the rock back about four feet. Isn't anything but sandstone so it only took a couple of hours." Bubby pointed up. "And you've got yourself a little place to park. I just extended the shed roof over to the rocks and put in a gutter."

We followed him up the stairs. The bedroom windows were newly caulked and several new floorboards were obvious. Bubby opened the side door and swung his arm out dramatically.

The footbridge spanned the gully with a graceful center span arch of several lengths of timber. The railing and floorboards gleamed whitely in their new raw lumber finish.

"Bubby, it's beautiful!" I exclaimed. "How did you get so much done in such a short time?"

Bubby displayed his slow grin. "Well, I got some cousins and I kinda bribed 'em. Wilfred and Hezekiah will both do a happy day's work for a quart jar."

"Where did the bed come from?" Culden asked. I hadn't even noticed a bed but there stood a wonderful double bed with bulbous turned headboard and foot.

"Mr. Sibley was a genius with a lathe. When he died the executor, Mandy Sibley, told me to store the bed in the barn and if the place ever sold, it was part of the property. She didn't want renters using it, though."

On closer inspection the woodworking of the bed was terrific but the mattress looked a bit lumpy.

"That's her original mattress," Bubby said, "feather ticking on a rope spring." He shoved down onto the mattress and his fist virtually vanished. "You might want to get a new one for her."

I unpacked my car and Culden drove back to town to fill a small grocery list for me. Bubby pulled out his notebook, licked his pencil, and totted up the woodcutting. "That was one good tree, Mr. Five. I figure we'll finish with ten cords. A little over six for you. That sound good?"

"Fine Bubby. How long will six cords last me?"

"Depends on how cold it gets. 'Course, you also got the natural gas." My puzzlement was obvious.

"Your land has two wells on it," he explained. "One of 'em pumps all the time and you're entitled to a share. I turned on the valve a couple of days ago so the hot water tank could heat up."

Will wonders never cease?

"You owe me thirteen dollars," Culden announced as we unloaded grocery bags from her car. As I put staples in the new cabinets, I discovered a quart Mason jar. "Oh my, that's a housewarming present from the other side of the Bristo clan. We'll have a taste after dinner."

Dinner turned out to be peanut butter and jelly sandwiches since I didn't own a single pot or pan. We ate on the front steps and admired the babble of the cascade.

Later, Culden came back with a jelly glass full of the slightly amber liquid. "We'll have to share, as this seems to be your only glass. You've got to do some serious shopping, buddy."

We settled into the porch swing and listened to the faint squeak of chain against eyelet. "You know, Culden, it's supposed to be bad luck if a porch swing doesn't squeak. Where did you get this one?"

"You'll have to visit Moyer Run… it's a holler about four runs south and it's full of craftsmen. A man named Dreyfus Harman makes swings and porch furniture all by hand. You're going to need at least four rockers for this big porch."

I took a sip of the 'shine, surprised when it didn't burn my throat. "This is pretty good stuff. Does Bubby make it?"

"No. My guess is it's from Denton Bristo, Bubby's cousin. I'm told he used to run a still on this mountain but God knows where he works now."

Culden snuggled against me as a cool breeze blew down the hollow. "I can't get over how nice everyone's been to me," I told her.

"Oh, you've met the good ones. There's a whole clan of *mean* Bristos and your friend Banker Norris is a hypocrite of the first order," she mused. "And God knows what the Underhill faculty is all about. It's almost like working at two institutions."

"How did you come to get hired?"

"I met Livvy Ferris at a symposium in Pittsburgh and she told me about the new College of Fine Arts and what she wanted to make of it." Culden ran her finger down my cheek. "By the way, don't call her Livvy 'til she tells you to. And watch out for her. I think she already has her eye on you."

• • •

Lightning bugs danced above the cascade and in the woods on the creek's far bank. Culden and I had finished the third jelly glass of *Old Bristo* and were feeling no pain.

"You think you can drive home OK, Culden?"

"Do I have to? Maddy's keeping Little Dicky and I... we... don't have anything important to do in the morning."

She was lying in my lap with her feet on the arm of the porch swing. She pulled my head down and kissed me, her always-active tongue pushing my teeth apart. I steadied us on the swing's edge then my hand wandered to her chest.

"Did you ever wear a brassiere, Culden?"

"My mom bought me one when I was twelve."

The waning moon cast faint light through the bedroom window. I came out of the bathroom and gingerly lowered myself onto the bed. The feather mattress enveloped me. Culden had used the downstairs bathroom and came up the steps quietly.

"Where are you, Five?" she slurred.

"I'm here. Here in the bed."

"I can't see you," she giggled as she pulled her shirt over her head. Tossing her hair, she stretched and then hooked her thumbs into her jeans, pushing them down slowly.

"I can see you," I gasped. "And you look better than you ever did."

She plopped into the bed and we both laughed as the rope springs made mouse noises and the wave of feather ticking rolled over us. Culden hooked her finger in the waistband of my underwear and slowly slid it under my hips. Then she touched my erection.

"God, I've wanted to do this for the longest time," she whispered, nuzzling her erect nipples into my chest. "Only…" pause, "I do wish you were Dicky Reb."

— § —

A blade of light from the east window cuts across my eyelids, turning the waking world pink. From the vicinity of my armpit a muffled voice says, "You're gonna need curtains." I look down, to see Culden's face displaying a shy grin. "We didn't *do* anything last night," she giggles.

"I remember! I shriveled up."

"Oh Five, that was an awful thing for me to say. I'm so sorry."

"It's OK Culden. It came from the heart, I know."

She wiggles a little and I can feel her taut nipples brush against my body. "But we're gonna do something now. Aren't we?"

"I've got to pee," I respond. "And we'll think about it."

I have to laugh returning from the bathroom. The feather tick mattress is a long groove and all I can see of Culden is her breasts. She peers out. "Looks like you've thought about it, all right." I ease over her but she shakes her head. "No. Me on top. I think you'd smother me." She rolls over and I slip into the mattress.

Culden pulls a leg over my hip and smoothly fits her body over mine and me into her. The familiar warmth and texture send chills down my spine. I begin to move.

"Nooo. No. Let me do the work." She starts a slow undulation and little gasps come out of her mouth. Quickly, she increases the intensity of her work and her gasps become louder grunts. "Huh, huh, huh." The grunts get louder and faster.

Culden raises up on her arms, breasts swaying above my head and raining drops of sweat.

"Huh, huh, HUH, HUH." She throws back her head and opens her mouth, "Aaaahhhhieeeaaa!" There's a sudden popping noise and our bodies jerk violently. Culden screams. I come. She collapses on my chest.

We lie there in a pool of sweat, gasping for breath. "My God, Five. That was fantastic! What did you do?"

"Well Culden. I think we just broke the string bed," I whimper.

"Ah, Five, I've wanted to do that since you first shared a studio with me. But you know something?" Culden says later. Simultaneously we say, "We can't do this again."

"I'm sure your staying here last night is all over town," I said.

"No. I doubt it. I promised Maddy that she'd never see Richard Thomsen again if she said a word. And Bubby is one of the most secretive individuals you'll find in West Virginia"

"Well, I'll give it the ol' college try. But it's going to be difficult."

"No it won't, Five. We'll find you a nice girl."

— 11 —

Communicating with the Outside World

I puttered around Five's Five the rest of the morning, unpacking and putting my meager belongings away. Indeed, the rope springs of the bed were frayed and broken. So I drove east to Petersburg to order a telephone and look for a mattress store. The phone was no problem as lines were already in from the previous tenants.

And the man at the mattress store told me it was my lucky day as their delivery truck was going to Seneca that very afternoon. After a hot dog and milkshake, I drove back to Seneca and to the Hilltop campus. Much to my surprise, the faculty parking placard read *Prof. Lowrey*.

"Morning, Professor Lowrey," Cyndy Byrd chirped. "Like your sign?" I nodded yes. "Culden's in her office and told me to send you right in if you come." *Culden? And I'm still Professor Lowrey?*

I tapped on her door, then eased it open. Culden indicated for me to pull it shut. "Now, wipe that shiteatin' grin off your face," she whispered. "I've got a couple of things."

"I'll say you do!"

"Five, goddamit. I swear I'll kill you if you don't stop." I held up my hands in mock terror.

"First of all, your mom called this morning. They've borrowed a truck and they're driving up tomorrow to help fix up Five's Five. Will you have a new mattress by tomorrow?" She had an anxious look.

"It just so happens," I said smugly, "this afternoon."

"Then your sister Eileen will be here by tomorrow night. I told your mom there wasn't enough room to sleep three extra people, but they're bringing a tent and everything will be just fine," Culden smiled at me archly.

"Jeeeesus," I muttered. "I hate to be forced into buying a bunch of furniture and stuff I don't really want just to accommodate them."

"Eileen can stay with me. Let your folks sleep in the tent. It'll be an adventure for them."

"Does that Dreyfus Harman guy have rocking chairs already built?" I ask.

"Oh yeah, he's got a whole yard full of furniture. You want to go to Moyer's Run today? Better go by the bank and get some cash. Mr. Harman probably won't take a check."

On the way to Moyer's Run, Culden told me her hiring was complete. "You'll meet them tonight at my house. Just drinks and crackers. Jaylene Fiore is going to teach sculpture and ceramics. She's got an associate degree from Mellon Art Institute. She's Livvy's find and comes with a good-looking portfolio.

"Stuart Poletz is a different story. He graduated from Marshall with a B.A. and has the weirdest, most quirky portfolio of little construction things and collages. But he's a fantastic printmaker and I think he'll be a great all-around gadfly."

Moyer's Run was another holler with the road following a winding stream up the ever-narrowing valley. Dreyfus Harman's cabin was hard to miss, with stacks of chairs, rocking chairs, stools, and other wooden furniture in the yard. No two rockers seemed identical but Culden and I picked out four that nearly matched for fifteen dollars each. Indeed, the affable Mr. Harman took cash but blinked owlishly when I asked about a personal check.

On up the road, we spotted woven baskets and colorful quilts in front of cabins very similar to my own.

"These folks set up stands at hairpin curves on the highways during the weekends," Culden said, "—either causing wrecks or selling quilts to tourists."

• • •

With the swing and four rockers on its wide front porch, Five's Five looked almost habitable. Inside were a fairly well-equipped kitchen and a beautiful bed with new springs and mattress. I walked across the bridge to the studio for a closer examination. The floor was swept clean, but the cracks between the puncheon boards were filled with sawdust.

I inspected the studio. The pot-bellied stove sat on a large sheet of tin with an asbestos cover. I shook its stack, which seemed solidly affixed through the wall. A pair of receptacles indicated that the studio was wired. It was a huge room, much bigger than any place where I'd ever painted before.

The honk of a horn drew my attention back to the house. Parked in the clearing was a truck from the telephone company. Paying cash obviously gets results. The phone man checked his hookup box and inserted the phone cord. *Some day customers will be able to do this themselves.* He also handed me a slim phone book for Grant County.

"I'll go down to the main line and get her hooked up," he announced. "It'll take me about twenty minutes, but stay close. I'll give you a ring to check the service."

Leaving the door open to hear the ring, I wandered the fringes of my clearing yard. No grass was evident… just rock, moss, and pine straw beneath the canopy of trees. *At least I won't have to mow a lawn.* At the far end of the clearing, I spotted another building: a small shed nestled in the bushes. *Could this be the barn where Bubby stored the bed?*

Just then the phone rang and I ran across the yard to answer. "Sounds like she works just fine," the lineman said.

The phone was a queer-looking Swedish *Ericofon* that sat on its own base. It intrigued me at the phone store but now I had second thoughts. I picked it up and stared at the dial set into the base. I dialed 'O' for operator in hopes of getting the Fine Arts Department.

"Operator. How can I help you?"

"I'm trying to reach the Fine Arts Department at Seneca University."

"One moment." Pause. "I have a Department of Fine Arts. Would that be it?"

"I think so."

"The number is S-E-1-8-7-5-5."

Immediately my second thoughts about the *Ericofon* hardened into fact. The dial had ten holes with numbers. No lettered prefixes. I was used to numerical dialing from D.C. and Baltimore. I tried to recall the phone at home and where the letters were located. I dialed the operator again and got the same woman.

"Hi, I've got a bit of a problem here with my telephone."

"It sounds as if it's working just fine to me," she responded.

"No. I just got a number from you but the dial on my new phone doesn't have any letters for the 'S-E'. Can you give me the numbers instead of the letters?"

"I am sorry," she said, "but Potomac Telephone is not equipped for all-numerical dialing."

"C'mon, lady. If the letter 'S' is in the same hole as the number '5' it's all the same."

"I'm sorry, but I cannot help you." She didn't sound sorry at all.

"Can you dial the number for me?"

"I can, and your bill will be charged ten cents."

Thank God Cyndy Byrd had a couple of years of college behind her. She understood my problem immediately and translated the number to 731-8755. She then put me through to Culden, who cackled as I described my plight. As it turned out, all the SEneca exchange numbers would start with 731 and all I would have to remember was the four end numbers. *Cool stuff.*

"You'll be coming tonight?" she asked. "About seven o'clock?"

"Oh, yeah. I wouldn't miss it. Can I bring anything?"

"Just yourself—and don't dress up."

I leafed through the information section of the new phone book. Long distance calls would have to be placed by the operator. *Perhaps I should have gotten the tin-can model with the string.*

Again I dialed the operator. A different woman this time. "Operator. How may I help you?"

"I would like to make a long distance call to Hockingport, Ohio."

"And what number are you calling from?"

"731-8444," I responded, turning the Swedish phone upside down to read my own number.

"And where is that?"

"Right here in Seneca."

"I am sorry, but..." and I interrupted her.

"Look, lady. My new phone doesn't have any letters on its dial. Just put your finger in the 7 hole and pretend it's an S. Then the 3 hole and pretended it's an E. Then dial. I think you'll be amazed."

• • •

"Hi, Mom, it's Five. I have a telephone."

"Five! Lordies but it's good to hear your voice. Did Culden tell you we're coming up tomorrow? The Captain's borrowed a pickup and we dug the old camping tent out of the garage. It's going to be a terrific time."

"That's great, Mom. Do you have any old pots and pans you could spare? I'm really living in an empty house."

"House? Culden called it a *cabin*. But yes, I'll bring a skillet and a sauce pan. Will that do?"

— 12 —

Meet the New Guys

Maddy Bristo was coming down Culden's walk with Hezzie and Little Dicky as I pulled up. "Gawfa Fi! Gawfa Fi!" Little Dicky yelled.

"Hey, big guy, give me a hug." I bent over and he put his tiny arms around my neck.

"He sure does love his godfather," Maddy said. I looked up to see her grinning archly.

"Maddy, don't forget what Culden promised you. I *am* his godfather."

"And when do we get to meet his poppa?"

"When his poppa gets back from whatever war he's photographing. By the way, thanks so much for putting me in touch with Bubby. He's been a tremendous help."

"Bubby likes you, Five. He's good people and he'll bust his butt for folks he likes."

Culden opened the door and gave me a little hug. "Come in and make yourself a drink," she said, gesturing to a side table.

"Booze!" I exclaimed. "Real booze! Where did it come from? I thought all booze in this place came in Mason jars hidden in mailboxes."

"There's a state liquor store in Petersburg," she replied. "Almost like Ohio... just a little more like a penitentiary." Just then, another knock on the door.

I poured some bourbon over ice as Culden opened the door to a short, skinny, and onion-bald man with the biggest horn-rimmed glasses I'd ever seen.

"Stuart!" Culden said. "You found it. Stuart Poletz, meet Thomsen Lowrey V, who'll never speak to you unless you call him Five."

"Everyone in Huntington calls me 'Hoopie' 'cause my dad owned a barrel factory and I worked there."

We shook hands. "I knew lots of 'Hoopies' up river from Parkersburg," I said. "Are you one of those?"

"Yep," he grinned. "The Moundsville Hoopies. Only Jewish-owned barrel factory in the Ohio Valley."

Another knock at the door drew our attention. This time it was a very tall woman dressed in red overalls over a turtleneck black sweater. Her straight brown hair fell in bangs over her classic Roman nose. She pointed at Hoopie and shouted, "Buddy Holly! You've losta your hair!"

"Jaylene Fiore," Culden announced. "Lately of Italian Hill in Pittsburgh and our soon-to-be sculpture instructor."

Jaylene's long fingers were surprisingly strong as we shook hands. "Gently, *cara mia*," I said, "my hands are my life."

"Mine, too," she cracked. "Culden—you got any good Chianti? Livvy said there were some Dagos down here that made pretty good wine." Culden pointed to a straw-covered bottle of the type that usually held candles in dark restaurants.

The last to arrive were Cyndy and her husband, Doug, a weedy man literally. He had a dense beard and wore a plaid shirt picked with burn holes. Bits of straw clung to the shirt and poked from his beard and thick mop of hair.

Both Byrds wore headbands and Cyndy's sported a black crow feather, giving her a Great Plains look. Her green beaded dress came to her ankles. Both were barefoot.

They each poured a water glass from the Chianti bottle, causing Jaylene visible anguish.

"You guys really live in a yurt?" Hoopie asked. "Is it authentic? You know, felt blankets waterproofed with yak grease?"

"Yaks are pretty hard to come by in this part of West Virginia," Doug quipped. "We got the plans from the *Whole Earth Catalog* and it's mostly tarpaper on the outside and carpet scraps on the inside. You guys'll have to come out and see it."

"Where is it?" Culden asked.

"Oh, it's way up off Laurel Run in the Fore Knobs," Cyndy answered. "Just south of Jordan Run. It's about seven miles. Some friends told us about it… great hardwood for firing, some super clay banks right in the creek."

"And we've got a fresh spring for drinking and a waterfall to bathe in," Doug added. Their enthusiasm for life in the woods was obvious.

"Who did you buy the land from?" I asked.

"Buy it?" Cyndy exclaimed. "We didn't buy it. We're squatting."

"Damn!" Hoopie coughed as smoke escaped from his nostrils. "You really went to school with Jim Dine? Damn! He's my hero."

"It was just for a year in 1957," I answered. "He came to OU from some school in Massachusetts or somewhere. But while he was there, he really set the place on fire."

"I love his fans and ties," Jaylene commented. "I saw a tie series in New York. And Oldenburg's goat."

"Why can't work like that be done in clay or stone, Jaylene?" I asked.

"I did a jockstrap series," Doug Byrd added. "Real smooth glaze on the outside and this totally outrageous rough raku on the inside." Cyndy laughed at the memory.

In a room filled with smoke, Doug startled us. "Anyone wanna go out on the porch and smoke?" No one responded. "Aw shit, you guys. I got some fine weed in the car. Just a little one."

"Go ahead," Culden said coolly. "Not in the house. Not on campus. OK?"

I entertained with tales of Bubby's prowess and knowledge. And how to drive by a certain Bristo mailbox, deposit four dollars, blink your lights and drive on up the road to a curve then return. A quart Mason jar of Grant County's finest would be waiting.

"And you bought a house with a studio attached?" Jaylene asked. "When can we see it?"

"Ahh... work in progress. My family arrives tomorrow and God only knows what will happen. My sister wants to paint the place bright yellow..."

"Good taste," Hoopie interrupted.

"...but as soon as it's ready, I'll have an open house. And Doug—I've got five acres of forest you can smoke in."

— 13 —

Invasion of the Fixit Family

From the ring of keys I'd received at the closing, I found one for the Master padlock on the shed door. The door opened without a squeak. A dust-covered window spilled a faint umber light, revealing various shapes covered by sheets. In one corner, a feed trough built into the wall told me that this *had* been a barn, albeit a tiny one.

I pulled a sheet off a large shape and found a leather couch. Before anything else, I went back to the house and dialed Danny Bristo's office.

"Danny, there's a little barn up here and it's got furniture in it. I've already found a leather couch. Do you suppose I own that too?"

"Five, you got a free and clear title to all properties, as I recall Banker Norris reading. Bubby told me about the bed and I'd guess the rest of what's in that building is yours also."

With a flashlight I returned to the shed. The couch was black leather and seemed remarkably soft. I found a two-wheel dolly beneath the feed trough and manhandled the couch into the sunlight. Another sheet draped a club chair covered in brown leather and patterned with cracks. But as I ran my hand over its surface, I could feel it was still soft and supple.

I had furniture. Obviously, the renters had not wanted all this old stuff in their house.

A little drop-leaf table and two chairs would do for the kitchen, although they badly needed refinishing.

The shed gave up a side table, two table lamps, and a marvelous floor lamp with a graceful gooseneck and a splendid tasseled *art nouveau* shade.

Hauling my trove out into the clearing, I dropped onto the couch and put my feet up, immediately falling asleep under the dappled shade.

• • •

I was roused by engine noises and the honk of a horn. I'd slept nearly three hours in the open air. Another honk was followed by splashing noises as a vehicle crossed the ford. Suddenly, a gray Chevy pickup truck appeared in the clearing.

Hurrying to meet them, I realized how dumb my yard must look with furniture scattered around. Mom hugged me and then… wonder of wonders… so did the Captain.

"Five, it's just darling," Mom exclaimed. "It's the prettiest cabin I've seen in West Virginia and God knows we've seen a lot of them this morning."

"Is that stream navigable all year round?" Captain grinned at his droll joke.

"Oh, show us around," Mom said, "I'm so excited to see it."

We slowly toured the property. "Floors should be sanded and oiled," the Captain noted. "And the roof and siding needs to be protected."

"Sissie Eileen wants it painted yellow," Mom smiled. I frowned.

"I have a handy guy named Bubby who made all these repairs, rebuilt the studio bridge, and split ten cords of wood in less than two weeks. He said the existing siding has been stained with some kind of water seal stuff... same for the roof."

We stared at the house. "Besides," I added, "I kind of like its natural look. Why don't we put up the tent and relax and talk about it?"

I'd all but forgotten the Lowreys' camping tent, a huge walled affair that once slept all four of us on vacations. We found a level spot and erected the tent, then put two folding canvas cots inside. I was anxious about the thin spots of the tent's roof where sunlight showed through.

"It hasn't rained since I've been here, but if it does we can move the cots under the back porch lean-to."

I could tell from the rattling that Bubby's pickup was crossing the ford. He climbed out and approached us in his usual uniform of overalls and T-shirt. "H'lo, and you must be Captain Lowrey IV," he said as he shook the Captain's hand. "And you're Miss Ellie, Five's mom? You ain't old enough to have a young'n that big."

"Bubby Bristo is a talented man, but now I realize he's also got to be Irish with all that blarney," I grinned.

"Maddy told me your folks were on their way," Bubby said to me. "Thought I'd drop over and see if I could lend a hand." He eyed the tent. "Y'all gonna sleep in that? Sure hope it don't rain."

From the bed of the pickup, he pulled down a huge belt sander. "I'd planned to sand those floors today, then give 'em a coat of tung oil."

Captain said, "We were talking about painting, or staining, the outside of the house. But I'll need a ladder."

"If you don't mind doin' the sanding," Bubby said, "I'll run back to the house and get my ladder... and mix up some stain."

• • •

The big belt sander made fast work of the floor and then Captain sanded the floorboards of the studio bridge and the floor of the studio. Bubby was like a third member of the family, scurrying back and forth for supplies.

"I'm sure sorry about the shed, Mr. Five," he explained. "I was just so excited about gettin' the bed set up that I plumb forgot to tell you about the other furniture. That was all Mr. Sibley's and it's yours now."

We moved the furniture under the roofed car port. Bubby worked a big mop from a bucket of tung oil and treated the floors. "She'll be dry in an hour," he said. "These heart of pine floors just soak up the oil."

The sun was drifting behind my mountain when another horn sounded down the holler. "That's got to be Eileen," Mom said. Sure enough, a white-on-yellow Chevy Bel Air stopped at the ford. She blew the horn again in short beeps.

I walked down the lane to the ford. Eileen was standing behind her open door. "Do I have to drive my beautiful car through this... this *river*?" I nodded yes. "Five, you said it was pretty. This is a damned creek. It'll get my car filthy."

"Sissie, it's only four inches deep. Your tires'll be cleaner than they've been since you bought that thing."

"It's your ass if you're lyin' to me, buddy."

65

— 14 —

The Work Party's Over

Two days later, Five's Five was transformed. Eileen got her way by painting the door and window trim a pale yellow. The interior walls were finished in the same shade, making the cabin much brighter. The outside walls glistened in their new coat of tung oil, which Bubby said would be back to its natural finish in a few days. Both roofs were coated with a blackish, thicker mixture.

Eileen came back from Petersburg with what she called an antiquing kit and repainted the little table and chairs in a burgundy color, then sponged a second lighter color over it. The result *did* look antique.

I was finishing chopping brush away from the creek bank when Eileen came down to tell me Culden had called a faculty meeting. "For right now?" I asked, wiping sweat from my bare chest.

"I think she'll give you time for a shower."

• • •

Cyndy Byrd was wiping tears from her eyes when I entered the office. "Mornin' Five," she whimpered.

"Cyndy, what's wrong?"

"Ohhh," she wailed, "the provost is having a party tomorrow night for the new Fine Arts people and Doug and I aren't invited." Pause. "Is it because we're... hippies?"

"You're not hippies," I countered. "You're just... free spirits."

"Whatever! But we're still not invited. I'd even shave my legs and armpits."

The Byrds' non-invitation plight was low priority. "Cyndy is the *only* secretary in the school right now and Livvy wanted to keep the crowd strictly academic," Culden said. "Besides, I'm not sure I want Doug Byrd smoking joints on her lawn."

The topics whirled around preparations for the coming fall semester, procuring supplies, finding Hoopie a place to live, building a kiln... and before we knew it, noon was upon us. My first real faculty meeting, and it was fun.

"That's it for today," Culden announced. "Next week, we'll start on curriculum assignments. The provost is determined that every Seneca student will have taken Art Appreciation before he graduates."

Catching her arm as we left the office, I asked Jaylene if she had any small carving tools.

"God, I've got dozens. Dull, sharp, wide, flat?"

"Could I borrow a couple?"

"Sure! Come into my lair," she snickered.

"Damn, but sculptors are as messy as painters!" I exclaimed. I chose a couple of tools that looked liberated from a dentist's office. Culden appeared in the doorway.

"Five, can I get a ride with you out to your place?"

"Sure. But why?"

"Your mom called and invited me out to lunch."

"Paper plates again," I responded.

• • •

"Look at the marker tree," Culden pointed. The big tulip poplar trunk sported a row of five green reflectors. "Five's Five. That's pretty neat. First left after the reflectors."

Another surprise awaited as we drove up the bank from the ford. Along the edge of the creek bank sat a long table, its top covered with checkered oilcloth. Mom, the Captain, Eileen, Bubby and a woman I didn't recognize, Maddy with Hezekiah, and Danny Bristo sat on the trestle benches.

"Surprise!" everyone yelled.

"Gawfa Fi, 'prise," Richard Thomsen Ellis yelled.

"Godfather Five, surprise," another voice yelled. Holding the baby in his arms, Richard West himself stepped from behind a tree. The four of us hugged and danced. "How 'bout this big guy?" Dicky Reb exclaimed. "And this gal? Ain't she something?" he beamed at Culden.

Bubby explained the yard table. "The Captain saw one at my place the other day and paid me to build this one. By th'way, this is Tibby, my wife." The woman rose from her seat and extended her hand. We shook and she gave me a shy smile. "Anyways, I been buildin' these yard tables seems like forever. As long as you can snag two, three mine props. These're ten-footers so that's how long your table is."

The yard table was covered with food. Sliced ham and turkey. Baked beans. Potato salad. A big bowl with some kind of tossed salad. Jars of pickles and pickled beets. And a blackberry pie.

We ate with gusto, everyone exclaiming over the tossed salad. Culden and I shared a look as we simultaneously thought of iceberg chunks and orange dressing.

"Five, you'll never believe it," Mom exclaimed. "Just above your first rapids is a pool filled with this delicious watercress. We pay two dollars for it at home."

"What is the dressing, Ellie?" Culden asked.

"That's Eileen's," she responded.

"I found a great store over in Petersburg," Sissie Eileen answered. "Same place I bought the tableware and glasses." For the first time, I realized we were eating from real plates. "It's olive oil, extra virgin from Italy," she giggled. "Just olive oil, lemon juice, pepper and some salt."

With the table cleared, we all sat around and smoked and sipped a taste of Bristo 'shine. I got up and strolled to the barn. Using a piece of clockspring wire for torsion and Jaylene's carving tool, I quickly picked the little padlock on the smallest chest. Sure that I could do it, I resnapped the lock and carried it to the yard table.

"Ta-daaa," I announced. "Y'all have surprised me and I'm grateful for it. Now it's my turn for some surprises… and they will be." Pause. "This is the smallest of three chests in the barn and I don't have a clue what's in them."

I quickly inserted torsion bar and pick and the cheap lock popped open obediently. With great drama, I opened the breadbox-size chest. Inside were books and papers. Everyone gathered around but I put the chest aside. "Can someone help me carry another one out?"

Bubby jumped up and we chose the biggest chest. Without rehearsal, I picked its lock and again raised the lid slowly. It was apparently full, with a chenille bedspread sitting on top. The women oohed and aahed and we removed beautiful single-bed quilts one by one. Seven in all.

"These are beautiful," Maddy exclaimed.

"Really works of art," added Culden.

"And my surprise is…" I thumped my hands on the table in imitation of a drum roll, "each lady gets to pick one for her very own. I want to keep whatever's left."

The middle-size chest was surprisingly heavy. Dicky Reb and I grunted as we manhandled it out to the table. Its lock took a little more time and everyone sighed when I finally popped it. As the lid was raised, the distinctive odor of Hoppe's gun solvent wafted from the chest. Packets of oily cloth and greasy rags filled its interior.

"Guns!" Bubby exclaimed. I nodded. "Do you know anything about guns, Mr. Five?" I nodded.

I unwrapped the first packet to find a leather case with *High Standard* stamped into it. I unzipped the case and in its velveteen enclosure was a beautiful .22 caliber pistol, gleaming satin silver.

"My gosh, will you look at that," Bubby breathed.

"But look at the grips," Dicky Reb exclaimed. "They're really beautiful."

"I knew Mr. Sibley collected guns," Bubby said, "'cause I bought a flintlock rifle from him one time. He must've carved the custom grips for this one."

The grip was dark brown with swirling stripes of brown, carved to mold into the shooter's hand. A tiny checkered pattern covered the right side while the left grip was smooth with a swooping thumb rest. I cleared the chamber and checked the clip holder to ensure the pistol was empty, then hefted its perfect balance.

The second package was a High Standard single-shot target pistol with a rosewood grip that totally enclosed the barrel and mechanism. Whistles and inhalations welcomed its unveiling.

Next was a cloth-wrapped satin silver revolver with a concealed hammer. I recognized it. "A *Lady Smith* .32 but

70

look at the grips." Usually the two-inch S&Ws have tiny grips and I've always found the weapon hard to hold. This silver beauty had a one-piece grip that covered the back of the frame. It was carved in flawless walnut. "If this beauty belongs to me," I stated, "I'm keeping it."

More packages revealed spare clips, a speed loader for the Lady Smith, boxes of ammunition, and a cleaning kit. In the bottom of the chest was a longer cloth-wrapped package running from corner to corner.

It was slightly heavier than the handguns and wrapped in two layers of oil-soaked rags. What came out was a sawed-off shotgun with an elaborate carved pistol grip.

"A vermin gun," Bubby whispered. "Mr. Sibley sure did love them things. Made one for me and probably four, five more for my cousins. Looks like he kept the best one for himself.

"Pretty nice one, too," he went on. "Mr. Sibley only made 'em from .410s and this one looks like a Browning."

"I've seen sawed-offs before but never this small. What's it for?" I asked.

"Like I said, vermin," Bubby answered. "Put a rock salt load in each barrel and you can kill snakes or rats or scare the crap out of intruders. Couldn't kill anyone with it 'less you stuck it in his ear. Course no one knows what's in your load and it could easily be number four shot." He looked in the breech. "I'll get you some rock salt loads."

• • •

Night was coming on and the Lowrey clan sat on the front porch, smoking, rocking, and reliving the work party.

"I can't tell you guys how much all this means to me," I said sincerely. "I'd still be working next October if I had to do it myself."

"Don't forget Bubby," Captain said. "That man is worth a dozen… and Five, he's a real friend."

"I know it, and he just won't let me pay him anything. I told you how little he charged me before you all got here."

"Five, he's got special skills," Sissie Eileen said, "but so do you. Why don't you do a portrait of Bubby and Tibby? I know Dicky Reb shot at least two rolls today and I'll bet he'll get you a print to work from."

Mom also contributed. "That's a great idea. Their cabin is ever so plain, although Tibby has planted lots of flowers and made colorful curtains."

• • •

When their lantern went out, Mom and the Captain giggled like teenagers in the darkened wall tent. Eileen and I swung gently on the porch, sipping a tiny taste of the 'shine.

"Lordies, Five, they have had *sooo* much fun. Did you know they're going to go home by way of Blackwater Falls and camp for a couple of nights there?"

"They're just like different people," I said, "now that they're not worried about us so much."

"Oh, they still worry. They just don't show it." Pause. "It was really good to see Dicky Reb. Culden was really surprised when he pulled in last night. I slept on the couch but it was sort of embarrassing. Culden makes a lot of noise!"

"I've heard. You want to sleep here tonight? I'll take the couch."

"Could I?" she asked. "That would be great." Another pause. "Five? Did you and Culden ever…"

I placed my finger over her lips, silencing the question at birth.

— 15 —

Evening at the Provost's

The Captain lost no time in breaking camp and the Lowreys were on the road after one cup of coffee. Eileen also got an early start, even though she was only going home to Hockingport before returning to teaching and grad studies at Miami University.

"I hope you'll like teaching, Five," she said. "I really enjoy it even though it's just little kids. And it's so neat that they want you to paint as well as teach. What a great way to pick up a doctorate."

She was barefoot as she got into her Bel Air. At the ford, she stopped in mid-stream and went around the car, washing each whitewall tire in turn. "Thanks for the free carwash, brother. I love you." As the white-on-yellow Chevy vanished down the road, I felt terribly alone.

• • •

Provost Livinda Ferris' residence was at the end of Deans' Row and was almost as big as the president's home. A big terrace overlooked the steep cliff and valley below. In the eastern distance, the lights of Petersburg began to glow against the darkening sky.

Doctor Cruz-Garcia greeted me at the door. "Good evening, Five. Livvy has me playing butler for the moment. Please come in."

"Good evening, Dean."

"Jorge, Five, on this informal basis," he responded with a thin smile. "You've met Wayman, of course." He then introduced me to a very round woman. "Sarah Lumley, our Dean of Women, this is Thomsen Lowrey V, but he answers only to Culden and to the name of Five."

"Hello, Five," she said with a velvety voice. "Welcome to Seneca. I've heard a lot about you—and pretty much all good stuff."

"I'm S.G. Caufield, Dean of Students," a straight-backed man of medium build and Prussian demeanor said to me.

"Any relation to Holden Caufield?" I quipped. Perhaps S.G. hadn't read *Catcher In The Rye,* as my little joke went spinning off into space.

"S.G. only smiles when he's torturing miscreants," a voice whispered in my ear. "Hello, Five, and welcome to my home." Livinda Ferris looked stunning in a dark blue cocktail dress with a Chinese slit up one side, exposing a lot of great-looking leg.

"Come get a drink before the bar is overwhelmed." She guided me by the elbow. "And look who's serving canapés! Little Jenny Whitestone from Dryfork." I recognized the waitress from the Faculty Club. "And your favorite bartender, Gerald Warren, who now knows a Gibson from a gimlet."

I accepted the Gibson, deliciously made, out of respect for Livinda's lessons to the bartender.

"Culden will be here in a little while," Livinda said. "I'm so glad her husband could come tonight as well."

I sputtered my response. *Had there been a wedding I missed?* "Richard is an old friend of mine," I said stiffly. "We were fraternity brothers at OU."

"Oh really? What house? I was a Kappa here but I'm afraid they don't want me as a faculty adviser."

"Alpha Chi Epsilon," I responded. "But I'm not very active as an alum."

"That's a shame. Their chapter here is on the fringe of being in trouble. They could really use a mature adviser."

"That's not me, believe me," I responded. "I'm sure you'll hear the story someday... but not tonight, please."

"Don't worry. I've already heard it from Culden. I'm still not sure you couldn't help the ACE house in Seneca."

Hoopie Poletz joined me, and Livinda turned to greet new guests. "Great place isn't it, Five? I'll move in here any time the Petrifying Provost asks me."

"You scared of her?"

"Shitless. She's one of the most imposing women I've ever met."

"Hey, Jaylene, you clean up pretty well," I said as our sculpture instructor joined us. She too wore a cocktail dress that revealed curves always hidden by her sweatshirts and smocks.

"Hi, Five. Did that carving tool work OK?" I explained what I'd used it for and they stood open-mouthed at my story of the treasure chests. "Where did you learn to pick locks, Five?" Jaylene asked.

"Ohhh, I worked one Christmas vacation in a locksmith's shop."

Dicky Reb and Culden arrived. Culden's face was flushed and I could tell the two of them hadn't been fully dressed very long. "Livvy thinks Reb's *your husband*," I hissed in her ear. "Thank God I didn't blow it. Doesn't she know?"

"Of course she knows," Culden responded. "She's just being my friend and looking to avoid... you know."

The crowd had thickened and Livinda returned with new faces to introduce. Con Stedman, chairman of the Music Department, newly moved from Liberal Arts to Fine Arts. "No *respectable* university should exist without a football team and halftime show," Livinda quipped. "Con's band puts on a great halftime show." Stedman, a handsome man in his forties with sandy hair, smiled and nodded.

"I'm Alice King," a thin, plain woman with brown hair in a bun, said to us. "Professor of Vocal Music."

"And this is another of our new faculty for next fall," Livinda announced. "Gillian McDearmid will organize and teach the new dance curriculum."

"And help train my majorettes and cheerleaders," Stedman chimed in enthusiastically.

Rich black hair hung past her shoulders, and Gillian McDearmid was one stunning woman. She wore a black leotard with a plaid skirt that I suddenly realized was a kilt.

"Ahh," I said to her, "are you by any chance from Scotland?"

"Oh, was it me shoes that gave me away?" she responded with a tinkling laugh. I stared down at her shoes, a pair of dance slippers, then got her joke. "And you are?"

"I'm Five Lowrey from the Visual Arts Department."

"Ahh, the painter. I've heard lots about you. Pleased to meet you," as she took my hand.

Gillian McDearmid's tiny hand was warm and firm and I'm afraid I held it too long.

"You're actually going to train majorettes... and cheerleaders?" I asked.

Gillian grinned. "I'm not too sure what a cheerleader is. But I really wanted this position and I'm afraid I sort of agreed to almost anything in the interview."

"Why did you want this position so much?"

"I'm from the Highlands and I love the mountains and glens. I like to climb and did a lot of potholing in university."

"Potholing?"

"You know, caving. Over here they call it spelunking."

"The only caves I've ever been in are Lascaux and Ruffignac in France and Smoke Hole Caverns down the road just last week."

"Did I hear Lascaux?" Livinda Ferris joined our conversation. "I'm leaving for three weeks in France right after commencement. Five, can you recommend any places to visit? I would love to see Lascaux."

"Sure, Doctor Ferris."

"Livinda, Five. And don't you have a gallery in Paris? I'd love to see your work there."

I reached into my jacket pocket and produced the case with my *Galeries Stansbury-Marchant • Beaux Arts et Photographie* cards, scribbling Gigi's and Anna's names on the back.

"My, my. Boulevard St. Germain. I am impressed."

Gillian McDearmid looked impressed as well.

"And if you want to see some fascinating country, Gigi knows the south of France quite well. Her family lives there and she even owns a tiny castle in the Dordogne."

As the evening wore on, I concluded that the Fine Arts faculty was a congenial group… Gillian McDearmid perhaps the most congenial of all.

— 16 —

Commencement Day II

The small group of new Fine Arts faculty sat on stone benches in front of the archway of Old Main. The archway, usually filled with parked bicycles, was clear and swept clean. Behind us on Eden Fields, the university orchestra played a medley as proud parents and onlookers found their seats for Commencement ceremonies.

Finally, Mendelssohn's *War March of the Priests* signaled ceremony, and far below, from the Underhill campus the academic procession came into sight. Leading the procession was Ed Gales, Seneca's basketball coach and the tallest faculty member. Towering in a resplendent scarlet and gold gown and carrying a five-foot golden mace, he turned at the steps and began the steep climb.

Following the faculty came graduates from the Underhill schools—Engineering, Arts and Sciences, and Mining. As the steps crossed the serpentine, each landing was crowded with spectators including a large number of hippies.

The sweating, red-faced faculty members finally hit the summit. "Christ," Hoopie muttered, "it's the Seneca Death March."

The Underhill graduates were halted as the faculty cleared the passageway and the graduates of the College of Liberal Arts filed from their Old Main wing. Next year, we would join the faculty from our wing, and in four years we would lead our students into the procession.

As the last of the robed graduates passed through the arch, I looked down the hill. Only four or five small groups of hippies remained.

"I suppose it's politic for us to watch the ceremony," Culden announced. "How 'bout sitting in the last row so we can escape quickly?"

We strolled across the plaza of Eden Fields, entered Piper Stadium by a side gate, and found ourselves at the upper level. The procession was entering the stadium from a corner tunnel below us.

The colorful array of faculty robes was followed by the black robes of undergraduates, although I noticed each gown had scarlet and gold piping on its right sleeve. "Pretty fancy for undergraduates, eh?" Culden whispered to Reb and me.

"Can we design our own regalia?" I asked her. "The brown hood literally looks like shit."

Awards were made, followed by the validectory, then some academic from Johns Hopkins gave a bland commencement address. Finally, 900 graduates trooped across the stage and after the last was back in his seat, President Skinner pronounced them graduated. Mortarboards filled the air and the Fine Arts faculty sneaked out.

• • •

"Well, whaddya wanna do, Marty?" Hoopie drawled the favorite line from the 1950s movie.

"It's a beautiful day," I commented. "Y'all could come to my place if everyone brings something and helps clean up."

"How do you get there?" Jaylene asked.

"Why don't you all meet at Culden's in about a half hour? Will that give everyone time to change, buy a six pack, or bake a chicken?" I asked.

"Can I ride with you, Jaylene?" Hoopie asked.

"If you can keep your hands to yourself," she answered.

I stopped at the A&P store and picked up ingredients for spaghetti, then headed for Five's Five. By the time the Fine Arts caravan arrived, I had garlic sautéing and onions and peppers chopped for the sauce. Culden, Reb, and the baby came in. The baby was waving a long loaf of French bread.

"Gawfa Fi, hi, hi!"

"Hi, Little Dicky, you brought the bread, eh?"

"Five, we've got to come up with a new name for this kid. *Little Dicky* is kind of... ah, well you know," Reb said. "Little Reb would be OK with me. Culden suggested R.T. Got any ideas?"

I removed the bread from R.T.'s grasp. "Where did he get this?" I asked.

"I drove into Petersburg to that store where Eileen got the olive oil and dishes. It's a terrific place with all sorts of exotic foods," Culden said.

Jaylene and Hoopie entered. The sculptor carried a giant bottle of chianti and Hoopie lugged a case of Rolling Rock. Last to arrive was Gillian McDearmid. "I didn't know what to bring so I'll just work extra hard. I can make a salad."

Sautéed ground beef joined the other ingredients in my biggest saucepan, a gift from Mom and the Captain. Water was set to boil in a huge pot Culden had brought. The group wandered around the cabin admiring the place.

"Culden, show them the upstairs and the bridge," I suggested. They climbed the stairs and a minute later I heard a collective gasp.

"God, Five, it's a regular estate," Hoopie yelled down. "Fantastic." His shouts were joined by squeals of delight as they walked the bridge to the studio.

"What a terrific place!" Jaylene exclaimed. "And you haven't even got the studio furnished yet."

Gillian chimed in. "I love it, really love it. Now, where's the lettuce? I'll start a salad."

"Lettuce?" Oh lordies, I forgot lettuce.

Culden saw my expression. "Have you found that place where Ellie—" aside to Gillian "his mom—found the salad?"

I shook my head no, but said to Gillian, "Come on, let's go forage some salad." I admired her cute wiggle as I followed her across the bridge. She wore white shorts and a man's work shirt tied at the waist, exposing a trim midriff. I led the way out the side door of the studio and up the path that followed the creek bank.

"Oh, Five, this is just like the Highlands," she crooned. "It's beautiful, but do you know where you're taking me?"

"Not exactly, but if my mom could find it I surely can. She said it's just above the first cascade."

And in another minute, Mom was right. The solid rock bed of the stream was cut by narrow channels filled with green vegetation. The rapid current moved the leaves in rhythm. I was glad I had brought along a market basket.

"Watercress!" Gillian exclaimed. "My word, but there must be half a hectare of it!"

"Surely not that much, but there's a lot." I sat to roll up my pantslegs.

"No! Stay! I'll just take off my Plimsoles and get what we need in a sec."

"What're Plimsoles?"

"You call them tennis shoes, silly" she laughed. "Or sneakers."

Gillian waded into the stream and began gathering bunches of cress. "I've never picked it before but it comes right up when you tug the roots." She tossed me a double handful. It smelled wet and fresh and peppery. I took a bite.

"Man, it's delicious just as it is," I exclaimed. We filled the basket quickly and I went to the edge of the stream to give Gillian a hand.

"Oooh, it's slippery on the bottom," she said. I grabbed her hand and felt myself sliding as her feet went out from under her. "Eeeeek," she squealed as she sat in the shallow stream and watched me slide in beside her. "Aww, I'm sorry Five. Why didn't you let go of my hand?"

"I thought I could catch you, but… and besides, I wanna hold your hand."

"Aww, a Beatle lover," she said in her low tinkle voice. "I wanna hold your hand also."

Gillian and I leaned into each other and kissed lightly on the lips.

• • •

We took a lot of kidding from the rest of the crowd about swimming in our clothes.

"I guess that's how they do it in Scotland," Reb chimed.

"Noo! We Scots are thrifty so we take a bath and wash our clothes at the same time."

Gillian changed into a pair of my sweatpants with the drawstring nearly doubled and an old basketball shirt from Hockingport High. The ensemble was at once sloppy and erotic.

The crowd had moved outside and opened wine and beer. I tended the spaghetti pot while Culden and Gillian assembled the salad. "Real olive oil. Lemon juice. A touch of vinegar, black pepper," Gillian chanted. "And sliced tomatoes and chopped onion."

"Five, you're going to have to make a store run," Culden warned. "You're nearly out of vegetables."

"Aw, I think I can exist on watercress."

Culden grinned, "Watercress and... love. I told you I'd find you a new girl."

• • •

To fight off darkness, someone had hung a lantern from a limb over the yard table. A car radio provided music for Gillian, who was performing a sinuous dance on the tabletop.

Dicky Reb and I sat inside, watching Gillian's performance and leafing through Mr. Sibley's papers from the smallest chest.

"Man, I hate to leave tomorrow but..." Dicky lamented. "R.T.'s growing so fast! He already calls me 'daddy' instead of 'pa' and that's just in five days."

"Where are you headed next?"

"Mmmm. I think Southeast Asia. Johnson is committing more troops every month. Vietnam is where the action is," he said. "Or maybe the West Coast. I've got a tightly laced Ivy League editor who's always been convinced I was a beatnik since I joined *Look*. He's sure I'd fit right in with the crowd at Berkeley," he said.

Gillian had done a leap off the end of the table and was now pounding through the dust of the clearing with short, sharp steps. The sweat pants drooped low on her butt and the cutoff jersey exposed a lot of her middle.

"That's some woman," Dick commented. "You could do worse." He paused and grinned at me, "although she is kind of flirty." I arched my eyebrows in question. "She kinda tried to cop a feel after dinner. Culden slapped her hand away from my crotch. 'Course we were all feelin' no pain."

As we turned through the pages of Mr. Sibley's papers Dick said, "You know, Five, I'd also like to shoot these people and mountains. That Bubby's a natural. 'Course, Paul Fusco has already done it for us and Gene Smith shot the country doctor for *Life*."

"I'll keep an eye peeled for a story idea for you," I said.

"This Sibley guy was a real character, too," he commented. "I guess he was a, whattayacallit, spelunker, eh?"

"Yeah, these look like maps of caves. The horizontal layout at the top and then a vertical view as well. This one's labeled *H3 Sibley's Hole* but doesn't tell where it is. And this one, *H2 Lazarus Pit,* looks immense." I paused. "The university has a spelunker club, or something, and Gillian said she's a potholer. Maybe I'll try to find out more."

Gillian changed out of her sweats and jersey in my room and shook hands with me as she left, wearing damp shorts and shirt.

"Thanks so much, Five. This was a terrific party. Good night."

Reb, Culden, and a sound-asleep R.T. were the last to leave. And finally, once more I was alone.

— 17 —

A Trip to Laurel Town

By mid-morning Monday, Culden was alarmed when Cyndy Byrd hadn't arrived for work. "She's been so punctual but that fit she threw last week about the party has me worried," she said. "I think I'll take a ride up there. You wanna ride along?"

"Better yet, let me drive. The 2CV looks more like a hippie vehicle than your red wagon. I'm hearing some of these folks are not of the love and peace persuasion."

We drove to the village of Jordan Run and got directions to go south again and take the first right-hand turn. The Laurel Run road was as obscure as my lane but considerably longer. Taking the wrong fork three times ran us into dead-end hollows and abandoned coal mines, the hand-dug kind the locals call cat holes.

A crude sign displayed a peace symbol and the inscription "Friends Welcome." Beyond was a lean-to with three or four people sitting in its shade.

"Mornin'," I greeted them. They returned silence and nods.

"Do y'all know where the Byrds live?"

"Do *y'all* mean the potter and his woman?" a girl with filthy blonde hair mocked me. I nodded yes.

"Keep takin' the left turns. You'll find their shack at the end of the road, top of the hill."

The road kept narrowing and deteriorating. The 2CV took it gamely in low gear. We passed a number of other structures that might have been homes. Two small kids were playing in the yard of one place, naked as the day they were born.

We finally reached a clearing and what was obviously the Byrds' yurt—black tarpaper with bright glyphs painted on its surface. Cyndy opened the door at the sound of my engine and came hurrying out.

"Culden, Five. Ohhh. Did you come to fire me?" She had the beginnings of tears in her eyes.

"Fire you? For missing a day of work?" Culden said sharply. "No… I was concerned."

"Oh thank God. Well, I can blame Mr. Shit-for-brains over there," she nodded and we saw for the first time Doug's sleeping form on a broken-down lawn chair. His mouth was wide open and one leg was bent under the chair.

"He got himself stoned yesterday afternoon and tried to drive home without going to town for gas," she growled. "Our car's down there on the mountain somewhere."

"Well, we'll take you to work and perhaps he can get the car going again before quitting time," Culden answered. "If not, someone'll bring you home."

Cyndy brightened immediately. "Great. As you can see, I'm dressed. I was even thinking about walking down the mountain and hitching a ride." She grinned. "Would you like to see the place first?"

The Byrds' place was an interesting concept in living. The yurt was covered with large pieces of tarpaper and carpet remnants, with a single window and a windowed door, both used and liberated from some other house. The single room had a living area and a curtained sleeping area. A rear door led to a cooking shed with a small stone firepit and grill. Near the cook shed was a piece of one-inch pipe that snaked through the woods, and a dribble of water ran into a barrel. A long-handled drinking cup hung from a tree.

"Water for drinking and cooking," Cyndy said proudly. "And in winter, we'll be able to heat it for washing and bathing." She strode on up a path and revealed a stone bank with a decent little waterfall. "And here's where we bathe right now."

"Ahh, where do you...?"

"Oh! Down the hill... Doug 'liberated' the outhouse and we took nearly a week to dig the hole."

"And Doug's studio?" Culden asked.

"Well, right now everything's outdoors. His wheel and the kiln are down there below the waterfall. We get the clay from up the hill about a quarter of a mile."

We walked back through the yurt and into the front yard. Cyndy went over and gave the yard chair a kick. "Wake up, asshole." The chair collapsed on Doug's leg and he rolled off it with a cry of pain.

"Wha... wha...?" he mumbled. One eye opened slowly. "Hey, Culden, Five," he said sheepishly. "Where? Are you going? Darling?"

"These folks are takin' me to work," she growled, "and you'd better be there to pick me up or else."

"Don't have any gas," he responded.

"Well push it out of the weeds and coast down the hill and thumb up to the service station... or walk." She pointed a finger at him. "Just be there."

Doug looked around the yard. "You got Five's car? I've got a Georgia credit card."

Culden gave me a questioning glance. "Don't ask," I said to her. To Doug, "you have a jug?" He muttered a yes.

"Then let's go."

The Byrds' old Ford was indeed in the weeds, just a few yards from a hippie camp. We watched as he siphoned a gallon from my 2CV into a stoneware jug. Then we drove off without another word.

"That shithook," Cyndy stormed, "I'll never know why I hooked up with him... stay with him!"

"Where did you meet Doug?" Culden asked.

"Antioch, in Ohio," she answered. We both laughed at the idea of Cyndy and Doug on one of the nation's most liberal, most radical campuses with all the other hippies.

All the way down the hill, people waved us either the peace sign or a single middle digit. "They're friends," Cyndy called out time after time. "Friends welcome, you asshole. Can't you read?"

"Does this *community* have a name Cyndy?" I asked.

"Yeah! They call it Laurel Town 'cause it's on Laurel Run. But some of these people are starting to call it Berkeley East."

— 18 —

Sign of the Times

With no summer classes, Seneca University was deathly quiet. Maintenance men climbed ladders to paint the trim on buildings while others scraped peace signs and other protest graffiti from the walls. The biggest noise was the hum of lawnmowers skittering across Eden Fields.

After a couple of weeks at home and Athens, I returned to Seneca and joined the rest of our faculty in preparing the Visual Arts Department for its first fall semester. The two north studios had been freshly painted and Hoopie had built a dozen sketching benches with the help of the university's shop.

"Damn, but I'm glad to see you, Five," Hoopie said. "Culden says we'll need at least fifteen of these critters. How do they look?"

I stepped over one of the low benches and shifted my weight back and forth. "Solid as a rock!"

"Hell, they should be. The carpenters insisted on bolts instead of nails."

A scream had us both through the door and looking down the hall for the source. Jaylene burst out of the faculty women's restroom and beckoned us. As we went by the office wing, I yelled in to Cyndy to call security.

"You won't believe this," Jaylene gasped, "but take a look!" She held the door open.

Three naked young women were standing there, dripping from the shower.

"Who the hell are you guys?" one of them screeched. "Can't a person have some privacy?"

"And just who the hell are you?" Culden screeched back as she burst through the door. "Get some clothes on, and right this minute."

"I don't have the soap off me, bitch!" another answered.

"And 'bitch' just got your ass arrested," Culden responded. "Five, you and Hoopie guard this door and make sure they're here when security gets here." To the naked girls, "I mean it. Get some clothes on and right this minute."

The women didn't look much better with clothes on. They sat defiantly on the hallway floor until Sergeant Glencoe arrived. One of them was smoking and her companion pulled a damp joint from her skirt, lit it quickly and took a deep drag, then killed the roach on her shoe. They wore peasant skirts and deep-cut blouses plus a variety of headbands. Only one wore shoes.

"All right, ladies, what's going on here?" Glencoe started.

"We were just takin' a shower and this dyke here burst in and screamed at us," the shortest of the three said indignantly.

"And what gave you the idea you could take a shower in a university building?" he asked.

"C'mon, man, get with it. I've showered in at least a dozen universities. Why is this one any different?"

"Why are you different?" the sergeant asked. "Come on ladies, let's come up with some identification."

Glencoe read aloud as he jotted down information from each ID card. "Jane Edodoe, Little Rock, Arkansas," he paused. "Would this be a valid Arkansas driver's license, Jane?" The little blonde remained silent.

"Matilda Grossman, New York University," he read from a student ID card. "Susan Liston, University of California, Berkeley.

"And where did you *ladies* come from?" he asked, "and where are you going?"

The tall, thin woman with long black bangs answered, "Pittsburgh. We've been attending a student seminar at the university where, I might add, they allowed us to shower."

"And we're not going anywhere," the scruffy blonde answered. "We're here!"

— 19 —

And the Livin' Is Easy

After the first encounter with the hippie chicks we had a doorbell installed and locked the outside doors. Anyone could still enter the Fine Arts Building from Old Main's covered walkway but the faculty restrooms were kept locked.

Cyndy had told the hippies the directions to Laurel Town but didn't encourage them to go to the top of the mountain.

As the war in Vietnam intensified, we witnessed the increasing presence and intensity of the hippie culture. Signs appeared on campus advertising the Sexual Freedom League and Students Against Warfare, even though the campus wouldn't have students for another six weeks.

One morning in early July, people began drifting in to Eden Fields. By noon, Seneca U. was experiencing its first *sit-in*, although there were few outside their crowd to watch it. Smoke hung in a thin cloud over the mass of hippies and the smell of marijuana was strong. Incomprehensible speeches were made with competing bullhorns. Sergeant Glencoe stood in the archway of Old Main and silently surveyed the scene.

• • •

At our fourth faculty meeting, Culden announced that Seneca's freshman enrollment had passed a thousand students for the first time. "And..." she grinned, "sixty-one of them have indicated Fine Arts as an intended major. We'll certainly lose a few of those but let's plan for at least fifty freshmen."

That afternoon, Jaylene, Hoopie, and I borrowed two university pickup trucks and drove southeast to Ablemarle County, Virginia. I drove one truck with Jaylene as a passenger. Hoopie drove the second and brought along a town girl, Hope Massingale, for company.

"We are so lucky," Jaylene said, "to find this mine. I mean, soapstone isn't rare or anything, but to have one of the country's biggest quarries within a two-hour drive, oh wow!"

"Oh, wow!? You sound like a hippie. What's so great about soapstone? I thought sculptors used marble."

"Jesus, Five. Didn't you take any sculpture? Soapstone's the ideal medium for teaching sculpture. It's fine-grained like marble and responds to the chisel but it's softer and easier to carve. And... if a student makes a mistake or breaks a work, soapstone powder can be mixed with epoxy glue and the piece can be repaired."

Soap Mountain was an amazing place with three large vertical gashes carved out of its side. Two were whitish, and the other was a dark gray. The soapstone man was delighted to show us around, since Jaylene was obviously going to be a lucrative account.

We saw white soapstone and what he called "black pearl" from the Soap Mountain quarry. He showed us a pink variety from New York state. And after Jaylene had made her decisions, he gave us a twenty-pound block of porous soapstone for fire starters. "Just soak a chunk of this in coal oil for a couple of days and you can light it instantly for a week or more," he told us. With more than half a ton of soapstone blocks in the two trucks, we headed back for Seneca.

. . .

On a foggy Saturday morning, my hopes of sleeping late were jarred by the sound of a vehicle making its way up Gerwig Run. I waited for it to cross the ford, then roused myself when it kept on up the other side of the creek. I crawled into some clothes, then crossed to the studio and up the creek trail.

As I got closer to the creek, I heard a single voice singing a tune I couldn't recognize. At the watercress riffle, Livinda Ferris was seated on a rock removing her shoes and socks. She wore short shorts and a T-shirt emblazoned with a Tricolor and *Galeries Stansbury-Marchant*.

"So, Livinda, how was France?" I called. Her head jerked up and she flashed a big smile.

"Terrific, Five. Your *friends* were so nice."

"And what are you doing up here? Planning to poach some watercress?" I grinned to show her I was joking.

"Not without asking you," she replied. "Both Culden and Gil have told me about your fantastic watercress ranch and I thought I'd drive up and see for myself."

"Well, come down to the house and I'll put some coffee on. Then we'll get you some cress."

"You realize I've never seen your place," Livinda said as she sat barefoot on the yard table's top.

"Well, you left for France so quickly after graduation," I responded. I showed her the house, excusing my messy bed before leading her over to the studio.

"Five. It's really a great place," she said. "I think Gigi might even be jealous."

The coffee was done when we returned to the kitchen. I poured two mugs and we retreated back to the yard table. "Bubby Bristo built this table," Livinda exclaimed. "I have its cousin in my backyard."

"Bubby did about ninety percent of the rehab on this place," I said. "Did you know Mr. Sibley?"

"Oh, yes," she said. "He was a famous personality. Always exploring caves and hollows, writing journals, carving whimsical animals. He was a guest speaker at the university every year. It was sad when he disappeared."

"Disappeared? I just naturally thought he had died."

"He *was* declared dead after being gone for fifteen years," she said. "That's two years longer than the law requires. Everyone just figured he fell in some cave."

I went into the house and returned with the box of Sibley's papers. We looked at the cave maps and journal entries. "Lazarus Pit? Does that ring any bells?"

Livinda put her chin in her hand and wrinkled her brow in thought. "Not really. Although there was a Civil War saltpeter mine called Lazarus Mine in a cave over on Skidmore Mountain. And look at this journal entry about Sibley's Hole. His description sounds like the road up to Skidmore."

"How can you tell?"

"Five, I grew up in these mountains. I used to be a caver in undergraduate days. Besides, Skidmore Bald is a famous make-out spot."

I rode back up the creek with her and we waded in to harvest some watercress. She put the leaves in a bucket of creek water.

"I wonder if this stuff could be transplanted," Livinda mused. "We have a big rivulet like this in Braddock's Branch."

"Where's that?"

"Oh, it's the stream that runs through my dad's farm. If we could cultivate watercress, it might make Seneca's Faculty Club famous."

"Anything would be better than iceberg lettuce chunks. My mom concocted a terrific dressing using olive oil."

"Yes, Gillian told me. I need to talk to you about that." She paused. "I'm planning a small dinner… tonight. I wonder if you could come?"

"I've got a date," I lied.

"Terrific," she responded, "bring her."

"Well… we have other plans."

"Ohhh. Well, you were my first invitation, so… how about tomorrow night?"

"Sure," I said hesitantly. "What time?"

"I'll call you tomorrow sometime."

• • •

I was just picking up the phone when it rang in my hand. "H'lo!"

"Five? It's Gillian McDearmid."

"I was just getting ready to call you. You beat me to it. Would you like to go to Petersburg this evening, maybe something to eat and a movie?"

"Strange. I was thinking the very same thing. That's why I decided to ring you up, figuring you'd never get around to calling me."

• • •

The pizza was delicious at Cazzo's, where Gillian—*call me Gil*—and I discovered we had mutual favorite tastes: peppers and anchovies. After, we sat through *The Graduate* and finished the evening with a walk along Petersburg's main street.

"I can't imagine any man being seduced by an older woman like that! Can you?" Gil asked as we walked hand-in-hand down Water Street.

Driving home, Gil asked, "How do the French come by their reputations as great lovers when they drive cars like this?"

"Meaning?"

She put her hand over mine as I shifted from third to fourth. "This tranny stick, right in the middle. This little car wasn't exactly designed for snogging now, was it?"

"Snogging?"

"You know, what you Americans call making out. Playing kissyface."

"Well," I drawled, "if you don't mind the tranny stick in your ribs, I guess it might work."

"And definitely no shagging," she said. "And that's where the French get their reputation!"

"I'm afraid to ask. What's shagging?"

"That's snogging taken to the next level."

• • •

Gil's apartment was in the upstairs of a frame house occupied by an older couple. When we pulled up in the driveway, a bluish light still showed in the living room window. "They're telly fanatics," she said, "stay up until one

97

or two in the morning. Sadly for me, I get to share all their programs as they don't hear too well."

She leaned over and put an arm around me, wincing as the tranny stick did its job, "Owww! No snogging in this car."

We walked to the side door to her enclosed stairs. Again we embraced and exchanged a kiss. Gil squeezed me tighter and whispered, "Now this is what we call snogging. Except anyone can see."

She turned the key in her lock and we went into the little anteroom that led to the steps. Through the other door, the sounds of Lawrence Welk rattled.

"Come on, better upstairs," she muttered into my neck.

"Perhaps this is enough… ah… snogging for one night," I whispered.

"As you wish," Gil said coolly and turned to walk up the stairs. "Good night and thanks for a fine time

— 20 —

Dinner and a Tête-à-Tête

Sunday was a quiet day. Bubby Bristo arrived and announced he was ready to start on the swinging bridge. So I helped him connect the cables with short support cables. By noon, he started bolting the floorboards to the cables and told me he could finish by himself.

I made us some sandwiches and then went to the studio to set up an easel. The studio furniture now consisted of easel, a small table for supplies, and a broken-down chair I'd rescued from the shed. By three o'clock, Bubby yelled for me to come and see.

The bridge crossed Gerwig Run in a graceful arc, just wide enough for one person. On the far side, the walkway was about four feet above the ground. On this side, it ran right into the path.

"All she needs now is an approach on the other end," Bubby said. "I thought about runnin' the boards down to the bank but the hillbilly way is to just build a set of stile steps." He stared at the bridge. "On t'other hand, if you gotta carry groceries or stuff, maybe we want to continue the walkways."

I walked out onto the bridge. Like Gigi's bridge in France, it bounced and swayed but the drop to the creek below was only about thirty feet.

Bubby and I celebrated the bridge with a taste of 'shine. He looked around Five's Five with an air of proprietary interest. "Yessir, Mr. Five, I think we've done some real good. Mr. Sibley would be proud."

"Bubby, I think using 'we' is overstating the case a little. But I'm grateful. I can't tell you how grateful."

"Well, Tibby and me can't have kids and I've always… well, I've always wanted a boy to help me around the place and like…" he stammered. A scarlet blush crept across his face. "And Tibby, she sure likes Miss Culden and that baby."

We sat silent for a minute or two, sipping and smoking. Then Bubby changed the subject.

"You been up to Laurel Run lately?"

"It's been a few weeks," I answered.

"Them hippies is really packin' in to that holler," he stated. "And they've just about taken over Jordan Run town. They've opened a 'commune store' and thrown up a couple of other shacks. Gas station's about all that's not taken over."

"I think they're fairly harmless, Bubby," I said thoughtfully. "I've been on a lot of college campuses in the last three years and they don't seem much harm. Just a lot of noise. And now, free love."

"Damn, but I don't think I'll want any free love from those scroungy women in Laurel Town."

I walked Bubby down to his pickup. He rummaged in the cab and produced a small cloth bag. "Oh yeah, almost forgot. Here's those rock salt loads for the vermin gun I promised you. I did a dozen, but keep 'em dry or the salt'll turn solid and you'll kill someone by accident. Just as good as a deer slug. "And if you have any trouble, give me a ring straight on. I can be over here 'fore you know it."

• • •

Listening to the chime of Livinda Ferris' doorbell, I wondered at the lack of cars in her parking circle. She opened the door with a big smile. "Good evening, Professor Lowrey." A shawl covered her shoulders and hung down to a peasant skirt like the hippie girls wear, only a lot prettier and cleaner.

"Hello, Doctor Ferris. Ah… where is everyone?"

With a hand on my arm, she ushered me into the house. "Well, *we're* everyone. I decided it would be more fun than a crowd, and besides, I've wanted to have a *tête-à-tête* with you since I returned from France."

Reluctantly, I followed her out to the porch where a small table was set for two, illuminated by a pair of tall candles.

"Ah, Livinda…"

She interrupted with a finger to my lips. "Call me Livvy, Five. Or Liv."

"Ah, Liv…" I surrendered. "Tell me about France."

"Drinks first," she said, and removed the shawl to reveal a peasant blouse with a very low neckline.

I gulped. *Plastics,* I thought.

• • •

Loosened up after my second expertly prepared Gibson, I listened as Livvy sat on a wrought iron bench beside me and talked. She told me about meeting Gigi and Anna, about traveling to the Dordogne and staying three nights in Gigi's tower.

"And you've only got four paintings left in the gallery," she went on. "The girls say you've got to get back to work. All of the nudes have sold."

She lit a pair of filter cigarettes and handed me one. "I also heard about your adventure, at least a little of it and I got to meet Josephine Baker. What a woman!"

Livvy opened a bottle of wine, explaining, "This is one I found in the Périgord. *Château Corbiac Pécharmant.* I think you'll find it exquisite but we'll let it breathe a little." I didn't want to break Livvy's $50-a-bottle wine bubble by telling her that all I'd really enjoyed in France was *marc* and Calvados, so I kept my mouth shut.

She served a bowl of soup sitting in a bed of cracked ice. "My own recipe and I hope you'll like it."

I dipped my spoon and savored an odor of onion from the creamy cold soup. I sipped.

"Lord, it's delicious! Creamy onion soup?"

"Not quite," Livvy answered. "It's ramp, a West Virginia delicacy. Kind of like a wild onion but they smell to high heaven and will have you chewing Sen Sen for months."

"But these aren't strong at all," I commented. "They're just delicious."

"If you pick them when they first appear in April, they're very mild and delicious. I froze these and they worked pretty well. By mid-April, they're big and strong. Richwood has a ramp festival every year and they even put ramps in the newspaper ink. The post office quit mailing the ramp edition of the paper because they made such a smell."

Livvy poured the wine and excused herself. In a few minutes, she appeared with two steaming plates and I recognized *pâté de foie gras* and roasted potatoes just as I'd enjoyed in the Dordogne.

"You've really prepared a Dordogne feast, Livvy."

"I've always loved *foie gras* but when Gigi fixed this in the Dordogne, I was gone. It's the height of decadence."

"Gigi was in the Dordogne with you?"

"Oh, yes. The three of us had a great time... Anna is a wonderful woman and so is Gigi." She grinned. "They told me a lot about you. About Darcy... and Andy... and Peggy... they even hinted about some other things."

I could feel my face burning.

"Aw, I've embarrassed you. I'm sorry." She jumped up and scooped away our empty plates. "Salad coming up."

"My French is pretty skimpy but I've named this *la salade Dordogne de Cinq avec le cresson*. Five's Salad Dordogne with watercress. The dressing is a homemade mayonnaise with olive oil," Livvy said proudly.

"And I recognize the truffles. Jesus, Liv, did you buy out the whole Dordogne?"

"In case you haven't heard, Five, I *can afford* to buy out the whole Dordogne. Do you like the salad?"

"I can taste ramps again, right? Or is it my memory from the soup?"

"Tiny slices of ramps, slivers of truffles, croutons and cress. Pretty simple. If we can find a steady source of watercress, it's going on the Faculty Club menu."

"Not with my name on it! No sir!"

"OK, we'll just call it Salad Dordogne."

The delicious salad was followed by a Continental course of fruit and cheese. Livvy picked up her cigarettes and lighter and announced we would adjourn to the lower terrace. I didn't even realize there was a lower terrace.

Between two *chaises longues* sat a small table with a bottle of Courvoisier and two balloon glasses. She directed me to a chaise and then bent over to pour the cognac. The view down her blouse was to infinity, and I realized she was totally naked beneath.

We leaned back in the chaises, sipped, and smoked. The lights from Seneca below twinkled and from time to time grew fuzzy as the cognac burned at my brain.

Stubbing out her cigarette, Liv got up slowly and moved to the foot of my chaise. I moved my legs to make room for her. She slowly moved up, her hands on each side of my body and her blouse gaping open. Her exquisite breasts and her belly beyond gave me strange but familiar feelings.

"Ahh," I gasped, "Mrs. Robinson. Are you trying..."

"Hah," Liv guffawed, "to seduce me? Hah, hah," her laughter broke into helpless giggles. She sat up on the edge of the chaise and looked down at me.

"Mrs. Robinson, eh? But that *is* one of the greatest lines from any movie I've ever seen." She lit another pair of smokes and put one between my lips. "I admit that *was* a plan in the back of my mind. And I'm not going to let it go away but... Mrs. Robinson?" She poked me on the shoulder. "You louse! I'm only three years older than you!"

She leaned forward and we exchanged a gentle smoke kiss. Before I could respond more, she jumped up and walked to the rail of the terrace. "Another time, Five. Another time, count on it."

"I'm sorry for the comment, Liv," I said lamely.

"Don't worry. As an 'older woman,' I'm used to rebuffs but... I do want to talk to you seriously about some things.

"I know what you did in the Army." Liv leaned against the terrace railing and talked. "Or at least a lot of what you did. I even saw you one time at a radical rally in Pittsburgh."

"Livvy, be careful of what you say. What I did is classified information. You shouldn't know."

"Five, when you're the daughter of Busby Ferris, you can find out almost anything. And I do not mean to sound conceited. It's just fact. Anyway, I'm glad to have someone with your background and experience here at Seneca. The influx of hippies is bothersome. So far, militant radicals have confined themselves to bigger schools, land grant schools. So why Seneca University?"

"Liv, I think it's just a cultural change. In the Fifties, they called us apathetic. But now there's a real war in Vietnam, discrimination in the south, discrimination against women, all of these social issues that are waking young people up." *Lord, I'm not as drunk as I thought I was.*

I continued, "I wasn't here long enough to see your students last year. But this fall, I think we'll see more kids dressed like hippies, carrying on like hippies. We'll probably have a sit-in or two and some anti-war protests."

"Is there anything special we should do to be ready?" she asked.

"Man, I don't know. I think perhaps asking the Seneca Police for more than one cop would be a start."

At her door, she turned out the light and leaned into me. I circled her waist and she looked up. "That was a wonderful evening," she said, "even though it didn't go strictly according to plan. You're a nice man, Thomsen Lowrey V."

"I share the feeling," I whispered. "And I really did love the dinner... even if everyone else didn't come."

"We'll do it again," she said, nibbling on my neck. "I might even invite Gil next time. Did you have a good time last night?"

"How did you know?"

She kissed me firmly. "Five, there's one thing you've got to realize in a town this size. You can't get away with anything so long as you drive a car like that little French monster."

I kissed her on the forehead. "Good advice well taken." I smiled and said, "Good night, Mrs. R."

— 21 —

August Interlude

The West Virginia woods turned from lush green to a dry olive drab and a haze of dust covered the mountains, creating spectacular sunsets. August was a time to hope that dry summer would soon give over to autumn.

We worked hard in the Visual Arts Department, prepping canvases for painting, assembling slides for Art Appreciation, kerfing and splitting soapstone, and finally, the arduous task of preparing lesson plans.

At my home studio, I painted. From prints Dicky Reb sent me, I completed a portrait of Bubby and Tibby Bristo. I accomplished several washed watercolors of Five's Five to send to Gigi and to family members for Christmas.

Using my erotic memories of dinner with Livvy, I accomplished four different nudes which I shipped quickly to Paris. Livinda would have to go back to Paris to see herself in my work.

Although Gil and I dated occasionally, Livvy didn't give up her seduction campaign. She would leave obscure little notes beneath my windshield wiper. Who reads parking tickets? An unsigned recipe for cold ramp soup arrived via campus mail.

Gil appeared in my doorway one afternoon. "Do you want to go to a spelunkers' meeting this evening? They're going to discuss looking for lost caves."

Thoughts of Sibley's Hole and the Lazarus Pit came to mind. "Sure, why not?"

"Great. It's at the Student Center at seven o'clock. How about coming over before and I'll feed you something?"

Bacon, lettuce, and tomato sandwiches on toast washed down by beer were the 'something' Gil fed me. I brought the little Sibley chest and together we spread out the papers and journals on her coffee table.

"These are good maps but he doesn't tell how to find the caves," she commented. "This will be perfect for tonight's meeting. Can we show them?"

"That's why I brought 'em along. I don't think there's any mystery involved," I added.

• • •

Derrick Birdsong was short and husky, and wore the traditional horn-rimmed glasses of a scientist. As we shook hands, he smiled at Gil with an appraising look. "Welcome to the Seneca Grotto of the NSS," he said.

I figured NSS meant National Spelunking Society and kept quiet. I later discovered the S stood for Speleological, which sounded a lot more scientific.

Seven more people—four women, three men— eventually arrived and Birdsong called the meeting to order. He introduced me as Gil's guest and ran through some other mundane business.

"I guess we need to introduce Five here a bit more. He's the new painting instructor at the University and bought Hiram

Sibley's old cabin. And tonight, he's brought a trove of Hiram's papers and journals which we should be interested in."

It was the first time I'd ever heard Mr. Sibley referred to as Hiram and I resolved to check it further.

The papers were passed around the group. Each person scanned them in silence.

"Do you know any more than what you've got here, Five?" Birdsong asked. "For instance, have you explored your own mountain? All of that land belongs to Westvaco and will probably be part of the National Forest Service sale. Perhaps Sibley's Hole is right in your back yard?"

"Livinda Ferris told me there's a cave on Skidmore Mountain called the Lazarus Mine," I answered. "Used to be a Civil War saltpeter mine."

"What was saltpeter used for?" Gil asked.

"It was a primary ingredient in gunpowder," a scientific-looking woman answered. "Comes from bat guano, and many caves in Virginia, later West Virginia, were mined by both sides."

"I know Lazarus Mine," Birdsong commented. "Been in it a couple of times. The old trenches are interesting but it's hardly the cave that Hiram shows in this drawing."

Nothing significant came of the discussion, and talk moved to the group's next exploration trip to a cave called *Schoolhouse.* "As you know, this'll be our most challenging trip of the year," Birdsong said gravely. "This is indeed a climber's cave. I think we'll all agree it's one of the toughest in the country."

Gil's eyes were glistening as she listened to the dangers and difficulties of Schoolhouse Cave.

"Schoolhouse is an old saltpeter cave and Gil, you and Five are welcome to come along for the ride. The entrance room is easy, with lots of mine artifacts and the 'jumping off place' is a good wall, just tough enough to test your climbing skills." He paused. "How much further you go will depend upon what you can show us on the first wall."

Walking back to my car after the meeting, Gil was quivering with enthusiasm. "What do you think, Five? Does this sound like something you want to do?"

"I'm not really sure," I responded. "I'd really like to find Hiram Sibley's caves but I don't know about this Schoolhouse place. It sounds really rough."

"Well, I want to go. That Birdsong guy sounded like he doubted my abilities. I want to show him I'm a real potholer."

"Tell you what," I said. "Mr. Sibley left some stuff in my shed that looks like miner's gear. You want to go look at it?"

• • •

With my battle lantern lighting the way, we walked through the darkness to the shed. The beam showed a pair of yellow helmets with big lamps hanging on the front. Several coils of rope hung from a rafter. A cloth bag full of jangly hardware was suspended from a nail.

Gil took a helmet and plopped it on her head. Her eyes vanished beneath the brim. "Needs some adjusting," she muttered.

"What are these light things?" I asked.

"Carbide miner's lamps. Also potholer's lamps," she answered. She unscrewed the bottom of the brass lamp and sniffed its contents. "Ashes. But if you put carbide rocks in here, then fill this part with water, then open this valve, a combustible gas is formed."

She ran her hand across the reflector face of the lamp and produced a big spark. "Just like a big cigarette lighter. The lamp should burn for a couple hours on a load of carbide."

She stood there in my lamplight with a goofy grin on her face. "I think we've got a good start. Can we go to Petersburg this weekend and get some more gear?"

• • •

Gil and I were snogging on the porch swing. I could smell the acrid odor of used carbide on her hands and somehow, it seemed sexy. Then a sound came to us and we pulled apart.

"What was that?" she whispered.

"Voices for sure," I answered, "from up the creek." Then a twanging set of notes echoed through the forest. "What the hell is that?" I said.

"It's a *sitar* or maybe one of those Chinese guitars, I think" she answered. "The hippies in Edinburgh like to play them."

I walked to the end of the porch and looked up the creek. The darkness was broken by a faint yellow flickering. I went into the cabin and dialed Bubby.

"Bubby, it's Five. Someone's got a fire goin' up the creek from my place and I don't think they're coon hunters."

"Five, give me ten minutes. How far up the creek?"

"I'd guess maybe a couple hundred yards. Why?"

"In that case, give me seven minutes. Take the vermin gun with you and don't really wait for me."

I jacked two shot shells into the vermin gun and told Gil to lock the door and stay inside. Instead, she picked up one of Sibley's carved walking sticks and hefted it. "This'll make a fine shillelagh," she growled. "I'm coming."

Using a penlight to pick our way, we crossed the bridge, went through the studio, and up the trail to the swinging bridge. Gil went first and picked her way across the swaying structure without a sound. On the other side of the creek, we headed on uphill, glimpsing the firelight through the woods.

As we got closer, the occasional twang of the noisemaker was broken by laughter and indistinguishable words. I looked at my wristwatch. It had taken more than ten minutes but I saw no sign of Bubby.

Finally, we were close enough to make out voices and laughter. We walked quietly to the edge of the clearing and peered at the fire. A naked man lay on his back with a naked woman kneeling over in a classic pose of fellatio. Another naked woman straddled his head and was twanging on the musical instrument in time with his tongue.

"Garm!" Gil whispered.

"Kama Sutra in the flesh. This might be fun." I whispered back.

• • •

The campfire activity seemed endless and repetitious. Finally, in my deepest voice, I said loudly, "Would you people tell me what you think you're doing here?"

The blowjob girl popped up from her work and I recognized her as the little blonde from the shower. The man tried to say something but his mouth was still obscured.

"What the fuck?" blondie screeched. "Who's that? Cob, you sonofabitch, is that you?" The other woman clambered off the recumbent man and stood up. She had large breasts and a protruding beer gut.

"Cob, that better not be you," she whimpered. "This isn't funny."

His erection drooping, the man scrambled around in the bush searching for something. He finally found a shirt and draped it in front of him.

"It's not Cob," I intoned. "It's the owner of this land and I'm not very happy having you people building fires here."

"Fuck you," the guy shouted. "It's our land as much as..."

The report of my vermin gun and the sound of the rock salt rattling through the branches above them made all three drop to the ground.

"Stay there. Do not move," I said, jacking another shell into the sawed-off. I repeated, "This is not your land and I do not want you to come here again. Do you understand?"

"Fuck you anyway," the guy said.

"You tell him, Pig," a woman's voice muttered. "Haven't you heard of the summer of love?"

"Shut the fuck up, Piglet," the guy responded roughly.

"How did you get here?" I asked.

"In our wheels. How the fuck did you think we got here? Walk?" Blondie answered.

"Well, you've got two minutes to get dressed, get in your wheels and get the hell out of here," I said with as much threat as I could put into my voice. I stepped from the brush into the firelight.

"Hey, you're the guy from the college," blondie shouted.

"What guy?" the man called Pig asked. "What're you talking about, Blondie?"

So her name is Blondie too?

"Fuck him, Pig. He's just some asshole teacher at the college. You can take him, Pig."

Pig's look of challenged determination changed when I raised the twin barrels of the vermin gun.

"I am standing by this piece of shit of a vehicle," a new voice sounded from the other side of the clearing. "You obviously don't understand the landowner here," Bubby's voice boomed. He stepped into the clearing with a .12 gauge double-barrel pointed at the trio. "Don't bother to dress. Just get in this crappy machine and go away. Don't ever come back."

The hippies scurried for the woods and I could hear doors opening. I shined the battle lantern in that direction and saw a dark brown Volkswagen van. As the driver spun it around, a hand came out a window and threw us a bird.

"Give 'em one for the road, Five. You ain't gonna kill no one."

I fired at the retreating van and watched it jump like a wounded animal. A taillight winked out as it vanished down the road.

"Looks like they left their banjo," Bubby said nudging the sitar with his foot.

"I wouldn't touch that thing, Bubby. God knows where it's been," Gil warned.

"Aw, it's private property. I guess I'll return it to 'em tomorrow," he laughed. "That was sure quite a show they were puttin' on before you butted in. Better'n any of those movies they showed the night before Tibby and I was married."

"That's sexual freedom at its finest, Bubby." I paused, "But how do you know where to take their banjo?"

"Ah, they all live up in Laurel Town. I've seen all three of 'em around. That Pig fella seems to be kind of a chief." He stopped. "Filthy bastards."

I thought for a second. "Bubby, you were here before we got here. How did you get here so fast? And… you didn't come up Gerwig Run?"

"Five. You don't realize it but we're next door neighbors. Almost three miles driving but just over the ridge on our old moonshine trail. I drove 'til I could see the firelight, then walked the rest of the way. I think you'd better explore your mountain."

• • •

"Wow! That was more excitement than I expected from an evening," I said, handing Gil a mug of coffee.

"Do you think you've made some enemies?" she asked from behind her mug.

"Probably. But remember, they're for peace and love. We just witnessed the *love* part tonight. By the way," I started for the door, "I'm going to bring that bag of climbing hardware from the shed. We should look at it before we go to Petersburg."

Back in the kitchen, I pulled open the drawstring and gently opened the bag to spill its contents on the table.

"Carabiners!" Gill exclaimed. "And expansion bolts. Crack bolts and cams." She held up a device shaped like a figure eight. "This is for belaying and rappelling... going down a rock face. And this is a Jumar. It clamps onto a rope and allows you to pull yourself up. Looks as if Hiram Sibley was a pretty serious climber."

As all of the hardware came out of the bag, it was followed by a folded square of paper. I unfolded it to reveal a topographic map with Seneca near its center. It had been refolded so many times it almost fell apart. Its surface was covered with dried mud and numerous annotations.

"And will you look at this H2 and H3, halfway down the road to Seneca Rocks on Skidmore Mountain," I exclaimed. "I think we've found a key to Hiram's journals."

"And here's your place," Gil poked her finger at Gerwig Run. "And look here, there's an H1 not more than two miles up the mountain." She yawned and stretched. "I think you'd better get me home. This has been a long night."

I didn't argue.

— 22 —

Knowing a Cave
from a Hole in the Ground

Culden was waiting for me in the parking lot the next morning. She looked ready to cry. "Why the long face, Culden?"

"I just heard from Dicky Reb," she said with a croaky voice, "he leaves for Vietnam tonight."

"Oh God, for how long? And where?"

"Saigon for sure, but *Look* wants him to shoot combat situations. He said it would be no more than six months. Oh Five, I'm so worried," she flung her arms around my neck and burst into tears. "Five, I'm such a damned fool," she blubbered.

"Why, Culden? Dickie's the one going to Vietnam."

She sniffled and looked up at me with reddened eyes. "Richard asked me to marry him when he was here." Sob. "I said, 'Oh, no, Dickie. You go on with your career and I'll go on with mine. Just come and see us as often as you can. We argued about it... a lot. He *really* wants to get married and... I sent him off to Vietnam."

• • •

Culden's tears had dried and her spirits lifted by the mid-morning faculty meeting. Everyone else seemed busier than I so I volunteered to take a truck into Petersburg to pick up a shipment of clay and some other supplies. I had packed all the caving gear in a cardboard box that morning.

I crossed the walkway to Canby Auditorium and found Gil alone onstage, barefoot and in a burgundy leotard. Watching her was a pleasure as she moved through a dance routine, stretching and moving sinuously. She stopped and walked over to a tape recorder and hit the rewind button. I applauded.

"Good morning, Five!" she called. "You surprised me. I was just working on my lesson plans."

She sat on the edge of the stage and wiped her brow with a towel. "One nice thing about teaching dance, you don't have to write a long lesson plan. Just remember the steps."

"I've got to go to Petersburg to pick up some clay and stuff," I told her. "Wanna ride along and we'll go to the mine supply shop?"

"Sure! Let me get some shoes on. Do you think I can go like this?"

Her nipples fought the wet cloth of the leotard. "It's certainly OK with me," I responded.

• • •

Gil and I wrestled three crates of clay from the Railway Express dock into the bed of the pickup. Then we drove to Clark County Mine Supply. I carried the carton in and explained to the clerk what we needed. He was more than cooperative after one glimpse of Gil's costume.

"These are good lamps," he told us, "top-of-the line by Mine Supply. And expensive helmets with clip-on locks. You won't accidentally bump one of these babies off your head."

We bought two pounds of miner's grade carbide and flasks for keeping the stuff dry, plus some spare flints and striker wheels for the lamps.

"I'd like to help you out with the other stuff," he said with eyes never leaving Gil's chest, "but we don't carry that climbing gear. You know, there's a little climbing shop down at Dorcas."

• • •

The Piton Climb Shop was a fascinating place in a refurbished old barn about five miles south of Petersburg. "Gary Criswell," the young owner stated as he shook our hands. Glancing at Gil's sweat-stained leotard he said, "Looks as if you've already been climbing."

I opened the box and he gently poured its contents on the counter. "Good lights. Carbide you can depend on. Great hats. They're climbing hats, you know. Not miner's helmets." He sorted through the various pieces of equipment. "Do you know how to use the Jumar?" he asked.

"I've used one in Scotland, although I learned with the Prusick and French Prusick knots," Gil said.

Gary sorted through the rest of the gear, snapping the gates on carabiners and looking for flaws. "This is great equipment. How did you come by it?"

I told him about buying Five's Five and finding the gear in the shed.

"Hiram Sibley!" he exclaimed. "Man, he's a legend. You know, he was the first person to summit all the Seneca Rocks pinnacles? His only problem was he was a loner. Caved and climbed solo… and that's probably what got him."

He hoisted the two coils of rope. "So these ropes are probably at least eleven years old. If they were kept dry, they might be OK since they're great quality stuff. You want me to stress-test 'em for you?"

Gil nodded and Gary played out about ten feet of rope, then connected two sections to a machine with an air compressor. "We'll do the nine-millimeter first. It's a light line but should hold either of you if it's still OK." He turned on the compressor, then touched a button and the machine's arms pulled tight, stretching the rope. We watched as a dial moved to above 300 pounds. Gary turned off the machine and the rope went slack. "Pretty good piece of line. No use taking it past the breaking point." He tested the ten-millimeter rope and stopped when it pulled past 400 pounds without breaking.

"I'd say you could get two, three good years out of these if you don't abrade them much."

We left the Piton with new coveralls, much lighter and more supple than the canvas ones we'd seen at the Mine Supply store, kneepads, a pair of boots for me, and some other small gear. Gary waved us away with a promise that he'd try to get to Schoolhouse next Sunday.

"Aren't you excited, Five?" Gil exulted. "Now we've got to get you some training. Why don't we explore your hollow and see if we can find H1? We could start after work today and have all day Saturday."

• • •

The hollow that shelters Gerwig Run got steeper after we passed the hippies' fire circle. The creek became more of a torrent as it tumbled down the hill. Soon, we were climbing from sapling to sapling on the edge of a steep ravine. We found no sign of a trail.

"Perhaps the going'll be easier if we go up the hill a ways," I suggested.

"No, the creek will probably lead us to the cave, if there is one," she answered. "If we find it, we can make a trail on the way home."

Finally, the hollow narrowed to a steep gorge with trees on each side joining to form a dark canopy. We could hear a louder rush of water. I climbed up a big boulder, then reached down to give Gil a hand. Her eyes got bigger as I pulled her up and she could look between my legs.

"Did you see, Five? Did you see this waterfall?"

I turned slowly to keep my balance and saw for the first time Gerwig Run plunging out of a hole in a sheer rock face. The triangular-shaped hole was much bigger than the creek and on one side, a rock ledge ran into the darkness of the cave.

"I think we've found H1," Gil said, giving me a hug and a kiss on the back of the neck. Our climbing helmets clanked together.

• • •

We sat on a flat rock just outside the cave mouth and quickly devoured our supper sandwiches. Then Gil dug out the carbide lamps and unscrewed the top of one.

"First, we carefully fill the top water chamber. Then, we'll pour the carbide in the bottom chamber," she said opening the carbide flask. "Fill it about two thirds, then spit into it to get the acetylene going. Then screw the chamber back onto the lamp tightly. It's really important that the carbide stays dry until you're ready to start the lamp. Make sure this needle valve is tightly closed. When everything is screwed down tight, we'll open the needle valve just a little. Water goes into the carbide chamber and you'll hear it hissing."

Indeed, Gil held the lamp closer to my ear and I could hear a distinct hissing of gas being formed. "Then we turn the jet valve," she said, twisting another knob on the lamp's top. She placed her palm over the light's reflector and with a sweeping motion, produced a loud *pop* and a thin jet of flame. I applauded.

"Now you try."

I proved remarkably adept at filling and lighting the carbide lamps. We hooked them onto our helmets and stepped toward the ledge at the cave mouth. "We'll just take a peek inside," Gil said, "then decide what to do next. I'll lead if you don't mind, and you must be careful not to burn me on the ass."

In the waning daylight, the carbide flames seemed puny but their reflectors threw good soft illumination inside the cave. The ledge was about two feet wide and five feet above the rushing creek. Gil crept around a curving boulder where the ledge narrowed and I followed her steps precisely.

"Looky there," she shouted. "The creek comes from over there." She pointed across the narrow cave to a window where the water poured out of the wall. Most of it splashed down toward the outside but another flow vanished into a hole deeper in the mountain. The ledge continued around a curve toward the right.

Then we came to the place where the ledge ran into a nearly vertical wall. Gil aimed her head up the wall to illuminate another hole about fifteen feet up. At eye level, our lights revealed a carbide fresco on the rock. *H1–Sibley.*

"So we've found H1," I said.

"Yes, and I'll bet anything there's more cave beyond that passage up there. But not for tonight. Let's go back and do some learning."

The mouth of the cave was like a railroad tunnel, with wings of rock protecting the gorge on each side. Gil scrambled up one of the wings, picking her way from rock to rock, handhold to foothold. I watched her carefully, trying to remember her exact placements.

"Just don't look down," she warned. "Concentrate on the next place you'll put a hand or foot."

I managed to make my way up the embankment and sat at the top beside her, our legs hanging over the edge. "That wasn't so bad," I wheezed.

"We'll be scrambling up that little face like monkeys after two or three trips. In the meantime, I'll put a small blaze on this tree. Tomorrow, we can put an anchor and a help line down to the mouth."

We climbed down a wider, more gentle ridge that paralleled the creek. From time to time, we'd look back and make note of the route as we'd see it coming up. Suddenly, we broke from the brush onto a flat area that was obviously a roadway. "Bubby's moonshiner trail," I reckoned. "If we go this way, it should takes us right back down to the cabin." And it did.

I sat on the top step of my front porch and Gil sat two steps down, her head back in my lap. We smoked and sipped at a shared glass of 'shine.

"I'll swear, Five, but you're getting me absolutely addicted to this stuff. And I've suffered some real addictions," she said.

"Like what?" I asked.

"Well, I can't go thirty minutes without a fag."

"I'm good for at least an hour," I responded, making her laugh.

"Have you ever tried marijuana?" she asked quietly. "I love a good joint but thank God I'm not that addicted."

"I've tried it. All it did was make me dizzy," I said. "A lot like my very first cigarette. What other addictions do you have?"

"Sex!"

"Me too!"

She unzipped the front of her caver's suit and sniffed. "I stink."

"So do I. Should we take a shower?"

"Let's do."

— 23 —

Black as an Owl's Colon

I awoke suddenly to the hoot of an owl somewhere close, louder than the noise of the cascade. I must have moved because I suddenly felt a silky arm graze across my chest.

"Do you hear that?" Gil whispered. "In Scotland, some believe an owl's cry is bad luck… even a warning of death."

Running my tongue gently across her breasts, I whispered back, "In West Virginia, some say an owl hoots when folks are making love."

"Ohh, I like your version better," she gasped. "Make him hoot some more."

I rolled into the hollow of her lithe body and gently entered her. Gil reached her hand down and ran wet fingers behind my scrotum. What a sensation!

"My but you're a pretty man," Gil teased. "I recognized that the first night I saw you."

"My but you're a pretty woman," I answered. "But I didn't recognize it until you got in the shower with me."

"Selfish lout," she mock-punched me on the shoulder. "Just for that, no more snogging all day and definitely no shagging. And... I'll let you make coffee and fry me some eggs."

I rolled to get out of bed, brushing her stomach with my lips as I did so.

"Eggs later," Gil yelled, and she grabbed the back of my head and pulled me down.

• • •

In the front yard, we laid our gear on a blanket. "We'll take only what I think we'll need and a couple of ropes for training."

I locked the cabin and we set off up the trail for what we were now calling Sibley Cave. At Bubby's road, we turned north and walked a couple of hundred yards. "Do you remember where we came into the road?" Gil asked.

"No, but I left a flat rock in the middle of the road. Unless someone's moved it, we should know." We found the rock but could barely make out the broken weeds and brush where we'd emerged the night before. I entered the brush and immediately turned right, paralleling the road.

"Where are you going?" Gil asked.

"Let's keep the path secret for as long as we can. I'll go this way for about fifteen feet, then zig back the other way, then start up."

Following our blazes and other marks, we quickly reached the anchor tree above the falls. Gil reached into her bag and brought out a big screw with an eyelet on its end. Using a short length of stick through the eyelet, she drilled the screw into the base of the tree.

"We'll dirty this up and pile leaves over it when we leave," she commented, "and no one will ever know it's an anchor tree."

I watched as she clipped a carabiner into the eyelet, then ran a length of rope through and down the rock face. "We won't need to belay on this little face. This is just a guide and safety rope. It'll come in handy when we're tired at the end of the day."

While we spent the morning with Gil teaching me techniques, I could tell she was anxious to get into the cave. After a light lunch, we suited up and made our way to the entrance ledge. Familiar this time, the ledge seemed wider and shorter. Gil studied the entrance wall for about three minutes.

"I think we can free-climb it," she announced. "Watch my placements and try to follow them. If that jutting rock is solid, it'll be the place to boost yourself over the top."

Basking in her confidence in me, I watched as she placed a hand above her head and then boosted herself with her first foot placement. Gil moved carefully and when she hoisted herself over the edge of the passage she had made the free climb in about two minutes.

"It's a passage," she yelled, "and it looks like a long one."

My confidence waned with the second handhold and I dropped down for another try. My boots seemed thick and heavy, my fingers weak. Hanging over my head, Gil talked me up the free climb pitch. It wasn't nearly vertical and I labored to make it to the jutting rock.

"That's a good foot placement you've got there," she said, "so just rest for a second."

With all my strength, I pushed off from the foothold and did a pull-up that was tougher than anything in basic training. But the effort was worth it. I lay on the dry dirt floor of the upper passage.

The passage was high enough for us to walk upright. It curved slightly to the right and presented a slight upward grade. From time to time, we had to pick our way around piles of rock from ceiling collapses. "When do you think this stuff fell, Gil?" I asked at one arduous pile.

"Perhaps 200 years ago. Perhaps yesterday."

After several hundred feet, the passage opened onto a large room filled with rocks as big as my car. The breakdown sloped upward to the ceiling, perhaps fifty feet above us.

"Time to rest," Gil said. "Sit here and I'll give you the ultimate caver's experience."

I sat beside her on a flat rock, expecting some erotic physical contact. Gil pulled off her helmet and adjusted the needle valve that fed gas to the carbide lamp. Slowly the flame grew smaller, then went out. She removed my helmet and repeated the maneuver. Then we were in total blackness.

Silence. Black silence. The feeling of vast space around us... but not claustrophobic. Just the lack of sensation except for the sound of our breathing. "Isn't this incredible?" Gil whispered. "And every time you put out the lights, it'll be a wonderful experience but nothing like the first time."

Then I heard the gas moving in her lamp and with a pop of the lighter, the cave was restored to illumination.

After studying the rock pile for about twenty minutes, Gil led me in picking a route to the top. Amazingly, very few boulders in the jumble were even wobbly. When this ceiling came down, it came with a vengeance.

As I neared the top, my lamp revealed a black horizontal stripe behind the rock pile. "Look Gil, is that the passage? Or another room?"

"I think it's another chamber," she said. Excitement tinged her voice. The stripe seemed less than six inches high. Gil marched to her right, the lamp searching the black stripe. "You go to the left," she ordered. "See if there's a higher place."

I picked my way around a big boulder whose top almost touched the chamber ceiling. And there it was, a hole about two feet high and wide enough for a person to crawl through.

"I found something," I called. Gil's footsteps echoed through the chamber as she clambered toward me.

"A crawlspace," she exclaimed. "You found it. You've got the honors," she said. I insisted she go first and reluctantly, she got to her hands and knees and began making her way into the crawlspace.

"Oh Five," she exclaimed as the soles of her boots vanished into the hole. "Come see! It's something wonderful."

On a plateau the size of a ping pong table, Gil and I sat and stared in wonder at the huge room below. A wall fell off beneath us to the floor of the room. The ceiling soared above. And within the range of our lamps, a garden of what Gil called *speleothems* glistened.

Huge sheets of crystallized rock hung like drapes to our left and right. The ceiling was festooned with stalactites which in some places had grown to join with the forest of stalagmites rising from the floor. Colors could be made out in our dim lights... pale yellows and reds... but the overall theme was white with crystal highlights.

"It's a *live* cave," she whispered. "Until here, it's been a dead cave probably because of the roof fall. Listen." Indeed, we could hear the faint trickle of falling drops of water, adding their mineral load to the accumulation of millions of years.

We explored the ledge carefully and I spotted an eyebolt and carabiner at one end. Gil stomach-crawled to the edge and peered over, using her hat as a flashlight. "It's not a steep pitch and someone has made a number of trips to the floor. The carabiner is the same brand and size as Sibley's hardware. I'll bet he's the one who made this path."

"Can you sketch this when we get back, Five?"

"Not in detail… just from impression. This is nothing like a person's face. It's just… fantastic."

"Well, we'll want to draw a sketch map. We can use the 70-meter rope to make rough measurements." Gil paused and grinned at me wildly. "To heck with Schoolhouse Cave tomorrow. I want to be back here at the crack of dawn."

— 24 —

Crack of Dawn

Dawn hadn't cracked, but lightning was flickering across the ceiling, followed by ominous rumbles of thunder as I awoke. I rolled over and blew softly on Gil's cheek but she only rolled away, taking most of the sheet with her. Getting up quietly, I went down the stairs and lit the burner beneath the coffeepot, then went to the front porch and lit a Pall Mall.

Limbs and leaves were bending under a steady wind and the lightning was flashing beyond my mountain. Although it was nearly six o'clock, no predawn light showed. We were in for a big storm.

Throwing on a pair of shorts and shoes, I took my car keys and went out to the *deux chevaux*. I drove it across the ford and then walked upstream to the swinging bridge. By the time I got there, solitary raindrops were crackling the trees. I crossed the creek and around the studio deck and back to Five's Five by the studio bridge. Letting myself in the side door, I stripped off my clothes and sneaked back into bed.

Gil turned and snuggled against me just as the first real rain began to rattle against the shingles over our head.

• • •

The storm was unrelenting. Windblown rain pounded against the side of the cabin. Lightning crackled and from time to time, I could hear the crash of a limb or a tree in the forest. Immediate thunder made the windows rattle.

Gil and I lay there on our backs, arms crossed and hands gently caressing the other's body.

"I love storms," she said softly. "And this is one of the best ones I've ever seen."

"Or worst, depending upon your point of view. And… I'm going to have to go get the coffeepot off the fire before it boils dry."

"Do that," she ordered with a smirk, "but I'll bet you're not going to stay down there for a cup of coffee."

• • •

By the time light finally reached the narrow hollow, the fierce storm had blown through and we were left with a steady downpour and a raging creek. Gil was pleased that I had moved the car to the other bank.

"No going back in the cave today," she said. "But I'd love to see the entrance. Can we go up there and take a look?"

"After we eat something," I said, cracking eggs into a sizzling skillet.

We pulled ponchos over shorts and T-shirts and started up the path. For all its ferocity, the storm had not left much windfall and we made good progress through the soaking woods. Arriving at the anchor tree, we peered over the edge.

"Holy shit!" I exclaimed. A six-foot triangular-shaped plume of water spewed from the side of the rock face. The entire entrance was filled.

"The mountain's got to be full of caves and stream cracks," Gill laughed. "Wouldn't you love to see that from inside the cave?"

"Do you think the crystal room will get wet?" I asked.

"No, because it's uphill from the entrance. Perhaps a little more water but nothing like that torrent."

Ponchos or not, we were soaked by the time we got back to the house. I dried off but Gil stripped nude and performed dance steps in the rainy yard. I sketched the scenes as quickly as I could.

"How can you dance with no music?" I asked as I handed her a towel on the front porch.

"The music's in my head. How can you draw or paint without a photograph?"

"I understand."

"And I understand, sweet man, that it's been a wonderful weekend but I need to get home and ready for work tomorrow." She wrapped the towel around her middle. "God, I don't think I have anything clean to wear. Come on. Take me home."

Gillian dressed in her yellow caving suit and we marched past the studio to the swinging bridge. Bubby's wisdom in repairing it was evident, as the creek was a roaring torrent just two feet below the walkway.

On the way down the lane, I had to run through two places where water had covered the road by a few inches. Gil laughed at the 2CV's little windshield wiper motor which ran both wipers from an eccentric crank.

We pulled up by her apartment. She leaned over and kissed me, avoiding the tranny stick. "Wanna come in? One last snog?"

"No. Like you, I have things to do if I want to keep this existence up. And I imagine one last snog would lead to another addiction. Seriously though, do we tell anyone about the cave? I'm so excited about it."

"I know. I'd love to take everyone I know up there and show them." Her brow wrinkled. "But just for now, let's keep it a secret."

— 25 —

Victory Over Bare Stupidity

I spent my Sunday afternoon sketching my memories of the Crystal Room and working on a map of the cave. For the first time, I was challenged to translate recall into lines on paper.

Then I opened Hiram Sibley's journal and, with a crow-quill pen and India ink, I went to a blank page and began my entry regarding H1. As I wrote, I avoided giving the cavern a name. I couldn't claim it since it wasn't on my land and Gillian had as much right to think of a name as I did.

So our magical cave continued to be H1. Sibley hadn't bothered to record his findings on the cave other than to mark it on the topo map. *Was it the first cave he'd discovered?*

His entries for H2 and H3 were also strange. He hadn't dated them or given good descriptions as to their locations. It was Livvy's recollection of the Lazarus Mine on Skidmore Mountain that provided the only clue, but Hiram's description didn't mention a saltpeter mine. And H3, Sibley's Hole, described what I now suspected to be a 'dead cave' and hinted at connecting to a larger network. Weary from the weekend's activities, I closed the journals and resolved to put caves out of my mind for the work week.

• • •

It rained for two more days, so everyone continued to prepare for the oncoming wave of students. Driving to work Wednesday morning, I was surprised at the traffic on the highway to town. Old buses, VW vans, and near-wreck cars were driving south, loaded with people.

"Did you hear the news?" Hoopie asked me as soon as I got into the office. "The Seneca Town Council is hearing an ordinance today and the hippies are going to demonstrate."

"What ordinance? Just like that one some asshole in Berkeley tried to pass? Making it illegal for a woman to appear in public without a bra?"

"I'd go down there and help 'em demonstrate if I didn't think I'd get fired," Culden commented from her doorway. "Just because some dumbass druggist got an eyeful of boob when some hippie chick was buying condoms. Now the whole town's righteous about brassieres."

I added, "From what I've seen on other campuses, the counterculture mode of dress should just about be getting to these quaint hollows. Wait'll they get an eyeful of that!"

Word trickled up the hill that the demonstration outside town hall was growing. After lunch, we shut up the Fine Arts Building and all drove down to watch.

Three town cops were guarding the door to town hall and Sergeant Glencoe was surreptitiously jotting in his notebook. About sixty ragged young people in all manner of clothing marched in a long oval on the sidewalk in front of Seneca's government building.

Since the jail was in the basement, anyone arrested would not have far to travel. The hippies were very careful not to block anyone's access to the sidewalk but when an occasional demonstrator would stumble off the curb, one of the cops would immediately blow his whistle and motion the hippie back to the sidewalk.

We were all taken aback when Gillian McDearmid emerged from town hall and made a pumping motion with her fist. Immediately, one of the hippies turned on a boombox and the strains of *White Rabbit* blasted over downtown Seneca.

"Christ! Is *she* part of this?" Culden muttered.

"Well, she's sure not wearing a bra," I commented. Gil was in her usual leotard and skirt combination and her nipples were obvious.

"Make love, not stupidity!" was the chant that went up from the demonstrators, competing with Grace Slick and the Airplane. Their pace picked up with the music, and their crude signs jumped up and down. "Make love, not stupidity!" The cops began to fidget as the demonstration became less orderly.

Suddenly blouses and T-shirts went flying through the air and six topless women scattered from the circle of marchers. The hippies cheered. The onlookers cheered. The cops were stunned and seemed planted in place.

I was thankful to see Gil making her way toward us, leotard intact.

"Hi, guys, isn't this great?" she called.

"Are you demonstrating?" I hissed in her ear.

"Not really, but I did help out. I gave them the signal when the council started debating the ordinance." She smiled at us, "but I *have* demonstrated. At Holy Loch against nuclear subs. At Lakenheath against the bomb. I even danced nude in Princess Street Gardens in support of women's rights."

"I hope that's in Scotland," I commented.

"Oh yes, Edinburgh. They have a really comfortable wing for women in the nick."

Two dozen topless women racing around Seneca's tiny downtown evidently awakened the town council to the folly of its thinking. I later found out the hippies had called the Elkins TV station but they didn't have the guts to run bare-titty footage. After an afternoon of excitement, it was still lawful for people to walk the streets of Seneca without a brassiere.

• • •

Gil and I explored the cave later that week. I made many sketches and we belayed down the path into the Crystal Room. It was there that Gil and I decided to name the cave *Sibley's Crystal Cave*. We found a narrow pathway worn among the stalagmites and gypsum flowers. From a couple of niches, flowers of long calcium needles sprouted out. I picked up several broken needles from the floor but we were careful not to touch the fragile displays.

In the rear of the room, we found a small lake that seemed to vanish into the lowering ceiling. Clear as vodka, its bottom was composed of calcium formations that looked like fried eggs, perhaps three or four inches deep. Gil removed her shoe and rolled up her pants leg to insert her foot in the pool.

"Man, it must be four feet deep," I commented. "Your foot isn't near the bottom."

"And it disappears beneath this wall," she added, "which means there's likely another room beyond, if we could get to it. I think the water level is up from the rain, but we'll find out when we return."

• • •

I was surprised when Gil refused to stay for dinner and some snogging. "I just can't, Five. I'm sorry but I have something else to do tonight."

So I went back to Sibley's journal, added to the cave map and began to translate my sketches into a cartoon on canvas. My mind pondered how to paint the Crystal Room and what media to use to capture the sparkling speleothems.

The owl was hooting as I turned out the light and crawled into bed. I don't think I was quite asleep but I must have been, because the telephone was ringing. As I stumbled down the stairs, I resolved to get an extension for the bedroom.

"H'lo," I mumbled.

"Five? Five Lowrey?"

"Yep, who's this?"

"Five, it's Josefus Kostic."

"Benjo? Where are you? Are you still a spook?"

"Not on the phone, Five. I'm in Washington but I'm planning to fly down to Petersburg. To see you. Can you meet me at the Grant County Airport tomorrow morning about ten?"

"Sure can. Should I bring Culden? I know she'd love to see you."

"No. We'll talk about that tomorrow."

— 26 —

The Sphinx Beckons Me Back

As the Piedmont DC-3 banked for its final approach, I thought about Benjo's call. Josefus "Benjo" Kostic was a pledge brother of mine in ACE and joined the Army's CIC after graduation. I followed in his footsteps a year later to avoid the draft but in my almost-five years in the CIC, we'd seen each other only once.

Benjo climbed down the aircraft stairs and we shook hands, then gave each other a big old European backslap hug.

"Man, Five, you sure look good. Dad's kept me up on your activities in Athens."

"And where the hell have you been? I joined the spooks so we could get together and then I never saw you but one time."

"Ahh, you don't want to know... and of course, I can't tell you," he grinned. "Here and there. Iran for a few months. Vietnam. Man, *there's* a clusterfuck for the CIC. And the past year, I've been on your old beat... hunting radicals on campus."

139

"Well, shit, Benjo, you just missed one of the great demonstrations of the counterculture. Topless chicks protesting a brassiere ordinance."

"Yeah, well..." he grinned again. "Is there somewhere quiet where we can talk?"

"Sure, these mountains are vast but there's supposed to be a pretty park down by the trout hatchery."

We lit up and leaned back against a picnic table overlooking the stream and the hatching beds beyond. A weeping willow swayed above our heads and hid us from view.

"Five, I'm here on business. Your business and... I don't know if you'll like it or not," he said somberly. I didn't respond as he handed me a familiar brown envelope.

"These are your orders. You've been recalled to active reserve."

I started to open the envelope. He put his hand on my arm. "Let me explain 'em instead of you reading the jargon. Army Intelligence Center wants you undercover at Seneca University. I don't have a need to know but something big is happening here."

"Something big at this jerkwater university? Damn, they've only had ROTC for about six years!"

"Whatever, AIC is concerned. You won't have to change anything about your job, your teaching, just keep your eyes open and report what you see."

"Agent Reports? Written ARs?"

"Nope. Just verbal."

"And who's my control? Where'll he be?"

"You're lookin' at him. I'm going undercover in Morgantown... WVU. They don't play Seneca in football, do they?"

"Naw. The Mountaineers are out of our league. But we do play OU and Marshall this year. I think they're shooting to get into the Mid American Conference. Now, are you going to get to stay for awhile, see my place? And how about Culden?"

"Yep. I can stay the weekend. And the story for Culden is I'm stationed in D.C. and have some leave time I've got to use or lose.

• • •

"No shit, real moonshine?" Benjo held his nearly clear glass up to the afternoon light. "Stuff's pretty tasty. Do you think I'll be able to get this in Morgantown?"

"It's the same damn state and I think 'shine is one of the Mountaineer traditions. I'll ask my friend Bubby. He probably knows some folks up there."

I had toured Benjo around Five's Five and suspected he was thoroughly impressed. "With E-7 pay coming in, you'll be a rich man." He admired my paintings and was especially taken with the nudes of Gil.

Finally, we got down to more details on my new secret life.

"We've seen a build-up of counterculture types this summer," I told him. "Interestingly, they've settled just up the highway about four miles and taken over a whole hollow."

"Laurel Town," he said quietly. "We have an operative undercover there. He'll be contacting you soon."

"Shit, I hope it's not my secretary... or her doped-out husband," I commented.

"No, I don't think so. Our guy's name is John Piggot. He's ex-Army, former Criminal Investigator, and a pretty good hand—a little older and he poses as a Viet vet. Like many of these hippies, they don't know his real name. He goes by 'Pig.'"

"And he's got a big dick, too, when it's hard." I laughed. "Pig! I ran that bastard and two naked chicks off my land just a few weeks ago." I reached up and pulled the vermin gun out of its doorway slot. "Gave 'em a going away shot with this. Think I blew out a taillight on their VW bus."

"Christ, Five. You can't go around shootin' at people!"

"Just watch me. It's the code of the hills, and besides—it's just loaded with rock salt."

• • •

Culden's arrival was greeted with more hugs and kisses. Benjo had been responsible for the plan that apprehended Culden's OU attacker in our college days and she had professed love for him ever since.

"And I've got news," she cried. "Shitbrain Richard West got blown up in Vietnam!" Tears welled in her eyes and Kostic and I were in shock. "Land mine blew his jeep clear into a rice paddy," she said grinning through the tears.

"You're not joking, but he *is* alive. You wouldn't be grinnin' otherwise," I chided her.

"He's alive. Minus two fingers of his left hand and a big chunk out of his ass. But he's alive and coming home."

By the time Gil arrived about eight, the three of us were totally hammered on moonshine. Benjo grabbed Gil and planted a passionate French kiss on her. She responded, then dug back into her car and came back with makings.

We watched in fascination as she rolled a big joint and sat cross-legged on the porch swing to light up. The grass burned slowly after each of us toked, and the joint kept making the rounds. Gil accepted a glass of 'shine and rolled a second joint.

It was after midnight when I awoke, took a leak off the porch step, then staggered upstairs and fell onto my bed. At three o'clock, chilled air woke me. I grabbed a pair of blankets and went down to the porch, covering the snoring trio.

Sunlight and raucous birdcalls woke me. For some reason, my head wasn't bursting. I went downstairs and put a pot of coffee on the burner. Then I looked onto the porch. The scene made me go for my Nikon. On the porch floor, Benjo lay between Gil and Culden, their heads on his arms and each of his hands covering a breast. Each mouth formed an O and they snored nearly in harmony.

Shaved and showered and with a mug of coffee and a Pall Mall, I sat on the swing and observed my trio of friends. Gil rolled slightly into Benjo and his hand responded by slipping under her T-shirt. *This was getting a little bothersome!*

Culden's nose twitched and I could tell she was catching the odors of caffeine and nicotine. She opened her eyes and looked sheepishly at me. I smiled and she smiled back. Gently, she moved Benjo's left hand away from her breast and got up slowly.

As she scooted onto the swing and took my coffee away, she whispered, "I guess that'll be the last five-fingered left hand that boob will feel… for a long time."

Bleary-eyed, Culden drove off to reclaim her child and, hopefully, nurse her headache. Gil remained snoring on the porch. Benjo and I moved to the studio to let her sleep and have some privacy.

"I'm instructed to give you your credentials," he said rubbing his forehead. "I don't suppose you've got a classified safe here?"

"No, but I know somewhere they'll be just as safe," I said, thinking of Bubby Bristo. "When should I use them? I thought I'd just be an informant."

"Don't know. Just know I'm supposed to hand 'em over. Do you have a sidearm? Any weapon besides that little snake gun?"

"Ohhh, yeah. I unlocked the gun chest and one at a time, produced the two High Standards and my little Lady Smith .32. Benjo sucked in his breath in admiration. "The little revolver I'm going to keep," I told him, "but I'm thinking of selling the other two."

"Wow, Five. I'll buy the target pistol if I can afford it. And I can sure find some gun collectors that would go for the automatic."

"What do you think they're worth?"

"The automatic? With the custom grips, probably a thousand, fifteen hundred."

I whistled.

"And I'd give you fifteen hundred for the target pistol," he said, "if I can make payments."

We hiked on up the trail and I showed him the mouth of Sibley's Crystal Cave and the waterfall. By the time we got back, Gil was sitting on the bench of the yard table with her head in her hands. "My God, what did we do last night?" she moaned.

"I think we… ah, you… smoked half the pot production of Jamaica and we had a few nips of Old Bristo," I said. "Don't you remember?"

"I've *got* to lay off that stuff. I wasn't the only one tokin', was I?"

"Nooo! You definitely had some help," Benjo said.

"Here, drink this," I ordered. She took the coffee mug and sipped, then grimaced. "What's in this?"

"Just a tiny slug of Old Bristo."

• • •

Benjo took the wheel of Gil's car and drove them back to town. I went to the studio and dabbled for a couple of hours, then took a nap. By late afternoon, I rang the Smoke Hole Lodge but got no answer from Benjo's room. Gil's phone rang and rang but no one picked up.

I drove over to Bristos' with my painting of Bubby and Tibby and my CIC credentials.

"Mr. Five, it's just wonderful," Tibby exclaimed as she walked around the matted and framed painting. Bubby was busy pounding a nail into the wall to hang the painting. "Look how pretty you made me!"

"You're a beautiful woman, Tibby," I answered earnestly. "You're both beautiful people."

"I also have a favor to ask," I continued. I told them about my CIC role and being called back to undercover inactive reserve. Bubby agreed to find a place for my credentials where I could get to them quickly. Then I drove home and crashed on my bed.

— 27 —

From Quiet to Chaos

"Hey, I'm Coach Art Bruce! Welcome to Seneca," the burly man with a Marine flattop haircut pumped my hand. "I go around campus on my first day back and greet all the faculty. Everyone says that's a sure sign of fall."

"Five Lowrey, Coach. You start practice this week?"

"Yep, the horses will be here starting tomorrow. You like football? I understand you went to Ohio U? You know we play them third game?"

With a promise of midfield season tickets, Coach Bruce whirlwinded off to pump Hoopie's hand and go through the same drill.

I walked over to Gil's office but found it locked.

• • •

Another figure loomed in my door. This was a young man in khakis, coat and tie. "Professor Lowrey?" he pronounced my name correctly. When I nodded, he stepped into the office and took my hand. "I'm Josh Tinkler, president of the student body."

"And president of Alpha Chi Epsilon?" I asked as the gave me the familiar *peculiar* grip.

"Welcome to Seneca, Brother Lowrey," he grinned.

"I'm glad to meet you, Josh, but I'm not really very active with ACE these days," I commented.

"Sorry to hear that," he said earnestly. "I was hoping I could prevail upon you to help us out… as chapter adviser." He paused. "Brother Klipford at OU called me about you. He told me a little about The Thirteen affair."

"That was a long time ago," I responded. "And this is my first teaching job so I want to devote as much time to it as I can."

"Well, good luck. And give me a call at the ACE house if there's anything I can do to help you."

The afternoon was filled with visitors. Susan Longmeyer, president of Kappa Kappa Gamma and of Panhellenic Council, came by to say hello. Presidents and chairmen of various student clubs came to introduce themselves.

Late in the afternoon, a familiar figure knocked and walked in. He was cleaned up from the last time I saw him, and wore clothes. "Professor Lowrey? I'm John Piggot and some friends told me to look you up."

"Hi, Mr. Piggot. Are you a student? A little older perhaps, so you're not a freshman?"

"Yeah, I'm transferring from Southern Illinois—thinking about taking a couple of art classes."

"Where are you living?" I countered.

"Got a place up at Jordan Run. Been living in Laurel Town, but with fall coming on, I decided we'd be more comfortable inside."

"We?" Which one makes we? Blondie or Piglet?

"Yeah, my girlfriend. I think you've seen her a couple of times… name's Blondie and she got caught taking a shower here."

• • •

Still no answer from Gil's telephone. On the way home, I drove by her place and knocked on the door but no one answered. Then I drove over to Culden's to ask her if she knew anything.

"No, all I know is Benjo called this morning to say goodbye. He said Gil had some errands to run in Petersburg and she would take him to the airport. They didn't want to bother you 'cause you were probably hung over."

We took R.T. to the Linger Longer for hamburgers and fries. "I think we're really ready to roll, Five," Culden told me. "I'll get our advisory assignments from the dean tomorrow. I think you'll probably have five freshmen and three upperclass students."

Lord, I'd completely forgotten Faculty Adviser duties. "When do we start?"

"Monday's the first day of Freshman Week. I know one transfer upperclassman has requested you specifically as his adviser. A guy named John Piggot."

"Yeah, I've already met him. He's a hippie."

"For real?"

"Oh, yes, he's the guy that was doin' the two girls on my creekbank," I reminded her. "Remember, Gil and I ran them off with the vermin gun?"

"Oh, Lord. Do you think he'll be a problem?"

"Nope. He seems like a really gentle person. Might even major in art."

• • •

Although I kept looking, I couldn't find Gil for the rest of the week. The Music Department secretary only knew that she'd taken a few days off.

Seneca University's campus became even more busy as Freshman Week and registration drew closer. By Friday, clumps of sorority girls flitted around Eden Fields, trying to pick the best spot for their orientation tables. Shirtless hippie men meditated in the sunlight. Geeky-looking students carried card tables and painted signs.

Across it all, the sounds of music battled with each other. As the breezes shifted around the open plaza, *The Times They Are A-Changing* would gain a few bars of supremacy over *White Rabbit,* which would be replaced by *Me and Bobby McGee.* Occasionally the twang of a sitar would butt in. The breezes also brought the faint aroma of burning pot.

Under a giant tulip poplar tree, a small group had set up tanks and a tie-dyeing station. Everyone seemed to be wearing tiny round spectacles with blue or pink lenses. It was very hard to tell students from the hippie tribe, and no one seemed to care. A few see-though blouses revealed that brassieres were going out of style.

Livinda Ferris sidled up to me as I watched the scene. "It's really something, isn't it? I've never seen the likes of it here before," she said. "And most of these kids are campus leaders." Then, "I had a visit from Special Agent Kostic earlier in the week," she said in a lower voice. "He briefed me on your situation, Five. Frankly, I'm relieved but I do worry about your teaching."

"I'll do my best, Livvy. But please keep this quiet."

"Oh, don't worry. Kostic was very emphatic about it being classified information and in the national interest."

• • •

Later in the afternoon, an ancient and brightly psychedelic-painted school bus pulled into our parking lot and about two dozen hippies piled off, rapidly mingling with the crowd. What a weird group they were… long gowns and flowing shirts, headbands, face paint, and some of the widest bell bottoms I'd ever seen.

Four people carried a small platform and set it up near the tie-dyeing station. Guitars appeared and, with a couple of feedback squawks of a sound system, someone opened with a very good version of Jim Morrison's *Light My Fire.*

Puff, the Magic Dragon followed, by a trio that sounded a lot like Peter, Paul and Mary. With every verse that emphasized *Puff,* billows of smoke wafted up from the growing crowd.

On the edge of Eden Fields, groups of parents with their freshman children looked on with awe. The boys and girls of the class of 1970 looked as if they would love to join in, if only the old folks would go home. The 'hippie lifestyle' had arrived at Seneca U!

As darkness fell, candles were lighted and the scene became even more psychedelic. I retrieved my sketchbook from the office and settled on the steps of the Fine Arts Building to capture the scene. I felt pressure on my shoulder blades and turned to discover Gillian standing behind me.

"And so begins the *semester of love,*" she whispered. "Isn't it something?"

I motioned for her to sit beside me. As she sat, I noticed her dirty bare feet protruding from beneath her long pleated skirt. An elaborate gold chain hung across the sweat-stained curves of her leotard.

"Where have you been, Gil?"

"Out there dancing with the tribe," she said. "But now I want to go home. Take me home, Five."

— 28 —

Gillian Spirals Down

By 'home,' she meant Five's Five, not her town apartment. I drove slowly and she curled into the seat, eyes closed.

"Meditating?" I asked softly.

"Unh-unh," she muttered. "I've been on a trip and now... I'm reliving it in my head."

"Are you OK?

"Unh-uh. I have *been* OK and now I'm back down."

"Gil, you're not making a whole lot of sense."

"Sensible talk. Sensible singing. Sensible dancing," she sing-songed. "Did I leave any grass at Five's Five?"

As I drove across the ford, she told me to stop. She opened her door and fell out of the car, face down into the shallow pool. I pulled the car up to the bank and then ran back to pick her up, just as she gasped and vomited. I carried her soaked body up to the yard and gently placed her in the soft grass.

"Gil, are you all right?" I whispered. She shivered, then opened her mouth and began to snore.

She didn't wake up as I manhandled her limp form up the stairs. I settled her gently on the floor and began to strip off the sodden skirt and leotard. Her feet were filthy and her legs badly needed shaving. I carried her into the shower and turned on the cold water. She sat there, head between her knees with the icy spray pouring down.

I stripped to my skivvies, turned the water to warmer and crawled into the shower. Gently, I soaped her dirty body noting that her armpits could stand a shave as well. Finally I rinsed her off and dragged her out of the shower to towel her dry. Nothing erotic about this. I felt like a male nurse.

Pulling a sweatshirt over her head, I then carried her to the bed and tucked her in. I grabbed a blanket and went downstairs to the couch.

It was three a.m. by my watch and I lay there on the couch listening to Gil's sobs from the bedroom. At long last, I climbed the stairs. She was curled in a fetal position and sobbing steadily.

"Gillian? Gil, are you all right?" More sobs.

I sat on the edge of the bed and ran my hand over her shoulders, down her arms. Finally, her crying subsided and she drifted back into sleep.

I went back downstairs and tried to sleep but the blanket seemed too little and a cold draft was coming from somewhere.

• • •

Sitting on the porch at dawn. Coffee was steaming from my mug and I lit another Pall Mall, blowing a cloud of smoke into the chilly morning. I heard the commode flush upstairs. Finally, her footsteps on the stairs told me that Gillian McDearmid had survived her night.

"Mornin," I said gently. She stood in the doorway, the sweatshirt damp and stretched to her thighs.

"Mornin'. Can I have a sip?" I handed her the mug and she lifted it to her mouth with both hands. She returned it to me and gently settled into one of the rockers, pulling her knees up to her chin.

"Anything you want to talk about?" I asked quietly. She nodded yes but didn't say a word.

We sat there in silence. I got up and poured her a mug of coffee, refilling my own.

"Thanks," she whispered, but we continued our silent vigil.

"It's so pretty here," she mused. "How could I have thrown it all away?"

"I don't understand," I responded.

"Oh Five," she bawled. The coffee spilled onto the floor as she waved the mug. "Oh Five, I feel so awful. I feel like an utter shit."

"Do you want to tell me?"

"Oh Five, I went home Sunday afternoon and had couple more hits. Then I walked over to..." she paused and broke into another spasm of sobs, "...over to the Smoke Hole and... went to Benjo's room. We smoked some more and drank some more and we... we fucked. Not made love, just fucked."

I met this revelation with silence.

"The phone rang several times and I knew it was you. But he wouldn't answer it."

She looked up at me. "Five, don't hate him. It was all me. I'm a slut and he's just a guy."

"Gillian. Benjo's been gone since Monday. It's Saturday morning. Where have you been?"

Gil wailed and swayed back and forth in the rocker, tears running down her cheeks. "I was out of pot so I drove up to Laurel Town. I met some people there and we partied. We smoked and sang and fucked and I had the time of my life... 'cause I'm a slut and I always have been."

• • •

She took another shower and fixed her unruly hair some. After a decent breakfast, Gil looked almost human, even managing a faint smile.

"I guess I've really screwed it up, eh?" she said. "You know what makes me really sad?"

Silence.

"That I'll never get to see Sibley's Crystal Cave again."

"Why not? A week of debauchery didn't make you any less a caver or a climber." I guess this was said to make her feel better, because I really didn't have my heart in it.

"Aw, it just won't be the same. I think you'd better take me home now."

— 29 —

Chaos into Order

Monday morning I turned from my lane onto the highway and was surprised to see Pig standing on the roadside, a red gasoline can in his hand. The gas can was Benjo's prearranged signal for a meeting.

"Need a ride?" I called through the open window.

"Often do. I'm out of gas," he gave the countersign.

Seated, he lit a cigarette and settled back. "I saw you at the *be-in* Friday night," he commented. "You were sketching. Several people thought you were a narc or the fuzz."

"I'm a painter. I thought it was a remarkable scene, and soon, several people will be able to see the painting."

"Well, I told them you were a pretty straight guy."

"You want to talk to me about something?"

"Several things. You know my woman, Blondie?" I nodded yes. "Well, it was one wooly week in Laurel Town. I found out Blondie is doing that pothead sculptor up on top of the hill."

"Doug Byrd? My secretary's husband?"

"Yeah, that's the one. You'd better be ready for some trouble there." Pause. "And then there was this dancer chick there most of the week. Really wild scene. She did a lot of people all week, smoked a lot of dope, even hit a tab or two."

"Tab? LSD?"

"Yep. She was pretty screwed up when the Coasters put her on the bus Friday night. I heard she ran a train on the bus."

"What are the Coasters? That gang in the painted schoolbus?"

"Yeah, they just came in from the West Coast or the desert somewhere. I have a feeling they're not all about peace and love," he answered.

"What have you heard about the university? Why all this interest from the hippie tribe?"

"Man, this is an ideal academic commune. Way out in the sticks. Lots of open land to squat on. Not much law," he recited. "But something else is going on… I don't know what yet… but something big is going on."

I let Pig out at a gas station and drove on to work. *Something big?*

• • •

Once again, Cyndy Byrd was fighting tears as I entered the office. I peered in the other offices and realized I was the first one in. I poured a cup of coffee and went into my sanctum. Cyndy followed me with a newspaper-wrapped package in one hand.

"Guess what, Five? Today's my birthday."

"Well, happy birthday, Cyndy. I wish I'd known. But tell you what, I'll buy you some lunch."

She ignored my offer. "Wanna see what my husband gave me… made me… for my birthday?" She unwrapped the newspaper and thrust an extraordinary ceramic sexual organ at me.

"A dildo? Doug gave you a dildo?"

"I guess," she gulped. "Actually, it's a bong." She pointed to the testicles which were hollow to hold the weed. "So whoever uses it as a bong looks like a cocksucker." She sobbed. "But it's more than that. It's a message. I know he's been boffing that Blondie slut for the last week."

Again silence. My best part of valor.

"Do you think Culden will fire me if I leave him?"

"Why would I fire you?" Culden asked from the door. "Leave who?"

Cyndy twirled and put the bong close to her lips. "Doug. Because he's telling me to suck off. He's found another bitch."

Culden pursed her lips. "You mean get a divorce. Leave him like that?"

"It's not a big deal," she gulped. "We aren't married."

Culden and I both gasped. So did Jaylene and Hoopie now standing in my door.

"So you're not really Cyndy Byrd?" Culden asked.

"Oh, yeah. I sure am. But he's not really Doug Byrd. He's Douglas Kaminsky, and he hasn't had a really good erection since he started smokin' pot," she stormed.

• • •

We four Fine Arts faculty had our feet on the lounge coffee table, four cigarettes going. "Lord give me strength," Culden said. "Too much drama and the semester hasn't even started."

"Cyndy's got all her belongings in the office closet," Jaylene said. "Not a whole lot. Just clothes and some toiletries."

"She can't sleep here, even though we do have a shower," Culden said. Hootie and Jaylene got up and left the room.

"I know someone who has some room and may just be looking for some company," I volunteered.

"Gillian McDearmid?" Culden asked. "I saw you with her on the steps Friday night."

"Culden, you're very observant... and very astute." I told her the whole story.

"So now we've got to find you another girlfriend," Culden sniffed. "That's really very sad. But she's hinted that she was kind of a wild child before she got here."

"And I can't bring myself to blame Benjo," I added. "I mean, I slid right into the sack with Gil. It's only natural."

Culden and I walked across the lawn to Canby Hall to find Gil sitting desolately on a piano stool. She smiled faintly at us.

"Gil? How would you like to do us a big favor?" Culden asked. Then she explained Cyndy's plight.

"I don't see why not," Gil answered. "I'm sort of fragile myself," with a firm stare at me, "right now. Perhaps we'd be good for each other."

• • •

Marilyn Kretzman was a tiny woman with clear hippie eyeglasses and stringy black hair. Otherwise, she looked like the sophomore advisory client that I expected.

"Professor Lowrey. I've always wanted to be an artist but I'm afraid I don't have much talent. Can talent be taught?" she asked shyly.

"I'm not sure, but I can sure try. Why don't you sign up for Drawing 1 and we'll find out, probably long before the drop and add deadline."

And junior Jim Gillespie was the exact opposite. Outgoing, carefree, and not very academically inclined. "I drew this from a matchbook cover," he said proudly, and passed over a sketch of the pretty girl from the Famous Artists School. Many years ago, I had drawn from the same matchbook cover, impressed my faculty adviser and began my career in art.

"Frankly, I'd just like to get in a class and draw naked ladies," he grinned.

"I think, Jim, you're likely to see more naked ladies on Eden Fields this year than you will in a class."

• • •

"Five, come on quick, you've got to see this," Hoopie nearly shouted. He and Jaylene ran down the hall for the front door with me following.

"Goddamn, if this isn't something." On the serpentine bike path, students were bent over their handlebars, laboring up the hill.

"There's one," Jaylene said, "pointing to a comely girl wearing a strange, brightly patterned blouse. The neck was deeply scooped and the arm holes descended halfway to her waist. Her pedaling posture let the blouse gape open, exposing her entire naked freshman chest.

"It's called a butterfly blouse," Jaylene said. "I saw pictures of them in Vogue. But man I never thought they'd expose *that* much." Another butterfly cyclist puffed her way past us and Hootie whistled under his breath.

"Boy oh boy, but I think I'll need a smoke break out here every time the class bell rings," he chortled. "And I hope winter never comes."

— 30 —

Someone Kicked the Hive

After the relatively quiet summer months of preparation, the frenzy of Freshman Week was if someone had kicked over a hive of bees. Eden Fields was swarming with students attempting to recruit new members for their causes... library volunteers, blood donors, language clubs, religious organizations... and some new ones. *Students Against War,* the *Mole People, Students Doing Something,? Underground.*

Manning these tables were people who looked like the Laurel Town hippie tribe. Livinda Ferris walked up to me with a wan smile. Several dogs ran around the green and one, with a neckerchief around his neck, chased after Frisbees tossed by his hippie master.

"Good morning, Five. This reminds me of a Brueghel," she laughed.

"Elder or Younger?" I returned.

"Oh, wow, right on your toes, aren't you? Pieter the Elder. Perhaps an *adoration* or a *village festival.*" She plucked at my sleeve. "How in the world are we going to keep track of these people? I can't very well go around asking for identification."

James Patterson

"I'm hoping that our students will turn out to be better-washed than the visitors from Laurel Town, at least in a week or so," I commented. "Smell will tell. But I do remember wearing the same ratty sweater for about three weeks straight... back in my undergrad *beatnik* days."

Livvy shuddered. "When we've got registration complete, we'll be able to use ID cards to control admission to classes and so forth, but that's five more days. I can just imagine... what's that girl's name over there?" she pointed to Blondie, who was helping Doug Kaminsky display rows of small ceramics.

"I can just imagine her showing up at the Kappa house for rush," she added mirthlessly. "By the way, I haven't seen Gillian for some time. I understand she took a few days off last week."

"Liv? How did you come to hire Gillian?"

"A friend at Aberdeen University told me about her. Said she was a very talented woman, very exciting dancer." She pursed her lips. "She said Gillian needed some help, a change of scene. I got the feeling she was sort of wild as an undergraduate. Why? Are you and Gillian having some problems."

"You might say. I don't want to go into it now, but Gil does need help. And I'm not the one to help her any more."

• • •

My freshman counselees were just as lost for a plan as I had been at Ohio University in 1954. One of the girls told me she had come to Seneca just to escape her parents' desire that she major in religion. Another freshman woman showed up in full hippie regalia, even though she was only three days out of her home in a place called Pocatellico.

Hoopie told us of a counselee who had been accepted at Davis and Elkins College but drove through Seneca on his way and decided to enroll here.

Three mornings were taken up with three freshman convocations, where President Skinner and Livinda made identical speeches and introductions. The freshman class nearly taxed the seating capacity of every building but the stadium and fieldhouse, both judged too impersonal. So the entire faculty was introduced three times at Canby Auditorium.

On Wednesday night, the faculty gathered at the Faculty Club for an introduction cocktail party. We mingled and reintroduced ourselves at a personal level. Coach Art Bruce was a center of attention as football fans pumped him about the team and the home opener against West Virginia Wesleyan in two weeks. Gillian McDearmid looked stunning in a simple black dress. "Hello, stranger," she greeted me.

"Hi, Gil, how are you surviving Freshman Week? And your new roomie."

"OK, I guess. And Cyndy's a great gal. Lots of common sense... which I obviously don't have. I've reintroduced her to a razor and we got her hair cut and curled."

"Yes. We've noticed she's cleaned up really well. I can't tell you how much we appreciate it."

"Oh, she's good for me too," she shrugged. "Five? Can we go back to the cave sometime."

"Sure we can, Gil."

"And can we go back..." she hesitated "...in other ways, too?"

"Gillian, I really can't say. I don't really know."

• • •

"They call us 'tons of fun' and we deserve it," the rotund Professor Emily Gestaat announced. She and four other fat ladies laughed at their big joke, causing at least twenty chins to quiver in unison.

"We got the name five years ago when we did a chorus line for the faculty Christmas party," Betty Desoto announced.

Erick Hinterhauer, professor of engineering, and Derrick Birdsong cornered me to ask about the Sibley journal and the lost caves. Tall and storklike, Hinterhauer didn't impress me as someone who would enjoy crawling through passages in a dead cave.

The crowd kept swirling from conversation to conversation, getting increasingly louder as the booze went down. Sweating, I stepped out onto the balcony that overlooked Piper Stadium. I was alone and the cool breeze felt good as I lit up a Pall Mall.

I heard a door open behind me but paid no attention. Suddenly, a hand swept around my head and plucked the cigarette from my mouth. Livinda Ferris slouched against the rail and puffed my cigarette.

"Culden just told me about Gillian's escapade," she said. "Does this mean you and Gil are… no longer a *thing?*"

"If we ever were," I answered. "Somehow, I think Gillian's synapses are a bit tangled. I feel sorry for her, sort of."

"Well," she exhaled and flipped the cigarette away. "I feel sort of sorry for you and…" She leaned into me and drew my head down for a big kiss. I responded, sort of, as her tongue busied itself trying to find an opening. We kissed for a long moment, drew back to stare at each other, then fell into another embrace.

The noise from the party increased as a door down the balcony opened. I peered from the corner of my eye and glimpsed Gil standing there, slack-jawed. Then she spun and hurried back into the building.

"Uh-oh," Livvy muttered, "*that* was ill-timed."

• • •

Registration on Thursday was almost anticlimactic after the Freshman Week activities. For the first-timers, confusion was the order of the day. Each faculty member fielded questions as students puzzled their way through class schedules. The Fine Arts faculty was particularly busy as kids tried to determine if this field of study was something they wanted to pursue.

Freshman Kathy Anders approached me and timidly announced she would major in Fine Arts. "Will we study religious paintings?" she asked. "I'll have to have something to tell my parents."

Horny Jim Gillespie also came to my desk. "You were right about the titties, Professor Lowrey, but I'm still gonna major in art."

• • •

Thursday night, the faculty four drove over to Petersburg for pizza and beer at Cazzo's. Culden brandished a sheaf of papers. "We won't have a final summary until tomorrow afternoon," she said, "and of course, we've got two weeks 'til drop and add. But it basically looks good for a new department," she said with a big smile.

Culden and I would teach two classes of Art Appreciation each for the next two semesters until we had everyone in the tent with the new required course. She handed me my class summary and I read.

Art App, MWF, 9 a.m., Art App, MWF 11 a.m., Basic Drawing, MWF, 2 p.m., Intro to Painting, TTS, 10 a.m.

"As you can see, Five, I gave you an hour's break in Art Appreciation. And I'll take the Tuesday through Saturday classes. We can trade days next semester," she told me. "And next semester, we'll add Figure Drawing and intermediate painting as new courses. By next year, we'll have a full curriculum and I hope we'll have a couple more staff people to help."

As she went over Hoopie and Jaylene's schedules, I studied my registrations. Each Art Appreciation class had the maximum of 300 students. We'd need some proctor help for testing and I knew from experience that roll-taking was worthless with that kind of crowd. Only a series of pop quizzes would keep the seats filled.

My basic drawing class had sixteen signed up. And the painting introduction had twelve. According to the standards set by the university, a class couldn't be made if six or fewer signed up.

Dropping us off in the parking lot, Culden had one last word. "Everyone get a good rest this weekend. We may not have another peaceful one until Thanksgiving."

• • •

The peace and quiet of my Saturday lasted until lunch. I'd spent the morning working on several canvases. Jaylene had given me some soapstone dust I used to blow over a gray wash. The resulting sparkles were an approximation of the interior of Sibley's Crystal Cave.

Bubby Bristo arrived at lunchtime so I whipped up another bologna sandwich for him and popped a second beer. He proudly displayed the hideaway box he'd made for my credentials and .32 revolver.

"I just duplicated this cabinet closest to the door," he said, pointing to the overhead kitchen cabinets he'd built just a few months before. "And I made her just a gnat's ass narrower on the inside." He rapidly unscrewed the old cabinet and replaced it with the new. It looked exactly the same.

"Now, if you need to get to your weapon in a hurry," he grinned, "just give her a whack right here." He hit the end of the cabinet with his fist and the side popped open to reveal a felt-lined compartment for my Lady Smith revolver, a shelf for ammo and a shelf for my credentials.

• • •

I was touching up specks of white soapstone with a varnish glaze when the phone rang. I picked up the extension.

"Hello Five, can you stand a visitor for a brief time this afternoon?" Livvy Ferris asked.

"Sure, I'm just painting."

"Great! I'll be there in about twenty minutes."

She drove up on time in a red MG-TC roadster that I'd never seen before. Her hair was pulled into a ponytail and she wore rolled-up blue jeans and a red-and-gold Seneca U. sweatshirt. This outfit made her look about sixteen.

We sat on the porch in rockers. "I'd like to see what you're working on. Is it anything for Stansbury-Marchant?"

"Could be," I responded. "I really don't know where this one is going."

"I got a letter from Gigi today," she said.

"That's better than me. I haven't heard from her since my last shipment of work."

"It got there. She said to tell you she's really pleased with the work, especially the nudes of me."

Livvy's eyebrows were arched like cats' backs. "When did you do nudes of me? And… did I say it was OK?"

167

I swallowed but nothing went down. "Er, you kinda posed the night… ah, the Mrs. Robinson night… remember?"

"Five! That's called taking advantage."

"Well, hell, Liv. Isn't that what you were trying to do to me?"

"There's a lot of difference between staring down my blouse and having me pose for you," she retorted, "but it's OK. I'd just like to see the work before the world does. Do you have a Coke? Or better, a beer?"

She followed me into the kitchen while I opened a Rolling Rock for each of us.

"Can I see what you're working on? Is it another nude?"

Liv stared at the cavescape for a long time, changing her position and squinting at the canvas. "It's interesting. Is it from imagination, and what are you going to do with it?"

"I'm thinking of putting a figure in it somehow. But the figure would have to be a flat color, black perhaps, to contrast with the formations."

She squinted again. "It's just on the verge of being kind of… well, tacky. Kind of like a black velvet painting." She laughed. "Why didn't you use sequins?" she asked archly.

"You've got to see the actual setting," I replied lamely. "It does sparkle so. But I just haven't quite captured it."

"So it isn't just your imagination!" I nodded. "It's a real place? Will you show me sometime?"

"Perhaps," I said cautiously.

"If you will, I won't be angry about the nudes in Paris," she said. "And—that's the second thing I want to talk to you about. I want you to paint my portrait."

"Well, that's certainly easy enough. I'd be glad to," I said.

"Head and shoulders," she said firmly, "nude from the waist up."

"Liv! I can't do that. You're the provost, for Christ's sake!"

"All the more reason to do it, assistant professor—without tenure, I might add."

"Livinda Ferris, you are a very scary person," I said with a quiver in my voice. "Tenure won't matter if this gossipy town—or your father—or President Skinner—finds out I'm painting their provost naked."

"Don't be scared, Five. I'm just a thirty-year-old girl who wants to be captured with what she's got right now. I've never heard you talk about whom you've painted. And they'll sure as hell not find out from me… for at least thirty years."

I put on a reluctant face. "Oh, OK. But I'm on record as being opposed to this politically."

"Good. Protest noted. Shall we start now?" She grabbed the hem of her sweatshirt and pulled it over her head, exposing a beautiful pair of breasts.

— 31 —

Please Appreciate this Art

A sea of expectant faces peered up from the seats of Canby Auditorium. Jaylene and Cyndy collected registration cards as my nine o'clock Art Appreciation class entered the big room. I had focused the slides in the Carousel projector, checked my notes twice, and I stood there, trying to look authoritative. A tinny bell rang. The doors closed. Jaylene lowered the lights. My teaching career was under way

"Thirteen thousand years ago..." I began as the slide of the great hall of Rouffignac appeared on the screen, "artists paid tribute to the animals they lived with and hunted. They did this by painting and carving the outlines of these creatures on the roof of a cave in southern France.

"Less than five years ago, I stood in that cave and stared up at this marvelous frieze of creatures. Not creatures from some prehistoric imagination but actual animals copied from life.

"What made this work even more remarkable... was that when this room was painted, the artists had to lie flat on their backs less than two feet from their canvas... the rock ceiling. And even more, the room is four miles from the mouth of Rouffignac through pitch dark passages with no running water."

I could feel a physical vibration in the darkened hall. I could feel that I *had them.* I peered into the room.

"It's dark in here. And early. But I want an honest answer from you." Pause. "Does anyone here find this picture and its story... boring?"

Silence for a second, then a growing murmur of "no"s filled the air.

"Well, folks, that's what Art Appreciation is going to be about. The artists themselves and why they created what they did. Art isn't a static thing—the end result of a painting— hanging in a frame. Art that way can be appreciated... can take our breath away... can be loved. But even more so if we know the stories behind the work.

"There are too many of you for us to spend all our time taking roll. So we'll rely upon pop quizzes instead. Fail to turn in a pop quiz and you'll lose five percent of your grade. And they will be *pop.* Perhaps as early as Friday's class.

"I'll want you to take notes, but not necessarily memorize. If I do my job well enough, you'll remember."

And with that, I brought up the next slide.

• • •

"Well, ball-buster, perhaps we should have discussed our theories of art appreciation," Culden grinned at me from behind her desk. She had beckoned me as my first class filed out of Canby. "Shit, Five. What am I going to do tomorrow to match that performance?" She threw a wadded piece of paper at me. "Damn, but I'm glad I hired you."

"Culden, you'll be just fine. If you want to use any of my material, please do. I just thought the cave painting opening might get their attention."

"Wow, did it ever! If I hear a single person snore in my class tomorrow, I'm going to give you all four sessions of Art App."

"That was *really interesting,* Five," Cyndy chirped at me as I went to my own office. "I was supposed to come back here and tally the registration cards but I stayed right there beside Culden."

"Thanks a lot, Cyndy. I'm just glad to have the very first one out of the way. How many students did we have?"

"I counted 294 cards and only saw three people leave. Two of 'em came back, so perhaps they had to pee." She looked up quizzically. "By the way, have you seen Gil? Yesterday? Or today?"

"Well, no. Last time I saw her was at the faculty party Wednesday night."

"Yeah, I heard about *that.* Sort of. She came home early and we smoked a couple of joints. Did something happen? She was gone when I got up yesterday morning and she didn't come home last night. I thought she might've been with you."

"Not likely! I don't think Gil and I are… ah, going together any more."

"You heard her Intro to Dance class didn't make? Only three enrolled. She seemed pretty down at being left with majorettes and cheerleaders," Cyndy added.

• • •

Exhausted after three classes on my first day, I headed for home. My second Art App class had gone nearly as well as the first and the twenty-two Basic Drawing students showed interest, if not aptitude. Marilyn Kretzman held her charcoal stick properly without coaching and Gillespie filled his newsprint pad with enthusiastic abandon.

Everyone else's classes had seem to go well. Hoopie had a surprising turnout for Intro to Collage and Jaylene's Intro to Clay Modeling classes had waiting lists.

I turned from the highway onto Gerwig Run lane and slowed when I spotted a familiar red gasoline can near the edge of the woods. I rounded the first curve, where Pig stepped out of the brush. I rolled down the window and he leaned in.

"Remember I told you about that dancer girl? Well, I've been thinking about it and realized she's the woman that was with you *that night*. Right?"

"Yep, that's right. What about her?"

"She your woman?"

"Not exactly. She's a professor at Seneca."

"Well, she showed up at Laurel Town yesterday... lookin' to buy some weed or hook up with someone who was willing..." He hesitated. "She's pretty fucked up, man. She'll take anything you can put in her... marijuana, LSD, a hard cock. I took her in last night and she's still asleep in my shack. Seems like a pretty nice chick when she makes any sense."

I sat there behind the wheel, staring straight ahead. *What to do about Gil?*

"Pig, can you get her down to my place without stirrin' up any shit?"

"Ah, yeah, nobody pays much attention to me... nobody messes with me. I'll bring her by about seven if that's OK."

I decided to call Livinda. "Miss Provost. This is your favorite portrait artist," I said. "We have a problem... could be a big problem."

"What's happened?" she asked.

"Gil's gone AWOL again. Someone described her as 'being pretty fucked up' and he's bringing her to my place at seven this evening."

"I'll be there."

Livinda arrived about ten 'til seven and pulled her car nearly into the woods. Darkness totally descended as I described my meeting with Pig without giving away his role in Laurel Town. About seven thirty, the clatter of Pig's VW bus echoed up the creekbed. He stopped short of the ford.

I waded across and Liv stayed out of sight in the yard.

"She didn't wanna come," Pig said. "Started to holler and raise hell so I had to tap her a little one. She'll be all right, though." I pulled the recumbent Gil from the bus's interior and without a word, Pig started his engine and turned back down the lane. I carried her back through the creek and laid her in the mossy yard.

"Who was that?" Liv asked. "And did I hear him say he hit her? Is she unconscious?"

"He's just an acquaintance from Laurel Town," I answered. "Someone who didn't want to see Gil get hurt any more than she is."

Gil groaned, then sat straight up with a wild expression. She made a couple of incoherent noises, then looked at both of us in fright.

"Doctor Ferris? Five? What's going on?" she muttered.

I put my hand on her shoulder. "Easy, Gillian, you're here at my place and we're going to get some care for you." The girl burst into tears. I pulled her to her feet and we helped her stagger into the house.

"If you want to take her upstairs and give her a shower, it's fine by me," I said. "She really stinks."

"I brought some clean clothes. Mine will be a little big but they'll do," Liv said. "Why don't you make some coffee?"

A few minutes later, Liv came back down the stairs. "She says she can shower by herself. I guess we've got to show her we can trust her, although I really don't. You know I had to tell her that her classes didn't make—that she doesn't really have a teaching job this semester?"

"Yeah, Cyndy told me."

"Dance seems to be her only interest," Liv said.

"Yes, that and caving. She's wild about caving." I hesitated for a second, then decided to tell Livvy about Gil's and my discovery of Sibley's Crystal Cave.

"The cave in your painting? I thought as much. Where is it?"

"Right at the head of Gerwig Run. The creek comes right out of the mountain."

• • •

Gil resembled a gnome, huddled in Liv's old jeans and a Pitt sweatshirt. But a clean gnome. She held the coffee mug in both hands and trembled as she put it to her mouth.

"I told you once I had addictions," she said to me through quivering lips.

"Gillian, do you want to beat these addictions?" Liv asked. "You know, your problems at Seneca aren't *that* great. We can find *something* for you to do until next semester, and I'll bet your dance class will be full."

"Oh Liv, that's so nice of you to say but I know you're just *saying* it. I couldn't stand the idea of cheerleaders and majorettes. And that unctuous Stedman man. I'm sorry but I don't think I'm cut out for Seneca."

"Well, let's not make that decision tonight. I'm taking you home and we'll talk about it some more. You won't run away, will you?" Liv asked.

"No, I won't run away. I think you and Five are the only real friends I have." She gave a brave, tiny smile. "And I'm so happy for the two of you."

— 32 —

The Strange Becomes Routine

The teaching butterflies were gone by Tuesday. My Intro to Painting class went smoothly, with 16 students listening attentively as I discussed media and tools. Several students had brought along portfolios of high school work and John Piggot proudly displayed a concert poster he'd done in California.

"Anyone who wants to see more of my stuff," the shaggy older student said, "can just take a look at my bus."

I sneaked into the back of Culden's second Art App class and was pleased to see another full house and my boss doing a great job. After the bell rang, we walked to the student union for grilled cheese sandwiches and Cokes.

"Great news, Five," she told me. "Richard is being discharged sometime this week. He'll be getting a month's leave from *Look* and he's going to spend it here."

• • •

Cyndy Byrd stopped me in the hall Wednesday morning. "The provost was over last night with Gil. I helped them pack a little suitcase for her to take to somewhere called

Woodstock. The provost said to tell you she'll talk to you tonight."

Without great detail, I told Cyndy what had transpired on Monday night. "Are you OK in Gil's place alone?" I asked.

"Oh yes, and the provost said she would take care of Gil's portion of the rent while she's away. She's really a nice person and… I think she *likes* you," Cindy added with a grin.

• • •

I made it through my first Art App class Wednesday morning but found I'd run through my lesson plan too fast and finished with about seven minutes to spare. Throughout the hour, people kept coming and going in the darkened hall but those who had seats stayed put.

Between classes, I helped Hoopie sort through piles of old magazines he had collected for his collage class. "What about Playboy? I kind of hate to have them torn up," he lamented. "And Penthouse?"

"Man, I don't know. I guess it just depends upon what tack you want your future collagists? Collagers? to take." I answered diplomatically. Don't forget this is academia. The grove of free thought."

We went back to the student union for lunch. I was becoming addicted to their twenty-cent sandwiches and quarter hamburgers. Hoopie asked me to sit in on his collage class, where I beheld the weirdest-looking assortment of students anyone could image.

Hippie costume was uniform of the day but several of these kids had long hair braided in Medusa-like strands. Still, I could tell they were students because the room didn't smell like Laurel Town. A few of the students addressed their instructor as 'Stu' so I decided to be more careful about using his nickname. Their discussion swirled around the subject 'what is creativity?' and I could see he had corralled the cream of the creative crop.

Antsy and not willing to go home, I ambled around the campus. Looked into the field house for the first time and marveled at its size. I sat on the field house steps and sketched Eden Fields from a new angle for me.

Shouted cadences and the thump of drums drew my attention to the footbridge by Piper Stadium. I walked across it and, on the far side of the South Fork, discovered the practice fields. A circular ramp spiraled straight down while two long sloping ramps led to each end of the field. At the far end, a raggedy group of musicians marched into a tentative formation under the direction of Con Stedman.

At the other end, Coach Art Bruce was watching his Warriors do calisthenics. I strolled down the helix end of the bridge and was passed by two football players panting up the ramp. As I approached the football field, Art Bruce gave me a wave and beckoned me to a set of three-row bleachers. "We may not have a lot of skill," he yelled at me, "but we'll sure as hell be in great shape." He dispatched another pair of players to 'give me two laps on the spiral.'

Watching individual drills and a thirty-minute scrimmage made it apparent that certain skills were rare. Still, the Warriors were big and shouldn't have much trouble with West Virginia Wesleyan.

I trudged with Art Bruce up the spiral walkway behind his team, making their sweating, panting way back to the stadium dressing room. The late afternoon sun cast long shadows and painted the turning leaves of Eden Fields in even richer hues of gold and scarlet.

"That's why I picked gold and scarlet when we started football," Bruce said. "Those leaves just mean the spirit of Seneca to me."

Behind us came the *Fighting Warriors Marching Fifty* in column and stepping quickly to the cadence of the drummers. I would discover this was an afternoon tradition: returning from band practice in formation.

The Fine Arts office was closed and locked when I returned after five o'clock. A phone message advised me to call the provost. No one answered her office phone so I called her at home.

"Hello, this is Livinda Ferris," she said crisply.

"Hi Liv, it's Five. You're back from... where, Woodstock?"

"Yes. Are you at home?"

"No, I'm still on campus."

"Good! Then why don't you come over for a drink and I'll have Mary fix us a bite to eat?"

"Is Gillian still there?"

"No. And I want to talk to you about her."

"OK, I'll be there in about ten minutes."

Livvy's maid, Mary, met me at the door and escorted me to the terrace. Liv had on a gray flannel skirt and a dark blue sweater set. She handed me a frosty Gibson and we clinked glasses.

"So tell me about Woodstock," I said.

"It's really Buena Vista Treatment Center on Massanutten Mountain in Virginia. It's a very good place. I know. I spent four months there myself."

My raised eyebrows and quizzical expression asked it all.

"My junior year in high school," she said slowly. "My parents sent me there to, ah… dry out."

"And you, an old alumna of Buena Vista, committed Gillian?"

"No! She committed herself. Five, she really wants to get clean. I mean it. The girl is, as she puts it, really fucked up and she wants to get unfucked," Livvy said vehemently.

"How long will she be there?"

"She can leave any time she wishes," Liv replied. "It's a good program. Very positive. Very much on the offensive. They don't just drug these kids up and let them sleep away their time." She gave me a hopeful look. "I arranged for her tuition and expenses to be paid through the end of the semester. Her last words were of you. How sorry she is and how much she'll miss you."

Over cold chicken and hash brown potatoes, I steered the subject away from Gil. "How did you get to be provost, Livinda?"

"At least thirty senior professors ask themselves the same thing every day," she smiled. "The simple truth is, my father and his friends wanted control of the Seneca board of trustees. They had the votes and elected me as the alumni trustee. No one batted an eye at that.

"My father, his crony Ollie Monkton, and his other friends are all looking to leave their mark. Turning Seneca into a major university was the way they chose." She laughed and took a sip of hot tea. "Daddy's big mistake was bringing me on the board. I quickly pointed out that his 'new university' with its science campus under the hill, its big fieldhouse and stadium, and its half-assed teams, was a shell. A Potemkin village. A super high school."

"And so…" I led her on.

"And so, I said I would resign from the board and write a big article for the *Journal of Higher Education* exposing Seneca unless he put me into a position of power. A position where I could bring some cultural personality to Seneca. Make it a real university.

"We had just hired Frank Skinner, so I settled for provost at age twenty-nine."

— 33 —

Ground into the Gridiron

Saturday was a crisp mid-September day. Liv showed up at Five's Five to supervise progress on her portrait. After her first sweatshirt-free posing session, I had been firm about her keeping her clothes on. This morning she wore a scarlet cowl-necked sweater and gray slacks.

"It's really looking good, Five," Livvy opined. "Did you ever see the portrait of my mom? It hangs in the library. It's weird, but you're making me look quite a bit like her."

"Livvy, I didn't even know you had a library. And no, I haven't seen her portrait. Where is your mother?"

"Oh, she's flitting around Europe somewhere, Provence, Positano. Who knows?"

In the portrait, I had Liv posed in a two-thirds reverse view, looking over her shoulder. Since she insisted on a nude pose, one breast was exposed. I had turned the sweatshirt into a drape that swept around her waist, hinting that she was completely nude.

"You've made my neck look so long," she exclaimed. "I rarely wear my hair swept up like that."

"The big question," I posed. "Will you like it?"

"Oh yes, very much. But I'd still like to see the ones from your imagination."

• • •

I'm sure we were a beautiful sight in Livvy's MG-TC, its high wire wheels under flowing fenders supporting bug-eye headlights. She had put the top down and the cool September morning felt great as we sped off to the campus and a tailgate party.

On football days, it was permissible to park on the grass at the edge of Eden Fields. Liv drove up to a huge red maple tree and carefully parked by Culden's big red Dodge woodie.

"This is why I insisted we hire Culden," Livvy called. "Because of that great station wagon. Any other color, Culden, and you might not have made it." Everyone laughed.

"Aces high," a voice called. I turned to see Richard West, left arm in a sling, hoisting a beer can with his good hand.

"Dicky Reb!" I yelled. "You've made it. Terrific!"

Dick tucked the beer can into his sling and we shook, him using the peculiar grip. "Go easy on that," I whispered. "I'm keeping a very low ACE profile in this place." Then in a full voice, "How in hell are you?"

"I sit very tenderly these days but that's improving all the time. And… I'll still be able to hold a cigarette and flip a bird with my left hand." He held up the heavily bandaged hand. "The pain goes away a little each day. And the docs say I should be able to grip a camera with two fingers and a thumb."

As the women opened real wicker picnic baskets and spread a red tablecloth on the grass, Dicky regaled us with the story of his Vietnamese mishap.

"We were riding on this dike road in the Mekong Delta when some mortar fire started walking across the rice paddy. My driver, a Viet guy, was startled and swerved to the edge of the dike and WHAM! I'll never know whether it was a mortar shell or a mine but the jeep became airborne and us with it. I must've flown five hundred feet through the air…"

"It was four hundred feet this morning," Culden giggled.

"…and landed in this rice paddy. Splat. Two fingers gone clean at the second knuckle and a big pain in the ass." He pointed gently to his right buttock. "About a three inch gouge there. Medics thought it was a piece of shrapnel. That was their biggest worry, me getting an infected ass from landing in a shit-filled paddy."

• • •

Some Kappas came by and cajoled us into buying bright gold corsages of leaves and tiny mums for Livvy and Culden. Students and fans began walking across Eden Fields toward the stadium, their costumes a symphony in scarlet and gold.

Bloody Marys were poured, spicy and redolent of vodka. "My maid is the original Bloody Mary," Liv told us. "She loves football season so she can concoct these for home games, then spend the rest of the afternoon sleeping it off." The rest of the meal consisted of meatloaf sandwiches, deviled eggs, potato salad, and homemade pumpkin pie.

I patted my stomach and said, "Gee, but I'm glad you invited me, Madame Provost. Is there time for a nap?"

My question was answered by a clash of cymbals and rattle of snare drums. The Fighting Warriors Marching Fifty emerged from the Canby basement and strutted across Eden Fields to a rapid drumbeat. I had expected full band uniforms but they wore red plaid trousers, white shirts, and straw boaters with scarlet and gold ribbons flying. Their footwear was white, but a motley collection of bucks and tennis shoes.

In the middle of Eden Fields, they struck up a tune I'd heard all week wafting up from the practice field. Livvy leaned into my shoulder, "That's the *Warpath March*," she said softly, "proud composition of yours truly… eight years ago."

"Liv! I didn't know you were a music major?" I exclaimed.

"I wasn't. Just the spoiled daughter of a rich trustee who wanted a fight song for his new university."

"And where are the majorettes?"

"You'll see," she said mysteriously.

We joined the crowd and filed into Piper Stadium at a mid-level gate, then followed Liv as she climbed higher in the stands. Just beneath the press box was a section with real seats instead of the aluminum bleachers.

"We'll say hello to my dad," Liv announced, "and some of the other board members, then we'll go sit with the real people."

I shook hands with Busby Ferris, Ollie Monkton and President Skinner. Ferris was a big man with a full chest and just the beginning of a gut. His grip was firm as he looked me in the eye and muttered something I couldn't make out.

"Aren't you all going to sit here, honey?" he asked Liv. "I think we'll have enough seats for your friends."

"No thanks, Dad. I think it would be better for me to mix with the alumni. Five and Culden each have fifty-yard-line faculty tickets."

"Of course. You all enjoy the game."

Our midfield seats gave an excellent view from about twenty rows up. The teams had already left the field after warm-ups and now the Marching Warriors pranced onto the goal line to the tick of a drumstick on a snare.

Liv leaned against me and said in a low voice, "I've talked Dad and Ollie out of their dream of a bigger press box and a president's box beneath it. The money we've saved is what funded your department this year."

With a feedback squawk, the public address announcer got our attention. "And nowwww..." echoing *nowwww* across the valley... our pre-game show featuring the *Fighting Warriors Marching Band* and the world-famous *Mountain Mamas...*"

The crowd cheered mildly as a long row of beautiful girls in skimpy metallic scarlet costumes strutted from the tunnel and lined up behind the band.

"God, there's more majorettes than band members," Dicky Reb observed.

The PA man continued... "and featuring Lucinda Latimer, world champion baton twirler and our *Golden Girl of the Glen!*"

With that, the band burst into the *Warpath March* and the Mountain Mamas pranced through their formation with the Golden Girl doing a fantastic strut, her head almost touching the ground and her gold-sequined suit shimmering in the sun. A more enthusiastic cheer greeted the show as Lucinda twirled and danced, then threw the baton high in the air and... missed it when it returned to earth.

"Oh God," Liv moaned to our little quartet, "this kid's got a bigger scholarship than any athlete, and she misses. World champion, my butt! Little Lucy was a twirler at Big Creek High School this time last year."

The Marching Warriors moved out from their goal line formation and as they moved in line down the field, some members accelerated while others held back.

"This is Dad's pride and joy," Liv commented. "He went to an Ohio State game once and came away determined to... well, just watch."

Suddenly, it dawned on us that the band was forming a capital S. The band moved to midfield and, for a second, crossed the line of Mountain Mamas, briefly forming a dollar sign. Livinda grimaced.

"Very impressive," Culden commented.

"Very *über* high school," Liv responded. "I think it's just cheesy."

The band struck a harmonic chord and the crowd automatically got to its feet as the PA man said, "And now, as the sun kisses the morning fog in our proud mountain range, let us join in singing the praises of our Alma Mater... *Morning Mountain Mists.*"

Culden, Dicky, and I shared a look of perplexity as Livinda's clear voice joined perhaps another 20,000 in a very tasteful hymn of praise. The alma mater was short and melodic, a surprising event for what Liv had termed an *über* high school. Applause followed the final chords.

"Did you write that one too?" I asked Liv.

"Lord no," she replied. "Some congregational preacher's wife wrote the poem and her husband put it to music back in the Twenties. Isn't it beautiful?"

Again the PA man... "And now, to honor America, please join in singing..."

• • •

A tiny band of Wesleyan fans cheered as their Bobcats came on the field. In their black helmets and orange pants, they looked more like a high school team. The crowd was much more enthusiastic as the Warriors emerged from their tunnel, clad in scarlet helmets, white pants, and scarlet jerseys with Princeton stripes of gold down the arms. They even had scarlet and gold socks while Wesleyan's kids had skinny bare calves below their baggy pants.

The Warriors won the toss and received the ball. Running off tackle slants, they were on the Wesleyan 12-yard line in five plays. Then our quarterback dropped back to pass. The ball was tipped and a Bobcat defender snatched it and ran alone for an 88-yard touchdown interception.

Behind by seven, the mighty Warriors became a different team. Wesleyan held them for five consecutive punts, then recovered a fumble on the Seneca two and scored a second time. By the fourth quarter, Seneca trailed the underdogs 31-0 and fans were beginning to leave the stadium in twos and threes.

"Can we leave early?" Dicky Reb asked Culden. "I'd rather be playing with R.T. than watching this. It's as bad as OU."

Liv looked at him and smiled wanly. "If you don't mind, let's stick it out. It wouldn't look too good for me to be leaving early, especially with my fellow trustees up there." She squeezed my arm, "and I won't make you come to any more games with me. I have a feeling it's going to be a long season."

• • •

We left Liv to go the alumni reception by herself and I rode with Culden and Dick to pick up the baby. Then we drove out to Five's Five to finish off the afternoon. It was still warm enough for R.T. to wade in the creek, and we watched him as he splashed and grabbed for crawdads.

"What's with this provost lady, Five?" Dick asked me. "She's a real nice woman. Are you guys dating?"

"Well, not exactly," I said.

"They would be if Liv had her way," Culden broke in. "Five's paintin' a pitchur of Livvy, and I hear it's a racy one," she added in a high, sing-song voice.

"And what happened to that Gillian gal?" he continued. "I didn't see her today. I thought you guys were pretty close."

Culden and I took turns relating details of Gil's misadventure, even to the extent of the first bad Saturday night.

"I mean, Dick, we were *destroyed*. Moonshine and pot in great quantities," she said. "When I woke up the next morning, Gil and I were lying on the porch floor with Benjo in between us."

While Culden took the baby inside to dry him off and put on a fresh diaper, Dicky Reb continued to question me.

"You mean Benjo beat your time with this Gil girl?"

"Well yeah, but it wasn't like we were pin mates or anything. And I don't think Benjo even realized what was happening. I can't blame him. Gil was already addicted to many habits, including sex."

— 34 —

Love-in in the Meadow

With R.T. sacked out in a makeshift cradle, I left Culden and Dick at the cabin and drove into town to pick up some pizzas. Teetle's, one of Seneca town's three pizza joints, was busy so I enjoyed a beer and read the inevitable bulletin boards. One poster drew my attention in particular.

When I got back to Five's Five, Dick said, "Your friend Livvy called. Asked you to call her back at home if you get time. Nothing important, she said."

Munching a piece of pepperoni, I dialed Liv's number.

"Hey, Five. I want to thank you for being so patient this afternoon. I know you would've loved to go home at halftime."

"Liv! It was nothing. After six years of Ohio University football, today's slaughter was kind of refreshing. How was the reception?"

"Irate. Half of the board is ready to fire Coach Bruce right now, and most of the alums that were there would fall in line. Thank heavens Gerald Warren was tending bar. I've taught that young man well," I could hear the laughter in her voice. "What are you doing?"

"Ah, Dick and Culden and I are enjoying pizza from Teetle's. There's plenty. Want to come out?"

"No, thanks. I'm pooped."

"I did see something at Teetle's that was interesting," I told her, motioning for Culden and Dick to pay attention. "There was a poster for the Mole People's first annual Fall Festival tomorrow. It advertised arts, crafts, food, fellowship, and friendliness."

"First I've heard of it," Liv answered. "Wasn't the Mole People one of the new student groups?"

"I think so, but I believe it's part of the hippie tribe. The festival's in the Jordan Run meadow—from dawn to when the fun runs out, the poster said." I paused and said loudly, "This isn't a date, but... do you want to go?" Culden and Dick nodded enthusiastically.

"Sure! I'll see you in the morning, say about ten? Grubby clothes?" Livvy said.

"You got it."

• • •

I sported a tie-dyed T-shirt over paint-spattered jeans and tennis shoes. Culden wore a similar outfit while Dick wore jeans, combat boots, and a photographer's vest over a T-shirt. His sling was gone and he wore a dinged Leica M2 around his neck. Liv arrived in a relatively modest butterfly blouse, sheer harem pants over sandals, and a headband over frizzed-out hair.

"Holy shit," Dick said, "it's Janis Joplin herself."

The four of us piled into Culden's wagon and hit the road for Jordan Run. The village had changed considerably since my last visit. Two new frame buildings accompanied the gas station and commune store. On the wooded hillside behind the town, A-frames, yurts, and other *Mother Earth News* structures were popping up.

Across the highway, a meadow reached a quarter mile to a bend in the creek. The field swarmed with people and activity. A thin haze of smoke drifted about a dozen feet above the ground. Frisbees floated through the smoke and dogs barked and fornicated at the edge of the crowd.

No one paid us much attention as we drifted into the crowd. Dick operated his Leica with one hand, shooting and thumbing the wind lever. "You'll have to change film for me, Five," he said. "But this is great stuff."

We saw the familiar faces of Laurel Town hippies and Seneca students and stopped to talk with some. The Kappa girls who'd sold us corsages the day before were decked out in granny glasses, bell bottoms, and peasant blouses.

The Tri-Delt chapter had a bench and deep-fryer and were making Indian fry bread for sale. Doug Kaminsky had a display of ceramic wares on a blanket. In a sling lawn chair behind him, Blondie lolled indolently. As we approached, Doug insolently rolled a joint and lit up.

"Hello, Doug," Culden greeted him.

"Hi, Culden," he said pleasantly. "How's Cyndy doing?"

"She's doing just fine," I responded for Culden, who looked about ready to spit on him. "Actually, better than just fine." I looked at Blondie. "Hey Blondie! How're you? I almost didn't recognize you with clothes on." The girl stared blankly at us.

"Don't pay her no mind," Doug commented. "She's not quite… with it, awake, just yet."

Dick leaned over to shoot a picture of Doug, the nodding Blondie, and the ceramics-filled blanket.

"You guys want to buy a bong?" Doug asked. "I've got a special on 'em today."

We strolled slowly across the meadow, stopping to listen to musicians—guitarists and flute players, bongo drummers, and one very talented guy with a sitar. We came upon John Piggot strumming a dulcimer with a big feather, accompanying a waif who sang *Aura Lee* in a plaintive voice.

"Hey, Professor Lowrey, good to see ya," he said pleasantly, never missing a note. "And Doctor Ellis. How do you like the love-in?" He looked at the vocalist and nodded, "This is Whisper. She's knows just about every mountain song ever… and I think she's got a nice voice."

From beneath the curtain of her long brown hair, Whisper looked up and smiled shyly.

"These folks are from the college, Whisper," Pig said gently. "You wanna walk along with 'em for a while?"

Without apparent motion, Whisper rose, sort of levitating beneath her dress, which touched the ground. She took Pig's hand and smiled. We continued to walk toward a large crowd of people gathered around a low place in the meadow. The crowd was cheering and whistling as a group of naked folks rolled in a pool of gray mud. Some were entwined. Others struck poses like statues.

The click of Dick's Leica drew no attention as he moved around the edge of the crowd to capture the scene. Livvy nudged me with a grin. "Looks like a lotta fun. Want to join in?"

Nudity was the order of the day by the time we reached the creek. Downstream, a gray slick drifted away where the mud bathers had washed. Several couples were making out in the water, and heaving naked buttocks showed another couple fornicating in the weeds.

"I think I'd best get out of here," Liv muttered. "I'm absolutely positive none of these kids are Seneca students—right, Five?"

"Oh yes, ma'am. Absolutely right, ma'am."

On the way back, Pig said to me in a low voice, "Does Lazarus mean anything to you?"

I shook my head. "Why?"

"It's just a word I've heard around the commune, that's all. Something to do with the university." With that, he and Whisper disappeared into the dusty afternoon, hand in hand.

• • •

We left the love-in and headed south for Five's Five. With a proprietary air, Liv led Culden and Dick up to the studio to show them the portrait. "Five says it's not finished," she complained. "I think it should be, though."

We settled on the front porch, where I poured glasses of homemade lemonade. Dick and Culden sat in the swing and I took a rocker. Livvy sprawled on the steps, allowing me an excellent view of her butterfly blouse.

"Who was that young man, John Piggot?" she asked.

"Pig? He's a student of mine," I answered. "He's a junior—transferred from Southern Illinois University."

"You call him Pig?"

"That's his name in Laurel Town," I responded. "He seems like a pretty good guy and he's got some artistic talent as well."

"Mercy, but that was a beautiful creature with him. Whisper! What a name!" Culden exclaimed.

"She's got a terrific face," I added. "I'm going to see if Pig can convince her to pose."

"Aww, Five," Dicky guffawed. "You just wanna see her body."

"Well, he's seen mine," Liv said quickly, "and a fat lot of good it did anyone except to get my portrait made."

— 35 —

Lazarus Rumors

Seneca's football team lost to Marshall College 7-6 the next week, and the following week, journeyed to Athens to get thumped by OU 63-3. By mid-October, football fever at SU had diminished to a low-grade sweat. *Talking Leaves,* the student newspaper, openly advocated the firing of Coach Art Bruce.

The trees had completely turned by mid-October, and students enjoyed rolling down the campus hill into piles of leaves. A pall of woodsmoke hung over the Seneca valley for several days as townspeople burned their leaves.

About 10,000 silent fans turned out the following Saturday to see the Warriors host Fairmont College. Bruce's boys played Fairmont a tough game until the final quarter, then gave up two touchdowns for a 14-0 loss. After the game, I joined Livvy at the alumni reception where three dozen people gathered in small, hostile knots and grumbled.

"Liv, remember a few months ago when you told me about the Lazarus Mine?" She nodded. "Do you know of anything the university is doing that involves Lazarus?"

"No. Not offhand. Of course, we have geology projects all over the place with caves and the mountains. Why?"

"Ah, no special reason. Just something I heard the other day."

"Something you heard in… ah, your special… ah, activity?" I nodded. "Well, I'll keep my ear to the ground. We have a board meeting Tuesday, and we're holding it in the Arts and Sciences building. I'll let you know if I hear of anything."

• • •

Monday morning was bright and chilly, and students making their way to eight o'clocks found the serpentine blocked at every landing by protesters. It was Seneca's first big war protest, and the disgruntled students had to make their way straight up the steps or around the hippie blockade to get to class.

At nine o'clock the crowd, now numbering a couple hundred, milled on the lawn in front of Felton Hall, the administration building, and chanted "Ho, ho, ho! We won't go!" and "Hey, hey, LBJ, how many kids did you kill today?"

One woman waved an upside-down American flag from its staff. Several people hoisted a man on their shoulders, where he lit a Zippo and burned what he claimed was his draft card. The crowd surged up the steps toward the entrance to Felton. A girl screamed as the crowd pushed her into the door. There was the sound of shattering glass, another scream, and the crowd ran in all directions.

The form of a woman lay in the doorway, her screams rending the cool October morning.

• • •

"No, she wasn't a student," S.G. Caufield told the press conference of three reporters. "Her name is Nancy Corum, and she *was* an expectant mother. According to the police, she miscarried on the way to the hospital. That's all I can tell you."

Reporters from the *Elkins Inter-Mountain* and the *Clarksburg Telegram* were on their way to Seneca when Nancy "Piglet" Corum was pushed through the shattered doorway and suffered multiple wounds. The camera crew from WBOY-TV in Clarksburg filmed the protest and caught Piglet's screaming form in the doorway.

I was at the edge of the room, at Livvy's request, but other concerned faculty and administrators made me inconspicuous.

"Doctor Caufield? Doesn't Seneca University have a responsibility to its students to protect them from this sort of violence?" the young reporter from Elkins asked.

"Seneca is a free market of ideas, as any college or university should be…" Caufield launched.

"Including chickenshit Davis and Elkins," Liv whispered in my ear.

"…and anti-war protest is another form of free speech. Our students are entitled to see our Constitution in action." A smattering of applause sprinkled around the room.

"Doctor Caufield?" the blonde TV reporter shouted, "How many security officers does the university have, and do you plan to hire more?"

"One. And yes," Caufield replied. "I can't take any more of your questions now."

• • •

A muddy government Chevrolet was waiting in my yard when I got home. Benjo Kostic sat in a rocking chair, smoking and writing in a notebook.

"Hey, Benjo, why didn't you let me know you were coming?" I greeted him coolly.

"Shit, Five, I've been on the road for four hours from Morgantown. This state's roads are for shit. It's less than a hundred miles as a crow flies. I wish to fuck I were a crow. Why didn't you tell me you were throwing a protest this morning?" he continued. "Come to think of it, why haven't you told me anything in the past month or so?"

"Nothing to tell. Hippies are pretty quiet. Football team is lousy. Come to think of it, I haven't heard from you since you disappeared from here that night with Gillian."

Benjo's face reddened and he flashed me a sheepish, lopsided grin. "Oh! And how is Gil?"

"You don't know?" I asked coldly.

"Know what? Is she OK?"

"Well, sort of, in a drug rehab center over in Virginia. We're hoping she'll whip her problem and get clean."

"Oh, shit, Five. I had no idea. I *am* sorry."

"So am I, Josefus. So am I."

"I mean, I had no idea she was your girl," he said earnestly. "She showed up that night and we all just started tokin' and I thought... well shit, I don't know what I thought."

• • •

After a dinner of tuna fish and crackers, we sat at the little table and Benjo asked me about this morning's protest. "You say a couple hundred. Did you count?"

"Naw. But it was about the same size as one of our football pep rallies."

"How did it get violent?"

"I'm not sure it really did. They just swarmed around a little bit. Someone burned a supposed draft card. Then they pushed up the steps like they were trying to get into the building. Piglet just happened to be in the front and got shoved through the door."

"Piglet?"

"Yeah, that's her hippie name. She's one of the two that our man Pig was doin' the night I ran them off."

"Well, you've got a lot more action down here in the woods than we do in Morgantown," he commented. "And the word is, you're going to get even more."

"What do you mean?"

"There's a big anti-war protest planned for the twenty-first in Washington. Agents from all over the country are reporting talk about something called the *Seneca Convocation*. It's starting to sound like this might be a staging area although God knows why anyone would drive these shitty roads to get here."

"Do you want to talk to Pig? He has classes tomorrow and we could contact him."

• • •

Cyndy led Pig into my office and announced him. "You wanted to see me, Professor Lowrey?" he said in a loud voice. As he stepped into the office, Benjo appeared from behind the door and closed it quietly.

"Morning, John," he said quietly.

"Morning, Mr. Kostic. How're they hangin'?"

We got right to the Seneca Convocation. Indeed, Pig had heard rumors of thousands of protesters heading for our valley.

"How many thousands?" I asked. "There aren't that many hippies in the country."

"I think we've got to change the way we think," Benjo countered. "This isn't really a hippie thing."

"Right," Pig added. "The hippie movement is cosmetic. Window dressing for the whole sentiment of dissent."

"So we've got radical students protesting all manner of issues. Dow recruitment. The draft. Sexual freedom. Civil rights. The war in Vietnam." Benjo paused. "And they're not just radical students. Students are inflamed about these things, kids who were going to sock hops just a few years ago."

"You mean Jordan Run meadow could be a transient home for thousands of kids? Not just hippies?" I continued to be skeptical.

"*Will* be," Pig answered. "It's nearly a sure bet that Don Sealy will be here to lead the Seneca Convocation to Washington."

"The president of Students Against Warfare?" Benjo asked.

"The very same."

• • •

Provost Livinda Ferris, Benjo, Pig, and I sat in a restaurant thick with a miasma of grease in the town of Moorefield, about ten miles northeast of Petersburg. The three of us had taken turns briefing Livvy on our activities.

"Since you're the man on the ground, Pig," she said, "we have to depend upon you for information. What I've heard so far sounds fairly scary." She turned to me.

"Five, as of right now, you're the newest member of the Academic Security Council," she continued. "The only member to be exact—since I just invented the organization—but we'll use it as an excuse for you to attend all the meetings involving this march."

"I've been told I'll be part of a team to meet with the university," Pig said. "Don Sealy wants to use the university as a staging center."

"My first reaction is *no way*," Livvy said. "But if this crowd is predominantly students, Seneca would seem pretty callous to turn them away."

"You want to check IDs again, Liv?" I joked. "Don't forget, they're all going to look much the same."

"If only we could! How are you and Pig going to stay in contact?" she asked.

"We'll see each other in class. I've dropped English Lit and added Basic Drawing, so we'll be in contact every day," Pig announced. "Also, I have a project I want to work on with him which would give us an excuse to meet at other times."

"What's that?" I asked. "What project?"

"I want you to do a portrait of Whisper, and I want to watch and learn from it," he said seriously.

"Ohhh, I don't think so," Liv drawled. "Five, you *need to be careful* using minors as models."

Pig leaned over the table and stared into Liv's eyes. "Whisper Gaskins is a 27-year-old woman—very much a woman, and besides—I want to capture her before she becomes famous."

• • •

Benjo hit the 'shitty roads' to return to Morgantown and we drove back to Seneca in separate cars and at staggered times. I was the last to leave and by the time I got to my office, Cyndy had a phone message to call the provost.

"Five, the Seneca Convocation is for real. Don Sealy has called once and wants to call again. Do we have a chapter, or whatever, of SAW on campus? What's SAW stand for anyway?"

"Students Against Warfare," I answered. "They had an organization table up during Freshman and Registration Week but I don't know if they're an official campus organization. Can't you find out?"

"I can, now that I know what SAW is. This Sealy guy is supposed to call back at four o'clock. Can you be in my office to listen in?" Sealy's phone call was short and to the point. He arranged a meeting with the provost and "whoever else it takes to make a decision" for the next afternoon.

Pig led Don Sealy, Alexander Rolling Thunder, and Arthur Boxx into the main administration conference room. Seneca was represented by Livinda; S.G. Caufield; Josh Tinkler, student body president; Sergeant Jack Glencoe; and me.

Sealy was dressed conservatively in khakis and a blue chambray workshirt. Arthur Boxx wore a threadbare brown suit, shiny at the elbows and knees. Rolling Thunder wore jeans and a beaded vest, exposing his massive bare chest and arms.

"Doctor Ferris, I'm here to tell you that we expect as many as 10,000 people to start arriving in the area on Tuesday the 17th. This will be the Midwest contingent of the Antiwar Demonstration scheduled for Washington on October 21."

"Mr. Sealy, we barely have 10,000 people in all of Grant County. How long are they going to stay and where are they going to stay?" Liv asked.

"You have a chapter of SAW, my organization, on campus. On behalf of that group, I would like to request the use of your practice fields beyond the stadium. Students

Against Warfare would, of course, be prepared to pay rent on the property."

"Rent?" S.G. Caufield perked up.

"Yes. The rate we're paying host colleges and universities is $1000 a night, which would be about $5000. And SAW would post a damage bond of $10,000 with your local bank," Sealy added.

"What about water, hygiene, food?" I tried to be practical.

"We'll provide portable toilets—about one for every 150 to 200 people. And water trucks. The participants are told to bring their own food."

"And security? Will you provide police and fire protection?" Jack Glencoe chimed in.

Sealy nodded yes.

"No fires," Livvy stated. "It's autumn and the last thing we want is a forest fire."

"We're thinking about cooking and feeding in the Jordan Run meadow," Pig spoke up. "Most of these people will be in buses or cars but just getting back and forth will take some time and energy."

Liv folded her fingers into each other and leaned over the conference table. "Mr. Sealy, what happens if we say no to your proposal?"

For the first time, the big Indian spoke up. "Why, Madame Provost, I would guess they would just use your land anyway and it would be up to you to put them off."

— 36 —

Convocation of Hippies
and Hillbillies

Pig arrived at Five's Five the next afternoon with Whisper in tow. She wore a powder blue dress that caressed the ground. Its weave was loose as burlap and its folds clung to her tiny figure.

"I've explained to Whisper what we want to do, and she's really excited about it." Nothing betrayed Whisper's excitement on her blank face. But what a beautiful blank face—with huge gray eyes, a tiny button of a nose, thin lips on a generous mouth, and a firm chin.

I showed them around the cabin, then the studio. Whisper picked up one of my art books and settled into a chair.

"Ahh, Pig, does Whisper ever speak?" I asked as we stepped out to the studio deck.

"She's not mute, if that's what you mean. You heard her sing." He smiled. "And she can make her feelings known. She's just very shy, very quiet."

"Is she, ah… your woman?" He nodded yes and grinned.

We set up two easels in the studio and Whisper took her place on a stool. Pig's first objective was to capture this child-woman's face. I sketched quickly, letting her hair drape over each shoulder. Pig worked at his own easel, wielding a conté crayon. I was pleased to see that he had captured Whisper's features very accurately, and wasn't too tight in his rendering.

Whisper was one of the best models I've ever used. She sat absolutely still for as much as a half hour. From time to time, she would give us a faint smile, but never a frown or sign of complaint.

We adjourned to the front porch. The October breeze was scourging the final leaves from the late-color trees, a blizzard of browns and yellows. I wouldn't have too many more days of sitting on the porch.

"What I have in mind is Whisper in several different locations," Pig said. "If we could just capture this curtain of blowing leaves…"

Whisper nodded, smiled and sipped her coffee.

"Can you sing something for us, Whisper," Pig asked softly.

Without a breath, Whisper's bell-like voice began the refrain from *Barbara Allen*. Pig and I sat there as the girl sang each of perhaps a dozen verses with perfect pitch and enunciation. We mimed applause and Whisper responded with her sweet smile.

"How many songs do you know, Whisper?" I asked. She widened her eyes and glanced at Pig.

"She must know hundreds," Pig responded. "Every time I ask her to sing something, it's always a different one."

I showed them the sketches I had made while Whisper was singing *Barbara Allen*. I had caught tiny nuances of expression that her face never showed except when she sang. She put her hand on mine and warmed me with a smile of approval.

• • •

"Coach Bruce, this is not a request," Liv said sternly into the phone. "It's an order. Your team will practice in the stadium this week." She grinned as she mimed the irritation on the other end of the line. "Arthur, it's mid-October. The grass is already nearly dead." Another pause. I could hear Art Bruce's protests. "And I'll be sure the athletic budget gets a thousand dollars for your inconvenience."

The protests ended and Livinda put down the phone. It was the day before the Seneca Convocation and she was giving the football team and band the bad news about their practice fields. Con Stedman didn't need a budget bribe to move band practice to the ROTC drill field on the Underhill Campus.

Livvy's secretary tapped on the door. "Sergeant Glencoe's here," she announced. We joined Jack Glencoe and walked across Eden Fields.

"How many extra people do we have, Jack?" Liv asked.

"Petersburg loaned us six, and I've got six auxiliary people who won't carry weapons," he responded.

We walked across the footbridge and looked down on the practice fields from the top of the helix pier. At the far edge of the woods, workmen were unloading brightly-painted portable toilets and placing them in rows. A huge black 1949 Pontiac Torpedo sedan came boiling onto the practice field, kicking up a roostertail of dust.

"Here comes the Chief," Glencoe said as Alexander Rolling Thunder got out of the car. "Man, he looks like a one-man security force." Rolling Thunder loped up the helix and greeted us without losing a breath.

"Morning, folks," he said. "Looks like Dan's people are already at work." He surveyed the fields and then settled with both hands on the bridge railing. "And this looks like an ideal spot to set up security to keep 'em all down there and not up here."

"That was my plan, Mr. Rolling Thunder," Glencoe said. "I'll have two people right here all the time."

"It's Alex, Sergeant. And I'll place a bike at each end of these long ramps and a couple of people at the bottom of this spiral."

"A bike?" Livvy asked. "You'll have motorcycles?"

"Oh, you bet!" he laughed. "We've hired the Hell's Angels from Pittsburgh and Cleveland. They're our security team."

• • •

By the time my two o'clock class was done, the sun had vanished and a steady wind was blowing mist out of the north. The temperature had dropped by fifteen degrees. I trudged across campus and back across the footbridge. Rolling Thunder waved from below and began loping up the north ramp.

"Hey there, Professor," he shouted. "Looks like it's gonna get wetter. I hope these kids are used to campin' out. We've already got some early arrivals."

Across the field, a VW hippie bus and several automobiles were parked close to the toilet rows. A motorcylist rocketed over the practice field toward them.

"Is that one of your security people, Alex?" I asked.

"Yep. These motorcycle sonsabitches are just itchin' to bust some heads. I hope this was a good idea of Dan's."

"Just so they don't let them burn the woods down."

"Not much chance of that if the weather brings us some rain." He paused and eyed me as if he were measuring me for a scalping. "Pig tells me you're a pretty good guy. That you've been around the campuses some. Do you have any causes?"

"No. I'm a teacher now. And a painter. Those are my causes."

"Well, this is a pretty hard time to not stand up for *something*. God. but this is beautiful country. Reminds me of home."

"Where's home?" I asked.

"South Dakota. The Black Hills."

• • •

Tuesday morning. Traffic was clogging downtown Seneca from all four directions. Chartered buses and private vehicles all followed big arrow signs that led to the practice fields. A huge banner hung from a pair of sapling poles announcing *Seneca Convocation: On To Washington*.

The rain of the night before had turned the entry road to the practice fields to mud and big ruts were forming as bus after bus pulled in. A Seneca patrolman and a Hell's Angel teamed up to direct vehicles to parking spots.

I spotted the big black Pontiac and pulled up beside it. "Morning, Alex! Looks like you're under way."

He leaned out his window and frowned. "I've already got about nine thousand people here and the word is many more are on the way. Thank heavens The Diggers have arrived. They've set up an infirmary tent and are working on a feeding tent.

"I've talked to the provost and she sounds just a little irritated. I think this is more than she expected. I know it's more than I expected."

I went directly to Felton Hall. Livvy's secretary just jerked her head toward the door. "She's snappin' mad, Professor so watch yourself," she warned.

"What a freaking disaster," Livvy screeched as I entered. "Have you seen that, Five? How could I be so stupid?"

"I talked with Rolling Thunder. He says it's a lot bigger crowd than they'd expected. But they do seem fairly well organized."

"Organized? It reminds me of Andersonville and this is just the first day," she continued to screech. "There are going to be sick people, starving people, even dead people on our practice fields. What a dumbass I am." She gulped in air. "Oh Five, I've really done it. Some 50-year-old provost would never have approved this fiasco."

"Come on Liv, stop beating yourself up," I grabbed her by the shoulders. She slipped into my arms and the tears flowed. "Let's drive up to Jordan Run and see what the situation is there."

• • •

We found Pig in charge of a huge fly tent covering six open grills made from split oil drums. Teams of men were bent over shovels, creating pits beneath the tent. I spotted Bubby Bristo's pickup but didn't see Bubby anywhere.

"What's Bubby Bristo doing here?" I asked Pig.

"He came over this morning with a truckload of split wood and volunteered to help us make *burgoo*. Now he's down there helpin' the women whip up biscuit dough." Pig put his arms around our shoulders and steered us away from the other helpers.

"Personally, I'm afraid someone had his head up his butt when he planned this thing. Without Bubby, I don't think we'd have been able to feed anyone more than soggy crackers. There's lots of talk," he looked around, "about pulling out and heading for Washington early."

Bubby emerged from the smaller tent, his overalls covered with flour. "Hey, Five, Livinda, did you come up to help make burgoo?"

"What's burgoo?" I asked.

"The way Bubby makes it, it's delicious," Livvy laughed for the first time of the day. "The Bristo burgoo feed is a famous annual event. But Bubby," she looked at him quizzically, "for 10,000 people?"

"Cousin Denton is coming up with six more barrels as soon as he can torch 'em in two. We've got lots of creek water which'll be great if I can keep these damn people from bathin' and crappin' upstream. The 'mountain Bristos' sold that Indian fifteen hogs and they're slaughterin' right now. The Indian bought four steers from someone up near Streby, and the chicken ranch at Maysville is sending down a couple hundred hens. These kids have to kill and pick them, but there are plenty of hands for that."

Bubby paused and looked around. "I was down at Seneca about an hour ago. I think this bunch up here is better off workin' than those kids huddled under their tarps." He pulled out his notebook. "Let's see. I still need about three hundred pounds of potatoes, a hundredweight of onions, about the same for carrots."

• • •

A steady drizzle washed us on the way back to the campus. On the practice fields, groups of kids were huddled under makeshift lean-tos, but most had climbed back on their buses. Their faces were gloomy as they stared out the rain-soaked windows.

The first bus pulled out about four o'clock. It was rapidly followed by another dozen or so. The practice fields were a quagmire, and not nearly so crowded.

Alex Rolling Thunder stood at the top of the helix and turned on a bull horn. "OK, people. Let's have your attention. There's a place up the road about five miles called Jordan Run. It's a local commune and the people there are working their asses off to get some food prepared.

"This is not a good place to camp," he boomed across the practice fields. "There's lots of space at Jordan Run and you can get a hot meal there if you want to go tonight. We'll be moving the portable johns up there starting right now."

A chorus of voices echoed across the misty field below. Jeers. Boos. Cheers. But a couple of buses immediately cranked up.

"We have three more nights here," Rolling Thunder boomed. "Or you can go on to Washington and take your chances on The Mall. Whatever you do, please be in Washington on Saturday. The nation needs you."

• • •

Back at Jordan Run, we found the half-barrels sitting in the pits atop thick beds of glowing coals. A steady line of hippies trudged back and forth from the creek with water buckets. Several mountain men were systematically butchering hog carcasses on a trestle table, the rain washing away the blood. Hippie girls and radical students were peeling onions and potatoes.

Hoopie Poletz and Cyndy Byrd pulled up in Bubby's pickup truck and unloaded bags of carrots and boxes of salt and pepper. Dicky Reb and Culden appeared with R.T. in tow. Dick shot steadily with his one-handed Leica as the cooking unfolded around him.

Horns blew as more vehicles entered the meadow, but its thick grass kept the mud down. A truck with portable toilets arrived and, under Pig's direction, they were established below the cooking area and away from the creek. Finally, a water truck arrived and the bucket brigade could find something else to do.

Liv returned with several mountain women who set up more trestle tables and stacked an assortment of bowls and dishes. "We don't have nearly enough dishes to serve everyone," she told Bubby, "so I guess we'll just feed them in rotation."

A hinged barrel served as an oven, and dozens of large skillets filled with biscuits were put in to bake. Guitars and other instruments appeared and the hungry onlookers gathered around and sang *If I Had A Hammer* and other popular folksongs. The drizzle abated and the narrow patch of sky above the hollow broke out in stars.

"You realize the burgoo has to cook all night," Bubby said. "But it'll be ready for breakfast, and it'll be damn fine, too."

Rolling Thunder made this announcement on his bullhorn, but instead of booing, the crowd started unpacking food they'd brought from home. No one would starve tonight.

Into the burgoo pots went wholesale lots of potatoes, onions, whole chickens, chunks of beef and pork. Carrots and greens followed. As Bubby and his crew stirred with stout saplings cut from the woods, the soup began to throw off tantalizing odors.

The campers eagerly attacked biscuits and camp food. Small campfires and many lanterns illuminated the tent city that spread across the meadow. From time to time, a bottle rocket would launch.

"This gets more Brueghelesque all the time," Liv said.

• • •

Dawn found the hungry crowd forming a line at the burgoo tent. The hippies seemed to form in groups according to their bus. By mid-morning, most of the buses were gone and the meadow held only small groups which were packing up their tents and tarps.

"I think we're going to be out of your hair, Doctor Ferris," Rolling Thunder said to us. "Most of the buses have left for Washington, and the rest of these kids are going to leave today." He paused to stroke his long black hair. "I checked with Arthur Boxx last night. He has deposited the escrow check in your local bank and said Seneca could make a claim against the whole amount."

"Ten thousand dollars?" Liv asked.

"That's right. It should cover the damage to your practice fields, whatever other expenses the university has, reimbursement to these people for the food, and a couple of thousand left over for use of the facilities," he said with a grim smile. "It'll work out to about a dollar a head, but it's the best we can do. We're going to pile up some big expenses in D.C."

Pig and Whisper came up to us as the crowd continued to thin.

"Five, Doctor Ferris, we're gonna be off to D.C. in a little while. I think my old bus will make it. But we'll be back next week. I don't want to miss too much class."

I punched him lightly on the shoulder. "Don't worry, Pig, I think my roll book will show you in good attendance. Just be careful, and have a good time."

Livvy threw me a mock glare. "You'd falsify the academic records of Seneca U.?"

"And you'd blackmail a faculty member into doing a job by threatening to withhold his tenure?" I responded.

— 37 —

Pigskin and Protest

Even though she didn't invite me, I joined Livvy for Saturday afternoon's tailgate party and the game against Bucknell. October had turned from bright hues to a cold, damp gray. As kickoff time neared, the stadium crowd couldn't have numbered more than 5,000 or so, mostly alumni huddled under blankets.

Livvy led us to the president's seats, protected from the wind by the press box, and we tucked our blanket over our laps. The Warriors took the field clad in all-white uniforms rather than their traditional red-and-gold jerseys. "I guess Art's desperate enough to try anything," Oliver Monckton muttered.

As the Bucknell Bisons came onto the field in their all-blue uniforms, a light rain began to fall. The president and trustees huddled beneath the shelter of the press box, and Liv and I moved to sheltered seats as well. The rain's intensity increased as we sang *Morning Mountain Mists* and it was a full downpour for the National Anthem.

Seneca won the coin toss and tried to receive the kickoff, but the ball bounced away and into the end zone, where a

Bucknell player covered it. With eight seconds off the clock, Seneca trailed by seven points. A scattering of boos and jeers echoed through the rain.

The next kickoff went into the end zone and the Warriors broke their huddle on the 20-yard line into a single wing.

"Single wing!" Busby Ferris scoffed. "This should be interesting."

The direct snap to the tailback bounced off his chest and a huge pile covered the ball. The Warriors' white uniforms were now the rich black of mud. Seneca recovered, and on the next snap the tailback squished through the Bucknell line and broke free for an 82-yard touchdown run. The Warriors missed the extra point.

The game ended with a 7-6 mudbath loss for Seneca. I was interested in hearing Ollie Monckton talking with a couple other trustees about a coaching change. One of the names I overhead was 'Duerhoff,' who could be none other than my old buddy Bear—now an assistant coach at Pittsburgh after a career-ending injury with the New York Giants.

• • •

Livinda and I met Culden and Dicky Reb after the game and we slogged to Liv's house. "Here's a nice sweater that belongs to Daddy," Liv said as she handed me a genuine Irish knit turtleneck. "Thank God for the blanket. We'd be soaked without it and the press box."

Drinks in hand, we settled down to watch Livvy's color television, one of the few in Seneca. Instead of a major college football game, we were greeted with frightening images from the anti-war demonstration in Washington. Clouds of tear gas made the scene as hazy as the football game we'd just endured. Policemen wielded long truncheons, flailing away at hippies.

A rock sailed out of the crowd and shattered a cop's plastic visor. Blood flew. The cops charged and another round of tear gas was fired. The National Mall was a battlefield. The scene switched to the turmoil around the Reflecting Pool and Lincoln Memorial. Don Sealy of SAW was vainly attempting a speech, but screams and shouts and the popping of tear gas canisters nearly drowned him out.

"Look, look there to the right!" Dicky Reb yelled. "It's Whisper."

Indeed, Whisper Gaskins was resolutely walking to the podium, her tiny hand in Pig's. Pig leaned over and whispered in Sealy's ear. Sealy shook his head, looked at Whisper, then shrugged and stepped away from the microphone. Pig drew the microphone down and Whisper stepped up and flashed her beatific smile. Then her mouth moved.

"Amazing Grace, how sweet thou art"… echoed across the Reflecting Pool, onto the National Mall, and across the nation on television. And, amazingly, the noises of protest and riot quieted as Whisper's bell-like voice commanded the attention of all. We sat open-mouthed as Whisper sang through the hymn to an absolutely silent crowd, estimated at half a million. As she hit the final note, another woman entered the picture with a guitar.

"My God, it's Joan Baez!" Culden said. Indeed it was, and Baez struck a chord that led to the second verse of *Amazing Grace.* Whisper jumped to harmony, and the two voices blended in a beautiful mix. They finished to scattered cheers which grew to a thunderous applause. With a slight smile, Whisper turned and left the podium hand-in-hand with John Piggot.

• • •

Walter Cronkite intoned, "A national tragedy was perhaps avoided this evening when a mystery woman brought to a halt fighting and disruption on the National Mall with only the beauty of her voice. Folk star Joan Baez joined the mystery girl for a second verse of *Amazing Grace* and when they were done, so was the riot.

"Authorities estimated that more than five hundred thousand Anti-War protesters gathered on the Mall in a mostly peaceful demonstration until a Molotov cocktail was thrown at a police car. Forty-five protesters were arrested and another twenty were hospitalized, as well as five police officers.

"The mystery singer vanished from the podium and disappeared into the crowd surrounding the steps of the Lincoln Memorial. Baez is reportedly seeking her identity, in hopes of making a recording with her."

• • •

On Sunday night, a big crowd watched on Livvy's color set as *60 Minutes* ran footage of the anti-war demonstration and Whisper's performance. Her identity remained unknown but hippies interviewed from the crowd recalled her singing at the Seneca Convocation and hearing the name "Whisper." Several people identified John Piggot as a Seneca hippie leader named "Pig." It seemed that Seneca had not escaped the national spotlight. Dean Sarah Lumley flatly declared that Whisper was not a Seneca student. Livvy and I remained silent as other faculty members debated how the university could capitalize on her fame.

"Perhaps she can coach football," Wayman Minteer cracked.

I broke in. "I know Whisper, and she's a very shy, very reserved woman. And I know her friend and he would not appreciate your joking about her."

"Is she from around here?" Minteer questioned.

"Yes. She lives in Jordan Run and her boyfriend is a student here," I answered. "I think the best course of action would be to wait and see how this thing plays out. I don't know how she'll respond to the publicity."

We found out Monday morning, when Pig showed up for his first class. The art faculty greeted him with cheers and back pounding.

"Pig, that was absolutely marvelous," Culden praised. "Tell us all about it—how it happened."

"Well," he drawled, "several of the Seneca people, including Alex Rolling Thunder, had asked Whisper if she would sing. But that would be way later in the program, after Joan Baez. But when the rioting started, Alex came to me and asked if she could possibly try to quiet the crowd.

"I said she couldn't talk 'em into being quiet, but she could sure try to sing. Whisper told me it was OK and you saw the rest."

"Did she come home with you?" I asked.

"Why, of course," he answered. "Laurel Town and Jordan Run is where we live." Pig grinned at us. "But we did watch *60 Minutes* with Joan Baez, and there's a guy from a recording company coming out later this week."

"How does Whisper feel about making a recording?" Liv asked. "How will she handle interviews? Publicity?"

"Doctor Ferris, just because Whisper doesn't say a lot doesn't mean she's some kind of freak. She talks when she has something to say." Pause. "You'll hear her talk some day."

— 38 —

Wedding Bells
and Jack-o'-Lanterns

On the last Saturday of October, I threw Five's Five open for my first big social event—a Halloween party. Liv and her maid, Mary, came out at noon to help prepare food. Bubby Bristo showed up with his truck full of pumpkins, and the art faculty spent the afternoon carving jack-o'-lanterns that would line the lane and the ford.

One of the 'mountain Bristos' showed up with a trunk full of Mason jars, which we stored in the icy water of Gerwig's Run. By five o'clock it was nearly dark and everyone had left to change into costume. I kept mine simple. A coonskin cap donated by Bubby and a pair of bib overalls worn over red long johns. A little stoneware jug filled with 'shine completed my costume.

Soon the lane was filled with headlights and my forest became populated with strange creatures. Liv's maid came in a genuine French maid costume, with white cap and lace apron and proceeded to serve hors d'oeuvres to guests. Livvy wore a variation of her hippie costume, deep-cut peasant blouse and no bra. President Skinner outdid me with a genuine buckskin mountain man outfit, and carried a long rifle.

The football coaches got a big laugh when they entered with a coffin holding the 'corpse' of Art Bruce. Culden and Dicky Reb appeared, Culden in a slinky Vietnamese *ao dai* and Dicky Reb in his old drum major suit. A sinister owl showed up, at least seven feet tall, and absolutely silent. Everyone speculated who was inside, but the owl remained at the edge of the yard and watched the proceedings.

Cyndy Byrd appeared in a harem outfit, revealing most of her attributes, much to the delight of Hoopie, her escort. He wore a Napoleon hat and red underwear. Another pair of mystery figures made an entrance… a tall one in a black cloak and pointed hood, and a shorter one in a red cloak and hood.

The crowd grew with people I didn't even know. I could spot several citizens from Jordan Run or Laurel Town, including Blondie; but I could not find Doug Kaminsky. Susie Longmeyer, the Kappa president, showed up with a gaggle of her sisters, all dressed as nuns. My student Marilyn Kretzman appeared in a biblical costume and declared she was the Virgin Mary, "but not for long."

Bubby, Tibby, and cousin Wilfred appeared out of the woods, obviously having walked over the moonshine trail. Bubby took in my outfit and guffawed. He wore a scarlet Warriors cap and one of Art Bruce's coaching jackets. A whistle and clipboard left no doubt who he came dressed as. Tibby had on a white gown with a long gauze train which gave her a ghostly appearance. Wilfred impersonated a hillbilly by donning a pointed felt hat over his usual garb of workshirt and patched jeans.

Livvy had recruited Gerald Warren to tend bar, and he kept up a continuous run to the creek for more moonshine. In addition, I had stocked bourbon and vodka, but most of the guests preferred Old Bristo. Out of the woods came three more mountain people, Bristo cousins, I reckoned— two men and a woman. They carried a banjo, a dulcimer, and a guitar, and without a wasted second, sat on the porch and began the music.

Immediately, Bubby shuffled into the yard clearing and did a fancy buck and wing, never moving his upper body. The crowd gathered in a circle as one after another took a turn in the middle, improvising fancy steps or drunken steps, whichever they could manage.

"I've seen Bubby dance like that in church," Livvy whispered in my ear. "We do have to go see his service some Saturday night."

When the music brought Culden into the circle, she did a bawdy shuffle and exposed a lot of leg in her *ao dai*. Then she swung over and grabbed Dicky Reb's hand, pulling him into the circle. Culden waved for silence and the musicians stopped their tune.

"Folks, this is Five's party but Dicky Reb has something to say, and I don't think it'll hurt Five's feelings."

Richard West took off his tall shako and held it under his arm. He looked at Culden, then dropped to one knee. The crowd gasped.

"Miss Ellis," he said in a cracking voice, "I would be greatly honored if you would consent to be my wife."

The crowd roared. Culden wiped a tear away and pulled Reb upright, then grabbed him in one of the most passionate kisses I've ever seen. I threw my arms around the two of them in a big hug and the music struck up a lively air. The three of us danced around in a staggering jig and finally fell down in a pile.

The musicians took a break, and Hoopie Poletz asked to use the guitar. He sat on the step and strummed a quiet tune that seemed familiar but no one recognized. The two hooded figures drifted closer to the steps and then the unmistakable voice singing...

Abroad as I was walking, down some greenwood side,
I heard a young girl singing, "I wish I were a bride."

Whisper was back. Hoopie softly accompanied her through all six verses of the English ballad. When she was finished, she gently removed her hood, smiled, and dropped her head. The crowd cheered and whistled. Whisper held up her hand for silence and said softly, "Thank you very much."

• • •

I walked to the edge of the woods where I'd last seen the giant owl. Broken limbs and brush marked a trail into the woods. After a couple dozen yards, I stumbled upon the owl suit, a big pile of feathers. The trail led up the mountain, and I knew in an instant who the wearer was.

I asked Bubby, Culden, and Livvy to keep the party going, then went into the cabin, where I picked up my battle lantern, and headed up the path. Not exactly sober but definitely not drunk, I made my way up the moonshine trail and turned toward Sibley's Crystal Cave. I didn't try for silence as I hurried along the trail and reached the anchor tree.

A carabiner-and-line was fixed and I flashed the battle lantern into the gorge.

"What do they say in West Virginia when an owl hoots?" Gillian called up to me. She was sitting on the ledge in the mouth of the cave, wearing her black leotard. "Are you going to come down, Five?"

I nodded and gingerly made my way down the rock face, using the safety line. Gil shined a flashlight at the face to mark my footing. I walked onto the ledge and sat beside her.

"Hi," she whispered. "Was it OK that I came to your party? Livvy told me about it."

"Of course," I responded with genuine emotion. "I just wished I'd realized who you were."

"I just wanted to see the Crystal Room one more time," she said. "Will you come with me?"

"No helmets, no equipment?"

"We know it's an easy free climb. And we've got two lights. C'mon, Five, be a sport."

I shrugged as she got up and started into the cave. I left my coonskin cap on the ledge and followed her.

Gillian went up the rock face like a lizard, but I had more trouble. At the pull-up point, she reached down and helped me over the ledge. We rested a minute, then started up the passage and across the piles of breakdown. Gillian wore her dance slippers and skirted the rocks with ease. My clodhoppers made me feel more clumsy. At the top of the rock pile, Gillian headed directly for the opening to the crawlspace, flopped on her stomach, and vanished into the hole. I followed without trepidation. When I emerged, she was already shinnying down the line from Sibley's anchor bolt. My brighter battle lantern illuminated the floor of the Crystal Room beneath her.

"I don't think I can make it without a rappel device," I called.

"All right. You just stay up there and watch," she answered.

Her flashlight flickered in and out as she passed through the speleothem formations. I followed her progress with the battle lantern, surprised that it would reach across the Crystal Room. The ceiling lowered as she reached the far side.

"I'm at the pool now. Can you see it?" Gillian ran her flash across the surface of the pool. I could barely pick her out in the beam of my light. She put her light on a rock and then leaned over to remove her shoes. In a quick motion, she stripped off her leotard.

My light picked up her dim shape as she lowered herself into the pool and grabbed her light. Then she disappeared.

Screaming her name, I watched as the glow of Gillian's flashlight flickered and faded beneath the surface of the pool. I looped the watertight battle lantern over my wrist and tried to clamber down the rock face, using the rope. After several slips and near-falls, I reached the bottom. By the time I had picked my way across the path of the Crystal Room's floor, ten minutes had passed. I sat at the edge of the pool to remove the cumbersome shoes, then shed my overalls and long johns. I lowered myself into the pool and marveled that the light continued burning.

Swimming under the ledge, I discovered an underwater crawlspace. After less than 30 seconds of holding my breath, the lantern revealed Gillian's naked legs ahead. I surfaced beside her, gasping for breath. Her flashlight glowed weakly, its batteries on their last legs.

"Thought my torch was watertight," she mumbled. "Wasn't. Thought there'd be another big crystal room." Her voice was weak, almost a sob. "There isn't."

My light revealed a very small low chamber. Gillian and I lay on a short bench, almost a beach, above the pool.

"Are you OK?" I asked, rubbing her shoulders and neck.

"Guess so. Hard to breathe. I think the air's bad in here." She turned to look at me. "There's something in here."

I directed my light to the far corner of the chamber, just at the end of the beach. A lumpy form lay against the juncture of ceiling and wall. I crawled up the beach and to the shape. The remains of a skeleton, covered with rotting shreds of a wet suit, lay pinned by a huge rock jutting from the wall. One outstretched arm covered a plastic emergency flask available in any military surplus store. I gently removed the flask and examined it. The initials "H.S." were painted in red enamel on the outside. Beneath the skeleton, a length of rope extended onto the beach. I pulled at it gently and was amazed when it did not disintegrate, revealing about five feet of climbing line.

"Gil! It's Hiram Sibley. You've found his tomb. But we've got to get out of here. Can you swim?"

"Yeah, but I don't... don't know where." Her voice was weak and incoherent.

"I'm going to tie this line around your wrist. Then I want you to hold tight to it as well," I instructed. I watched her carefully, and she seemed to understand. "The passage can't be more than 15 feet long. I'll tie the other end to my ankle and start through the passage."

Gillian nodded.

"When the line goes tight, you take a deep breath and hold it. I'll pull you through."

With the line tight around my ankle, I gently dropped into the pool and aimed the battle lantern at the underwater passage. Kicking with one leg and pulling with one hand, I made good progress into the passage. The line went tight and I could feel vibrations that told me Gil was also in the water. I pushed the plastic flask ahead of me with the hand that held the light.

Progress wasn't as fast going out, and my lungs were burning when I could see the black surface of the Crystal Room pool. I stood on the bottom and gently reeled Gillian in. She burst out of the water, gasping and puking. I held her tightly and untied the line from her wrist, then pushed her slippery body up onto the ledge of the pool.

It was all I could do to pull myself out of the four-foot depth but Gillian gave me a hand and I finally scraped my way onto the ledge. I took her leotard and used it as a towel, briskly rubbing her shivering body dry. Then I bundled her into my red long underwear and used the leotard on myself.

Once I got semi-dry, I donned the bib overalls and pulled on my woolly socks. Gillian pulled on her dance slippers and wrapped the damp leotard around my bare shoulders. I tucked the flask into an overall pocket.

"Come on, Five, we've got to get out of here—fast," Gil told me. She took the battle lantern and aimed it at the passage ledge high above. We picked our way across the room, following the path as well as we could in our haste.

At the rope, Gillian handed me the battle lantern. "Light my marks and I'll climb first. Then we'll hoist the lantern up and I'll help you." I lit her path as she climbed catlike up the steep rock face. For someone who seemed nearly drowned, her recovery was remarkable. I knotted the lantern handle to the climbing rope and Gil quickly hauled it up.

"Tie a bowline in the end of the line," she called down, "and put one foot in it." I followed her instructions. "Now, start climbing and I'll pull on the line at the same time."

Gillian's wet body had made the rock face slippery and I clambered and clawed my way up. Each time I would make a foot of progress, Gil would tighten and shorten the line. I doubt that I could have climbed it by myself, but finally I reached the top and tumbled onto the ledge, gasping for breath.

We made our way through the exit crawlspace and out of the cave to rest for five minutes on the ledge where I'd first joined Gillian. We took turns wearing my coonskin cap.

As we began shivering, Gil muttered, "Hypothermia," and rose to attack the last rock face. This one seemed easy after the cave ordeal, and within minutes we were on the trail back to Five's Five.

"What on earth were you thinking, Gil?" I panted as we hit the moonshine road.

"Five, I've got to leave Woodstock pretty soon," she answered. "I just wanted to see the Crystal Room one more time. When I got there, it suddenly struck me that there might be a bigger crystal chamber beyond the underwater passage. Now we know. And we did solve the mystery of Hiram Sibley," she added.

"Yeah. That's something I've got to contend with. Let's keep it quiet when we get back. I wonder if the party is still going." The sounds of laughter and music from down the mountain answered that question.

• • •

Pulling the studio key from its hiding place, I let us into the warm and dark building. I pulled a blanket from a closet and threw it over Gil, who curled into a chair in front of the gas heater.

"I'll go get some clothes for us," I said, and crossed the bridge to the house. Only Mary, the maid, was visible and

I shushed her as I crept up the stairs. I changed into jeans and a sweatshirt and found an old warmup suit of Gillian's. Back in the studio, Gil's color had returned, and she smiled as I entered.

"One more snog and shag for old times' sake?" she grinned as she unwound the blanket from her naked body.

I grinned at her display, but shook my head no.

"Why not? I'm clean and sober... and I still love you, Five." But she stretched into a lithe pose and then reluctantly, put her leg into the warmup pants. "So it's really over, eh?"

"Yes, Gillian. It's really over."

"Is there someone else?" she asked quietly.

"No... no one else. It's been a great adventure but... it's really over."

Gil decided she wanted to leave without showing herself at the party. We crept through the woods to recover her owl suit, then crossed the swinging bridge and walked down the mountain to her car.

"Now, be sure to tell Cyndy I was here and got my things," she instructed, "or she'll think someone broke into the apartment."

"Where will you go, Gillian?"

"Oh, I've got a few more weeks at Woodstock. Then I'll take off for New York, maybe. Audition for some dance jobs. Maybe even go home to Scotland. Who knows?" She stood on tiptoes and gave me a chaste kiss and huge hug. "Thanks for everything, Five. And good luck with Hiram Sibley."

— 39 —

Hiram and All Saints Day

Bubby, Liv, Culden, and Dicky Reb were the last to leave the party. I gathered them around my living room and related the events of the night, leading up to the cave.

"We wondered where you'd gone to," Livvy stated.

"And when the big owl disappeared, we wondered who it was and why the two of you vanished," Culden added.

"I went looking for the owl. When I found the suit in the woods, I knew instantly who was wearing it," I said, not telling them how I knew. "I found Gillian at the mouth of the cave and she told me she wanted to take one last look at the Crystal Room."

I related how we did the fairly harmless free climb into the cave and then about Gillian's impulsive plunge into the pool. "We got out OK," I added, "but that's not the important thing." I produced the plastic survival flask. "Gillian—and I—discovered Hiram Sibley's body. The room beyond the pool is really his tomb. This flask was with his skeleton. I haven't opened it yet."

The flask was the size of a thin novel, with an o-ring screw top for use as a canteen, and a removable latch top for storing larger objects. I flipped the latch and its contents fell onto the table—a small notebook, a mechanical pencil, six waxed matches, a whistle, four paraffin fire starters, a smaller flask of carbide, and some spare lamp flints in a cloth bag.

The contents of the notebook revealed little except to pinpoint the location of H3 on Skidmore Road, 2.3 miles from the highway and uphill.

"Lord, that's pathetic," Livvy exclaimed. "The man really explored caves with this little bit of equipment?"

"He was a lively one, all right," Bubby said. "Climbed all the Senecas by himself, he did, and with only one coil of rope."

We talked quietly about getting the body removed from the cave for burial.

"Mr. Sibley never said anything to me about the Crystal Cave, and it was nearly in my own backyard," Bubby said. "I think it was his own beautiful secret."

"Recovering the body would involve a lot of work by some experienced cavers and divers," I said. "Enlarging a crawlspace and swimming into the chamber."

"My feeling is Mr. Sibley would just as soon let that chamber be his grave," Bubby said. "That fella Floyd Collins is buried in his cave in Kentucky."

"I kind of agree," Liv chimed in. "Five, could you take us to see this cave tomorrow? Then we could think of a way to memorialize him."

• • •

Sunday morning, Culden, Dicky Reb, and Maddy Bristo showed up first. Maddy and Tibby Bristo would babysit R.T. and Hezekiah while we visited Crystal Cave. Bubby and

Tibby showed up soon after. Livinda was the last to arrive, attired in an old caver suit and battered hard hat.

"Will we need all that gear just to see this cave?" Culden asked.

"No," I answered. "Gillian went in last night in a leotard and armed with a flashlight." To demonstrate how easy it was, I wore jeans and a sweatshirt, but had my helmet and carbide lamp.

We hiked up the trail through the forest, the trees bare except for the conifers. The morning had an air of celebration and the woods smelled good. At the anchor tree, the group stood in awe at the water pouring from the cave mouth. I demonstrated the hand and foot holds by climbing down, and rigged a belay rope. With the belay line attached under their arms, each member of the party made it down, even Dicky Reb with his healing hand. The group followed me along the ledge and then assaulted the entry rock face after watching me. The assist rope here was all we needed.

Carefully we hiked across the breakdown room and climbed the rock pile at its end. Then each of them followed me through the crawlspace to the ledge overlooking the Crystal Room.

"My word, it's gorgeous!" Culden exclaimed. "It's even prettier than your glitter painting," she nudged me.

"How do we get down?" Livvy asked.

"That line over there. I could rig another belay. Gillian and I got up last night, but it was a bitch for me," I added.

"Where's the pool?" Dick asked. I shined the battle lantern across the room.

"Over there by that wall."

"Let's go down," Culden said. "I want to see the whole room."

I rigged another belay line. This time, Liv went on belay on the ledge and gently protected me as I made the climb down. Then she tossed the belay end to me and I became the climbing partner.

"On belay," I called, winding the line around my waist and across my butt.

"Climbing," Liv called, even though she was coming down.

Soon the five of us were on the chamber floor, and I pointed out the path that Hiram Sibley had created. We crossed the room slowly, marveling at the formations and the glittering chunks of mineral reflecting our lights. The pool was still slightly murky from our thrashing climb-out the night before. We stood in silence and contemplated the wall that shut off the next chamber except for its underwater route.

"I see no need for anything more than a simple memorial plaque," Livinda stated. "He may have died in agony but I think Hiram died in his favorite environment."

"Amen to that," Bubby intoned.

• • •

As we crossed back through the Crystal Room, everyone played lights in every direction to explore the speleothem wonders. Culden stopped beside a curtain of flowstone and directed her light into a dark spot in the wall. "What's that?" she asked. "Looks like a doorway."

I walked across a stretch of broken stalactites, and found it was a door of sorts. "It's a passage. Bubby, you and Livvy come with me, since you've got helmets."

"I knew we'd need equipment," Culden groused.

We entered the upright passage and again found a worn floor that marked the earlier use of this area. The passage led steadily upgrade and narrowed, but the ceiling stayed at about seven feet. Finally, we came to an area where the passage appeared no more than a foot wide, slightly wider toward the floor.

"It's a keyhole squeeze," Livvy announced. "I can make it for sure. Let me see what's on the other side."

She eased into the squeeze, which did indeed accept her trim body, and eased through.

"I think all three of us can make it," she called. "Come on and see."

With rock walls pushing on my gut and butt, I managed to make it through the squeeze. Bubby crawled through at the slightly lower place. Beyond us, the battle lantern and our headlamps revealed the narrow tunnel working on upgrade.

What appeared ahead as a blank wall turned out to be a sharp right-hand turn in the passage. Finally, a few yards farther on, the passage emerged into a large chamber. Shining the battle lantern around, I finally recognized it as the breakdown room from a completely different angle.

"My God, we've walked out of the Crystal Room and skipped the crawlspace!" I exclaimed. "Liv, you and Bubby go back down the passage to get Culden and Reb. I'll go back to the ledge through the crawlspace and tell them you're coming.

Culden and Reb were obviously happy to see my light shining through the crawlspace above their heads. I told them about the passage. In a few minutes, we could hear Liv and Bubby talking as they returned through the tunnel. Soon the four of them were back in the tunnel. I retrieved the belay line and the safety rope and made my way through the crawlspace for the final time.

I watched in amazement as they appeared from the tunnel and continued to walk down the side of the breakdown room without climbing the boulders.

"It's a man-made path," Liv called out. "Do you suppose Hiram cleared it?"

Making my way carefully across the breakdown pile, I fell behind the other four and finally caught up with them at the entry wall.

"About time," Reb joked. "You wanna get somewhere in a hurry, just ask Culden."

"It's a really nice path," Liv said. "Smooth and not much grade. I built a little cairn by the place where it joins the big room."

"Five? I know we want to have a memorial for Mr. Sibley," Culden said. "But do you suppose we could get a ladder on this wall and another outside? This is where I'd like to have my wedding, too."

"You want to bring a lot of people in here to climb around?" Reb asked incredulously.

"Not a lot of people," she answered. "Ten, perhaps? No more than twenty."

"What about your parents? My parents? Relatives?"

"Ah, shit, Reb. Keep that up and I'll change my mind about marrying you. I want to get married in the Crystal Room. We can let my mom plan a wedding in Zanesville and not tell her we're married."

"I can build a pair of ladders," Bubby volunteered.

• • •

Planning Hiram Sibley's memorial was a lot simpler than planning Culden's wedding. We decided on the wording and Culden produced a flat slab of soapstone from the sculpture lab. A Bristo cousin who ran a tombstone business carved the inscription.

Livinda checked with the county authorities and I signed an affidavit to the presence of the skeleton in the cave. We got the clearance to make the cave Hiram Sibley's grave.

On November 1, All Soul's Day, our small group plus Mandy Sibley, Hiram's niece, hiked through the sunny woods and climbed Bubby's shiny new ladders. We climbed Sibley's trail up the breakdown room and entered Culden's Tunnel. At the squeeze, we discovered a wider passage and about six inches of chipped-off rock. Bubby grinned back at the group as we easily made it through his handiwork.

Bubby had placed votive candles in tinfoil cups to illuminate the path through the Crystal Room. At the Sibley Wall, we said a silent prayer in candlelight, then Bubby shined my battle lantern on the soapstone plaque, affixed to the wall with four bronze climbing bolts.

In Memory of Hiram Sibley
1917 – 195?
Creator, Explorer, Adventurer
Who Knew These Mountains
Inside And Out

• • •

Culden's mother announced her daughter's wedding would be held during the Christmas break in Zanesville. Although it was uncharacteristic of her, Culden gave her mother free reign with the plans.

Cyndy, Hoopie, and Jaylene were brought into the Crystal Cave wedding planning committee. On the next Saturday morning, the eight of us went back to the cave, with Reb carrying his equipment and a large tripod. The other six entered the Crystal Room by the trail and tunnel, while Dicky and I went to the crawlspace ledge. He set up the tripod and I carefully art directed, placing each person in the room below where Dicky wanted.

"I'll leave the shutter open for about a minute," he said. "So there's no need to hurry to fire your flashbulbs. Just pop one, then eject it. Wait a few seconds for the flashgun to cool down, and put another bulb in and fire it in the other direction.

"Remember, you want your body or a formation between the light and the camera." Dicky Reb made a total of three exposures before the group retrieved their spent flashbulbs and we left. Late that afternoon, he called and announced that the photo shoot had been a glorious success. "Just from looking at the negative, Five, it's going to be beautiful."

• • •

In Tuesday's painting class, John Piggot produced his portrait of Whisper. Wreathed in fog, she stood at the edge of my creek. He had captured her slight smile perfectly and I imagined I could hear the strains of *Amazing Grace*.

"She's signed a contract for two albums," he told me. "One an *a cappella* solo, and the other a duet with Joan Baez. God, but the money, Five. We can't afford to be hippies any more," he grinned.

"And tell Doctor Ferris that she'll sing the Alma Mater and National Anthem at the Ohio Wesleyan game. As long as she doesn't have to make a speech."

We talked some more, and as the bell rang he gestured toward my office. Once in, I closed the door and we lit up.

"We've got some new people at Laurel Town," he said quietly. "And there's more Lazarus talk, especially with the new guys. And there's some talk about the Mole People.

That's the student peace group that got set up during Freshman Week."

"What about the Mole People?" I asked.

"Just that they're going to start—and I quote—'carrying out their program' whatever that is. Are you sure you don't know anything about Lazarus and the university?"

— 40 —

Wedding Stalactites Chime

"OK, Five! I really leaned on Wayman Minteer. You won't believe it, but Academic Affairs is barely aware of what goes on at the Underhill Campus. Maybe we should rename it 'Lower Seneca University'," Livinda said wryly. "But he had his assistant check all the university contracts. Four years ago, the College of Engineering and School of Mining received a federal contract for over a million dollars for a classified project. Its name is *Project Lazarus*," she said seriously. We were sitting in her office with the door tightly closed. "Once Wayman sprang that little morsel loose, I had him dig deeper. Seneca has designed and begun phase one of Lazarus, a huge excavation of the Lazarus Mine cavern."

"What in God's name for?" I asked.

"It seems that there's a secret underground facility near White Sulphur Springs where the President and Cabinet and staff would go in case of nuclear attack. And our representatives in Congress were wondering why they had to stay in Washington, so Lazarus was passed."

"You mean… we're digging a secret bomb shelter for a bunch of congressmen?"

"And important federal records," Liv added. "But yes, that seems to be what Lazarus is all about. I talked to Dean Jack Gamble about it and he denies everything. Says there are no federal contracts and, if there were, they would be classified and I have no need to know. Does that make sense?"

"The need to know sounds OK," I answered, "but the rest sounds like bullshit. Still… the university bullshit and the hippie rumors do have a certain coincidental ring."

• • •

Culden, Liv, and Cyndy returned from the Piton Shop with wedding trousseaux. Culden's was a shiny white caving suit in some nylon material. The maid of honor and bridesmaid… Livvy and Cyndy respectively… would wear dark blue jumpsuits. Dicky Reb, and I, as his best man, would be attired in 'formal' black jumpsuits.

Although Bubby and I vowed that Sibley's Crystal Cave would never become an attraction, more than twenty invitations were out. My opinion was that once Bubby's ladders were removed, the cave would become difficult to reach and enter again. In addition, the wedding date was set for Friday, the 24th, when most of the students would be gone for Thanksgiving vacation. Bubby volunteered a generator and a Bristo cousin in Moorefield would rent cable and lights to illuminate the cave and trail to the Crystal Room. The debate was still on regarding the use of candles.

Dean of Men Jim Gerholt, who held a doctorate of divinity, agreed to perform the nuptials. Culden and Dicky Reb were busy writing the brief ceremony. In the meantime, all of us had to cope with the bother of teaching classes, reading papers, and the other mundane aspects of life.

• • •

"These next paintings are by a group of Sixteenth Century painters who are of particular interest to me—and I'm sure to you—in these particular times." My Art Appreciation class was still full, halfway through the semester; and on a particularly snowy November morning this was gratifying, to say the least. I clicked the Carousel remote and Brueghel's *Adoration of the Magi in the Snow* appeared on the screen.

"This is by the Flemish painter Pieter Brueghel the Elder, a master of genre painting. It is another Adoration but, as you can see, Brueghel has set it in a typical Flemish village rather than the Holy Land. Take note of the many tiny scenes within the painting, depicting human activities. Although village gossip has it that something wonderful has happened, the elders continue to eat and drink and the children play silly games. Only in the stable at the lower left is the serious business of greeting a newborn King going on." Click. Onto the screen came *Picture of a Country Wedding*.

"Look at the stupid expression on the bride's face in this work, *Picture of a Country Wedding*. Is she plastered? Or is she really dumb and just happy to have snagged a man? By the way, it's thought that the lout feeding his face with a spoon is the bridegroom. What a catch!" The audience laughed.

"I know this is a lecture course, but I want to ask a question." Faces tilted up in expectation. "How many of you were at the Jordan Run Meadow or the practice fields for the Seneca Convocation a few weeks ago? Come on, let's see some hands. We're not taking names."

Nearly half of the 300 students raised their hands.

"Do these paintings resemble anything you saw there?" The crowd burst into laughter.

"Brueghel and his sons, Pieter the Younger and Jan the Elder, delighted in painting allegorical subjects using the

Flemish or, if you will, Dutch peasantry on their canvases. Wouldn't the Brueghels have delighted in the hippies, their dogs, their lovemaking in the weeds, their joy of life?"

The bell rang and the big hall emptied of buzzing students who had a greater appreciation of Flemish art.

With Livvy's portrait finished and delivered, the Brueghels lecture inspired me to start a painting of the hippies at Jordan Meadow. Working from photos Reb had taken from the hill above Jordan Run, I prepared a large canvas at Five's Five with a Brueghel-like perspective… a raw landscape to be filled with hippies in their daily activities.

As the wedding day drew closer, Culden, Reb, Livvy, even Cyndy, stopped by to kibitz and make suggestions. The first figures I inserted into the painting were Pig stroking the dulcimer with a feather, and Whisper in her characteristic long dress, her mouth open in song. I included Bubby Bristo tending his burgoo pots in the foreground with Tibby supervising a crew of people peeling vegetables.

The Jordan Meadow painting was then populated by eleven Kappas, clean and fresh, mingling among the hippies doing good works, each wearing a key in her hair. This touch made Livinda Ferris very happy.

Doug Kaminsky was included, sitting on a blanket arrayed with his phallic bongs, his long hair being braided by Blondie. A group of naked women cavorted beneath a makeshift shower. Was it hygiene or exhibitionism that caused this strange penchant for public showering? Dogs ran and leaped for Frisbees and sniffed each other. I was constantly urged to include a pair of dogs mating, and finally did.

I populated the scene with hippies I didn't know, doing their normal activities. Drinking, smoking dope, sleeping, eating, making out. I placed several couples in the weeds at the edge of the meadow, a bare butt or opposed pairs of feet indicating their activity. I marveled at how much the scene resembled the peasant population of Brueghel's paintings.

• • •

At Sibley's Crystal Cave, Bubby's 'ladders' had been constructed as full-formed steps with handrails. Bubby also offered to drive wedding guests from his house across the moonshine trail, to avoid the steep climb from Five's Five.

The Moorefield Bristo cousin arrived and looped cables from my cabin, where a huge generator was installed, to the cave. Inside the cave, he illuminated the path to the Crystal Cave with 25-watt bulbs every dozen feet or so. Tibby Bristo worked with him to artistically illuminate the Crystal Room, where guests would stand for the ceremony. She also produced candle holders made from aluminum foil.

The wedding party ate rehearsal dinner on Thanksgiving at Livinda's house. On Livvy's patio we held a short rehearsal with the Rev. Dean Gerholt, and everyone discussed last-minute plans for getting the guests to and into the cave.

Reb and Bubby showed up at my place at two o'clock. Reb looked handsome in his nylon jumpsuit with a white carnation affixed. Bubby wore work pants and a black shirt, the closest to formal dress I'd ever seen him in. We rode in Bubby's truck, the bed outfitted with bench seats, to his place and then ascended the moonshine trail.

A step platform had been built at the trailhead to allow passengers to disembark from the truck. Bubby returned home to await the guests, and Reb and I made our way up the trail and down the steps to the cave entrance. Hoopie was drafted as an usher, and the three of us climbed the steps and followed the lighted trail up and then down to the Crystal Room.

Three o'clock came, and all the guests were standing in a semicircle around the stalagmite we had chosen to serve as an altar or podium. From the back of the room came the soft notes of Pig's dulcimer and then the bell-clear voice of Whisper singing a familiar refrain:

Abroad as I was walking, down some greenwood side,
I heard a young girl singing, "I wish I were a bride."

When she finished the old English folk song, the lights dimmed to total darkness and the silence of the cave engulfed us. After a few seconds, Hoopie applied his Zippo to the small soapstone fire lighter and slowly walked toward the tunnel, lighting candles as he went. The reflections of the Crystal Room sparkled in the growing candlelight.

Reb and I stepped from behind a curtain of flowstone as the first zither notes of Pachelbel's *Canon in D* announced the entrance of Cyndy, followed by Livvy. Then *Here Comes the Bride* rang through the chamber. The electric lights in the tunnel came up, silhouetting Culden as she marched slowly into the room and up to me. She took my arm and I moved between the pair.

After the preamble, Dean Gerholt asked, "Who gives this woman in marriage?"

I replied, "We do! Her best friends." Then I stepped back to stand by Livvy and Cyndy.

The vows were simple and original. And finally, Dean Gerholt pronounced Richard West and Culden Ellis West *husband and wife*. Reb lifted her short veil and they kissed.

We all turned to face the audience and a single note from the dulcimer sounded. Then, *a cappella*, Whisper sang *Ave Maria* and the wedding was finished.

• • •

Everyone got out of Sibley's Crystal Cave without incident or even getting dirty, except for baby R.T. who loved rolling on the clay floor of the cavern. Culden and Reb led the parade of guests down the trail through the darkening woods. At the trailhead, several Bristo cousins stood by the truck steps with paper cups and a jar of Old Bristo to sustain the guests while Bubby drove the bridal party out first.

The reception was an informal affair at the Faculty Club with a sit-down dinner. My wedding present was the painting of the Crystal Room, although as a joke I had dashed off a quick one on black velvet and covered it with sparkling glitter. A few students who had stayed on campus for Thanksgiving vacation peered in at the strange gathering and were invited in for dinner.

I complimented Pig and Whisper on the music and was surprised when Whisper responded, "Thank you very much, Five. And for the beautiful paintings, thank you."

"See," Pig chortled, "I told you she'd talk when she had something meaningful to say." Whisper just smiled.

Pig drew me aside and looked around the room cautiously. "I've heard from Mr. Kostic," he whispered. "He gave me two names and descriptions of guys to watch out for. Told me to pass it on to you." He paused and looked over at Whisper. "I think I've already seen one of 'em, hanging out with your Mole People here on campus."

"Is he a student?" I asked.

"No. But he looks young enough to be one. His name is Linus Friedman but everyone is calling him 'Charlie Brown.'"

"The other one is named Adam Mecklin," Pig added. "He's wanted by the FBI and everyone else for bombing a building in Madison, Wisconsin."

"The chemistry lab?"

"Yep! That's the one," Pig said. "Have you heard anything about this Lazarus business?"

"Livvy's looked into it," I answered, "and the university does have a project from the federal government. Does Benjo think this Mecklin guy is coming here?"

Pig nodded and wandered back to Whisper as Culden and Reb walked up to us, with little R.T. in hand.

"Fi, Fi! Dark cave," the kid gurgled. "R.T. like dark cave."

— 41 —

Things Go Boom in the Night

The following week was busy for me as I covered Culden's Art Appreciation classes while the newlywed family went to Sanibel Island for their honeymoon. I could just imagine R.T.'s "bea, Fi, beach" as he toddled along the Gulf picking up seashells.

Livvy called one evening to tell me Buena Vista had informed her that Gillian had checked out and left for parts unknown. "She promised me she'd keep in touch," she complained, "and now she's gone. I thought you ought to know so you won't be surprised if she shows up at your place."

"Why would she show up here?" I asked innocently.

"Come on, Five. You know she's still got the hots for you," Liv responded. "And she's not the only one."

I let that pass in silence but turned on the porch light which revealed a curtain of fast-blowing snow. "It's snowing here," I said. "Is it there?"

"Don't try to change the subject. Yes, it's snowing here. Will you take me to the Homecoming game Saturday?

249

• • •

Most colleges schedule some cupcake opponent for homecoming games on a beautiful fall afternoon. Not Seneca, which held Homecoming the first weekend in December. To add insult to chilly injury, we scheduled unbeaten Ohio Wesleyan.

Still, it was a beautiful Saturday and the students happily rolled huge balls off the field from the three inches of snow covering the yard line markers. Livvy and I sipped Bloody Marys at the Faculty Club and watched the kids below as they made the field sort of playable and threw snowballs at each other.

"This beats tailgating," she grinned. "I think I could make this a permanent tradition."

"Do we really have to go down there and sit on a snowy seat?" I asked. "Couldn't we join Culden and Reb in Florida?"

"I've got two blankets, and of course Dad will have the seats cleared for all the president's party. But… this is really nice." She paused and a serious expression masked her face. "I've heard a couple of disturbing things about the Lazarus Project. Such as, the University is making over three million dollars for project coordination. That's clear of any construction costs. And my father might have a serious conflict of interest as chairman of the trustees since his former company got the major contract."

"Ohmygod," I whispered. "And we have to sit with him this afternoon!" I paused. "Let me dump a couple more items on your worry wagon. CIC has identified two radicals who might be coming here—perhaps one is already here. The other is wanted for bombing the chem lab at the University of Wisconsin. Pig thinks one of them is posing as a student but the hippies are calling him 'Charlie Brown.' His name is Linus Friedman."

As the Ohio Wesleyan Battling Bishops took the field, Liv murmured, "God, maybe it's time to get out of the provost business. Let's have another drink."

Ohio Wesleyan's team was huge, looking even bigger in their all-black uniforms against the background of blinding snow. Perhaps making his last appearance, Coach Art Bruce led the Warriors onto the field, clad all in white with the sunshine glistening on their gold helmets.

"Five, that's not the last of my problems," she said. "Do you know a Denzel Duerhoff?"

"The Bear! Of course I know him. He comes from Hockingport! Why?"

"Well… as you're probably aware… barring a big upset today, the university will be looking for another football coach. Art has been given his notice by the board. Win today! Or go!"

"And The Bear?" I asked. "He's just an assistant coach at Pitt. Would he be qualified to replace Art? He's my age, for godsake. We went to high school together."

"Dad and Ollie Monckton are convinced he's a winner. After all, he was all-NFL with the Giants."

• • •

Liv and I walked onto the Faculty Club balcony and stood arm in arm as the partially filled stadium stood in awed silence while Whisper sang *Morning Mountain Mist*. We could see many people wiping their eyes as the alma mater was finished. Then… "To honor America, please join our own Whisper, national recording star, as she sings our National Anthem."

The chill of the balcony chased us back into the Faculty Club, where Livvy waggled her finger for another round of Bloody Marys.

Wesleyan kicked off and the Warrior returner was promptly downed at the seven-yard line. After three single wing plays, Art chose to have his boys punt for a 13-yard gain. The Battling Bishops took over deep in Seneca territory and scored on their first play from scrimmage. Liv waggled her finger again at the waiter.

• • •

"Why don't you sink Bear Duerhoff would make a good coash?" Liv asked, her fifth Bloody Mary reflected in her speech.

"I didn' say that," I returned. *Thank God I can hold MY liquor.* "I jus' shed he wash my age and doesn't have mush coashing 'sperince."

We grinned at each other in mutual recognition of non-sobriety.

"Lesh go," Livvy said. "Not to my place. Yours."

Fortunately, Saturday traffic in Seneca is pretty light, especially on a football afternoon. By closing one eye, I could hold oncoming cars and trees to a single image as I wove my way out of town to Five's Five. Bubby had plowed the lane the day before, and I crossed the ford by gunning the 2CV in low gear, then skidded sideways to a stop on the snowy lawn.

Liv staggered ahead of me, retrieved the house key from its 'secret' hiding place and unlocked the door. She mock-shivered and ordered me to build a fire. Logs were already laid in the fireplace over a small pile of fatwood splinters, and in minutes my fire was crackling away. She removed her wet shoes and put them on the hearth.

"Wanna see the *Jordan Meadow* painting?" I asked. "It's almost done, I think."

Liv nodded and headed toward the stairs in her stocking feet. "Aren't you gonna put shoes on? The footbridge'll be all covered with snow."

"It'll melt," she mumbled. "I won't."

The studio was really cold and I turned on the gas fire immediately. Liv took her soaked socks off and draped them in front of the stove. I removed the cover from the big *Jordan Meadow* canvas and plopped into the chair. She bounced onto my lap and said, "Mmmm. Freezing feet. Rub my feet, will you, Five?"

We stared at the painting, now literally crowded with hippies in all their glorious activity: body painting, waiting in line for burgoo, playing Frisbee, wallowing naked in the mud pit.

"Where'm I?" Liv mumbled. "I don't see me. I wash there. Remember?"

"Take a closer look at the body painters," I instructed.

"Ohmygod," she said. "That is me, even though you covered m'face with m'hair." Livvy's nude body was covered in a swirling pattern of scarlet and gold, the SU colors. Her honey hair swirled over most of her face, making her unrecognizable in the painting. "Are you in the *Meadow*, Five? Did you portray yourself?"

"I'm one of the body painters," I grinned. "Take a closer look."

She did, and laughed loudly. "Thash you! And you're painting my boob!" She giggled and wriggled her toes beneath my hands.

• • •

Livvy walked across the footbridge barefoot, her nearly dry socks in her hand. Back in my bedroom, she pounced onto the bed and sat cross-legged facing me. "I wonder what the score is now?" she asked. "You wanna lissen to the game on radio?"

"Nope. I want to take a nap," I said. "You should, too. 'Specially if you're going to the alumni reception this evening."

"OK!" she said brightly and drew one arm into her baggy sweater. Then she drew the other arm in and worked through some kind of maneuver. Finally, she put her hands back into the sweater arms, reached into the neck hole and removed a flesh-colored brassiere. "More comfortable to nap," she said, and promptly lay back in repose.

I walked down the stairs and lay down on the couch, its leather warm from the fireplace. Thoroughly aroused, I fell asleep instantly.

• • •

From an obscure dream, I awoke to the sensation of falling. Fully awake, I found myself braced against the smooth softness of Livvy's silk-covered buttock. She was sitting on the edge of the couch.

"You said nap, not an all-day sleep," she whispered in a husky voice. She leaned over me and continued to whisper, "Do you want to make out? Just a little?" Her breath smelled minty.

"You brushed your teeth," I muttered.

"Very astute. I hope that was *your* toothbrush I used," she whispered, "and not Gillian's."

Liv snuggled down on my chest, the softness of her baggy sweater doing little to hide the feel of her attributes. "Come on, Five. We can't waste the whole afternoon." Her lips planted little kisses across my forehead and down my cheeks."

"Gotta brush my teeth," I said, pushing her away.

"Hurry back."

As I brushed my teeth and splashed cold water across my face, the voice of SU's play-by-play announcer echoed through the cabin. "Even in the one-point loss, the Warriors played their finest game of the year, nearly upsetting the unbeaten Bishops and perhaps saving Coach Art Bruce his job." My radio clicked off.

I returned to the living room to find Livvy sitting cross-legged on the shearling rug in front of the fireplace. The baggy sweater lay at the foot of the couch. She was sitting with her arms crossed, clad only in flesh-colored panties. I stepped in front of her and she looked up with a smile.

"I want to see your body, Five," she said in the same low, husky voice. As sensually as I could, I slipped my crewneck sweater over my head. Livvy reached up and undid my belt buckle, then unbuttoned the fly of my slacks. Her breasts swung gently with the motion.

Stepping out of my pants, I let her slowly draw down my briefs. She leaned forward and brushed her lips across my erection. *Oh please, please, give me self-control.*

• • •

The alumni Homecoming reception was one of the jolliest of the football season. Art Bruce was making the rounds, shaking hands, slapping backs. Provost Livinda Ferris moved gracefully from group to group, never once wobbling or giving away a hint of *her* football afternoon. Like Livvy, I stuck to club soda. No one mentioned our absence from the game.

Busby Ferris, roof-bolt king and chairman of the SU trustees, gave me a friendly pat on the shoulder and cut the end off a fat cigar. "Livvy tells me you're a personal friend of Denzel Duerhoff."

"That's right, sir, we grew up in the same town, played basketball together."

"He must've been a great football player in high school," Ferris commented.

"Well… nossir. We didn't have football at Hockingport High. Bear played his first football at Ohio University."

"What do you think of him as a coach?" Ferris asked.

"Gosh, I've never seen him coach. I only saw him play twice for the Giants, once in New York and once against the Colts in Baltimore."

"Well, Pitt's got a winning team for the first time in six years and a big part of that is their defense. I think Duerhoff's responsible."

Before I could respond, the windows of the Faculty Club rattled and the boom of an enormous explosion followed. We rushed to the balcony to see debris raining down and a huge column of smoke boiling up from the ROTC building.

— 42 —

Turmoil in the Mountains

Thankful for sobriety, I drove at top speed past the burning building for home. Red lights flashed behind me as cops and firefighters converged on the scene. Leaving the engine running, I let myself into the kitchen, popped Bubby's secret compartment, and grabbed my credentials, orders, and holstered revolver. Special Agent Lowrey of the CIC was back in business!

A state policeman stopped me at the edge of the Underhill Campus and I flashed my boxtops. "If that is the ROTC building," I told him, "I'll probably be in charge of the investigation until some bigger Army brass gets here. Where can I find the top cop?"

Two more officers stopped my unlikely-looking car before I made it to the fire line. Fire Chief Griffin and Police Chief Lambeer looked skeptical as I presented my case, finally convinced when they read my orders and examined the credentials very carefully.

My orders also finally convinced Major Turnbull, USAReserve, and Sergeant Hinckly of the ROTC unit that I was an official CIC agent.

Livvy, her father, and President Skinner approached. "Where did you go, Five?" she asked. I slid my jacket back to give her a glimpse of the belt holster and Ladysmith .32 and she nodded. "Dad? Doctor Skinner? Professor Lowrey has something to tell you."

• • •

Benjo Kostic arrived by car three hours later, minutes before a helicopter bearing CIC Technical Response Unit agents and a squad of armed GIs landed on the practice field. This event triggered a new level of respect from Busby Ferris. For awhile, I had feared that President Skinner would probably fire me for working undercover in the guise of a faculty member.

A state arson inspector and a team of firemen picked through the smoldering rubble. As university buildings go, the ROTC building was tiny and its remains didn't cover a great deal of territory. The blast directed most of the debris toward the river, and a large drill field separated it from the rest of the Underhill campus. Soon, the arson inspector approached what had been established as a command center—a conference table dragged out of the engineering building.

"Well, we've found what we think is the P.O.O.," he commented.

"Point of origin?" I asked. He nodded yes.

"Pretty crude job, in my book," he continued. "At least two blasting caps. We found the remains of one. And probably two bundles of dynamite… one under the desk in the outer office, another in the rifle rack." He paused as if expecting applause. "Not very professional, as I said, but it got the job done. And… anyone can buy dynamite in this hill country."

• • •

"Was anyone killed or injured in the blast?" a reporter from the *Inter-Mountain* yelled. It had been decided that I would be the spokesman to the media, without identifying my undercover status.

"No one except for one alumna who fainted at the Faculty Club. She bumped her head and was treated and released at Petersburg General," I responded to her question.

"Are there any suspects?" the *Clarksburg Telegram* asked.

"No specific suspects at this time," I answered. "These are times of radical dissent and several groups have claimed credit for campus bombings across the country. Naturally, all of these groups will be suspect but we have no indication of any local affiliation with them."

A television light flashed on and a short brunette thrust a microphone in my face. "What about the Mole People?" she asked breathlessly. "We've received information that a group called the Mole People was responsible."

I turned to Livvy. "Provost Ferris, can you answer that?"

Liv looked gorgeous as she stepped forward. "The Mole People is a registered undergraduate student group at Seneca. Their charter indicates devotion to furthering peace and protesting war. That's all I can tell you." She paused. "Naturally, we would like to know where you received this information but… I'll just bet you'd say it's confidential and privileged."

The TV babe nodded yes.

• • •

With eight armed soldiers guarding the perimeter, we moved the command center into the chemistry building. By the time the big coffee pot had perked, several field grade officers had appeared in another chopper. Being the first agent on the scene, I conducted the briefing. Then Benjo and I fielded questions about local conditions and subversive elements.

"We have an undercover asset in the local counterculture community," Benjo said, "and last week, I gave him a heads-up on the possibility of two radical organizers coming to this area. They were identified as Linus Friedman and Adam Mecklin. Mecklin is wanted in connection with the Wisconsin bombing."

"Our asset informed me three days ago that Friedman, using the alias 'Charlie Brown,' has affiliated with the Mole People, an undergraduate student group," I interjected. "There are several uniquely-named dissident groups on campus this year plus *Students Against Warfare*."

The meeting went on until way after midnight. Then the field grades piled back into their chopper, leaving behind a Major Kinnard, and flew back to Washington.

Kinnard, Benjo, and I walked through the rubble at first light but found nothing in the way of a clue.

"Master Sergeant Kostic," I'm going to TDY you down here to wrap this up. I don't like the idea of having Agent Lowrey operating by himself—especially in reserve status," Kinnard said.

• • •

Sunday afternoon, Benjo and I drove down Highway 55 toward Skidmore Mountain. "That must be it ahead," I commented as a sharp peak loomed ahead of us. "The topo map says it's nearly 2,300 feet."

He turned the government Chevy onto County Road 28 and we wound along the steep flank of the mountain. I kept an eye on the odometer and had him slow down as we reached 2.3 miles. A steep, brush-covered bank flanked the road on the uphill side. I got out and broke a sapling to mark the location, then we continued on up the mountain.

A chainlink fence and gate topped with barbed wire halted our progress. A guard in fatigues emerged from a shack beside the gate, an M1 carbine at port arms.

"Shit," Benjo muttered. "He's not Army. Probably some security firm."

The guard approached the car from the passenger side and I rolled the window down.

"Sorry, gentlemen," he said, "but access is restricted beyond this point." He nodded to a *No Trespassing, Restricted Area* sign.

"Is this a government project?" I asked, ready to flash my boxtops.

"I'm sorry, but I'm not at liberty to tell you that," he replied smugly.

"Well, I happen to know it's a Seneca University project," I said. "What kind of authority will get us in? Will the provost do? Maybe Dean Gamble? Perhaps President Skinner?"

• • •

Livinda, Benjo, and I sat in President Skinner's conference room awaiting his arrival.

"One hire-a-cop with a carbine," Benjo said to Livvy, "and there's no sign of a military or government presence."

"Can we find out how far that fence line runs?" I wondered aloud.

"I've already checked," Liv responded, "with Dean Gamble. He said the project covers five acres. I've alerted him to be ready to go with us."

Skinner came through his open door and greeted us. I introduced Benjo again as a special agent from the CIC.

"Doctor Skinner, we have reason to believe that the bombing of the ROTC building is directly connected to a university project that's being kept hush-hush," Benjo said. He looked at Livvy.

"It's called the Lazarus Project, Frank. I've already pumped some information out of Jack Gamble but it doesn't appear on any of our budgets," she told him.

"Dean Gamble told the provost that it's a government contract. But we need to know the total scope of the project," Benjo said. "Five and I went down there this morning and were turned away by a private security guard."

Skinner folded his fingers and stared evenly at each of us. "I'm barely aware of Lazarus," he said softly. "Dean Gamble assured me that it was a project that would bring great benefits to the university but it would have to remain classified information. You young people now have my curiosity aroused." He paused. "What say we take a drive down to Underhill and the project?"

"I already have Dean Gamble on hold," Liv responded. "I'll call him and we can pick him up."

The security guard wasn't quite so smug when two cars pulled up. Skinner, Gamble, and Livvy produced their faculty identification cards. I never realized that the president of a university might have to prove who he is. To add weight to our arrival, I presented my boxtops and Benjo did a splash-dash show of his credentials, then flashed his badge.

"Special Agent Kostic of the United States Government," he growled. The guard's chin quivered.

"I'll have to call my boss," the guy said.

"That's me, son," Gamble responded. "I think you'll find the number on your call chart is SE-1-8447."

The guard ducked into his shack and came back with a clipboard. He shook his head in puzzlement. "What can I do for you?" he asked.

"For a start," Frank Skinner announced, "you can unlock that gate and let us in."

We drove for about 200 yards on a gravel road that was well graded and firm, arriving at a trailer with a sign that read *Project Office*. Liv climbed the stairs and knocked on the trailer door but, the day being Sunday, it was locked. Beyond the trailer was what looked like the mouth of a coal mine—a horizontal slot in the face of the mountain, about five feet high. This was also secured by a chainlink fence and barbed wire gate.

"As far as I know," Dean Gamble said, "this is a mine drift. We've got some low-wheeled hauling equipment and a wall-cutter at the end. The contract calls for us to provide access into the cave for records storage."

"That sounds pretty harmless," Skinner said. "Who is the contractor?"

"Mountain State Mining," Gamble responded. I looked at Livvy but her negative head shake told me it wasn't Daddy's company.

"All right. I want their top representative and all of you in my office tomorrow afternoon," Skinner said with authority. "Dean Gamble, bring the contract. Tell your contractor I want a complete accounting of the scope of this project. Say… two o'clock."

• • •

That night, Benjo and I arrived at Livvy's house for a 'light dinner' and informal get-together. I drove my own car in anticipation of leaving later than Agent Kostic.

Liv met me and led me into her library where Benjo sat, drink in hand and looking up at me with a grin.

"The provost has good taste in artists," he said archly. I looked up and there, on the wall opposite her mother's portrait, was my matted and framed painting of Livvy.

"Doesn't it look fine, Five?" she asked. "I got the matte and frame to match mother's exactly." She grinned. "Don't you think she'll be pleased?"

I was at once shocked and pleasantly surprised. The portrait *was* well done even though my model had insisted on having her breasts exposed. Then I looked at the portrait of Mrs. Ferris and realized that she, too, had posed semi-nude.

"It must run in the family," I shrugged.

We sat in front of a cheerful fireplace in the library. The dinner of fried chicken had been delicious and now Hennessy cognacs and Pall Malls completed a full evening.

"I can't help but think that Dean Gamble is being evasive," Benjo said.

"Me too," added Livvy. "That mine drift isn't much more than a cat hole. That's certainly not a three-million-dollar government project. It'll be interesting to see what comes out of tomorrow's meeting."

Benjo yawned. "It's been a busy thirty hours for me. Guess I'd better get back to the Smoke Hole and catch a few Zs." He rose and waved goodnight to me, then Livvy walked him to the door.

When she returned, she was slowly unbuttoning her blouse. "Five, I opened the garage door. Why don't you pull your car in there… and spend the night? I have an electric razor and some spare toothbrushes."

• • •

Monday morning found me in the Student Center, drinking coffee and smoking with Culden and Reb. Since classes wouldn't resume until tomorrow, we could afford a day of relaxation. They were tanned and clear-eyed, and full of funny stories about their honeymoon with a baby.

"But, shit, Five, how could I have been on the last day of my honeymoon when a big story is blowin' up right here?" Reb complained. "We hadn't been back in the house five minutes before *Look* was on the line. My vacation and recovery is over. I told my boss I already had a ton of good stuff from the Mole People Love-In and if they're connected in any way with the bombing, we may have a big leg up."

I told them everything I knew except for the SU tie-in with the Lazarus project and our meeting that afternoon. Just as we ordered another round of coffee, Livvy walked up and nudged me with her hip to scoot over in the booth. Her arrival led to another round of honeymoon stories.

"Does Culden also know Denzel?" she asked me. Culden looked blank.

"Denzel Duerhoff, 'The Bear,'" I explained.

"The Bear! Of course," Culden said. "Everyone at OU knew The Bear."

"Well, we have a board meeting at ten o'clock," Livvy said with her glum provost face on. "Looks like we're going to fire Art Bruce today."

"What *about* The Bear?" Culden asked.

"He may well be our next coach," Liv answered. "We've already invited him down for an interview."

— 43 —

More Than Just
a Hole in the Ground

After Livvy left, Culden punched me on the arm and laughed. "Well, Livvy chased you and chased you until you finally caught her." I tried to act nonchalant but Reb informed me they'd called Five's Five when they got home yesterday, with no answer.

"I called again about six this morning," he added, "wanted to know about the bombing. No answer then. What'd you do? Sleep in the woods?"

Changing the subject, I said, "You guys should know that Benjo is in town and has been assigned on TDY."

"Don't let him near your new girlfriend," Culden giggled.

"And speaking of that," I added, "Livvy's found out that Gillian is gone from her rehab center. No one knows where she went."

"What about the bombing? Can I cover it? I looked at the rubble this morning but there's no picture there." Reb caught his breath. "Can I tag along with you or Benjo when you investigate?"

"You'll have to ask Benjo," I responded. "He's the CIC agent."

• • •

The president's conference room wasn't large; and with Livvy, Benjo, me, President Skinner, Dean Gamble, and Warren Tonkins of Mountain State Mining, it was crowded. Tonkins was a fountain of obfuscation, verbally tap-dancing around every question. He promised to return with a full written report on the project as soon as he could get the *restricted* information released by the proper authorities.

"Mr. Tonkins, I *am* the proper authority," Skinner stated emphatically.

"With all due respect sir, I must talk to someone higher… someone in the federal government."

"We've seen the outside of the project," Jack Gamble asked, "but when can we go inside?'

"As soon as the restricted information is released," Tonkins answered.

Livvy, Benjo, and I stayed behind after the meeting.

"We've got to get into that cave—or tunnel—or whatever it is," Benjo said.

"I don't know when I've been so frustrated," Livvy announced. "The top operating officer in the university and I don't know shit except we've got a cat hole mine on a big mountain."

"Here's one idea," I countered. "Remember the little tree I broke? Two point three miles up Skidmore Road. Why don't we check out Hiram Sibley's other cave? The notebook we discovered on his skeleton has a pretty accurate description of how to get to it."

"And didn't you tell me he had made a sketch of the cave in his other papers?" Liv asked. I nodded assent.

"It's too late to go tramping through a strange forest," I countered. "And I've got class tomorrow morning. How about tomorrow afternoon? Liv, can you take Benjo over to the Piton tomorrow morning and get him some gear? We've got a helmet and lamp, but he'll need a caving suit and perhaps some shoes.

• • •

Tuesday classes were full, due to the university's policy of dropping a letter grade for anyone who missed the first class after vacation. My Intro to Painting group stumbled through the hour along with me. I took Culden's eleven o'clock Art App class, as Reb was leaving for New York that morning. I discovered that a week off had made me rusty, but the 300 students sat through my presentation without snoring aloud.

An unsigned note was tucked under the 2CV's windshield wiper.

Going with you two this afternoon. I'll leave the garage door open tonight.

Before I could start the engine, Liv slipped into the passenger's seat. She was dressed in her blue caver's suit and carried a duffle bag. She held up her hand as I began to protest.

"No arguments, Five. This is as much my secret project as anyone else's. Besides, I think I know of a place we can hide your car."

"Livvy, did Benjo get his gear this morning?" She nodded yes. "Then we'll pick him up at the Smoke Hole and go out to my place to get my stuff."

"I told him we'd pick him up about two o'clock, so let's go to your place first." She flashed me a wicked grin.

• • •

"Livinda! We have to talk." She was sitting cross-legged on the edge of my bed as we shared a post-coital cigarette. I had the sheet chastely pulled up to my chest.

"Five! We know each other well enough… now. You can call me Liv or Livvy."

"Seriously," I almost shouted. I reached over and touched one of her erect nipples. "*This* is driving me crazy."

"And seriously," she said, reaching down and touching my sheet-covered groin. "I'm being driven crazy, too."

"I mean, I can't even *think* of you without *that* happening," I whined as we both watched my once-flaccid member bounce back to attention beneath its tent. "Thank God I've got a podium to hide behind in Art App Class."

"You mean you think of me while you're lecturing?" she asked in a coy tone. "I'm flattered."

"Livvy, you're not talking. You're teasing… and it's not getting us anywhere."

"*Au contraire, mon amour,*" she whispered as she stubbed the Pall Mall and leaned down to me. "It's getting us everywhere. I've been crazy for you since we first met… since I first saw your painting of Gigi and Anna. I was crushed when you started going with Gillian. I can't help it, Five, that's how I feel." She let her statement hang there like a fog cloud over the bed. "How do you feel?"

"You know how I feel," I said carefully. "But we've got responsibilities, jobs, appearances. You're the provost, for chrissakes. We can't jump in the weeds and fuck like bunnies all the time."

She giggled. "I'm no stranger to sex, but I'm not promiscuous either. Believe me, this is more than bunnies."

• • •

I could tell Benjo suspected our tryst when we arrived at the Smoke Hole. Liv sat in the back seat and leaned over to point out the features of Sibley's Pit from the old explorer's sketch map.

"You smell good, Livinda," he said teasingly. "In fact, you *both* smell good. Like just out of the shower."

"That's enough, Special Agent Kostic," I growled. "Let's keep our minds on the mission at hand."

Livvy giggled again.

We were just over two miles up the gravel Skidmore Road but not quite to the place where I had broken the marker sapling. Livvy touched my shoulder. "Slow down. It's going to be coming up pretty quick, I think. It's been at least 15 years since I was on this road."

My mind whirled the math. "Why were you here then, Livvy?" I teased.

"Jackie Burke, my first serious boyfriend. He had his dad's car and we'd drive out here to play kissy face."

The roadside brush was thick, and Liv had to get out and walk before she motioned us forward. I drove slowly to where she was standing. I could see my broken sapling about 100 yards up the road.

"It's a dry creekbed but Jackie could make it in a '49 Ford. The weeds aren't too thick. Pull up there and Benjo and I will try to erase the tracks through the weeds."

We left the 2CV behind a huge boulder sticking out of the mountainside. The car's tracks were barely visible on the dusty roadside.

"OK, I'll lead," I said. "We need to go about 100 yards that way, and then uphill. Look for a giant hickory tree."

We trudged through the woods and climbed the steep hillside, using hands and feet.

"What's a hickory tree look like?" Benjo asked.

"It's got squirrel shit all around its base," I answered.

Sibley had been accurate in his description of the hickory tree. Its trunk was at least four feet in diameter, with giant roots reaching out over the hillside like octopus tentacles. On the uphill side, the roots dug deep into the mountain. We walked around the tree, pushing on its trunk.

"Not a quiver," Benjo observed. "It sure looks stable. But where's the cave?"

"Down here," Livvy called. We found her under the downhill roots, only her legs exposed. "It's going to be a crawl, but I think we can make it."

"A crawl?" Benjo asked. "Like on the combat range?"

"Except no live bullets flying overhead," I answered.

We pulled Livvy out by her legs and I bellied down the hole while she showed Benjo how to start his lamp. The crawlway was perfectly round and narrow, but big enough to make it through. A cool breeze blew up the passage toward me. The passage sloped downward as far as my light could reach. I pounded a piton into the rock near the entrance and we attached a safety line.

Not really happy about going headfirst, I led off down the crawlway. After about 30 yards, the passage grew until I was able to get on my hands and knees. I called up the passage for Benjo to come down. Finally, Livvy joined us and we hunkered in the low passage.

We continued to crawl on hands and knees for another few yards until the floor reached a pit. Our three lights showed the pit to be about two to three feet wide and almost vertical. We dropped a rock and listened as it hit the bottom.

"Two seconds," Benjo stated. "Anyone know what that works out to in distance?" Silence.

"What do we do? Rig a belay and rappel down?" I asked.

"I know how to do this. We used to do it as kids," Livvy said. "Rig a safety line but no belay. I know you two can do it if I can."

I drove another piton and fixed the line to a carabiner. Livvy dropped her legs over the edge to the far side of the wall. Then she eased her back into the near side of the wall.

"We called it *crabbing a crack*. Just drop one foot and then the other a few inches and let your back slide down. It's pretty smooth," she said, disappearing down the crack. After a few minutes, Liv called up, "I'm at the bottom and it's smooth all the way. We can stand up down here."

Benjo went second and I followed. We found crabbing wasn't difficult and was a pretty efficient way of navigating a crack passage. At the bottom, Liv sat on a lump of hard mud and waited for us to catch our breath. We all jumped as a vibration, followed by a low rumble, shook the cave.

"Earthquake?" Benjo shouted.

"I don't think so, Livvy answered. "I think it was a blast. Someone's exploding charges down here. That means mining."

Now able to walk erect, we followed the passage deeper into the mountain. After about 30 minutes, the passage started a gradual climb. And from the tunnel ahead, we could hear an engine noise.

"Turn off your lamps," I said. "Let's see how dark it is." We did so and after a few seconds of blindness we could make out a dim glow at the top of the tunnel. We lit our lamps again and slowly climbed the passage, which ended in a chest-high wall. I peered over the wall and gasped at what I saw below.

A vast chamber, probably 60 feet deep, was dimly lighted with electric bulbs. As we watched, a frontloader crept out of a tunnel to the right, its lowered blade pushing a pile of rubble into the room. The noise was deafening. We couldn't see the machine operator beneath his safety cage but he was the only person in the huge chamber.

— 44 —

Discovering a Secret Chamber

The machine operator was skilled as he tidied his load of rubble, then spun the machine and headed out the same passage.

"This explains the lack of outside activity," Benjo said. "Whatever they're doing, they're pushing the waste material into this chamber."

"I'm timing how long it takes him to return," I said, watching the second hand on my wristwatch.

"This chamber doesn't look familiar," Liv added. "But then, I was only in the front part of the Lazarus Pit where the saltpeter diggings were."

The frontloader returned roughly seven minutes later and repeated the operation, then spun and trundled away.

"Time him one more time," Benjo counseled. "Seven minutes is long enough to climb down this bank and find a place to hide."

Again, it was a little more than seven minutes before the frontloader returned. As soon as the machine vanished into its tunnel, we extinguished our lamps and scrambled down the moderate slope that led from the passage. At the bottom, our ledge was invisible in the dark above the string of lightbulbs.

"Right behind the, ah, tenth bulb from the tunnel," Benjo spotted our passage. "In case we have to go out that way."

A haze of dust filled the chamber as well as the tunnel the frontloader used. We hurried across the floor, thankful that there were other footprints in the debris.

When the machine's headlights appeared in the tunnel, we ducked behind a large boulder. The dumping and tidying operation was repeated and the loader disappeared into the tunnel.

We hurried in its path and entered the tunnel. Livvy pointed out tiny slot chambers every 50 yards or so for personnel to duck into as machines came by. With luck, we wouldn't be noticed even if we were caught in the tunnel. And we were. Around a curve, the headlights lit up the wall and we hopped into the nearest safety chamber. The loader roared by and we quickly ran to the next safety chamber.

Finally, the tunnel widened and the roadway followed a ramp which led to another huge chamber. In this one, at least a dozen workers scurried around the room. Some worked on lumber forms for a concrete pour. Others scraped at the floor and walls to achieve smooth surfaces. The noise level was very high for such a big room. Banks of portable lights furnished illumination for individual projects, leaving pools of darkness. We took advantage of these dark places to skulk through the room. Benjo ducked through a doorway in one of the long concrete structures, then waved us in.

"Looky here," he whistled. "It looks like a college dorm hallway."

Indeed, the long structure had a hallway flanked by doors on each side. Liv lit her headlamp so we could see in the darkened building.

"There must be a hundred rooms in this one building," I said.

"Let's count them. I'm sure there's another door out at the other end," Liv said.

When we left by the anticipated exit door, we'd counted 120 rooms. The exit door faced a concrete wall that rose to the cave's ceiling. In the wall was a huge doorway. I peeked around and saw another long building.

"Blast baffle," Benjo observed. "When they're done, this'll be a blast-proof door or doors."

Seeing no one, we scuttled through the big doorway and ducked into the next building.

The second building was nearly finished, with steel doors closing off most of the rooms. In other respects, it was identical to the first building. Another baffle wall led us into a chamber with a lower ceiling and branching tunnels. One tunnel had daylight at its other end and we could make out the chainlink fence.

The other led to the left, and we followed it. After a few yards, we came upon a trailer parked in a niche carved from the tunnel. Interior lights were on and Benjo took a careful peek through a window.

"Looks like an engineering office," he whispered. "I can't see anyone, but let's don't take any chances."

We tiptoed past the trailer and to a sharp bend in the tunnel, where we encountered a welded steel wall. A door inset in the wall was ajar and we sneaked through into the refreshing air of a winter's evening. I took note of the padlock hanging on the door's hasp. A narrow footpath led through a winding maze of rocks and bushes and finally ended against a chainlink fence. Flanking the inside of the fence was a perimeter path.

"They'll have dogs here when this thing is finished," Benjo observed. "Let's see if there's a way out."

We hadn't walked more than 50 yards when we came to a gully. The path crossed it on a three-foot culvert which ran beneath the fence. It was easy work for us to crawl through the culvert and drop into the woods on the outside.

— 45 —

Lazarus Confirmed

We let Benjo out at the Smoke Hole to report to Major Kinnard. I dropped Livvy off at her car by the administration building and then drove back to Five's Five. As I turned into the lane, I noticed the red gas can lying along side the road. I drove up the road slowly but didn't see any sign of Pig.

When I parked the car, he stepped from behind my little barn and gave me a short wave.

"I was just about ready to leave," he said. "I'm a little worried about Whisper being alone."

"What happened to you?" I asked, noticing the bruise on his forehead.

"I found out the hard way that Mecklin and Friedman are in Jordan Run. Mecklin overheard me asking about them. Of course, I didn't recognize him but when they came to our place, Friedman was recognizable. If the other one's Mecklin, he's a fat little fucker with thick glasses. One held me, the other one worked me over." He stopped and caught his breath. "Whisper went out the back door and ran to the store. Cob and Wayne Smead broke it up."

He pulled up his sweatshirt and displayed the bruises on his torso. "The bastards took turns," he growled. "I've got to take Whisper to Pittsburgh tomorrow for her first recording session." Pause. "I don't think we'll be coming back."

"We're really going to need someone on the inside," I said. "Are you sure you won't come back?"

"Naw. Whisper's not a hippie. She's just a little hillbilly girl from Omar Mine Number Three. She deserves more than Omar or Laurel Town, either one, can give her."

I nodded in agreement.

"But I do have a suggestion. Remember Susan Liston?"

"Blondie? Is that her name?"

"Yep. She's a runaway from California. Doesn't want to go back to her parents. And she's finding the hippie life isn't so great. Plus, she'll do anything for money," he grinned.

"Could she be trusted?" I asked. "And how would I contact her?"

"You'll be hiring a model or two for Figure Drawing, won't you?" Pig asked. "She does have the figure for it."

I told Benjo and Major Kinnard about Pig's decision the next morning. They both agreed we couldn't force him to stay undercover. Then I mentioned using Blondie as an informant.

"She knows I teach art at SU," I said, and related the shower incident. "If we paid her a regular fee for modeling and added some as an informant, she'd probably do the job and keep her mouth shut."

"You'd better check with Livinda," Benjo said. "This is getting our case awfully entangled with the university."

• • •

"I always suspected that John Piggot was your guy undercover," Liv said.

"It's a shame to lose him. He's a nice guy and had the makings of a pretty good artist," I replied. "But he had a suggestion that I think might work." I told her about Blondie.

"That's one of the girls y'all caught showering in the faculty bathroom?"

"The very same. She's been shacked up with Cyndy's ex-husband, ex-lover, but I guess she left him and now she's just hanging around the Jordan Run community."

"How would you hire her," Livvy asked, "even if I thought it was a good idea? Which I don't. And I won't approve it unless Culden does."

"Well, we can't use students," I responded. "Probably against university policy." Liv nodded. "So I thought I could put up a few help wanted signs... a couple downtown, another at the store in Jordan Run."

"What if your girl doesn't bite?" Liv asked.

"She's not my girl, and I've seen her body in action twice. I think she'll be a candidate."

Two days later, I thumbtacked a 3x5 card on the bulletin board at the Jordan Run Commune Store.

Help Wanted. Part-time model for art class at Seneca University.
Call Professor Lowrey. SE-1-8755

And two days later, Cyndy leaned in the door and said, "There's a Miss Liston on the phone."

"Hi, Professor, remember me?" she chirped.

"Sure do!" I responded. "Blondie, isn't it? You're the one who thinks cleanliness is very important."

She giggled. "What's this gig you're advertising? Will it be steady work?"

"I think it would be best if you came in and we talked in person," I answered.

"I'll hitch a ride as soon as I can get some decent clothes on."

Blondie showed up less than an hour later. Her hair was combed and she wore a tie-dyed skirt and a Haight-Ashbury tee shirt. Her sandaled feet peeked out from the hem of her long skirt. Cyndy closed the door behind her with a wink. "Well, hi. I thought that might be you," she greeted me. "You're the guy from the showers... and that night beside the creek."

"Good memory, Susan," I responded. "Take a seat."

She plopped into a chair, reached into her blouse, and extracted a pack of Chesterfields. I leaned over and flicked my Zippo for her.

"So what's this modeling gig?" she asked, as she blew a cloud of smoke across my desk.

"I teach Figure Drawing, and we're ready to have a live model," I said calmly. "Someone suggested you might be interested."

"That 'someone' being John Piggot?" another puff of smoke. "He's the only one who knew my name is Susan. You do know he's left town with his little songbird? Got the living shit beat out of him by Charlie Brown and his buddy. Then left town—fast!"

"You know Charlie Brown?" I asked casually.

"Just to see him," she responded. "But what about this modeling shit? How much does it pay?"

"Three dollars an hour," I said. "And you'd work six hours a week maximum."

"Ratshit!" she said vehemently. "I can make more than that with blowjobs."

"I could raise the money to about forty a week if you're willing to do some extra work. And keep quiet about it."

"What? Give you a blowjob?"

"No… I've seen you in action, remember? No, what I need is someone to keep her eyes open and have a reason to meet with me on a regular schedule. The modeling's legitimate and the other work has some risk… if you're found out."

"Spying? And risk? Like having Charlie Brown pound the crap out of me?"

"Exactly."

"Well, I *do* need the bread. Will I have to take my clothes off?"

"Yep. Next semester. And you'll have to be clean… I mean, no dope… no needle tracks."

She grinned. "I'm OK with that right now. But I'm shit-tired of washing in that goddam freezing creek. How 'bout I get a shower before every modeling session? With warm water?"

• • •

"Dean Cruz-Garcia has asked us—ah shit, *told* us—to have a faculty-student art show in the Student Center-Faculty Club gallery by the end of January," Culden told her three faculty members. "Do you people have enough work to be representative?"

Hoopie grinned. "Culden, I've got the big protest piece nearly finished and I can sure whack out some smaller constructions between now and then." Hoopie's *Protest Piece* was a life-sized coffin lined with charred remains of draft cards. He had been borrowing draft cards from students since the start of classes and photocopying them, then charring them. "The student work is pretty rudimentary, though."

"I only have the dancer sculpture," Jaylene said, "and it's nearly finished. Some of my students have done pretty good studies in class. I think I could piece together a fairly decent little sculpture show."

Culden looked at me. "You should be the star of the show, Five. *Jordan Meadow's* just about finished. I'll loan *The Crystal Room* and Livinda has volunteered one from her collection."

I gulped at Livinda's generosity. To my knowledge, the only work of mine she owned was the portrait hanging in her library.

"I have three studies of Whisper," I said, "and John Piggot left behind his portrait of her. I'd be proud to hang that. And I've got some pretty good other student sketches and one other post-modernist painting from Marilyn Kretzman that's going to be really good."

"Don't forget your *Ménage à trois*," Culden added. "I think that's the basic reason Cruz-Garcia wants a show… to be able to take another look at that every day."

"What about you, Culden?" Hoopie interjected.

"As you know, I haven't had much time to work this semester," she said laconically. "But I have a few things I wouldn't be ashamed to hang."

• • •

I hadn't seen Benjo Kostic in four days and was surprised when I found him sitting on my snow-covered porch when I got home. He had dusted the snow off one of the rockers and was sitting serenely, waiting for me.

"Christ, Benjo, aren't you freezing?"

"No. I've only been here a few minutes. Just thought I'd let the mountain air clear my brain," he grinned as he took one last puff of his Pall Mall.

"Where've you been?" I asked.

"Baltimore. Army Intelligence Center. Then down to D.C. and the Pentagon." He had a sly smile and continued, "Finally, to Senator Brand's office."

"And?"

"Brand wouldn't say specifically, but the Lazarus Project seems to be piggybacked on some covert ops bill for CIC and… that's why we've still got an interest in it. If our budget is paying for it, then we want responsibility."

"Who determined this?" I asked.

"Secretary of the Army. Secretary of Defense. And… Senator Brand. And… here's a new set of orders for you."

I opened the envelope and read the orders, relieving me from active reserve duty. I was a civilian again.

"And I'm on what looks like permanent TDY down here. Plus, I've got authority to recruit you as an asset. Cheapass Army just didn't want to pay your salary, I guess," he added with a grin.

While I heated soup, Benjo filled me in on details of his trip. "Army's going to dispatch a platoon to guard the site. What I didn't reveal was how we got into the project in the first place… you know, through Sibley's Pit."

"Why not?" I asked.

"Seems to me that we should have a means of surreptitious access… or an escape route if one's needed," Benjo answered.

Over tomato soup, Tater Tots, and Old Bristo, we talked about the investigation.

"Nothing's going to happen as far as we're concerned, with the CIC, that is. I'm on what seems like permanent TDY with a direct report to Major Kinnard in D.C. You're still on inactive duty unless I really need you. We'll run a soft investigation on the hippie community and whatever radical groups we can turn up. Speaking of which, how did you do with Blondie?"

"I think she'll work out," I commented. "She's a callous and greedy little bitch. And forty bucks a month is more than she's seen in a long time. She told me it worked out to about twenty blowjobs."

• • •

On Thursday night, Livvy invited me to dinner with the West family. Reb had returned from New York with an assignment to cover the hippies and possible student radical activity in the mountains. After a leisurely dinner and drinks, Culden and Reb left to recover the baby from Maddy.

Liv sent Mary home as soon as the dinner plates had been recovered, and later we washed dishes ourselves.

"Do you want to pull your car into the garage?" she asked.

"I'd be happy to," I grinned. "I even brought a change of clothes in hopes…."

"Let's enjoy the fire in the library," she suggested, grabbing a bottle of Courvoisier and a pair of snifters.

"I'll be right up," I said, "soon's I get the garage door shut.

I pulled the 2CV into Livvy's double garage, shut the door, and turned off the outside lights. Depositing my duffle of clean clothes, I entered the library, where a cozy fire was burning. I found Liv on the couch wearing a long velvet robe. Her bare feet were on the coffee table.

James Patterson

As she handed me a snifter of cognac, the robe slid open and I found her beautiful body painted by firelight. I slipped my hand inside the robe and she shivered.

"Lord, but your hands are cold!" she exclaimed. She took my hand and moved it from her breast across her stomach and lower. "This'll warm them up quickly," she murmured.

I couldn't get my clothes removed fast enough as we slid into a horizontal pose on the warm couch.

"Liv? Culden told me something I've been meaning to ask you about," I said softly as I moved my lips across her breasts.

"What's that, Lover?"

"That you've agreed to loan my portrait for the faculty-student show."

She turned her head and placed her lips on my forehead. "Do you mean the one over the fireplace?" she asked.

"I thought that's what *she* meant."

"Well, that would certainly be a death-wish act as far as *my* career is concerned," she said. "What I said was I'd loan a work from my collection."

"You have a collection of my work?" I asked incredulously.

"Two landscapes I bought in Paris," she answered, "and I just received one from *Galeries Stansbury-Marchant* in Washington. Do you want to see?"

She threw the robe around her shoulders and led me to the small room off the library that served as an office. Turning the light on, Liv turned me toward a wall to the left, and pointed.

"Voilà! Gigi said it was the first of the nudes of me you shipped," Liv said.

The painting was done in monochromatic tones of burgundy, and it showed a woman leaning toward the viewer, her naked breasts as I'd seen them beneath Livvy's blouse months ago. Her bare stomach and pubis receded with the perspective. Her head was down and waves of her hair fell over her face.

"No one can tell it's me," she grinned. "At least… very few people can."

— 46 —

A Question of Ability

When the bell rang, my horde of students headed for the exits of Canby Auditorium. By the time the lights came up, the big room was nearly empty. From the back came a slow clapping sound. I could make out a huge figure standing against the backlight of a doorway.

"Excellent job, Professor. Excellent job," Denzel Duerhoff shouted as he continued to clap slowly.

I ran down the aisle and grabbed my huge buddy by the neck.

"Bear! It's great to see you," I said. "Where's Paige?"

"She's with that pretty provost lady. Doctor Ferris told me to come over here and catch the tail end of your lecture," the one-time New York Giants linebacker said. "Sheeeit, Five. I'd-a never figured you for a professor. That crap about van Gogh's ear is fascinating. The only way I know of to lose an ear is to get your helmet ripped off."

Paige Duerhoff, The Bear's wife, had always claimed she did a good thing by changing her name from Dobrowski. She was a big, beautiful Polish woman who was wonderful to me in New York the day I went to see the Giants play.

The Bear got knocked silly in the final moments of the game against the Redskins and ended up in the hospital with a concussion.

After visiting him there, Paige took me to a great restaurant where a lot of other Giants players and wives were. She drank me under the table and then nearly carried me back to the Duerhoff apartment, where I slept for ten hours on the couch.

"I'm really glad you could bring her," I said to The Bear as we walked back to the Fine Arts Building. "I know Culden will be tickled to see her. And Dicky Reb West," I went on, "he's here, too."

"The photographer? What's he doing here?"

"For one thing, he's married to Culden and they've got a kid. Second, he works for *Look Magazine* and he's covering hippies and student radicals in this area."

Culden gave The Bear a huge hug and kissed him fervently, as usual, on the mouth. "God, it's great to see you, you big hulking bastard," she cried.

"I don't *hulk* anymore, Culden. I'm a coach now."

"Are you going to be *our* coach, Bear?" I asked.

He looked at me with a serious expression. "This place isn't much bigger than Hockingport, Five. I'm used to the bright lights... Broadway... even Pittsburgh when the smog's not too heavy. And I'm really afraid... that I'm too young for the job. Being a small frog in a big pond like Pitt is one thing but this is an awfully small pond."

"Come on, Bear," Culden took his arm. "Five and I'll give you a quick tour and convince you that this is the best damn university in Grant County."

• • •

The Bear was more enthusiastic after seeing the stadium, practice fields, training room, and a fast tour of the academic campus. We got him back to the admin building in time for his eleven o'clock meeting. Paige met us outside Livvy's office with hugs and kisses for Culden and me.

"I hear you've got a baby, Culden," Paige trilled. For such a large woman, she had an inordinately high voice. "And you and Dicky Reb are married. I think that's wonderful."

Livvy nodded at Paige and gave me a wink as she closed her door. We walked toward the Fine Arts Building.

"Doctor Ferris is a wonderful person," Paige declared. "She was just one of the girls with me, made me feel right at home. And… she's so young to have that position."

"Five thinks she's a wonderful person, too," Culden said slyly. "The provost is his *honey.*"

"Really, Five? That's so neat. Is it serious?"

• • •

"We should start an Ohio University alumni group here in Seneca," Livvy said as she toasted the five of us in the Faculty Club. "Especially, if the Duerhoffs become part of our family."

Dinner was filets mignon, bouillabaisse, twice-baked potatoes, and watercress salad, a surprise to me. The salad was covered in Liv's Dordogne dressing that brought out the peppery flavor of the greens.

"This is a special night," Livvy said to the table. "Not just because we have the Duerhoffs as our guests but this is the first salad using watercress from Braddock's Branch."

"No kidding?" I asked. "You *did* transplant it. And it grew?"

She grinned broadly. "You betcha… didn't grow a lot with winter coming on but the plants are healthy and our creek won't freeze." She went on to relate the story of my watercress riffle.

After dinner, The Bear and I went out on the chilly balcony and smoked cigars, looking down on the moonlit stadium. He clapped me on the shoulder.

"What'ya think, Five? Should I take the job?"

"Did they make an offer, Bear? I truly haven't heard."

"Oh, yeah! And the money is better than what I'm makin' at Pitt. Eighteen thousand plus expenses. That Busby Ferris seems to know what he wants. And Paige just loves the place, too," he said quietly.

"Believe me, it runs in the family," I responded.

He shrugged. "I'm just so damned 'fraid I'll fall on my ass. I mean, ten years ago I didn't even know how to put on kidney pads. Thought they were to protect my nuts."

I laughed at his memory of The Bear, limping around after an afternoon of the spine protector cutting into his groin at his first day of practice.

"So you fall on your face," I retorted. "After Art Bruce, I'll bet you could have two losing seasons before they canned you."

The Bear grimaced, then grinned. "Let's go back and join the ladies. I'll tell Doctor Ferris that we'll come. There's recruiting to be done."

— 47 —

Does a Bear
Coach in the Woods?

After dinner, the Duerhoffs and Liv and I went over to the gym to watch the first basketball game of the season. To my surprise, the fieldhouse was nearly full as the Warriors took on Morris Harvey from Charleston.

"Morris Harvey won the West Virginia conference last year," Liv told us. "I think they lost only one player, so they should be tough."

To everyone's surprise, the Warriors put on a last-minute rally and beat Morris Harvey by three points. After the game, the Bear talked for a long time with SU Coach Sam Fleckman. As we walked across the frozen campus, the new football coach said, "Doctor Ferris, there's one thing I don't understand. I've read the football roster and watched the basketball team tonight and… there's not a single black athlete. Is that something *I can overcome?*"

"Please call me Liv or Livvy, Bear." She stopped and turned to us. "Five can tell you, SU does have black students… not many… I think about 75 or so. But you're absolutely right about black athletes. I know it's not a conscious policy on the part of the board. I can speak for them. The man who replaced my dad as president of the company when he retired is black, and two of their top executives as well. I've never heard Sam or Art Bruce say anything in the way of a racial slur but Art never seemed to recruit among the black athletes." She put her hand on Bear's huge shoulder. "I'll tell you this. You recruit anyone you wish to. Other schools' black athletes have beaten this university too many times. It's time to turn that around."

• • •

Blondie was shivering on the Fine Arts steps when I arrived for work the next morning. She had a small duffle slung over her shoulder.

"Good morning, Miss Liston. You're early enough," I commented as I unlocked the door.

"I woke up and got to thinking about the luxury of a hot shower and… well, I just couldn't get back to sleep," she said.

"How did you get to town?"

"Oh, I hitched. Not many of these hillbilly farmers can pass up a chance to give someone like me a ride," she commented. "Although they're too shy to ask for anything in payment."

I let that one slide by. I unlocked the faculty women's restroom with the key Culden gave me.

"Jaylene and Culden both have eight o'clocks so no one will be here until, oh, nine-fifteen at the earliest," I said, leading her into the bathroom. "Here's a couple of towels, and there's soap in the shower. You can wear what you've got on this morning. And jeans and a tee shirt will be fine for the rest of the semester."

She gave me a nice smile and asked, "Look, I don't mind you knowing my name. But I'm on the run from my parents and I'd really appreciate it if you just call me Blondie in public." Blondie began pulling her T-shirt over her head, asking "Sure you don't want a little something? I mean, I really appreciate this."

I fled.

• • •

Cleanly scrubbed, her short blonde hair glistening, my new model sat quietly in the back of the classroom as my Figure Drawing class entered. Once they were all seated on their benches, I motioned Blondie forward.

"OK, people. You've done a good job of sketching from mannequins and still life subjects but now it's time to get started on the human figure. This is our model, and she likes to go by her nickname, 'Blondie.' For the rest of the semester, we're going to concentrate on her facial features and hands."

After a dramatic pause, I continued. "Next semester, we will see even more of Blondie as we begin study of the human figure."

• • •

Dan Bristo, Seneca's only real estate agent, had Bear and Paige in his car when I came out of the classroom.

"Mr. Bristo has been telling us about your place," Paige said, "and he's going to show us a couple of properties right now. Would you like to come along? We'd appreciate it."

"The first one's the old Herkimer place," Dan said. "It's in town, about ninety years old and in pretty good shape. The last of the Herkimer clan passed away a couple of months ago."

The house was a two-story brick with slight Victorian touches: bay windows on the ground floor and a tiny round tower extending beyond the second floor. A wrought iron fence extended around the yard. Inside, polished hardwood floors gleamed in the morning light and bright colors splashed across them from the cut glass window ornamentation in the living room and dining room.

"It's really nice," Paige exclaimed. "And plenty of room for kids when they come."

"How much?" Bear asked.

"The estate is asking sixteen thousand," Dan replied.

We then drove halfway to Petersburg and up a hillside lane to a big farmhouse overlooking the highway. Its wood siding needed a coat of paint and the porch was sagging. In addition, four outbuildings leaned in various states of falling down.

"This one needs a little fixing up, but…" Dan started.

"I'm not going to have time for fixing up," Bear growled.

"Dan's got a brother… Bubby," I said, "who's a wonder at fixing up. What's the asking price on this one, Dan?"

"Thirteen thousand, firm."

"I'll tell you what, Mr. Bristo." Bear had a gleam in his eye. "You offer that Herkimer estate twelve thousand for the house in town and we've got a deal."

• • •

That afternoon, I sat with Bear and Paige in the living room of Five's Five. We drank hot cocoa in front of the fire and watched big snowflakes drifting down. I told them about my experience in buying the Sibley cabin.

"We could easily put half of twelve thousand down, honey," Paige said softly. "Even more, if necessary."

"I paid cash for this place," I said. "Banker Norris almost choked."

Then the phone rang. I answered it and beckoned to Bear. "It's Dan Bristo."

After a few minutes of conversation, Bear looked up with a grin and gave us a thumbs up. "Twelve thousand, plus closing costs? That sounds OK to me, Mr. Bristo. Let me call you back in a few minutes."

"He needs an earnest payment," Bear said. "What do we have in the checking account?"

"About seven hundred," Paige answered.

"How about I give Norris twelve hundred?" I ventured. "You can pay me back as soon as you can."

"You'd do that?" Bear asked incredulously.

"Does a Bear coach in the woods?"

— 48 —

Sleighbells and Serenades

I've always liked December on campuses—any campus. Despite the fact that nearly all of Seneca's students lived at the bottom of the hill, the weeks approaching Christmas vacation were full of activity. The Warriors were on the road for three straight games, beating Alderson Broaddus, Shepherdstown, and Fairmont.

With a four and zero record, their last home game before the holiday was with unbeaten West Virginia Wesleyan, and Warriors fans became believers when the scarlet and gold coasted to an easy twenty-point victory.

I agreed to accompany Livvy and chaperone the Kappa winter dance, and we had a ball. I'd never danced with Livvy before and was pleased at her enthusiasm and grace. The Kappas stayed moderately sober, and the chaperones were the picture of propriety... until we got home.

• • •

Livinda murmured in her sleep and rolled over to wrap her arms around me. Then she snored in my ear. The curtains were open and I could see dim daylight behind the flurry of snowflakes. I eased out of bed and tiptoed to the bathroom, then stood at the window and saw huge drifts piling up on Liv's terrace below.

I crawled back into bed and pulled the covers over both our shoulders. Livvy's eyes popped open.

"You're awake? What time is it?" she groaned.

"It's nearly eight o'clock. Should I put some coffee on?"

"Mmmf. That'd be nice," she grunted. "Why's it so dark?"

"It's snowing like crazy," I answered, walking downstairs to the kitchen.

As I returned to the bedroom, I noticed Livvy's flannel nightgown in a pile by the bed.

"C'mere, Love," she called. I crept back into the warm bed and she jerked her body away. "Holy crow, but you're cold, Five."

"Surely I'll warm up," I responded, and rolled over to embrace her warm body.

• • •

"Five? What're you going to do for Christmas?" Liv asked later as we sipped lukewarm coffee in bed.

"Oh… go home to Hockingport, I guess."

"I'm going to be all alone," she said with a mock pout. "Daddy's going to spend the holidays in Paris with Mom."

"Why don't you come to Ohio with me?" I asked. "I know my folks would love to have you, and you could sleep in my room."

"With you? In your old boyhood room?"

"Well, not exactly. My old boyhood room is now my sister's old girlhood room. But I can stay at the Riverview."

"What's the Riverview? A nursing home?" she giggled.

"No, it's a nice little motel. Should be nearly empty at Christmas. Not many people come to Hockingport in December."

"OK," she said in a chipper voice. "We'll do it... and work out the sleeping arrangements later."

• • •

Bear returned with a check for my twelve hundred dollars, and closed on the old Herkimer place. He took Livvy and me to lunch in the Smoke Hole to celebrate.

"And I've got more good news," he said, his face breaking into a huge grin. "I've got a verbal commitment from a kid named Evermont Nixon from Wheeling. I'd been hound-dogging him for Pitt, but he said he'd come to SU if I were going to be coaching. Telling him he'd likely be my starting quarterback looks like it's clinched the deal," he added.

"But we've got two quarterbacks coming back," I mentioned.

"Not like Monty Nixon," Bear countered. "The kid's a great athlete, smart, runs like a deer, and is an unbelievable passer. And—he's black!"

Livvy clapped her hands softly. "You say he's smart. Is he a good student as well?" she asked.

"Good student? All A's and he's a guard on Wheeling High's basketball team. And he'll complete his high school credits this semester. He's planning to enroll in January."

• • •

On a Sunday night, we drove through the snowy woods for my first trip to Braddock's Branch. Busby Ferris was leaving for New York and Paris on the following morning, so it was the Ferris clan's—father and daughter—Christmas celebration.

Ollie Monkton and two other trustees, J.R. Tanner and Gwen Stump, were guests. Mrs. Stump, who was obviously Tanner's date, said to me, "I understand you and our Livvy are, eh, keeping company?"

"Yes, ma'am, we are indeed. She's a wonderful influence on me."

"Oh? How so?" The others, including Liv, looked at me with interest.

"Well, I've always been a wild and sort-of untamed artist type… you know the kind… loose women and late parties and hung over mornings trying to find my brushes and paints."

A slow grin started to capture Livvy's face.

"Well, Miz Stump. Livvy's changed all that." Pause. "I haven't had a hangover in oh, fifteen days."

The group roared, and I was pleased that Gwen Stump had a sense of humor.

• • •

"From what I've heard, he's dug a pretty big hole in Pitt's recruiting basket," Ollie Monkton chortled.

"Now Ollie, none of it counts 'til signing day," J.R. Tanner countered. "But if he comes through—wow!"

Bus Ferris beamed as if The Bear was his only son. "That running back from Stonewall. And a pair of bookends from Parkersburg South," he added, "and all four of 'em black kids. I'm so proud I could…"

"He hasn't told me much," Liv announced, "but The Bear's evidently scouting the coal fields of Kentucky and southern Ohio as well. He did say he wouldn't bring any ignorant kids to Seneca, though."

Later, the conversation turned to academic events of the fall.

"I'm really pleased with this semester and all you've accomplished," Ferris said to Livvy with a squeeze of her shoulders. He raised his snifter. "A toast to our provost." We all raised our glasses. "And her talented… friend." He gave me a glance and a smile.

• • •

Somewhere in the vast house, a clock tolled twelve times. I rolled in the huge bed and pulled covers up. There was a slight creak, and hallway light spilled through my door. Silhouetted in the doorway was my love.

"This is an old Ferris custom," she whispered, kneeling beside the bed. "We go around to each guest room and feel under the covers to make sure the guest is warm enough."

I giggled as her hand ran up my thigh. "Am I warm enough to suit you?" I asked.

"Not quite. Let's see what we can do."

• • •

The breakfast room was bright and full of cheer. I was the last to show up, and Liv greeted me with a cup of coffee.

"Pancakes, eggs, sausage, fruit—you name it, we've got it, Five," she said. "But eat hearty because we're going out in the woods."

"You're not going to Petersburg with us, Liv?" Bus asked.

"Oh, Daddy, Ollie can take you to the airport. Five has never seen the riffle. I thought I'd hitch up Esopus and we'd take the sleigh out there. After all, Five *is* the source of our watercress farm."

Breakfast finished, Liv and I made our goodbyes to her father.

He put a firm hand on my shoulder and said softly, "Take good care of her, son."

We bundled up and walked through the drifts to a stable where a skinny man in a leather jacket waited for us.

"Mornin', Miss Livvy."

"Good morning, Jake. Five, this is Jake Jericho. He makes Braddock's Branch run efficiently, most of the time." I shook Jake's hand.

"I've got Esopus ready to go. She hasn't been out of the stable since the snow started."

Esopus was a huge, dapple-gray mare… nearly as big as a Clydesdale. Jake led her out of her stall and she backed obediently between the shafts of a small green sleigh.

"What a sight this has got to be," I laughed. "Esopus is three times bigger than the sleigh."

"They're both antiques," Liv grinned. "We've had Esopus since I was what, Jake, fifteen?"

He nodded. "About that. She's a Belgian, and just as strong now as she was back in her yearling days."

"And the sleigh was built in Vermont in the 1890s. We had it sent back ten years ago to be refurbished by the same company."

Jake handed the belled reins to Livvy and tipped his hat. Liv gave the reins a twitch and the huge draft horse stepped out. The snowy woods muffled the sound of the sleighbells, and I felt like I was in a Christmas fantasy.

The Braddock's Branch riffle was huge. A wide expanse of stone, cut by dozens of channels. Short poles were pounded into the streambed and from them, lines were attached to coarse nets across each channel.

"The nets were my idea," she said proudly. "We seemed to be losing a lot of plants at first. I think because their roots weren't very strong. The nets would catch them and we could harvest. You know, watercress is delicious regardless of how young it is. We've got a big net upstream to catch limbs, twigs, woods debris," she said.

"My gosh, Liv. I had no idea. How much watercress is in there?"

"Jake figured we probably have half an acre. Should be an acre by next spring."

From the riffle, Livvy steered Esopus up a hilly lane. At the top, we came to a clearing and she halted the big mare.

"This is Braddock's Bald. And look, there are some deer." Indeed, at the far side of the broad meadow a dozen deer, including a large buck, stared up at us. The woods rolled down the mountain away from the meadow. In the distance, I could make out the sparkle of the riffle, and beyond, the Ferris home.

"Who's Braddock, Liv?"

"Braddock Ferris was my great, great, oh, great grandfather. He consolidated the acreage and built the farm, but not before opening the coal seam over on Braddock Mountain." She pointed to a looming peak, perhaps four miles away. "But now, it's time to get old Esopus into a warm stable and head back to the real world."

• • •

The real world was Monday of the last week of class. The week was filled with celebrations. The President's faculty party. The Fine Arts party. Faculty caroling.

As I had done for Halloween, I tailored my Art Appreciation lectures to the season, concentrating on nativities, adorations, and similar subjects. That first morning, I determined to add winter scenes and sleigh rides to the Wednesday class, the last of the year.

Blondie was waiting for me at the back of Canby after the second lecture. Her hair was still damp and she looked like any other student who'd suffered a late start on the morning.

"That was neat, Professor," she exclaimed. "I never heard anything that good at Berkeley."

"Did you attend U.C.?" I asked.

"Naw. My folks wanted me to, but I just hung out in People's Park and checked out—what'dya call it—audited? Any class I felt like. That way, I didn't have to spend the tuition money my parents sent me."

We walked across the courtyard to the Fine Arts Building.

"The reason I'm early is I've got some news," she said softly. "That Charlie Brown guy and his buddy, and a couple of the Mole People, have left town. Yeah! Yesterday afternoon, they piled into Charlie Brown's old Ford and split. Only thing is, Charlie left most of his stuff with Doug the potter. So I think he'll be back."

"Doug Kaminsky? The guy you were, ah, hanging out with?" I ventured. "And these Mole People you mentioned. Are they students?"

"No," she responded, "they're just hippies. Or at least, pretend to be. But they're the ones that organized that student group at the first of the semester."

I called Benjo and relayed Blondie's information.

"Well, it is almost Christmas vacation," he said. "Perhaps they're goin' home for the holidays. Or to Fort Lauderdale."

"Interesting that they have a couple of Mole People recruiters in the hippie camp," I commented. "We both know from experience that's not too hard to pull off."

Benjo responded, "I've run a check with the Army Intelligence Center. So far, we don't have a record of any other Mole People organizations. There is something called the 'Weather Underground' but it's not considered a threat of any sort. By the way... even the Smoke Hole is cutting into my per diem. Do you have any thoughts on a place I could stay?"

• • •

"It's going to be lonely here," Cyndy said. "The Wests are going home to Ohio and so are you. Jaylene and Hoopie are going to Huntington."

"Cyndy, is Gillian's old apartment still empty?" I asked.

"Yes, but it's not really an apartment. Just a room and a little toilet."

"I've got an idea. How would you like a roommate?" Her eyes lit up. "He's a nice person and..."

"He?"

"Yes. It's Josefus Kostic. Benjo. The CIC agent, and he's on temporary duty for a while."

"I know what he looks like. He's OK." Cyndy put her chin in her hand, then slowly grinned. "Have him come in and we'll have an interview."

Benjo passed the interview with flying colors and moved out of the Smoke Hole the next day. The next evening, the Fine Arts faculty, Benjo, Cyndy, and Livvy ate pizzas at the Wests', then walked over to the steps that led up to the hill campus. The street was blocked off and a crowd had gathered at the foot of the steps.

Rows of paper bags, each holding sand and a candle were lighted up each side of the steps.

"They're called *luminarias*. I saw them in the Southwest a few years ago and thought they'd make a nice tradition," Livvy told us.

From the portal of Old Main, the combined choruses of fraternities and sororities came down the steps for the annual Seneca Christmas Serenade.

The music and the sight were wonderful, and we all wiped our eyes from time to time. Suddenly, the holidays were upon us.

— 49 —

Over the River
and Through the Woods

Livvy didn't have much trouble persuading me to drive one of the farm cars to Ohio. Her MG and my Citroën were small and drafty. I was surprised when she showed up the next morning with a Jeepster station wagon, one of the ugliest cars of the Fifties.

"It's not that much to look at," she said, "but the heater works and it gets good mileage." The back of the wagon was partially filled—a couple of suitcases and some wrapped presents.

To my further surprise, the Jeepster wagon was fairly comfortable and responsive. As we drove through the mountains toward Elkins, the snowdrifts along the road seemed higher. The temperature was colder and patches of black ice gleamed on the surfaces of bridges.

We passed through Buckhannon and into the lower hills of West Virginia. Like most of the state's roads, Routes 33 and 47 followed the contours of the land and were narrow and winding. The overcast of the mountains gave way to bright sunshine. As we drove past Freeport, I pointed out the Hughes River.

"I used to go to Boy Scout camp over there," I pointed. "Camp Kootaga. A long time ago."

"I can't image you as a Boy Scout," Livvy giggled. "I was never anything but little Livvy riding her pony."

We crossed the Ohio River at Parkersburg. "There's a towboat down there," I pointed toward the upstream side of the bridge. "It's not as big as the one I worked on, but you get the general idea. And welcome to Southeastern Ohio," I called out. "Not a whole lot different from West Virginia."

"Yes it is, Five," Livvy joked. "Look at these people," as we drove through Belpre, "they're all wearing shoes."

At Little Hocking, I turned off on county 124 and parked along the riverbank.

"That's Lock 19. It's where the Captain and I used to depart our boats when we got furlough. If we sit here long enough, we could see a tow lock through.

"Back in 1916, the Corps of Engineers was just finishing these locks and a terrible event happened," I told her. "One awful winter night, a packet named *Kanawha* couldn't keep control and was swept broadside over the light towers at the end of the lock. The river was way high but the downstream light tower poked a hole in her hull and the poor *Kanawha* immediately started to sink."

"Lord, right out of Mark Twain," Liv observed.

I took a dirt road up a hill and in a minute, we could look down upon the Ohio. "She turned turtle somewhere between the locks and that island down there," I pointed. "That's Newberry Island." We drove back to the bigger road and soon paralleled the river. "And that's Mustapha Island. The wreckage floated on down here and Mustapha was her grave. Sixteen people died that night."

• • •

Coming into Hockingport by way of the River Road brought us to the Lowrey house before we hit 'downtown.' It looked warm and inviting, perched on the high bank of the river. No cars were visible, so I drove on to the center of town and pulled up by the office of *The River Views,* the weekly paper edited by my mom.

The office was warm and fragrant with the odors of copypaper and paste, darkroom chemicals and cigarette butts. Leaning over the shoulder of a teenage girl at a typewriter, Ellie Lowrey looked as beautiful as ever, although a few strands of silver were showing in her auburn hair.

"How much for an engagement announcement, ma'am?" I called. Mom's head jerked and her face broke into a broad grin.

"You'd better be joking, Five Lowrey," she said in a mock-stern voice, "because when this paper runs an engagement announcement, a wedding damn sure follows."

We hugged, then she turned and regarded Livvy.

"Mom, you remember Livinda, don't you?"

"Five, you might recall that Livinda didn't make it out to Five's Five during our 'fix and furnish' visit. I surely *would* remember her!" Mom said, giving Livvy a quick hug.

"Hi, Mrs. Lowrey. It's good to see you, and thanks so much for inviting me."

Looking from one to the other, Mom frowned. "Stupid here *was* just joking, wasn't he? About the engagement announcement?"

"I hope so," Liv responded. "It's the first I've heard about it."

Mom introduced us to her 'staff,' Deanna, and instructed her to mind the shop "while I get these kids settled in." When we got back to the house, Eileen's yellow Bel Air was parked off the driveway. As we climbed out, she burst through the front door and gave me an enthusiastic hug and kiss. And another for her mother. Then she stopped and stared at Livvy and me.

"Hello! I'm Eileen Lowrey, the normal offspring of this family." She extended her hand.

"Sissie, this is Doctor Livinda Ferris, the provost of Seneca University and my guest for the holiday."

"Wow, but I am impressed. Hi, Doctor Ferris," Eileen said. "And Five… it's Eileen, not Sissie. Remember?"

"Please call me Livvy, Eileen. And it's good to meet you. I've heard a lot about you."

Sissie took Livvy into her old room while I kindled a fire. Mom stood watching.

"Five? You know we've got the attic kind of fixed up. Your old single bed is up there and the Captain put in a sink and toilet. There's no need for you to go to the Riverview…" she hesitated, "unless…?"

"Naw, Mom, nothing like that," I grinned and lied. "The attic will be fine and the chimney will keep me nice and warm."

• • •

The rumble of diesel engines rattled the window and the calliope toot of the Captain's personal whistle let us know that the *Aspinwall Queen* was thirty minutes from Lock 19.

"Let's all go in the Jeepster and give him a surprise," I said. "And I want Liv to see how the lock operates, so let's take off pretty soon."

The late-afternoon sun was failing quickly and we could see the beam of the *Queen's* searchlight probing the West

Virginia shore before the giant towboat rounded the bend in the river.

"Goodness, it's huge!" Liv explained.

"Biggest diesel on the Ohio, second biggest in the world," Ellie Lowrey said proudly of her husband's boat. "The Captain's up in that tiny little pilothouse on top of the skinny tower."

The *Queen* had to double her tow through Lock 19 so the Captain left the boat after the first string of barges was safely tied upstream. As his form disappeared beneath the lock wall, we all got out of the station wagon to surprise him.

"Holy Hell!" he exclaimed as he left the lock wall ladder, "Three beautiful women and a professor." Again, hugs and kisses all around.

• • •

After a huge dinner, I brought out a jar of Old Bristo and we sat around the living room, watching snowflakes blow past the bay window.

"There was a lot of snow down below Gallipolis," the Captain said. "Forecast is for it to keep blowin' up the valley all night and tomorrow."

"Wouldn't it be neat if we had a white Christmas?" Eileen said.

I explained to Liv that we didn't get the kind of snow down here on the flatlands that we enjoyed in the mountains.

"If we've got some snow tomorrow, can we go sledding?" Mom asked. "You kids'll have to sand the rusty runners on your sleds and I know we can probably borrow two sleds from the Gestners."

• • •

The wind howled and rattled the door to the 'widow's walk' that decorated the roof of our house. Snuggled in my childhood single bed, I slept like a cadaver. No creaking of attic steps disturbed my sleep. Five and Livvy were on their best behavior.

We were finishing breakfast when the phone rang. Mom picked up and listened, then grinned. "Five, it's Denzel. He wants to speak to you."

"Hey, Bear, Merry Christmas!"

"And you too, you little pervert."

"Well, you're in good form this morning. Where are you?"

"Five, I'm only six miles away. Paige and I came home for Christmas. We thought we'd go up to Tower Hill this morning and do some sledding. Do you and Sissie wanna go?"

"Bear, you read our minds. Our whole family's going. We'll see you at Tower Hill about, what—ten o'clock?"

Just outside Coolville, Tower Hill is named for the one-time fire lookout tower that sat beside Route 50. When I was a little kid, a restaurant was built at the bottom and customers could climb the tower for a spectacular view of the Ohio Valley.

It was a terrific hill for sledding, a steep slope at the top for exhilaration and then a long gliding path that wound among pine trees and finally stopped in a small meadow beside a frozen creek. Several cars were parked beneath the tower, now closed and boarded. Even the first two flights of stairs had been removed.

We could make out figures at the bottom, including one immense one that had to be The Bear. We pulled the sleds out of the station wagon. Three Flexible Flyers and a two-person toboggan.

"You kids go ahead," Mom urged. "We'll take the toboggan and then we'll take turns."

Livvy wrapped her scarf around her face, leaving just her eyes between the scarf and her mouth. She then took a short run and bellyflopped as if she'd been sledding Tower Hill all her life. I hustled behind her and we zipped down the hill. Paige Duerhoff waved as we roared up to their group. Liv dragged her foot to execute an expert skid and stop right at Bear's feet.

The Bear grabbed her off the sled in a gesture that was only known as the *Bear hug*.

"Sissie, you minx," he roared. "Give me a kiss."

"Why, Coach, I didn't know you cared," Livvy said from beneath her scarf.

Just then Eileen skidded in, to cause a look of astonishment on Coach Duerhoff's face.

After climbing back up the hill, everyone sat on sleds and puffed away.

"I'm gonna have to quit these things by spring practice," Bear groused. "And you, Provost, what kinda' example are you setting for your students?"

"Coach, wait'll you see *our* students in warmer weather. Pall Malls are the very least of my worries," she countered.

"OK, everyone back on the hill," Ellie the Sledder yelled. She and the Captain flopped on the Flyers and were gone, followed by Eileen and the Duerhoffs.

"Hop on the front," I instructed, indicating the toboggan. "I'll push. And scoot way up front. This is a tight squeeze."

I shoved a few steps and then hopped onto the sled, my legs on each side of Liv's hips and tucked beneath her knees. I reached around and plunged my hands beneath her jacket, then under her sweater. She screeched.

313

"Five, I swear to God you have the coldest hands and the damnedest sense of timing."

"Keep on yellin', lady. The others'll just think you're having fun."

She squirmed around and kissed me as we glided sedately down Tower Hill.

— 50 —

Peace on Earth
for a Few Weeks

After church on Christmas Eve, Eileen took me aside as the others were talking with the pastor. "That's a really good woman, Five," she said in her most serious voice. "I really like her. And it's not hard to see that she's crazy about you."

"Ah, Mom's all right," I joked. "She feeds me well but... well, she's already taken," I joked.

"You silly asshole," Sissie punched me on the shoulder.

• • •

On Christmas morning, we were all as excited as little kids and hurried through our coffee and homemade sweet rolls to get at the presents. Eileen went first by unwrapping my gift... a scarlet and gold Seneca sweatshirt. She laughed uproariously and insisted I open her present. I did, revealing a red and white Miami sweatshirt.

Livvy and Eileen exchanged long knit scarves, each in the other's school colors and the laughter continued.

"Here's one for you, Five," Livvy said, "but it's not from me. I just said it would get delivered."

From the shape, I could tell it was a long-play record but my surprise was obvious when the paper was stripped away. There was my painting of Whisper on her new album, *Whisper of the Mountains.*

"Pig sent it the day before we left Seneca," Liv told me. "It's an advance copy, but it'll be in record stores by the middle of the month."

I removed the shiny black record from its slip-cover and put it on the Captain's turntable. Soon our living room was filled with the sounds of Whisper's folk songs. Between us, Liv and I related the story of Whisper and her rise to fame.

Livvy's gift to me was a large-format book of Impressionist works, printed in France with tipped-in color plates.

"I had Anna Stansbury find it in Paris and ship it," she said.

"Well, turnabout's fair play," I said, handing her a wrapped package. She burst into laugher as my book was revealed. *The Watercress Book: How to Grow and Cook with This Miracle Food Source.* "There's something else," I added, pointing to the gift-wrapped square inside the book cover. Livvy unwrapped it to show my *Braddock Branch* logotype. "In case you ever want to go commercial."

"One more here for Livinda," the Captain announced. He held up a small package and handed it to her. Her eyes lit up as she tore the paper off and revealed a jewelry box.

"Oh Five!" she exclaimed, and opened the box slowly. Inside was a smooth disk of white crystal, a vein of scarlet running through a field of gold flecks. The disk sat in a graceful mount of silver fingers, attached to a silver chain.

"It's from Sibley's Crystal Cave," I said. "One of the Bristo relatives did the work, God knows which one. But he or she is talented."

"Let's find out," Liv said. "It's beautiful. We could sell jewelry like this in the bookstore." She gave me a hug and a big kiss. "I do love it, Five."

• • •

Christmas night took us all to the Duerhoff farm where Papa Duerhoff was impressed and amazed when Bear introduced Livvy as his new boss.

"Ach, Denzel. A big football coach has a pretty woman such as this for a boss? It's as good as being a farmer," he joked, slapping Mrs. Duerhoff on the butt.

We spent a day in Athens with Bear and Paige. We had a pizza lunch at The Tavern, then walked down Congress Street past the Sigma Nu house. On to the ACE castle and past The Begorra, which was closed for Christmas vacation.

"Makes you want to order a couple hundred Begorras and haul 'em down to East Green," Bear said. Naturally, this comment led to tales of my entrepreneurial days as a freshman. Then we entered the College Green and strolled under the elms toward Cutler Hall.

"I used to think this was the prettiest campus in the world," Paige said. "But now that I've seen Seneca, I think it's a two-way tie."

Even though it was vacation, the Fine Arts Gallery was open and we walked in. One hallway was filled with an exhibit of current students' work, some of which was very impressive. We turned the corner and entered the faculty and permanent collections.

"Five, Is that Andy Logan?" Paige asked. Indeed, the large portrait of an undraped girl looked exactly like Andy, but I recognized it as the portrait of Andy's mother, painted many years ago by Doctor Logan. "God, but it's the spitting image," Paige exclaimed.

As we moved to another wall, I was confronted with my own work. There, in an alcove of its own, was *The Light Show*. Darcy's expression, painted by the neon lights of Union Street, was as precious as ever. It was the first painting by a freshman ever to win a Best in Show and had been bought by Duff Phelps and displayed in The Begorra for years. Duff had obviously made a gift to the university.

"So that's Darcy," Liv whispered to herself. "You can see why she became famous."

After a brief pause at *The Light Show*, we moved on. My next painting was a variation of the sleeping girls in *Ménage*. Doctor Logan liked my portfolio so much that he asked for one of the three I'd done for the permanent collection.

This was followed by the first of Culden's abstracts, *Homage to Jackson*. Next was Mark Husted's *Line and Shadow*, for which my old friend Trish Spottswood had posed. Another Culden Ellis, this one called *Flood Tide*, which showed the tip of a giant tongue dripping saliva.

Then we came to my only graduate school painting, the nearly monochromatic *11/22*, the row of shocked and exhausted faculty members watching the televised passion play of JFK's assassination. And that was followed by *The Players*, the OU field hockey team in stages of sweaty, dirty disarray, posing in their gloomy locker room.

"That's Andy Logan," Bear pointed out the blonde with one breast exposed from her upraised jersey.

"That was brave to pose like that," Paige pointed out. "But as you can tell, the Logans are a pretty liberal family."

"Dicky Reb took the original photo," I said. "Those are the Braswell twins, Sigrid and Signe, in the back. They wanted to take everything off," I laughed. "Later Reb got them to pose out in the country somewhere and they almost got into *Playboy.*"

Liv squeezed my arm and pulled close to me. "You certainly seem to have a way, Five, of making women want to take their clothes off for you," she whispered.

• • •

As always, our farewells were poignant. Liv and I heading back to Seneca for President Skinner's New Year's Eve party; Eileen back to Oxford to get ready for school on Wednesday, since New Year's Day fell on a Sunday.

Finally, we were on the road for home. Livvy chattered on about my family and what a good time she'd had. She sat in the bucket seat with her legs folded beneath her.

"One thing I don't like about this car," she said, "is that gearshift. Why didn't Kaiser put it on the steering wheel like civilized automobiles?"

"What's the matter with this shift?" I said, putting my hand on the console's automatic shifter.

"'Cause I want to snuggle," she said, "and that damn thing's in the way." She paused. "And more, the back seat's way too narrow."

We drove through Belpre, then Parkersburg, and onto route 47 headed for Weston. Liv grew silent as the miles rolled by.

"There's your old Boy Scout camp," she observed. Snowflakes were beginning to fly. "It's snowing."

"Yep, snowing," I replied.

"It's snowing really hard, Five," she said earnestly. "I think we'd better find a place to pull off."

I looked at the tiny flakes, barely visible in the gray noontime light.

"Look," she said brightly as we entered Freeport, "a motel!" Indeed, there stood the Freeport Tourist Cabins—five tiny cottages flanking a larger building. "Oh Five, it's been sooo long. Can we stop? Please?"

The manager of the Freeport Tourist Cabins was happy to take my $15 in advance, obviously believing my story that the wife and I were exhausted after twenty hours on the road. "Just leave the key in the door if you take off early," he said with a smile.

I squatted before the tiny gas stove, which popped into action from its pilot light. Behind me, I could hear the rustle of clothes.

"Hurry up, Five," Livvy called from beneath the covers.

"God, how did you get undressed so fast?"

"I didn't have much on in the first place," she giggled. "I thought perhaps we could stop in Belpre or Parkersburg."

I crawled beneath the covers and Livvy was on top of me instantly, showering me with tiny kisses. Very soon, we were in the throes of 'bunny love.'

• • •

It was nearly four o'clock when we emerged from the tiny cottage to a world covered with white. Nearly eight inches of snow. I started the Jeepster and turned on the heater, then worked to brush the snow off the nearly vertical windshield.

Liv came out and got behind the wheel. "We're gonna need four-wheel drive in this stuff. I'll drive for awhile and then you can have your turn."

As we pulled away, she gave a sad smile to the little row of cottages. "Goodbye, Freeport Tourist Cabins," she said with a small voice. "I'll always remember you."

The highway wasn't plowed, but the Jeepster chugged steadily along in four-wheel. Two hours later, we reached Buckhannon and had a cup of coffee in a local restaurant.

"You look bushed," I observed. "Do you think I can drive in four-wheel?" She nodded yes.

I drove on to Elkins, usually a thirty-five minute drive, but this time an hour and a half.

"What do you think, Liv? Want to push on for home?"

"Well, the snow's let up and 33's pretty clear. We should be able to make it by midnight," she said with confidence.

But route 33 didn't remain clear. We struggled on through blowing drifts, and at 11:30 entered the tiny hamlet of Seneca Rocks. There we found the Seneca Cabins and woke the manager to take the last vacant cabin.

"Oh, man," Livvy said as we settled into our hard twin beds. "What a day! Two motels in one day. I can't believe it."

And with that, we were asleep.

I woke to the sound of splashing. Liv's bed was empty and the door to the tiny bathroom closed. A second later, Liv came through the door wrapped in a towel.

"Mornin', Love," she said, "I didn't drain the tub 'cause the water started going cold. If you can just wash, we're only twelve miles from home… and that tub is really tiny."

I followed Livvy's suggestions and washed in the tiny sink. Everything about this cabin was built to small scale.

As I dressed, Liv gave me a kiss on the cheek. "Scratchy, but at least you smell OK. Let's head for home."

• • •

New Year's Eve morning was blinding bright with snow cover everywhere and a clear sky letting every solar ray through. The road was clear and we made good time up 55/28 toward Seneca. As we passed the Skidmore Mountain

James Patterson

turnoff I said, "I wonder if Benjo's made any progress over the vacation. He was staying in Seneca."

"Oh, I'll bet he's made progress," she giggled. "Wasn't he moving into Gillian's old place? With your secretary?"

Seneca shimmered in the valley below us as we caught our first sight of the town. I drove right through and on to Five's Five. The cabin was frigid and filigree frost patterns covered the windows.

"Just like the *dacha* in *Doctor Zhivago*," I observed. I popped the pilot light and put a match under the fireplace grate, already built up with kindling and logs. "Do you want to stay for awhile, get some breakfast?"

Liv shook her head. "I just want to get home and into a really hot bath. Wash my hair. I'll see you this evening."

And our holiday vacation was over.

— 51 —

Startling Images

Never before had I resorted to the hand crank to start the 2CV. And never before had I imagined it to be such hard work. Cursing my recalcitrant machine and bruising my knuckles, I finally coaxed the Citroën to life. It sat there in its shed, quivering like mechanical jello. I went into the house, shaved, showered, and got dressed for the evening.

When I returned to the 2CV it was still idling, perhaps a little smoother. I raised the hood and pulled the radiator shade down, then got in and put the shift into reverse. The little Citroën lurched backward and then gave a loud *clank* and stopped. I jiggled the shift lever and raced the engine. Louder noise; no movement.

I looked beneath the car where a pool of some liquid was forming on the dirt floor of the shed. Shutting off the engine, I went back into the cabin and called Liv.

"I don't know much about cars," I told her, "but I think the transmission's gone."

"Don't worry, Five. It's not a big deal for me to drive out and pick you up. We'll probably do better with four-wheel drive."

• • •

The 'tons of fun' girls were singing raunchy versions of Christmas carols when we arrived at President Skinner's house. It was my first visit to the president's home and I was impressed that Livvy's residence was almost as big and almost as opulent.

It was really a gala party, with faculty members, staff assistants, even secretaries present. Benjo showed up as Cyndy's guest and gave me a thumbs up.

Liv and I told Culden about the Ohio Gallery and seeing her work on permanent display.

"I'm going to call Doctor Logan tomorrow and see if we can get your work and Five's on loan for the Faculty-Student show," Liv told us.

Reb West came back from talking with Benjo. "Five, I've come across something really interesting," he told me. "It was really Culden who put me onto it. Benjo wants to meet in the morning. Would your office be OK?"

Eggnog was consumed in great quantity as the evening wore on. A small combo played in one corner and I got to dance with Culden, Jaylene, Cyndy, and Liv, as well as various other faculty members. When the band took a break, someone put Whisper's album on the stereo and the crowd quieted to listen to the extraordinary voice.

The minutes ticked away toward midnight. Frank Skinner directed waiters to fill champagne glasses, and with just five minutes left of 1967, we all moved to the chilly patio, swept clear of snow. Arm in arm, everyone swayed as we sang *Morning Mountain Mists,* then the bell of Old Main began tolling and the combo broke into *Auld Lang Syne.*

From the mountaintop across the valley, a single skyrocket soared, its many starbursts creating a golden light over the snow-covered town.

"Happy New Year, Five," Livvy said, and kissed me passionately.

"Happy 1968, Liv," I responded.

• • •

Liv drove me home and stayed the night. We started New Year's Day by sitting on the couch with our feet propped in front of the fireplace, sipping cocoa and watching the snow flurries outside.

"Does it always snow this much up here?" I asked.

"Pretty much. That's why we have a sleigh at Braddock's Branch. There's a bigger sleigh wagon, too. We used to have hayrides on it. That's a lot of fun."

I took the empty cups to the sink and returned with my gift from her, the book on Impressionism. "Read to me, Liv. I know all the paintings but I want to hear what the French said about them when the artists were still alive."

Later, we walked through the snowy woods and across the moonshiner trail to the Bristo house. Bubby and Tibby welcomed us in and invited us for lunch. They were dressed in fairly formal clothes. Bubby wore a white shirt beneath a rusty black suit.

"Would you like to come to church with us this afternoon?" Bubby asked.

"We're not dressed for it, Bubby," Liv protested.

"You look just fine, Miss Livinda," Tibby commented. Liv had on a pair of ski pants and a Nordic knit sweater.

"Come on," Bubby urged. "It'll do you good and be a grand way to start the New Year."

• • •

The Pentecostal Word of the Truth church was deep in the far reaches of a hollow south of town. Liv and I sat under blankets in the back of Bubby's truck. We were surprised to see the number of vehicles, mostly pickups, surrounding the gray house that served as a church.

"Take a seat here in the back," Bubby suggested. "You'll be able to see everything but…" He didn't finish the sentence and strode toward the front of the church.

A stout woman began playing the piano and a fiddle player joined in. We all stood and joined in singing *Bringing In The Sheaves*. Then a thin woman stood and, to piano accompaniment, sang *Life Is Like a Mountain Railroad*, joined by the congregation in the chorus.

A couple of prayers, and then a tall, emaciated-looking man stood up and began the sermon. Liv nudged me and whispered, "Now the good part's starting."

From time to time the sermon would be interrupted by another man, shuffling forward and speaking gibberish in a high voice.

"Speaking in tongues," Liv commented.

While the preacher continued his sermon, the fiddle player began picking out a tune of tiny notes. The pianist joined in.

Suddenly, Bubby Bristo came forward and began the shuffling dance that we'd seen at my Halloween party. His upper body completely stiff, his feet bucked a double beat to the music. Someone added to the spectacle by crying out in tongues, soon joined by another and another.

Yet another man came forward, carrying a wooden box. Bubby's stiff upper body suddenly went into action as his dance grew more frenetic. He then shuffled up to the man with the box, who opened the lid. Bubby reached in and, never missing a step, withdrew a giant snake.

"Rattler," Livvy gasped. "And what a big one!"

Bubby danced around in a circle with the huge serpent held over his head. The music slowed and with it, Bubby's dance. Then slowly, he brought the snake to his face and opened his mouth. With two feet of snake on each side of his face, Bubby shuffled around in a circle with the snake in his mouth, his arms raised to heaven.

The church was a cacophony of tongues and "Praise God" shouts and music. Finally Bubby returned the snake gently to its box, wiped his brow, and returned to his bench.

Several more parishioners handled snakes and performed their strange worship. The pastor never did pick up his sermon. Finally, we joined in *The Old Rugged Cross* and the service was ended.

Bubby and Tibby introduced me to many of the churchgoers. Most of the mountain people knew Liv and greeted her by her formal name—Livinda Caroline.

Later I said, "I never new the *C* stood for Caroline. That's a pretty name. And all of those folks seemed to know you."

"Many of those people literally 'owed their soul to the company store,' as Tennessee Ernie sang, until Bus Ferris took over the county," she said. "Daddy may be arrogant and needy for recognition, but he's a good man and he's done good for the people in this county."

Over glasses of Old Bristo at Bubby's cabin, I expressed my admiration for Bubby's performance at church.

"Old snake's on our side," he drawled. "He represents the Devil but he knows the power of our God is mighty in that worship. Old snake's never bit anyone I can remember."

"Some say we liquor 'em up before worship," Tibby said. "But that's not so. I've seen 'im in the summer, grab a rattler out from under his rock. And worship with him, not one but many, handle him and the snake never loses his temper."

• • •

We elected to walk back to Five's Five. Hand in hand, we strolled through the woods, the silence broken only by an occasional crack of a branch or the thump of a falling snow clump.

"You know, Livvy, I've really come to love this country. That church service was one of the great experiences of my lifetime… not that I'd want to join their church."

"Now you see why I never really wanted to leave home," she responded. "These mountains do something to your soul." She squeezed my hand and looked into my face. "I hope you'll never leave these mountains."

• • •

"From what I know about tractors and trucks," Liv commented as she knelt behind my crippled Citroën, "I'd say your rear end is gone."

"And how do I get it to a repair shop?" I asked. "I think I saw one in Petersburg."

"Five, this may be the only Citroën 2CV in West Virginia. Does Citroën even have dealerships in this country?"

"Man, I feel stupid," I said, "but it's the first time I ever really gave it a thought. Maybe it's time for a new car?"

"I've been invited to the meeting in your office tomorrow morning," she said. "Afterward, why don't I drive you over to Petersburg and we'll go car shopping. You can certainly afford it."

• • •

Liv, Benjo, Culden, and Reb gathered around the little table in my office the next morning.

"As you know, I'm on assignment from *Look,* and I went up to Pitt and Penn State just before Christmas. I shot a couple of protests at State College and my editor had this set enlarged and sent 'em out. I'm supposed to write captions." Reb fanned six or seven 8x10 glossy prints on the table.

"Naturally, I'd never have thought anything about it, but when Culden saw the prints..." he paused and looked at his wife. She picked up the narrative.

"Look at this one," she pointed to the print. "I'm positive this girl is Gillian." In the photo, a dark-haired girl was in mid-leap, her curls twisting with the motion. Both hands were over her head, middle fingers extended.

"And this one," Culden produced another print. "What do you think, Five, Liv? Isn't that Gillian?"

"So it is. But what's it mean? What's Gil doing at Penn State?"

"This was a protest by Students Against Warfare. SAW seems to be taking the lead, even in protests out of their sphere of interest. This particular activity was for the Free Speech Movement and they screamed 'fuck' a lot."

"What's interesting to me," Benjo spoke for the first time, "is this picture here. He held up another print of Gillian in a crowd. "Look carefully at this guy next to her. He's kind of blurred but I'm sure he's Linus Friedman."

"If Gillian's back in the protest business," I said, "we've got something to worry about. She saw Sibley's notebook the night we found his remains. She knows where the other entrance to Project Lazarus is."

329

— 52 —

My First Semester Ends

My Intro to Painting class was full the next day, since it was the first day of class after vacation. I really didn't like the idea of having two more weeks of the old semester, then finals, but Livinda was the provost, not I.

I was surprised when Pig came through the door and took a seat at an empty bench. No one paid much attention to him. I put the class to work on a still life timed drill, and beckoned him to the hallway.

"Pig, Happy New Year, and what're you doing here?"

"Hey, Five." He gave the hippie handshake of clenched fists. "We're just driving through from Omar on our way to New York. Whisper went back to see her mother and get some of her stuff."

"You're going to New York?"

"Yeah, the *Today Show* has invited Whisper to be on. And we're going to talk to the *Ed Sullivan Show*."

"My God, Pig, that's terrific. And you're her manager?"

Pig blushed and grinned. "Well, yeah. And her husband, too. We got married down in Omar."

"Oh, wow, that is great! Where is she now?"

"In the car. She didn't want to cause a disturbance."

I called Liv and pulled Culden out of her office. We walked with Pig down to the Fine Arts parking area. Liv came running across the campus.

"Hi, Whisper," I said. "I want to thank you so much for the album. It's just beautiful."

"Hello, Five," she responded in her ever-soft voice. "You're welcome, very welcome. And thank you."

Whisper got out of the car and exchanged hugs with Liv and Culden. We persuaded the shy star to come into Livvy's office for coffee. Pig repeated their New York adventure and Liv made him promise to call her collect when he knew anything about the appearances.

When we left the admin building, the steps were crowded with students and faculty hoping to get a glimpse of Whisper, or even her autograph. She graciously signed everything handed to her. Then she entered the car, gave a shy wave to the crowd, and the Piggot family was off for New York.

• • •

The offerings of Petersburg's Ford, Dodge, and Chevrolet dealers were uninspiring. Liv even suggested I might like a pickup truck, but none of them showed any appeal.

"What about a Jeepster?" I asked. "I really enjoyed driving yours, and I could use the four-wheel drive."

"There's a Kaiser dealer in Moorefield," Liv responded. "Let's go."

Moorefield is just up the road nine miles and we were there in no time. The Kaiser dealership wasn't nearly as big as the ones in Petersburg but it did have several Jeepsters on the lot.

"Look at the convertibles, Five. Aren't they dear?"

"Yeah, but I think I'd need a wagon. Especially if it's going to snow like this every year."

"Does that mean you're going to stay for at least another year?" she asked with a grin.

"If I'm invited back."

Moorefield Kaiser had seven Jeepsters—three convertibles in pastel colors, three wagons in pastel colors, and a solid black wagon that didn't resemble the others. I balked at the prices quoted, over three thousand dollars for a convertible, $3500 for the hardtop.

"What's the black one?" I asked the salesman. "It doesn't look like the others."

"Oh, that's a sixty-five station wagon. Last of the line," he responded. "We ordered it special for a local farmer. It came in the all-black and he wanted the woodie version. By the time we got back to Kaiser, they'd quit building them at all. So he bought one of these new Jeepster models."

"How much for the '65?" Liv asked. "It looks kind of old fashioned."

"Well, the boss really wants to get it off the lot. I think he'd take $2500 for it."

"Can we test drive it?" I asked.

We each took a turn behind the wheel of the Jeepster, which still had its new-car smell. The four-wheel drive worked smoothly. The steering was sharp and responsive. I drove it back to the lot.

"Throw in tax and title, a full tank of gas, and I'll take it for $2100…" I said, "cash. I want to drive it away today."

"I'll have to talk to my sales manager," he said, Adam's apple bobbing.

"My best offer just went down a hundred dollars," I said. "Make it quick."

I drove my new vehicle to the Bristos' hollow and asked Bubby if he wanted my 2CV for anything. He followed me home. It was Bubby's opinion that the 2CV's transmission was shot but perhaps he could rebuild it, "using the planetary gear from a motor scooter or something." I watched as he towed the little Citroën away to become another fixture in his side yard.

• • •

The Warriors continued to be unbeaten, and basketball fever was starting to grip the campus. They trounced Slippery Rock and eased by Bethany on the road, then came home for easy wins against Bucknell and Gettysburg. Classes went smoothly through the last two weeks of the semester, and the cold weather seemed to have slowed the protest movement.

Gordon Logan responded to Livvy's request and shipped *The Light Show, 11/22, The Players,* and Culden's *Flood Tide* and *Homage to Jackson* for the Faculty/Student Exhibition.

It took two dollies to maneuver Jaylene's *The Dancer* to the Center Gallery. As I was fighting to keep the big sculpture from tipping, I realized who the model had been.

"Jaylene? This is Gillian, isn't it?"

"Well, yeah. But she didn't pose. I just made a few quick sketches."

Our faculty looked more like a funeral cortège as we carried Hoopie's *Ashes of Glory* casket to the gallery. And one by one, we got the paintings and other exhibition pieces moved.

My student, Marilyn Kretzman, arrived with a matted and framed work I hadn't seen before. "Did you do this at home, Marilyn?" I asked the thin girl. "It's quite good and… uh, a little unorthodox."

She looked alarmed. "Do you mean it can't be in the show?"

"Not at all. It's just that I've never seen an orange nun's habit before."

"Look carefully, Professor. I call it *Habit Forming* and well, look carefully," she said.

I did look carefully, and found Marilyn had quite a talent for subtlety.

Then the campus became quiet as finals week arrived and students hit the books.

• • •

"Well, you've survived six pop quizzes, your attendance has been terrific, and now it's time to tackle the final exam," I told my first Art App class. "Each pop quiz was worth 15 percent of your grade," I continued. A loud murmur swept across Canby Auditorium. "That means that you have 90 percent of your grade complete. This is totally arbitrary on my part but… you have been so attentive that I feel you've earned it."

In truth, not a single student who attended class had failed a pop quiz. During the semester, I lost only six people.

"So, here we go. I'm going to show ten slides. You'll have thirty seconds to write down the title of the work for one point. Two points if you correctly identify the title and the artist. This means you *could* raise your grade by a whole letter."

Applause.

• • •

If there's one thing about teaching I don't like, it's grading tests. Thank heavens art students don't have to write many essays. Culden and I had devised the final exam scheme but didn't count on our Art Appreciation classes being so successful. A bell curve of my early morning class was flatter than a fourth grader's brassiere.

"What the heck," Livinda told us. "So no one flunked. That's not important. What's important is did the students learn anything. Did they learn to appreciate art?"

We found out on Saturday night, the last day of finals and the opening reception for the exhibition. The private cocktail reception for faculty and artists was at six o'clock and by fifteen after, the room was packed. While many of the guests were dressed for dinner in suits and ties, the Fine Arts faculty went bohemian in black turtlenecks and jeans.

"My word," Jim Gerholt said, "who's M. Kretzman? That's remarkable. You can see the nun's equipment right through that orange habit."

"If you look carefully," I added.

I complimented Jim Gillespie on his modest portrait of a young woman in a green drape.

"Just wait, Professor," he said with great enthusiasm. "Next semester it's gonna be boobies and buttocks. I mean, look at all your stuff. Aren't you going to teach us how to do that?"

Hoopie's *Ashes of Glory* drew a great deal of attention, most of it favorable. "That's a powerful statement," Dean Cruz-Garcia said to Culden. "I think Stuart Poletz was a good choice on your part." Having overheard the statement, I made for Hoopie straightaway.

Culden's use of broad brushstrokes and drippings from a ladder drew a lot of attention. I told Livvy how I'd first met Culden, standing on a ladder, her naked body covered with paint splatters as she aimed her brush at the canvas on the floor.

To our amazement, students began congregating around the entrance to the gallery. Livvy ordered the bar closed ten minutes early, and Culden invited the student crowd into the show.

Jordan Meadow immediately drew a knot of onlookers. To see the detail in the big painting, they had to get nose-up to the canvas.

"Man, that's just like that Brueghel guy Professor Lowrey talked about in class," one girl commented aloud. A couple of Kappas squealed with delight as they recognized their semi-likenesses on the canvas.

John Piggot's portrait of Whisper was beautiful. Hoopie had matted it in a pale blue that complemented Whisper's gauzy dress.

"I guess I'm most proud of that," Culden said. "Pig's got great talent. And Marilyn Kretzman's the talk of the show."

"I heard a couple of kids discussing pointillism," I told her. "I mean really discussing."

"Five, I think it's been a heck of a semester," she said, giving me a hug.

— 53 —

Surely, Winter Is Followed
by Something

Culden stomped into the office on registration day, flinging snow and water in every direction. She was followed by Cyndy, Jaylene, and Hoopie.

"Christ on a crutch!" she shouted. "This is the coldest fucking place I've ever seen." She looked at me. "How did you get up that fuckin' mountain? We had to walk. This place ought to issue climbing ropes and axes."

"Man, I'm sorry," I said, not really meaning it. "I could've picked you guys up in the Jeepster. It came right up the hill in four-wheel, no problem at all."

"Well, Mr. Four-Wheel," Cyndy said, "Benjo wonders if you could pick him up. The government's Chevy won't turn over and he needs to talk to you. I'll take your place at registration and make sure you get some good counselees this semester."

Benjo was waiting on the drift-covered sidewalk trying to blow smoke rings with his frozen breath. "Shit, Five, Korea wasn't as cold as this," he gasped as he climbed into the Jeepster. "Cyndy called and said you'd be down in your fancy jeep. This thing turned out to be a pretty good buy, eh?"

"I still need knobbies, but it does get through this stuff pretty well," I said. "How are you and Cyndy getting along? She a good roommate?"

Benjo grinned sheepishly. "I'll say. She's a good cook and doesn't complain. Says that after living in a yurt for a summer, anything, anybody is an improvement. And there are other benefits…"

"I'll bet. Where are we headed?"

"Back up the hill. We need to talk to Livvy, maybe even the president."

• • •

Livinda was in full provost mode, explaining policy to faculty members, directing students to the right registration tables, looking harassed.

"You bet I'll take a break," she muttered as we approached. "I *just know* you two have something important to tell me. Let's go to the Center."

We trudged across snowy Eden Fields, following the narrow path tamped down by hundreds of student feet.

"I'd love to go to the Faculty Club and have a couple of Bloody Marys," she said, winking at me, "but it's not even nine-thirty." She led us into the student center snack bar.

"OK," Benjo said as we sipped our coffee and lit up. "Here's the government poop on Project Lazarus. It's an emergency shelter for 350 federal staffers and technicians with sustainable supplies for 30 days."

"That's probably what we saw when we were in there," I commented.

"Yeah, but that's not all. There's an area for records storage but... there's also an area for storing chemical and biological weapons."

"Holy shit!" I exclaimed. "No nukes? Why not?"

"Five, you know nuclear weapons come under a whole other classification and it's not in the AIC records. I was amazed when I found out about CB stuff."

"What does this mean, Benjo?" Livinda asked.

"It means that as long as Seneca University is a participating entity in this project, you have to consider the institution as a target—of saboteurs from foreign powers... of radical groups... even student radicals."

"And what do we do as a target?" Liv continued.

"Not much more than has been done. The Army will beef up the security force and we'll just have to keep our ears to the ground."

• • •

"Lord, Five, what did you do? Put up posters advertising naked women posing?" Culden grinned as she and Cyndy tallied registrations. "You have 30 students signed up for Figure Drawing. Even if we move the painting benches into the north studio, we'll only have seats for 25."

"Culden, we've got pre-cut materials for another ten benches in the basement. I could get maintenance to pound them together before classes start," Hoopie volunteered. Culden nodded her approval.

"I kind of doubt if all thirty of them will stick for a nine-o'clock," I commented.

"I don't," Hoopie observed, "not after they get a look at the model."

"Well, don't let it get out of hand," our department chairman ordered. "Cyndy just finished these class schedules. Looks like everyone made a class." She passed out our schedules. "As we agreed, Five, you've got the Saturday Art App duty for the spring semester."

My class schedule read:

Art App, TTS, 9 a.m., Art App, TTS, 11 a.m.,
Figure Drawing, MWF, 9 p.m.,
Intro to Painting II, MWF, 10 a.m.

• • •

"Sonofabtich, but it's a cold cocksucker out today," Blondie groused, as she pulled off her coat and unzipped her boots. "They had a fire last night on Laurel Run Road," she added. "Burned two shacks right down! So we've got about ten less hippies in Laurel Town this morning."

"Ten people were killed?" I asked, alarmed.

"Nooo. Shit, Professor Lowrey," she grinned. "Ten people just hauled ass for somewhere warmer."

She rubbed her hands together briskly. "I'm gonna shower now. You wanna join me?"

"No, thanks, but there is a warm robe in there for you."

"So today's the big day, eh? Little Blondie takes it all off."

"That's right. Just come in and sit in the rear of the classroom. When it's time, I'll introduce you and we'll go over the ground rules."

"No coppin' a feel, no groping, right?"

"Right. And wear some slippers until you pose. The floors are pretty cold."

Blondie sat demurely in the back of the classroom, bundled in the big white terrycloth robe and with fluffy pink rabbit slippers on her feet. The Figure Drawing class indeed counted thirty people, many of whom I'd taught the semester before.

Jim Gillespie was in the front row, practically drooling in anticipation. As I called the roll, I had each person stand and give a brief bio and state why he wanted to take Figure Drawing. At the end of this exercise, I advised three guys and two girls to take their academic interests elsewhere. The voyeurs huffed out of the room. That left me with my first-semester class plus three new people.

"Most of you know Blondie from last semester," I said, motioning the model forward. "Today, we're going to start the study and drawing of the human figure. Later in the semester, we'll have a male model but we're going to start with this young woman.

"Ground rules: Blondie is not a student here, but that does not mean she can be treated rudely. If anyone is caught treating her with disrespect, that person will fail the course and be dismissed from the class."

Mentally, I worked hard to recall Jan Dabney's introductory speech at OU lo, those many years ago.

"We'll start working in three- or four-minute poses. A lot will depend upon Blondie's stamina. Please refrain from talking to her while we're in a pose exercise."

"OK, let's get started. Blondie, will you take the podium?"

Blondie sort of sauntered to the front of the room, stepped lightly upon the podium, and stood with her back to the class, facing the north window. Then, with a dramatic gesture, she spread the terry robe wide, and slowly slid it down her body.

A collective gasp filled the room, led by me. I picked up her robe and draped it over a nearby chair.

"I can assure you that Blondie will have a little less drama from now on," I said. "Right?" I looked at her sternly. She grinned and slowly turned to face the class. I recalled the next lines from Dabney's introduction.

"I'm sure that for some of you, this is your first encounter with a naked person. We'll all become accustomed to the characteristics of this mature young woman. But until we do, I would like for you to act as if you *are* accustomed."

I pointed to Blondie's gorgeous breasts. "These are breasts. Everyone comes with a pair of them, and at puberty the woman's breasts assume a different shape and a different role." I made a twirling motion and Blondie turned.

"And these are her buttocks, perhaps not so different from what you see in your own mirror." Once more I turned Blondie. "And this," I said, gesturing generally toward her crotch, "is her pubis. Again, standard equipment for a mature woman." I thanked the Muses that Blondie hadn't shaved her public hair into a nifty pattern.

Finally, I put my hand toward her face and grasped her chin. "And do not forget, this is Blondie's face, the mask of her personality. The sum of all these parts. Let's get to work."

Jim Gillespie looked as if he were about to faint.

Blondie held the first three-minute pose like a statue. I wandered around the crowded room, noting the hesitancy of some, the enthusiasm of others. Gillespie surprised me with a very accomplished soft sketch that flattered Blondie's rounded form.

When I called the pose to an end, Blondie slumped on her posing stool, legs akimbo.

"Can I smoke?" she asked. "Of course you can smoke, Stupid," she chided herself as she noticed my Pall Mall.

"How was it?" I asked softly as I lit her cigarette.

"Tougher than I thought it would be," she whispered. "Can I look at their drawings?"

"After a few more poses. Let them—and you—get used to it."

She blew a smoke ring, scratched a breast, and said to me in a mock whisper, "But you were right. This is easier than giving blowjobs."

• • •

I was reviewing an assortment of Figure Drawing sketches in my office when I heard a knock at the door. I looked up to find a young black man peering around the door.

"Professor Lowrey? I have a counseling appointment. At ten thirty?"

"Oh, yes, please come in. Have a seat. And you are...?"

"My name's Evermont Nixon. But everyone calls me Monty. Coach Duerhoff said I should ask for you as my faculty adviser." Everything clicked into place. This was the Bear's quarterback recruit, enrolled a semester before his official graduation from high school.

"Well, welcome to Seneca, Monty. I hope you'll enjoy the university and make a success of yourself." *God, did that sound pompous.* "Do you have any academic goals?" I asked. "I know you're just a few days out of high school."

"No, sir," he said with a big grin. He nodded to the pile of nude sketches on my desk. "Are those part of a college course?"

"Errr, yes. Figure Drawing. Do you like to draw, Monty?"

"Umm, ah, I never thought about it," he grinned. "But I think I could learn to like it."

Since freshmen didn't have to declare a major, I managed to guide Monty Nixon toward a liberal arts schedule. Engineering was out, since he didn't like math.

I finished looking at the drawings, discovering two or three students with a feel for line and form, two or three more who were obviously embarrassed beyond committing anything definitive to paper. That would change.

The phone rang, and I agreed to meet Livvy at the Faculty Club for lunch.

As I crossed the gallery floor, I found her strolling through the exhibit.

"Five, I can't believe that in less than a year, Seneca has accomplished an exhibit of this quality. Last year, we'd have set out a box of Crayolas and let the viewers do their own," she said with a giggle. "Your work is even more fun for me since I'm personally acquainted with *some* of the subjects."

Over soup and salad, I told her about my session with Monty Nixon.

"Oh, I know. Doesn't he seem like the nicest kid?" she exclaimed. "Paige brought him up to meet me this morning. He's staying with the Duerhoffs until we can find him the right roommate."

"Someone who doesn't wear a gown and hood?" I asked, half seriously.

"Mmm. That's partially true," she acknowledged. "And how did it go with your hippie figure model?"

I related the high points of that morning's class. Her expression alternated between provostly concern and pure hilarity.

"I would've loved to see Blondie disrobe," she said. "But of course, when word gets around you'll probably have all sorts of people wanting to audit. And North Mountain will be filled with 'bird watchers' from nine a.m. three days a week."

I unfolded one sheet of newsprint and showed it to her. "I think this kid has some real potential. Another Varga or Petty, perhaps."

Liv looked at Gillespie's sketch. "Wow! Is Blondie really that built?"

"No, but Gillespie's imagination is."

— 54 —

Our Winter of Great Content

Through February, winter ruled Seneca and its university. Storm after storm came pounding out of Canada and the drifts grew higher. The Warriors stayed unbeaten, although two games were postponed until early March because of travel problems.

Blondie dutifully reported nothing from the hippie community except that its population was slowly dwindling. "I've even got a room of my own in the back of the store," she told me, "with a gas stove and a good sleeping bag."

The Figure Drawing class grew more confident, as did their model. Between poses, Blondie would stroll among the young artists with her terry robe open, leaning over this one and that, occasionally brushing a bare breast against an arm or a shoulder. This sexy tactile encouragement worked wonders, and the class improved its skills steadily.

• • •

The Norman Luboff Choir came for a concert in mid-February and stayed for three days, until the road to Petersburg could be cleared. The choir members wandered around the campus and looked in on classes. Livvy had Jake Jericho bring Esopus and the farm sled into town for a hayride. It was a great experience to have a famous choir riding through Seneca's streets, serenading the townsfolk.

• • •

Football signing day brought Seneca a recruiting class that had The Bear beaming. His 'pair of bookends' from Parkersburg South, plus Bobby Linhart, an all-state running back from Stonewall Jackson, brought Seneca's black athlete population to four.

Monty Nixon moved in with a chemistry major in Monckton Hall and survived his first racial incident without a fight. It was a name-calling by a town boy, and Monty's roommate put the bigot in his place with words alone. Monty worked out with the basketball team, but Coach Sam decided to redshirt him.

Livvy and I became an accepted pair by the Duerhoffs and Wests. The three couples socialized every weekend with dinner at one another's homes. But the provost and the art professor still attempted some degree of discretion, and sleepovers were fairly rare.

The three couples rented a big house near Cabin Mountain for a ski weekend. Dicky Reb and Liv were the only ones who had ever skied, and our first attempt at getting up the slope ended in laughter. The rope tow swung around a big wheel at the bottom of the slope and the idea was to straddle the rope and let it glide you up the hill.

"Sum'bitch almost took my nuts off," Bear howled.

"Let go, Bear. Let go!" Reb yelled as the rope dragged the Bear's recumbent form through the snow. But by Saturday night, we were gliding down Cabin Mountain's gentle slope with great confidence.

When we arrived back in Seneca on Sunday night, a warm breeze was wafting through the valley.

"False spring," Liv muttered. "If it keeps up, we'll have a big season for colds and sore throats."

Sure enough, the sun rose Monday morning and temperatures quickly climbed to the sixties. The drainage around the campus suddenly roared with water as the snow rapidly melted. The balmy temperatures continued, and by Wednesday night the snow was gone.

Thursday morning found the second session of my Art Appreciation lecture playing to a half-empty hall. Liv met me outside Canby for our usual lunchtime date and we picked our way across Eden Fields, cluttered with students sunbathing on the grass, tossing Frisbees, and generally having a good time. Several couples were in passionate embraces.

"Spring's in the air," I hummed. "Love is all around."

"I wish," Liv grumbled. "It won't last, mark my words. Spring won't be here until I get the MG out of the garage."

Friday was another gorgeous day, and attendance dwindled even more. Butterfly blouses reappeared, much to every male's delight. Even a few hippies came to Eden Fields to strum instruments and smoke a little pot.

Liv drove home with me Friday afternoon to help prepare the night's big spaghetti feed. By six o'clock, the sky was dark and thunder rumbled in the mountains. The Wests and Duerhoffs arrived in one car and used the footbridge, rather than risk the ford across the creek. Little R.T. sat in the porch swing between his parents and chortled with every lightning strike in the mountains.

"We've got to get some chairs like these, Denzel," Paige said.

"Does this guy make 'em to fit someone my size?" Bear asked.

"I'm sure he does," I responded. "We can drive over to Moyer's Run tomorrow and see."

"OK. 'Cause I'm damn tired of sittin' on these steps."

We all hurried into the house when the first huge raindrops splattered through the trees.

Later, as we washed dishes, the wind howled and blew sheets of rain through the yard. I bundled our guests into the Jeepster and four-wheeled through the ford to their cars.

Livvy greeted me at the back door with a towel.

"You're soaked," she scolded. "Come in and get those clothes off, right now."

"Yes, Mother."

"I'll mother you," she said, stripping my shirt off. "And mother you. And mother you."

We climbed into bed with the rain pounding on the roof. I opened a window slightly the better to hear the downpour and the rushing creek below.

I tiptoed my fingers across Livvy's back and shoulders, down her spine. She guided my hand around her hip and I finger walked through the soft brush of her pubis.

Livvy rolled over and pulled me to her. "Oh, Five, will *this* ever get old?"

• • •

Around midnight the rain softened. I rolled out of bed to use the bathroom and was blasted with a chill of air from the open window. I closed it quietly but saw the rain now coming down as fat, wet flakes. I popped the gas stove and set its flame to low, then crawled back into bed.

By morning, winter had returned. The woods were covered with nearly a foot of snow—big, wet piles without drifts. Heavy blobs of snow plopped from tree branches to the forest floor, forming what the skiers called moguls. The sun glinted through the bare branches of the forest, but without warmth. Livvy read and I made sketches of the snowy woods, whiling away the Saturday morning. The phone rang.

"Guess we're not going to go chair shopping today," Bear said. "We must have a foot of snow here, and it's packing up. I think I'm just going in to the office."

"OK. I'll see you later when I bring Livvy home," I answered.

After lunch, I four-wheeled us out of Five's Five and down the lane, packing deep ruts behind us.

"If this stuff melts a little bit, then freezes, it'll be a bitch to get around," I observed. As we crept into town, a strange sight confronted us. Students had rolled huge snowballs at the top of Old Main hill and then sent them down the steep embankment. The effect was of a striped hillside, white, brown, white.

We spun and skidded our way to the upper campus and found another strange sight on Eden Fields. Two big groups of students were rolling snowballs and packing them tightly to create what looked like forts.

"Oh, crap," Liv exclaimed. "A snowball battle. Ordinarily they can be fun, but with this wet snow, I'll bet we have some problems."

We walked over to the field house, where Bear's temporary office was and watched the scene below. With the walls completed, the competing crowds set to work rolling snowballs. From one parapet, the flags of several Greek organizations flew.

"Greeks versus GDIs," Bear observed.

The battle began calmly, until the Independents brought out a couple of water buckets and started icing their snowballs. The Greek side countered with the same tactic, and soon lethal ice balls were whizzing between the two forts.

Someone on the Independent side planted a flagpole on top of their parapet and unfurled a Viet Cong flag. Through the closed windows, we could hear the roar of disapproval from the Greek side. The ice-ball barrage picked up in intensity.

Then a squad of people from the Greek side ran out of their fort and across the no-man's-land, headed for the Viet Cong flag. Independents mounted their parapet and peppered the attackers with ice balls. Someone pulled an Independent off the parapet and fists flew as the two rolled in the snow.

"Better call Sergeant Glencoe, Livvy," I counseled. "It's getting rough down there."

She frowned, but picked up the phone.

The mêlée grew, with students throwing punches wildly and wrestling each other in the snow. Bear threw his coat on and grabbed an air horn.

"Sheeit, this is serious. Let's go," he said, leading us down the stairs. "I'll try to take that big kid in the red hat. Five, you get one of the Greeks and Liv, get that dipshit girl with the flag out of there."

We ran across Eden Fields and into the fray. No one seemed to notice our presence until Bear let off a long blast of the air horn. In the silence that followed, sirens could be heard. Bear hugged the Independent guy in a red watch cap to his chest. I grabbed a guy I recognized as being in the Interfraternity Council. Liv tugged at the girl defending the Viet Cong flag.

"Provost Ferris will take the names of anyone left on this yard when the police arrive, and discipline will follow," Bear growled. "And… if I recognize any of you turkeys as members of the football team… woe be unto you come spring practice."

Jack Glencoe pulled up in his squad car, red light flashing, and found the Bear, Livvy and me. The only evidence of any mayhem was bloody patches in the snow. Not a single student was in sight.

• • •

"Just blowing off some winter steam," Livvy told Dean Gerholt, who'd appeared in his office about an hour later. "And it was your typical Greeks against GDIs confrontation. The only thing really different was the appearance of a Viet Cong flag."

"Are you *sure* it was a Viet Cong flag?" Jim Gerholt asked.

"Oh, yeah, red and blue field with a gold star in the middle," I said.

"Where would one of our students acquire such a thing?" the Dean mused.

"We're not sure everyone on Eden Fields *was* a student," Liv responded.

• • •

The snow was gone by Monday morning, leaving only huge lumps of ice at the bottom of the hill and the melted remains of the forts on Eden Fields. The bright sun even showed some bright green tips of stubborn crocuses.

Blondie ducked her head into my office, looked around, then pulled the door shut behind her.

"Some of them are back," she said quietly. "Charlie Brown, Doug, a couple of guys I don't know, and that crazy girl."

"What crazy girl?" I asked.

"You know. The one with you that night up on the creek. The dancer pothead."

"Gillian?"

"That's her. Except I heard Charlie Brown introducing her as 'Snow Heather' to the others."

"Where are they living?" I asked.

"There's a farmhouse north of Jordan Run. Was a commune until it got cold. Charlie Brown said they'd moved in there."

• • •

Benjo listened intently to what I'd heard from Blondie, and scribbled a couple of notes.

"She didn't know if either of the other guys was Mecklin?" he asked.

"I don't think she's ever seen Mecklin," I responded.

"Reb has been pretty active in Laurel Town and Jordan Run, hasn't he?" Benjo asked.

"Yep. He's got that continuing assignment from *Look*, goes up there at least once a week."

"Would it offend his journalistic integrity if I asked him to go take a look, maybe get some pictures?"

"Not if he gets a story in the long run," I commented.

Reb was tickled to go back to Jordan Run, especially when we told him that a genuine radical might be in residence. I don't know what story he spun, but he returned with four rolls of film, three of which he shipped off to the *Look* lab in New York. The last he developed in the little darkroom he'd set up in his basement.

"I shot these last 15 exposures at their house," he said proudly. "Fortunately, Charlie Brown knows enough about photography to realize we shoot a lot of film. Here's the contact sheet, and I made some 5x7s of these four."

"Clear as crystal!" I exclaimed. "Great shots. Benjo, can you send these out to AIC to see if we can get identification on the other two guys?"

"Not a problem," he said. "God, I don't think I would've recognized Gillian, though."

Gil's appearance was altered with a very short haircut and her thick eyebrows had been plucked. She wore granny glasses. The giveaway was the leotard top she wore beneath her overalls.

"I'd recognize that leotard anywhere," I said.

Reb looked at the prints. "They called her 'Heather,' and when she spoke, I could detect a definite accent."

"Oh, it's our girl, all right," Benjo said, giving me a serious stare. "Our girl."

— 55 —

Spring Break Follies

As spring break drew closer, everyone's discussion turned toward vacation destinations. For the Fine Arts faculty and friends, Culden and Reb decided it for us by announcing that their second, or *faux,* wedding would be in Zanesville.

"Well, crap," groused Livvy. "I was really looking forward to Venice."

"Oh, Liv, you'll love Zanesville," Culden said. "It has a Y-Bridge that you'll find just as fascinating as the Grand Canal."

Livinda gave Culden a skeptical look.

The wedding went smoothly, even though Culden's little sister spilled the beans about the earlier wedding in Crystal Cave. Mrs. Ellis didn't seem to care, so long as her four-attendant, dresses-and-tuxes, and country-club-reception affair went without a hitch.

Little R.T. was a perfect ring-bearer, and Culden's niece captured the audience with her flower petal distribution, which took almost five minutes to get her down the aisle.

With Culden and Reb married properly and twice over, we arrived back in Seneca with three days to go before classes resumed.

When I returned to Five's Five, I found wet tire tracks on the slope up from the ford but no car in the yard or shed. On the back porch, a few muddy footprints were still damp. I'd had visitors, and not very long ago.

I retrieved the key and opened the back door. Nothing seemed missing or disturbed. In the living room, my desk was slightly messed up, but I couldn't recall exactly how I'd left it—until I realized that Sibley's little notebook was jammed into the desk bookshelf in the wrong place.

Opening it, I found the page that described the relationship of Sibley's Cave and the Lazarus Pit had been torn out. I immediately called Benjo. He and Cyndy showed up twenty minutes later.

We studied the footprints on the back porch, found some more in the mud, and determined two people had been there. The smaller foot had to belong to a woman.

"It had to be Gillian," I said. "She's the only one besides Liv that knows where I hide the key."

"That ties in with something I learned yesterday," Benjo said. "Gary Criswell—the guy at the Piton Climb Shop? I visited him about a month ago and asked him to call me if he had any interesting customers. He called and said Gillian was there two days ago with another guy that sounds like Charlie Brown. They bought climbing gear, lamps, and caving suits for her and four men, judging from the size of the suits."

"How did he know it was Gillian?" Cyndy asked.

I laughed. "Oh, he'd remember Gillian, all right. The first time we went, she was practically naked."

• • •

Jim Gillespie appeared at the first Figure Drawing class miserable with a fierce sunburn. So did Marilyn Kretzman.

"Fort Lauderdale?" I asked her. Marilyn beamed, and undid two blouse buttons to display the red skin down into her cleavage.

"It'll be a tan in a few days," she said.

"Did you run into Jim down there?" I asked. Marilyn's red face got even redder.

"Well, er," she stammered. "Yeah, we kind of went down in his car. A couple of sorority sisters also."

Blondie began posing and, after the first break, seemed to avoid looking at Gillespie's sketch although she wandered the rest of the studio. During the break, Jim came up, brandishing his sketchbook.

"How'd you like Fort Lauderdale, Jim?" I asked him. He threw me a big shiteating grin.

"Great, Professor Lowrey. Just great. Wanna see some of my pictures?" I nodded and he immediately fanned open the sketchbook.

The first three pages were Petty girl sketches of the girl the others called 'the nun,' Marilyn Kretzman. Except she didn't have a towel or anything else draping her little body and she definitely was not a nun. They were followed by nude studies of Marilyn's sorority sisters.

"Looks as if you've broadened your model spectrum a little bit," I commented.

"Oh, yeah, Professor," he grinned again. "And guess what? I'm not a virgin anymore."

• • •

Cyndy and I were in my office checking the after-vacation rolls for Art Appreciation classes when the door opened and Blondie peeked in. She then slid through and closed the door tightly. "I guess you'd both be interested," she said softly. "Doper Doug is back from wherever he was."

"Oh! And are you back *with* him?" Cyndy asked archly.

"No. I've had enough of that scene," Blondie said. "I just saw him unloading boxes of clay at the store last night. Charlie Brown and one of his buddies were helping him."

"Clay?" I asked. "Isn't Doug still up on the mountain, in the yurt? Doesn't he dig his own clay?"

"Clay?" Cyndy queried. "He couldn't afford a pound of clay, much less boxes."

"Well, that's what they said they were. They were bricks of clay, each one wrapped in paper."

• • •

Our weekend social group had grown to eight with the addition of Benjo and Cyndy. On a Saturday night, we were sitting around a big table in Cazzo's, Petersburg's best pizza joint. Seven of us were sitting back with full tummies watching Bear polish off the remaining slices.

"I got a call from Bubby Bristo this morning," Livvy announced. "He said the ramp shoots are about four inches high in his meadow."

"Whash a ramp?" Bear mumbled through a mouthful of pizza.

"They call 'em wild onions in Ohio," I said, "only these are kind of different. They're delicious."

"I'd like to get a crowd together tomorrow and go up to Braddock's Bald," Liv said. "Then we can have a big ramp feed at the farm. You'll all get to meet my mother, who's home from France, and Dad loves ramps. It'll be fun."

• • •

358

I picked up Hoopie and his date, Hope Massingale; Jaylene and her friend, Irma; and Benjo and Cyndy at noon on Sunday and we drove to Liv's house. She had the Duerhoffs and the Wests in her Jeepster. We drove out the country lane to Braddock Branch.

For everyone but me, it was the first visit to the farm. Green and red buds were nearly bursting on the trees and the forest floor was covered with bright green plants. Everyone seemed impressed with the watercress farm. Livvy removed her shoes and waded in to weed out last year's plants to give the new perennials room to grow.

We were joined by two more carloads of young faculty families for a lunch of hot dogs and beer, then set out up the mountain. The four cars labored up the narrow lane. We finally pulled into a clearing and Livvy got out.

"We'll have to four-wheel from here," she announced. "Five and I will take our loads up to the Bald and come back for you folks. It's only about a quarter mile so it'll be quick."

My memory of the previous visit was of Esopus pulling the tiny sleigh over a smooth forest lane. This four-wheel-drive trip was a challenge. The lane was basically a creek bed and we slipped and slid up the steep grade. At one point, a forty-foot drop encroached on the edge of the road, and everyone leaned toward the inside of the hill.

We unloaded our passengers. From her Jeepster, Liv produced cloth sacks and two bushel baskets. The trip down and back didn't seem as dangerous, and soon we had a full troop of ramp hunters standing at the edge of the meadow. Livvy led us a few yards along the fringe of woods, then stopped and pointed to a thin, bright green shoot.

"That's a ramp," she said, "and just about good eating size. When you pick them, get right down to the ground and ease 'em out of the ground. Otherwise, the greens will snap off just like a green onion." She deftly eased the ramp out of the ground and passed it around.

"Oh my gosh," Paige exclaimed, "that sucker is strong. Bear!"

She looked aghast as Bear peeled off an outer layer of tissue from the bulb and popped the ramp into his mouth.

"Goddam, I'll tell the world it's strong," he wheezed. Everyone laughed as he chewed with exaggerated expressions. "Needs salt."

It wasn't long before everyone had eaten a raw ramp out of self defense. Livvy had even brought a saltshaker. As we moved down the meadow, we found places where the thin green shoots were as thick as new grass. The pervading smell of onion was pleasant, but still powerful. Liv encouraged us to pick as many as we could since new ramps would be springing up within the week.

"And you'll soon know about mature ramps," she warned seriously.

• • •

That evening, Braddock Branch farm had an invisible cloud of *eau de* ramp hovering over it. Liv was a whirlwind in the kitchen, breading ramp bulbs and popping them into deep fat, snipping the green shoots for salad, creating the ramp soup that I had enjoyed so much last fall.

Busby Ferris was a genial host, presiding over the bar and a martini pitcher with the élan of someone who had just brought his prize wife home from Paris. And Louise Ferris *was* a prize, a mature replica of her daughter and in love with the French city.

"Livinda took me to your gallery last summer," she told me, "and I make a point of returning once a month."

She poked a trim finger into my shoulder. "I think you should know I suspected you and Livinda were seeing *a lot of each other* after I saw the first nudes of her." She smiled slyly. "And of course, now that I'm home and have seen the library, my suspicions are confirmed. And… I approve."

Busby turned over the bartending duties to Bear and moved to the flagstone patio, where an outdoor grill was built into the wall. He poked the glowing bed of coals, then moved to the kitchen pass-through and retrieved a platter of steaks.

Louise Ferris clapped her hands and called, "If anyone doesn't like a steak medium rare, I'd advise you to tell Bus right now."

The steaks were served with a layer of sautéed ramps and were delicious. The soup was delicious. The salad was delicious. And we left Braddock Branch stinking of ramps.

— 56 —

Return of the Hippies

Smoking a pre-pose cigarette, Blondie lounged in her robe and made a face. "Christ, Professor. I don't know how to tell you this, but…" she paused, "well, it's your breath."

"Blondie, I am sorry but it's ramp season, and I'm told my breath will improve in three or four days."

"Ramps? You mean those little green onions growing in the woods?"

"Yep! Those are ramps, and they're delicious. I've got some in my office. You're welcome to try one. There should be lots along Laurel Run."

After the first pose, Blondie followed me to my office. I handed her a ramp and saltshaker and she bit into it tentatively.

"Hmm. This *is* good. Better than green onion." She chewed the vegetable. "And your breath doesn't smell half as bad now," she giggled. "By the way, I think I may have a male model for you if you're still looking." I nodded yes.

"His name is Wayne Smead and he's pretty straight, for a hippie. From Minnesota. Lived in the woods all winter."

"Have him come in. I'll be glad to talk to him."

Wayne Smead was thin but well-built, and had a head of snow-white hair and a short beard to match. He wore jeans and a well-used Pendleton shirt with the sleeves rolled up. Even from across the desk, I could detect the slight odor of sweat and wood smoke. I outlined the nature of the model's job and proposed the same shower/three dollars an hour deal that Blondie got.

On Friday morning, Wayne appeared, with Blondie at his side. "I thought I'd come along just to make sure he's OK with this shit," she announced. I showed him a locker in the faculty men's restroom, a robe, and left him to shower.

Blondie settled on a taboret and lit up a Chesterfield. "We got another dozen or so people moving in," she announced, "most along Laurel Run. They've taken over last year's shacks and just settled in."

"Any more of Charlie Brown's friends show up?" I asked.

"Not that I can tell. A lot of kids from the campus are coming out for meetings... that Mole People bunch. You want me to try to join up?"

"No. Just keep hanging around and keep your ears open."

• • •

The class assembled. Most of them looked puzzled to see Blondie in clothes, but no one said a word.

"OK, people. By now I think you are pretty familiar with Blondie, her lines and curves." A small chuckle. "As I told you at the beginning of the semester, we're going to have a male model... today." Wayne peeked around the door in the back of the room.

"His name is Wayne, and the same ground rules will apply, as to your conduct with him. Wayne has never modeled before and I'll appreciate your patience with him."

I motioned Wayne forward, and he mounted the posing pedestal with a stricken look.

"OK, Wayne, just take a seat, be comfortable and remove the robe," I asked.

He sat. Slowly he untied the belt of the robe and shrugged it off his shoulders. The room was silent.

"Three-minute drill," I announced. The students bent over their newsprint pads, but stopped sketching as they looked up at the new model. His flaccid member was jerking to attention. "OK, smoke 'em if you got 'em," I called. "We'll take a few minutes." Wayne pulled the robe back on and hastily tied the belt.

"You OK, Wayne?" I asked softly.

"God, Professor Lowrey, I'm sort of embarrassed. I didn't think this would happen." He looked sheepish. "If you'll just give me five minutes, I'll be ready to go, I think."

"Naw, give *me* five minutes," Blondie nudged him. "I've got just *the cure* for what ails you."

• • •

Fat buds turned to tiny leaves in the course of a few warm days, and suddenly the woods were a hazy gray-green. In the late afternoon, the mountains rolled away in the west, each ridge a slightly lighter shade of gray.

Classroom windows were flung open and small lecture courses moved to the green lawn of Eden Fields, beneath the new shade of trees. I inwardly cursed my class offerings, chained to drawing benches as they were.

Butterfly blouses and short shorts reappeared. Hoopie began taking between-period smoke breaks with every class change.

And the hippies reappeared. As could be expected, there weren't many familiar faces, and the few I thought I recognized had changed. They congregated on Eden Fields in the late afternoon to play frisbee with each other and a few dogs, to strum guitars, or generally shoot the breeze.

And hippie dress again became the garb of Seneca students. Although she didn't like it, Livvy had to enforce student identification for a local rock band concert. A crowd of hippies stood outside and chanted their disapproval, nearly drowning out the performing band.

• • •

On a late-April Friday, posters went up all over campus for a Free Speech demonstration on Eden Fields the next day. The featured speaker was billed as Madalyn Murray O'Hair, the famous atheist. President Skinner asked Livvy to have extra security on hand.

I joined faculty and administration members on the Davis steps. Below us, Eden Fields was filled with small knots of students and hippies, lounging on blankets. The first speaker got my attention, Benjo's too. Linus Friedman took the bullhorn and harangued the crowd about First Amendment rights, especially free speech. We listened as Friedman—otherwise known as 'Charlie Brown'—aimed the speech toward us.

"Just try to curb our speech," his amplified voice echoed across the plaza, "and you'll see blood running down the Old Main steps."

"That should be colorful," Dean Minteer observed.

Murray O'Hair was scheduled to speak at noon, so by half-past, hunger was of more concern than free speech. The crowd was beginning to thin when the far-off keen of a siren was heard.

"She's got a police escort?" Livvy asked. The siren got louder and then a black van with flashing lights and a siren wailing pulled into the Davis courtyard. A self-important student wearing an armband waved the van on and it moved slowly across Eden Fields to the speaker's platform.

"Get the hell of our grass," S.G. Caulfield muttered.

Madalyn resembled a gray bulldog. In her forties, she wore a long gray dress and sensible shoes. She took the bullhorn from Charlie Brown and, without introduction, began to speak.

"Hello, Seneca University free-thinkers," her growly voice echoed from the bullhorn. "At least I hope your minds haven't been cluttered with academic shit to the point where you really think there's a God. As some of you might be aware, the Supreme Court of the United States voted eight to one to allow my son to go to public schools without being forced to pray or listen to so-called Bible readings." There was a smattering of applause. "But there are so many more battles to be won," O'Hair's voice boomed. "And free speech is one of them. Who is to say that I cannot say anything I wish from this platform? Who?" Again, scattered applause, a few cheers. "Fuck them!" she shouted. "How many of you have ever said *fuck* out loud? Here's your chance! Say it! Say FUCK!"

Delighted at this opportunity, the audience chanted "fuck, fuck, Fuck, Fuck, FUCK!"

• • •

It was that same April that my old girlfriend, Darcy Robinette, returned from her famous visit to Hanoi and became a nexus of dispute—cheered by the antiwar crowd—despised by the Hawks. She embarked on a nationwide speaking tour. Darcy had appeared in two awful movies, so the press made a big thing of the 'famous actress' visiting the enemy. Actually, she was far more famous as a fashion model. While in Vietnam, she had posed for *Paris Match* in several military-oriented fashion spreads.

Antiwar protest groups immediately launched her on a speaking tour of college campuses. In my gut, I felt doomed. Although it had not been announced, it seemed inevitable that Darcy would visit the mountains of West Virginia on her way east.

— 57 —

Mayday!

When the campus calendar for May appeared, the first day of the month was marked as 'No Classes: May Day.' "What's this May Day stuff?" I asked Culden. "We're already behind by two days because of snow."

"It's an old Seneca tradition," she replied. "One of the few genuine traditions this institution can claim. Since way back at the end of the Civil War, students have celebrated springtime by having a May Day event. For the last sixty years, it's become a big deal. Bigger than OU's prom, even."

"OK, so what goes on?"

"Well, it kind of *is* Seneca's prom. I don't know enough about it. We should ask Livvy."

• • •

"Oh, you're going to adore May Day," Liv said. "It's one of the neatest things that happen here."

"OK," I said. "Why am I going to love it?"

"Well, this isn't a requirement, but it's very romantic. Lots of people go to the woods in the dark hours before dawn to gather flowers and greenery." She grinned. "There are lots of nice traditions involved. It's an offshoot of pagan ceremonies and back when it started here, some of the Congregational scholars frowned upon it."

"How come?" Culden asked. "It seems fairly tame to me."

"Well, May Day celebrates the coming of spring and… well, fecundity. The pagans and Romans made a fertility rite of it. The original Maypoles were very phallic. Now, it's more of a competition and celebration. Dorms and the Greek houses all have their May Queen or King candidates, and their dance teams must compete in three traditional dances. Finally, the winning men's team partners with the May Queen candidates in a traditional dance that ends with the choosing of the May Queen."

"Do we have to wear tights or anything like that?" I asked, skeptical.

"No. but the groups and queen candidates spend a lot of time on their costumes. You'll see."

• • •

As I closed my eyes, I was glad tomorrow was a holiday. In April it had become more and more difficult to teach college students. Their attention spans narrowed. Classroom windows were open to let in fresh air and the distracting sounds of students who were not in class.

Academic progress was apparent. Their drawings were better. The paintings demonstrated skills mastered. Only in the Art Appreciation lectures did springtime have an effect. Attendance was about the same, and I turned a blind eye upon students sitting in familiar seats with totally unfamiliar faces. After all, we had pulled the same stunts at OU years ago.

James Patterson

My night ended with a tapping on the door that led to the studio. I quickly went to the bathroom and washed my face. With half-opened eyes, I cracked the door open and saw a small straw basket, full of flowers and ferns.

A giggle attracted my attention to the studio bridge. At the corner of the studio, Livinda Ferris watched, grinning. She wore a diaphanous white dress that came down to her ankles. Her feet were bare.

"Happy May Day, Five," she said, then turned and ran around the studio.

I picked up the basket and walked across the bridge, following her. As I rounded the studio, I got a glimpse of the white dress dancing into the woods. She was running.

So I chased her. After all, it *was* a holiday.

She ran into a clearing filled with spring ferns, and fell dramatically. By the time I huffed into the clearing, she was lying on her back, a vision in a white gown, with bright green baby ferns surrounding her.

"Happy May Day, Livvy. Now what do I do?"

"Well, you can start by kissing me."

• • •

Livvy pulled the thin gown over us to keep the early morning chill away from our bed of ferns. She rolled on top of me and ran a finger down the bridge of my nose, across my mouth and onto my chest.

"Now you know one of the most important May Day traditions," she said with a smile in her voice.

"You mean people all over Grant County are lying with each other in the woods?"

"Oh, no. It's the tradition to deliver a May basket to your one true love. What comes after is individual choice."

"And I am your one true love?"

"Oh, yes. Don't you know that by now?"

"And Livvy, you are my one true love as well," I whispered, pulling her to me.

• • •

From the wake-up call to all that followed, I wasn't exactly ready for Seneca's May Day celebration. At an hour before noon, the campus was packed with spectators, most of whom had brought their own lawn chairs. Our chairs had staked out our space overlooking Eden Fields and now we—the Wests, the Duerhoffs, Cyndy and Benjo, and Livvy and I—stood at the top of the Old Main steps. Livinda wore a long black skirt and a matching blouse with long sleeves.

Spectators filled the steps and lined the serpentine bike path. As the Old Main clock began chiming eleven, what looked like a walking tree emerged from a small group at the bottom of the hill. A reed quintet struck up what sounded like an English folk tune.

"That's Jack O'Green, the symbol of May Day. No one knows who he is except for the committee, that knot of students down there," Liv told us. "He'll lead the procession and ultimately crown the May Queen."

Jack O'Green was covered with vines and blossoms. He stood facing the south and the residences across the street. Then came a long string of young women, wearing pink gowns and carrying a long bright-red ribbon. All were barefoot.

"This is Delta Gamma," Liv announced. "They won last year's competition, so they're first in the procession."

Other groups appeared, each taking its turn to enter the procession. The sororities and women's dorms all wore long gowns of different pastel colors and each group marched linked by a long brightly-colored ribbon across their right

James Patterson

shoulders. In each women's group, a girl with a white gown was the last in line. The May Queen candidates, Liv told us.

The groups followed Jack O'Green up the serpentine. As they grew closer, we could hear the tinkle of bells tied to their ankles. After the last group of women joined the procession, louder bells announced the entry of the men's groups. Each group was dressed all in white and carried a long ribbon over their shoulders. Bells on ankles and wrists musically accompanied their progress.

Jack O'Green passed us, and I could see that his vegetation disguise was attached to a robe and hood of what looked like burlap.

As the DGs passed, the scantiness of their costumes was apparent. Physical attributes were hinted at and the undergarments of the shyer girls were obvious. We scurried through the arch and went quickly to our seats.

"It's the finest Maypole I've ever seen," Liv declared. "It's hollow on the inside so the rope that raises the ribbon ring never interferes with the dances. It's also fifty feet high." The white Maypole was the focus of attention in the center of Eden Fields, which was now surrounded by the colorful groups, sitting on the ground.

Even the hippie community was present, sitting in a more colorful knot behind the men's groups. As each group entered the circle, a page announced them and Jack O'Green led them to their seating area.

"I'll see you in a few minutes," Liv said as she slipped off her shoes and got to her feet. The page announced the first event, a demonstration dance featuring past May Queens and faculty members. With mock ceremony, Liv and three other black-clad women bowed to four men all in white. They all attached ribbons to the Maypole ring and then bowed again as the ring was raised to the top by the man we learned would be the interlocutor. He wore an all-green suit topped by a green derby.

Each dancer grabbed a ribbon, black for men, white for women, as the quintet struck up a lively air. Dancing intricate steps, and bobbing and weaving, the eight dancers swirled around the pole, their ribbons forming a pattern. The dance was done in less than a minute, with all eight dancers holding hands at the bottom of the pole. A breathless Liv returned to her seat. I gave her a hug and everyone applauded.

"That one's called The Harlequin," she said, "and it's a real bitch to do without a lot of rehearsal, which we haven't had."

"And you were once a May Queen. I'm impressed," I said. She hushed us as the first women's team approached the pole. "Don't bother me now," she added. "I've got work to do." She produced a clipboard and forms.

The interlocutor announced them as Alpha Gamma Delta. The eight Alpha Gams attached four dark blue and four gold ribbons to the pole and then did the familiar curtsies to each other as the ring was raised.

The interlocutor then announced, "Alpha Gamma Delta... will now perform The Chain." The quintet began to play, slower than for the demonstration dance, and the girls in their pastel blue gowns started into an intricate step.

"Each group has to be ready to perform any of four required dances," Liv told us in hushed tones. "They'll be judged on the grace of their movements, the accuracy of their steps, and the pattern on the pole. If a ribbon should break, that will disqualify the team."

The slower, intricate dance took nearly five minutes to complete, and the girls got a huge round of applause.

A total of nine Greek groups and five dormitories competed for more than three hours. The competition was broken up by skits performed by other members of each group. All of the skits were based on the themes of spring and fertility, and some were hilariously raunchy. The men's groups performed what Liv described as Morris Dances, twirling rapidly with their long ribbons held to their shoulders. Some of the Morris Dancers even managed a simple tune with the bells attached to their arms and legs.

After each performance, a page would hurry over and take Livvy's judgment form away. Finally, the competition was finished and a page rushed a scroll to the interlocutor. The quintet blew a small fanfare and the interlocutor unrolled the scroll.

"The winner of the Morris Dance competition is…" a long pause… "the men of Phi Delta Theta." The Phi Delts jumped up and celebrated while the crowd responded with catcalls and whistles.

"The Phi Delts will be labeled as pansies for the rest of the year," Liv laughed. "That's one of the traditions."

The page ran up with another scroll and the interlocutor repeated the ceremony.

"Winners of the 1968 Maypole dance competition…" pause… "the ladies of Delta Delta Delta." Great cheers and hugs from the Tri Delts as the rest of the women's groups applauded politely.

The finale was the presentation of the May Queen candidates and their performance of *The Queen's Dance.* Nine beautiful girls all in white attached their longer white ribbons to the ring, then gracefully walked away from the pole until the ribbons were almost taut. As the interlocutor raised the ring, the girls were drawn back toward the pole. A single green ribbon lay dormant along the length of the Maypole.

The music began and the women started a stately dance that had each of them weaving inside and out as they circled. Slowly their white ribbons formed an intricate pattern on the Maypole, covering the green ribbon. During the dance, each girl came to the outside and performed a graceful curtsy to the crowd, much to the partisan applause of the groups.

Finally, *The Queen's Dance* finished with each girl on one knee, her head bowed toward the Maypole. Livvy's judgment slip was grabbed by a page and hurried over to the judges' stand. Tension grew as the judges' scores were totaled. Finally, the interlocutor took a slip of paper over to Jack O'Green.

With a shambling grace, Jack came forward and stepped between the kneeling girls to the Maypole. He grabbed the tail of the green ribbon and gave it a vigorous pull, ripping the pattern of white ribbons from the pole to flutter down upon the girls. The quintet played a lively tune and the ponderous Jack O'Green did a lumbering dance around the pole. One circuit, two, three, and finally as his ribbon grew shorter, he settled it upon the blonde head of a kneeling girl.

Cheers and squeals erupted from the crowd and the short girl with blonde hair down to her buttocks rose to be recognized as the new Queen of the May.

• • •

As May Queen Alexis Devlin was crowned by the interlocutor and Jack, in what should have been the culminating event, the Mole People, hippies and students alike, slowly filed across Eden Fields, each carrying a sign:

You Dance While They Die. Stop The War!

Dicky Reb's photo of the protesters walking past the jubilant May Queen would later be a lead center spread in *Look*.

— 58 —

Rough Sledding With No Snow

Bear had asked me to attend his first team meeting as a sort of critic, even though the only locker room I'd ever been in belonged to the OU field hockey team. He outlined the team rules for spring practice and the basic three-week schedule.

"I've watched the films of last season's games," he told the footballers. "From what I could see, your biggest problem was a lack of attention to the task at hand—namely, practice and the actual game. In the Morris Harvey game, the punt returner was daydreaming or watching bugs—God knows what. And the ball came down and hit him on the head! Good thing he had his helmet on or he might not have graduated." Goose Fretzel, the veteran equipment manager, asked Bear what he wanted for a laundry schedule.

"When they get filthy, we'll wash," he responded, referring to the practice uniforms.

"But Coach Bruce wanted the players to have a clean uniform every other day."

"And Coach Bruce is selling cars in Sistersville," The Bear roared. "I'm Coach Duerhoff, and my team will play in the dirt and mud. That's the nature of the game."

But Fretzel wasn't to be deterred. "Well, we've got to order game helmets by next week or they won't be ready for the season."

Bear's eyebrows imitated croquet hoops. "They're *wearing* their game helmets! And if they're scarred and messed up, it'll look like they play tough football." Fretzel retreated as Bear turned to me and said under his breath, "Even if they don't."

• • •

"On three! Hut, hut, hut." On the third *hut*, two beefy linemen bounded out of their stance and attacked the blocking sled where Coach Bear Duerhoff held on. The sled budged slightly, then the right side lineman lost his footing and slipped off the pad. This resulted in a wild circle ride for Bear and the sled.

"Come on, Greski, one more time," Bear urged the fallen football player. Greski looked at the mud on his cleats, then slowly trudged back to the stance position.

By the third day of spring practice, Bear's Warriors had learned the difference between coaches. Coach Duerhoff didn't care about runs up and down the helix. "Football is played on a flat surface," he told his players. "If you deserve a conditioning run, you'll do it with wind sprints."

• • •

The first week of spring practice culminated in a scrimmage and only three of the 52 players who turned out had left the team.

Bear started Joe Freeman, a junior who would have been Art Bruce's quarterback the next season. Freeman fumbled once, was sacked twice, and threw an interception in the first two dozen plays.

"OK, Joe, take a knee. Nixon, get in the huddle and let's see what you can do with 'em," Bear called.

The young black kid, who should've still been in a high school study hall, buckled his helmet and ran onto the field. On his first play, he dropped the ball on a handoff. The second play was another fumble. Bear turned and scanned his sideline players as if he'd picked the incorrect Monty Nixon.

Nixon took the next snap, threw a terrific play fake into the line and scampered around end and half the field for a score. The offensive team cheered.

"Good job, Nixon," Bear said. "Just don't forget—you made that run *against* Seneca U."

• • •

Seneca fielded 55 players for the Scarlet-Gold game that signaled the end of spring practice. Six students had come out for the team after watching the first scrimmage.

Of the thirty-some offensive players, six stayed on the field to play defense. One of them was Monty Nixon, who had solidified his job as starting quarterback but went in at safety on passing downs.

Our gang of eight sat in the president's seats to watch the action on the field. Paige joined us with the news that Evermont Nixon had convinced four top players from the Wheeling area to join him at Seneca.

Nixon passed for five touchdowns, ran for another pair, and led the Scarlet team to a 49-21 victory. But the Gold team, composed of first-string defense, held the Scarlets on three goal-line stands, made two interceptions, and recovered a fumble.

• • •

"You ought to feel pretty good, Coach," President Frank Skinner told The Bear. "That's the most activity we've seen in that stadium in a couple of years."

Bear was the guest of honor at the annual President's Scarlet and Gold cocktail party. Skinner's house was on the other side of the ridge from Livvy's, and the patio overlooked Piper Stadium. Faculty and alumni milled around to congratulate Bear and speculate on next season.

Bear was reluctant to talk much about his recruiting class, as the real proof was still months away. But he fielded compliments with grace and never let his left arm leave the shoulder of a beaming Paige.

The art gang left early and walked over to Livvy's house. "Bear said he and Paige would join us as soon as the party is over. I told him I'd save a steak or two for him," Livvy said.

• • •

It was nearly midnight, and only the Duerhoffs, Livvy, and I remained, our feet on the patio wall. "I can't believe that Nixon kid," Paige said. "Can someone make All-American from a school this size?"

"Or win the Heisman?" I added.

"Four years is a long time," Bear said philosophically. "A lot can happen in four years. But he does have the tools!"

"And you were absolutely right about his smarts," Liv said. "He's pulling a 3.7 going into finals."

As the Duerhoffs got up to leave, our attention was drawn to the highway below. A long string of lights appeared down the valley and approached the town. We could hear the drone of heavy engines. As the first of the trucks passed beneath a streetlight, I ran to the phone and called Benjo.

"Somebody count them for me," I yelled out to the patio.

"Get your ass out of bed," I gasped, "and down on the main drag. The Army's got a convoy going through town."

"Where are you?" he asked.

"I'm still at Livvy's. I'll take her MG and pick you up in about six minutes if I can get through the convoy."

Liv pouted that she couldn't come, but handed me the keys to her MG. I zipped the little roadster through a fifty-yard gap in the convoy, then drove the back streets to the Linger Longer. Benjo jumped into the MG.

"Should we try to crash the convoy?" I asked. "They don't have road guards out."

"Naw," Benjo responded. "They're heading south and that means the probable destination is Lazarus. Let's just wait till they pass and follow along… surreptitiously."

"Livvy counted 15 trucks when I left. She said there were two Jeeps after the fifteenth truck, then more trucks coming up the road."

A pair of jeeps equipped with mounted machine guns rolled by. We sat as five more trucks went by. Finally, a gap, which was then filled with another pair of armed jeeps.

"Holy shit!" Benjo exclaimed. "I've never seen so many deuce-and-a-halfs before, not even in 'Nam."

We gave the convoy five minutes, then set out down route 55. In less than two miles we saw the taillights of the convoy blinking on the road below.

"They didn't turn at County 28," I said. "They're going further south."

"Yeah, but they've slowed to almost a crawl. That means they're turning somewhere," Benjo responded.

"Should we take County 28?"

"No," he said. "Pull over, and let's give them plenty of time to get off the highway. Then we'll mosey on down there and see if we can find where they turned."

• • •

Twenty minutes later, we saw a set of flares and a flashlight. I approached slowly as the MP waved us around a deuce-and-a-half along the roadside.

"Any problems, soldier?" I asked politely.

"No, sir," the young MP replied, "just a flat. We'll have it fixed in a minute."

As we drove on, Benjo asked, "Did you see the markings on that truck's tailgate?"

"Yeah, I did. CBR. Chemical, Biological, Radiological."

We continued down the highway, and soon we were in Seneca Rocks.

"Sonofabtich," Benjo said. "Not a sign of a turnoff anywhere. And we would've caught them if they'd come through here. Turn around, and let's take a better look on the way back."

On the way north, we didn't see any sign of the convoy, not even the crippled truck.

"Since that deuce-and-a-half with the flat tire didn't come past us, it had to have turned off somewhere. Should we go up County 28 and take a look?"

"Nope. I don't want to be goin' up that road in a red MG at this time of night. Let's go home."

I pulled Liv's MG into the garage, went upstairs and kissed her on the forehead, then drove my Jeepster back to Five's Five. Livvy never woke up.

— 59 —

Reaching the Boiling Point

Early the next day, Benjo flew to Washington to report to Colonel Kinnard. I studied a topo map that included Skidmore Mountain and found a road that wound its way up the grade from the south. But we had seen no turnoff the night before.

I called Liv and asked her to pick me up in her Jeepster. We then drove south again toward Seneca Rocks, just a sightseeing couple on a Sunday morning. We traveled slowly and I peered at every bush and rock on the right side of the road. Just like earlier that morning... nothing!

While we ate lunch at the Rocks View Café, an Army deuce-and-a-half rolled by, heading south. Its canvas was stowed and the bare roof racks exposed an empty bed. The truck had no markings except the U.S. Army and serial number stencils on the doors.

"Have there been many Army trucks like that coming by?" I asked our waitress.

"Oh, yeah. All morning. Must be some reserve unit going somewhere," she answered.

Two more trucks came by as we finished our lunch. We got back in the Jeepster and headed north. As we came to a curve in the highway, another truck passed us heading south. Rounding the curve, I caught a glimpse of an olive drab figure moving into the woods on our right.

"Slow down, Liv," I ordered. "Did you see that soldier? Drive pretty slow past where he went into the woods."

As we passed the place I'd last seen the soldier, I got a fleeting glimpse of a face peering out and a section of chain link fence or gate.

"Of course. What dumbasses we were! Not you—Benjo and I. They turned left instead of right."

"Check the road right here, Five. It looks as if it's been watered and scrubbed. It hasn't rained for several days."

"OK," I said, "let's go home."

• • •

On Tuesday morning, a naked Blondie gave me a nod from the posing platform. She'd been in the pose for about five minutes, so I called a break. She put on her robe and headed for the hallway, lighting a Chesterfield.

"Want one?" She offered the pack to me. I took a cigarette and let Blondie light it for me.

"I thought I'd better tell you," she said after a couple of perfect smoke rings. "All the shacks on Laurel Run are full and they're building some new ones. They've also got some school buses parked in the meadow. I can't figure it out. I like this place OK but it's not really a paradise… no coffee shops, no bookstores, no clubs."

"Do you think something's up?" I asked her.

"Yes, I do. I think you're going to be on the shitty end of some demonstrations."

• • •

I was painting in my studio when I heard a car cross the ford. Walking across the bridge, I heard the door slam and by the time I got downstairs, Benjo was opening a beer from the fridge.

"So, how was DC?" I asked.

"Very interesting. Interesting, indeed," he said. "We stumbled onto something that the Army doesn't want known."

"Like three dozen trucks rolling into the West Virginia hills at midnight?"

"Big movement. Edgewood Arsenal," he muttered. "They need more room for nukes there, so they've moved out a lot of old inventory. Just chemicals, no critters or nukes."

"What kind of chemicals?"

"You name it. Sarin, Phosgene, even World-War-I-vintage mustard gas."

"And they're putting it in Lazarus?" I asked incredulously.

"Temporarily," he responded. "They're building a whole CBR storage facility somewhere deeper in the mountains."

I told him how Liv and I had found the secret turnoff to Skidmore Mountain.

"They must have built a tunnel under the road. That was pretty poor security if the road guard let you see him."

"So what do we do?" I asked.

"My orders say do nothing, be observant."

"Blondie says the hippie community is really growing. New shacks. Buses parked in the meadow."

Benjo raised his eyebrows. "Why here? This isn't Haight-Ashbury."

"Blondie raised the same point. She thinks something is brewing. Demonstrations, perhaps?"

• • •

Whatever was brewing, a lot of people were having fun that May. The cut of the butterfly blouses got deeper and deeper. Coeds started appearing in class wearing virtually transparent blouses with no underpinnings. The hippies challenged the Delta Gams to a touch football game… in the nude. When it became obvious that such a spectacle couldn't be held on the practice field, the venue was changed to Jordan Run Meadow.

More people attended that game than had attended any Warriors game the previous season.

Streaking was a fad for a couple of weeks. Members of both sexes ran across Eden Fields, through classrooms and into the residential area. It came to a rapid end when one streaker got his equipment tangled in a fence he was trying to jump and ended up in the Petersburg hospital.

Hippies and student protesters held a sit-in demonstration to block the library steps one Saturday morning. No one paid much attention and the few serious students entered the library by the back door.

Every day at noon, Eden Fields was packed. The crowd was a hodgepodge of student radicals, hippies, straight students, faculty and staff, and the just plain curious.

"It reminds me of Speaker's Corner in London," Livvy observed, "except the speakers there are generally a lot brighter and certainly more polite."

Rumors began circulating about the coming appearance of Darcy Robinette, "Hanoi Darcy" as some called her. The phenomenon of a girl speaker appearing in Eden Fields, and everyone identifying her as Darcy, continued to grow. To my relief, none of these girls was the real thing.

"I think it will be fun if the little bitch shows up," Culden said one evening, as the eight of us ate hot dogs on the Wests' front porch. "Just to see old Five squirm," she added.

"Culden, you have no reason to call her a bitch," I argued. "She never did anything to you."

"Except model for you and ace me out of Best in Show my senior year," she growled. "And walked out on you. I think she's selfish and hungry for all the attention she can get."

Liv snuggled up to me and whispered, "It'll certainly be interesting if she does come, don't you think?"

• • •

Then, one Thursday morning, I went to Canby for my 11 a.m. Art Appreciation class and found just a handful of seats occupied. When the class bell rang and no one else entered the nearly empty hall, I dismissed the grateful class. Culden walked in just as I was ready to leave.

"She's here," Culden announced. "Hurry, or you'll miss what I'm sure will be an enlightening speech."

We stood on the Canby steps, overlooking the biggest throng I'd ever seen in Eden Fields. Instead of a bullhorn, Charlie Brown was haranguing the crowd through a genuine microphone and speaker system. I scanned the crowd around the speaker's platform but recognized only the familiar figure of Gillian McDearmid, standing by a black van.

As Linus Friedman ranted on, the restless crowd began to chant, "Darcy, Darcy, Darcy." The sound guy, in an attempt to overpower the crowd's chants, finally produced a terrifying shriek of feedback and Friedman threw up his hands. The crowd whistled and cheered. Charlie Brown motioned for quiet.

"OK, people, it's obvious who you want to hear. So I'm proud to present one of the few Hollywood personalities brave enough to take a stand on the Vietnam War... and go to Vietnam to take that stand." He paused dramatically. I noticed Gillian opening the van's side door.

"Direct from Hanoi, Darcy Robinette!"

The crowd's response was divided between boos and cheers. Everyone seemed sort of good natured. Darcy stepped out of the van and followed Gillian to the platform steps. She wore black tights and a bright red turtleneck. Her glossy brown hair was pulled into a ponytail held by a long red ribbon.

"Helloooo Seneca," she shouted into the mike. "I'm glad to be here with you." More cheers and boos. "You may call me a traitor," she began, "but let me tell you, the real traitors to our country are 200 miles east of here. And that's where I'm going." Applause. "Lyndon Baines Johnson, you may not be our next president..." Darcy paused with a dramatic arm gesture, "but you are our present traitor and... SHAME ON YOU!

"People, I have seen for myself the victims of LBJ's war policy—the dismembered women and children of Hanoi. The orphans. The victims of indiscriminate bombing of a city that only wants to be the capitol of a united Vietnam." Boos and hisses. "I have seen the villains of this war—the pilots who flew these weapons of death and are now held in what the military calls the Hanoi Hilton. These men are villains, but they are also dupes."

Darcy's rant continued for another five minutes as the crowd got increasingly boisterous. A water balloon hit the speaker's stand and Darcy jumped back to dodge the cloud of red water. At least I hope it was water. More objects flew through the air. A crowd of antiwar protesters pushed back some of the people throwing stuff, and fisticuffs broke out.

Darcy turned and followed Gillian back to the van, where both got in. The van slowly pulled away from the crowd and drove behind the Faculty Club and down the hill. The police moved in.

"Impressed?" Culden asked me.

"Well, she does know how to harangue. I hope it gets her to where she wants to go."

The Seneca cops arrested two or three protesters and the crowd dispersed after the Hollywood star left the grounds. I walked with Culden back to the Fine Arts Building. The phone rang as I sat down at my desk.

"Well, I tried to get over to you," Livvy said at the other end, "but I couldn't get through that crowd. I wanted to see how you reacted to your old girlfriend."

"That's enough, Livinda," I growled. "I really don't have a lot of patience for that sort of thing."

"Was it a thrill to see her, though? I thought she was quite a good speaker, and... quite pretty."

"Darcy's a beautiful woman, Liv," I said, "but it's been more than ten years. And... I think she should stick to modeling."

Just then, my office door cracked and the smiling face of Gillian McDearmid appeared.

"Liv, someone just arrived. I'll call you later."

• • •

Gillian swung the door open and Darcy walked into my office. Gil went back into the hall and closed the door.

"Hello, Professor," she said in her 'wanna play?' voice.

"Hello, Darce. When did you get into town?"

"Oh, last night. My new friend Snow Heather told me where I could find you. Of course, I knew you were teaching here." She grinned and settled into my counselee's chair, put a black-clad leg up on my desk.

"Did you hear my speech, Five?" she asked. "What I was allowed to make of it, I mean."

"Oh, yeah. You emptied the room for my eleven o'clock class. Quite dramatic." I looked at her face carefully. Tiny wrinkles accented the edges of her eyes, giving her beauty a mischievous aspect. "Does your speech ever go longer than that?"

"Oh, sure, I spoke for almost an hour at Berkeley. Of course, there aren't so many pro-war students out there."

I got my Pall Malls and popped up a cigarette toward her. She shook her head.

"I don't do that anymore," she said. "But how are you? Do you like it here?"

I took my time lighting the Pall Mall. "I love it here, Darcy. I really enjoy teaching."

"Snow Heather said you had *The Light Show* on exhibit here. I would love to see it. Is it still here?"

"No, we closed the show at the end of April. It's back in Athens."

"Snow Heather also told me that you're really tight with the administration here. How tight?"

I laughed. "Snow Heather. That's a beautiful name for a beautiful girl. Of course, Gillian McDearmid is a pretty name for the same woman."

"Everyone should have the opportunity to be called whatever she wishes," Darcy pontificated. "How tight are you?"

"Pretty tight," I said without commitment, "why do you ask?"

"Oh, I'm working with a producer on a new film… based on Desmond Morris's *The Naked Ape.* They want to set it on a college campus. This is as pretty a campus as I've seen."

"Well, I'm not *that* tight," I lied.

"Well, could you mention it to your friend, the provost?" she asked. "As a favor to me?"

Culden's knock saved me from commitment. She peeked around the door and said "Hi" to Darcy as if she'd never been away.

"Was that Gillian I saw down the hall?" she asked.

"No! That was Snow Heather," I responded. "Not quite as prosaic as Gillian. Culden, you remember Darcy, don't you?"

"How could I forget?" Culden said pleasantly. "And if I had, your speech this morning was a reminder. How are you, Darcy?"

"Fine, Culden. It's good to see you again."

"Five, I just talked to Liv. She's on her way over. She wants to meet Darcy."

"Liv?" Darcy's eyebrows went up.

"My friend the provost," I replied.

Liv entered my office and swept over to give me a kiss on the cheek. Then she turned and offered her hand to Darcy.

"Hi, I'm Livinda Ferris and, of course, you're Darcy. That was quite a performance on Eden Fields."

Darcy looked puzzled and offered her hand tentatively.

"Eden Fields is the name of the plaza out there," I explained.

"Hello, Doctor Ferris," she finally said. "I'm pleased to meet you."

To Culden and me, Liv said, "I talked with, er... Snow Heather... in the hall. She says she's going to travel with you for a while, Darcy?"

"Yes, she's going to Charlottesville and Williamsburg with me... perhaps Richmond and even Washington."

"Well..." Liv paused, "perhaps you can convince her to take a bath now and then. And lay off the chemicals... she's going to kill herself. Her eyes look like plague blisters."

Darcy got up and quickly took her leave. A sidelong glance at me and a quiet, "Promise?" and she was gone.

— 60 —

Calm Before The Storm

"Promise what?" Livvy asked in a cold voice. "It sounds as if I arrived just in time to save your virtue."

"No, I can vouch for Five," Culden said. "I had my ear to the door the whole time."

"Oh, thanks very much, ladies. I'm glad you both have so much faith in me," I grinned.

"And my promise—" I added. "I don't know if you're ready for this, Livvy."

"Try me."

"Well, Darcy has a producer who wants to make a film—from Desmond Morris's book, *The Naked Ape?*"

"I read that thing. How in hell could you make a movie out of that crap?" Culden said.

"Well, that's not all," I continued. "He wants to film it on a college campus, and Darcy thinks Seneca would be ideal. This is, in her words, 'as pretty a campus as I've seen.'"

"No way!" Livvy stated. "Absolutely no fucking way."

Livvy lingered just inside my office door. She put her arms around me and presented a light kiss.

"Didn't you feel just a teensy bit of temptation? Of lust? That's a very pretty woman," she said.

"Liv, it was more than ten years ago," I protested. "I didn't even have feelings four years ago when I saw her in Paris."

"Ahh, Five, I believe you. But she *is* a beautiful woman and I think she could easily be cast as a temptress."

She kissed me again, then pulled away as I moved to caress her breast.

"Don't forget, we've got the Rhododendron Ball Saturday night. You will pick me up? We'll have a couple of drinks first."

• • •

I rang the bell at Livvy's house and Mary opened the door.

"Miss Livinda says for you to go right up, Professor," she said. "Tell her I'll set drinks on the patio and see her on Monday."

I climbed the stairs and tapped on the door to Liv's bedroom.

"Hey, Five, come on in. I'm a little slow getting it together tonight."

She sat before her mirrored dressing table, finishing her hair. I went over and put my hands under her arms, cupping her breasts. I kissed her on the neck, and she shivered.

"Come on, Five. *Stop* that! I'll never get ready if you don't quit… right now!" I could feel her nipples tightening under my fingertips.

I reached down and untied the belt of her silk gown. Liv stood and stepped out of the gown, clad only in a garter belt and stockings. She turned and put her arms around my neck.

"You have a choice between drinks and... me! We don't have time for both."

• • •

The Rhododendron Ball is Seneca's other big social event of the spring, a combination of senior prom and faculty dance. In my tux, I felt elegant and appropriate as Livvy's escort. She wore a shiny, slinky, gray gown and her hair was in a pile on the top of her head. When we entered the decorated Student Center gallery, Woody Herman and the Herd were jamming away.

On another bandstand, a rock band called "The Galloping Scallops" waited its turn when the big band took its break. Livvy had reserved a big table in a corner of the room for us, Bear and Paige, Culden and Reb, and Benjo and Cyndy. As usual, Reb had his camera and worked his way around the room.

We jitterbugged to *Woodchopper's Ball* and *Big Noise from Winnetka*, much to the amazement of the younger students. Bear and Paige stole the show with Denzel flipping his substantial wife over his head and between his legs. After that performance, Bear was in demand as a dance partner for the rest of the evening.

Jim Gillespie brought Blondie up to our table. She was surprisingly pretty in a simple red cocktail dress and matching shoes.

"Hey, this is really fun. I'm thinking about enrolling next fall if I can keep my job." She winked at me. Liv just raised her eyebrows in question.

"My God," Culden said, "isn't that your male model, Five?"

Indeed, there was Wayne Smead on the arm of the president of Delta Gamma, a member of my Figure Drawing class. And Marilyn Kretzman was dancing up a storm with her date, Monty Nixon.

We left the Rhododendron Ball in the hands of the official chaperones and drove out to the farm at Braddock's Branch, where Bus and Louise Ferris would cook us a late dinner.

"What a great dance!" Paige Duerhoff exclaimed. "We never went to anything like that in New York or Pittsburgh."

"Except for a bad case of thirst," Livvy said. She passed around the first alcoholic drinks of the evening. "Still, we put on a good show for the younger folks and didn't get caught with a flask."

"I saw a few kids sneaking from pints," Reb said. "Even got a shot of one table waving a bottle of Jim Beam around."

"Were your two models the only hippies there?" Liv asked.

"I think I recognized two or three other people," Culden answered. "But how can you tell 'em apart from the students?"

We fed on scrambled eggs, sausage, grits, and toast, then everyone took their leave. Liv was just about to put the top down on her MG when the first raindrops began to fall. We hopped in the little car and she said, "Your place or mine?"

• • •

The rain was still beating on the shingles of my cabin when we woke the next morning. I went down and perked coffee, and brought the pot upstairs. We lay in bed to smoke, drink coffee, and watch the rain falling among the new leaves outside.

"Well, rats," Liv said, "I was going to take you over to Charlottesville today, but not if this is going to keep up."

"Why Charlottesville?" I asked.

"Oh, it's kind of a secret, but we're getting a new computer this summer. And UVA is going to transfer all our punchcard data onto magnetic tape."

"I've never asked much about your work," I said. "What kind of data? Student records?"

"For sure. And personnel data. Alumni. All that sort of thing." She poured another cup. "We've been getting it onto punchcards from written records for the past three years. That project is finished and now the damn cards are obsolete." She paused. "I just don't quite understand computers."

"Me neither. I'm sure glad the computer will never replace my sketchpad and paints."

"Do you want to come with me to Charlottesville tomorrow?" she asked. "Virginia has a beautiful campus."

"If I can get Culden to cover my classes, I'd enjoy it. She does owe me a couple from the honeymoon."

• • •

We loaded three big cases into the back of Livvy's Jeepster and set out for the University of Virginia.

"Hard to believe all those cards will be on one or two reels of tape," Liv said as she rolled us down the hill. "I'll really feel relieved to be rid of those punchcards."

We drove south to Seneca Rocks, then picked up U.S. 33 toward Harrisonburg in Virginia. A little farther on, Liv turned onto another highway and stopped at a toll booth.

"This is Skyline Drive. It's not as fast but the scenery is beautiful. And our appointment isn't until two o'clock."

We followed the curving road, pulling out at overlooks to admire the vistas from the Blue Ridge Mountains. Looking west, we could see across the Shenandoah Valley to our Allegheny Mountains.

Charlottesville and the campus of UVA were charming. Just as beautiful as Seneca, in a big university way. I unloaded the punchcards at the registrar's office and strolled The Lawn while Livvy took care of her computer business.

"I'd love to stay here overnight," she told me as we returned to the car. "We could go out to Monticello, but I've got a board meeting tomorrow afternoon and the usual crop of little meetings before. But I do know a great place to get some trout and biscuits on the way home."

The sunset was intense as we topped the rise and saw Seneca Rocks. Livvy's restaurant was a tiny cottage in the woods south of the little climbing village and indeed, the trout were delicious and the homemade biscuits never quit coming.

We stopped by Culden's house on the way back to campus.

"Everything in your classes went fine, Five. I think Gillespie's about ready to go commercial. His paintings of women are fantastic, with an emphasis on fantasy," she reported.

"Where's Reb?" I asked.

"He went up to Jordan Run to shoot some stuff. The hippies were having some kind of rally."

We drove on to the parking lot, where I picked up my car.

"I'm not going to invite you over," Liv sad, pecking me on the lips. "I'm pooped and have a big day tomorrow."

"Thanks Liv. I really enjoyed the ride and seeing Charlottesville."

"Goodnight, Love," she whispered.

— 61 —

Tear Gas in Bloom

The morning of May 21 was as brilliant as the sunset had predicted. I arrived for my nine o'clock Art App class and noticed for the first time that the rhododendron and dogwood trees that bordered Eden Fields were in full bloom. We had reached the Expressionist Movement in class and it seemed like too nice a day to explore the gloomy works of the Germans.

Nevertheless: "The works we'll see and discuss today represent the German approach to Expressionism," I began. "As you'll see, the Germans and their kin suffered a lot of angst, and it came through in brilliant shades of blacks and browns.

"Not exactly the riot of color presented by the *Fauves*," I went on. "There was a group called *Die Brücke*, or The Bridge, and their goal was to express their work as the future of art. The Norwegian Edvard Munch was a strong influence." The screen showed Munch's *The Scream*, which was followed by Schiele's *Death and Girl.*

"The Austrian Egon Schiele was expected to be the successor to the acknowledged leader of the German

Expressionists, Klimt. But Schiele was a tortured persona and did not live to see age 29. In this painting, titled *Death and Girl,* the artist has created a self-portrait as Death and his mistress, Walli, as the girl.

"After an incestuous affair with his sister, Schiele's career seemed welded to erotic depictions of young women, often pre-pubescent. At one time, his studio was the neighborhood hangout for delinquent children whom he often used as models. In 1912, he was arrested and imprisoned for pornography."

I continued the projection of Schiele images: the erotic *Girl with Black Hair* and the more mysterious *The Couple,* in which the woman peers from beneath the folds of a man's large coat.

"Schiele used his imprisonment as a portrayal of artist as victim, and the experience actually increased his fame. Sadly, he died in 1918 in the Spanish flu epidemic, three days after the death of his wife and unborn child."

• • •

"Professor Lowrey, I loved the way you compared the work of Schiele with the paintings of Klimt," Susan Longmeyer gushed. "That painting of *Judith II* by Klimt… it's so organized and flowing, but really spooky. But Schiele seems more like a wild man."

"Don't forget, Susan—Klimt portrayed Judith as a real beauty. You can tell that by her face and gorgeous bosom. But the real beauty in the painting is found in the way he treated her distorted, arthritic hands."

"Oh, yes," she cooed, "I can see how either artist could get his share of beautiful women."

"Thanks for the comments, Susan. Now I've got to get going."

"You know, Professor Lowrey, when I saw those Klimts and Schieles today, I thought of your paintings in the show last winter." The Kappa president wriggled her assets displayed by a cashmere sweater. "If ever…" she started.

"I've really got to go," I said, and fled.

• • •

Culden and I discussed my Art Appreciation lecture and Susan Longmeyer's not so veiled approach after class.

"Those *are* pretty erotic paintings by that bunch of German perverts," she commented. "They used to get me horny and I think it's a common reaction, especially among young students whose hormones are still tap-dancing."

"I know, but you know how I feel about showing the whole spectrum of an artist's work," I said. "Klimt and Schiele did create paintings with clothed models, but it would be a sham to show only those."

"You're right, Five, but keep your eye out for Longmeyer. I don't think she's really a wild girl but don't let her get into your office with a closed door, OK?"

I nodded OK, but our attention was drawn to the window. Somewhere outside, screams and shouts were growing in intensity.

"What the hell?" Culden asked. Our offices faced the front of Old Main and the steps leading down the hill. What looked like a protest group was knotted around the middle landing of the serpentine bike path, effectively blocking anyone's access up or down the hill.

We walked outside and down the first curve of the serpentine. It was definitely the group from Jordan Run-Laurel Town, out in full force. Most carried signs and, as we got closer, we could read them:

SU War Machine.

Grades, Not Gas.

And, most interesting, *Tell Us About Lazarus.*

The group seemed relatively peaceful, so Culden and I returned to the Fine Arts Building. Cyndy met us at the doorway.

"Five, call Benjo at home right away. Culden, you're supposed to return Dicky Reb's call."

We went to our own offices and I dialed Benjo's number.

"Yeah," he growled. "Is that you, Five?"

"Yep. What's up?"

"You've got a protest group on the steps, right?"

"Yes. Culden and I just walked down there. They seem pretty peaceful."

"Well, I've got a Special Agent Morris here with me. FBI. He's pretty sure that our man Mecklin has arrived and has something to do with this protest. Can you meet us... ah... at the Student Center? In the gallery?"

"No problem. You should get there in about five minutes. I'll be there."

"Reb's on his way to Petersburg to put some film on the plane for New York," Culden told me as I prepared to cross Eden Fields. "He said he'd got some pretty good stuff at Jordan Run this morning... hippies getting their stuff together for this protest. He told me to stay inside and out of the way," she said. "Out of the way of what?"

• • •

Benjo was right on time with a man in a dark suit, admiring the remaining paintings in the gallery.

402

"You must be Agent Morris," I observed, extending my hand. "You're probably the only person in Grant County wearing a suit today."

Morris glared at me and ignored my outstretched hand. "I'll change into something more suitable. I just got to, er... Grant County... a couple of hours ago."

"Bad start, Five. Agent Morris has followed Adam Mecklin down here," Benjo stated. "Now you two shake and we'll try again."

"Sorry, Agent Morris. Five Lowrey," I put my hand out again. "I'm just used to seeing Bureau people in suits—almost like a uniform."

"Arnold Morris, Five. Joe here has told me about you and briefed me on the situation." We shook hands.

"I got a tip from an informant that Mecklin had left State College, Pennsylvania, yesterday," Morris told us. "The informant is working undercover in a group called the Weather Underground. The tip was that he was coming to Seneca to help organize something. Three members of the Weather Underground did us a big favor last week by blowing up their bomb factory in New York and taking themselves with it."

"So they're definitely bomb makers?" Benjo asked.

"Yes indeed. We know for a fact that Mecklin was in on the Madison explosion," Morris said.

"Do you have a description of Mecklin?" I asked the FBI agent.

"Yep! Many! All different. But he does have some things working against him."

"Such as?" Benjo questioned.

"First, he's short. About five three. Second, he's round. I would estimate maybe two hundred pounds. Finally," he paused, "he has to wear these incredibly thick eyeglasses. Evidently blind as a bat without them."

"That fits with a description our informant at Laurel Town gave us several weeks ago," I mentioned. "Short. Fat. Thick glasses."

"Let's go back to my office," I suggested. "We'll find Agent Norris some more appropriate clothes and take a look at the demonstration."

• • •

Wearing an old windbreaker of mine, Norris stood in the window and scanned the hippies demonstrating on the hill below.

"What's Lazarus?" he asked.

"A classified Army project the university is involved with," Benjo told him.

"Hmmf. I don't see any short, fat guys with glasses," Norris observed.

As we watched, the demonstrators started up the steps toward Old Main. A quick head count totaled about fifty hippies. I saw Blondie straggling behind, bouncing a *Grades, Not Gas* sign up and down. Three bounces and pause for a count of twenty, three more bounces. Our pattern.

"I see our informant," I said. "She's signaling for contact."

"How can you do it?" Norris asked.

"If they march through the Old Main gate, the informant can duck into the covered walkway that leads down here," I said, careful not to identify Blondie by gender.

I stood inside the walkway gate and watched the demonstrators pass. Their shouts echoed inside the bricked entrance. There was a short interval before Blondie came, limping badly. She limped to a bench just outside the doorway and rubbed an ankle.

"Good work," I said *sotto voce*. "Just keep limping so no one notices."

"No time to talk. The little guy with glasses was back. He stayed with Kaminsky all night and I saw them go by in his truck early this morning. I think this demonstration is going to get rougher." She wiped her brow and limped away.

I relayed Blondie's message to Benjo and the FBI guy. Bells rang and I realized I'd missed my eleven o'clock class. Students swarmed onto Eden Fields to join the protesters. As we watched, a new supply of signs appeared and the protest became a real student event.

Out came the bullhorns. From somewhere, a bass drum was produced and a syncopated chant went up.

No Gas, Give Us Grades.
Tell The World About Lazarus.

They marched around Eden Fields in a big circle, the leaders and the drum in the center egging them on.

"Oh shit," Benjo muttered, "there's a TV truck." Indeed, the truck from the Elkins ABC affiliate was parked in the admin building courtyard. I could see a couple of the university trustees staring at the spectacle, then entering Davis Hall for lunch.

By one o'clock, the demonstrators nearly filled Eden Fields—at least two thousand—the majority of them being students. I tried to call Livvy several times but her secretary said that she was with the board and couldn't be interrupted. She did tell me that Livvy had called the Seneca Police and State Police to be on standby.

"I'm going to call Colonel Kinnard," Benjo announced. "I'm not in the chain of command at Lazarus, but I think that guard platoon should be alerted." I told him to use the phone in my office.

The protest crowd continued to swell. Now a big group was on the steps of Davis Hall and the chant of *La-za-rus, La-za-rus* echoed off the front of the building. Someone opened the front door of Davis and a swarm of protesters entered the building to the cheers of the crowd.

Cyndy came running up.

"Five—Ginnie, the provost's secretary, just called with a message from Liv. Three Seneca police are at the top of the inside stairs in Davis but she's afraid they're going to need more security to hold the building."

"OK, Cyndy, why don't you call the State Police barracks? Liv has already alerted them." She ran back into the Fine Arts Building.

• • •

Four State Police cruisers arrived by three o'clock. The crowd was noisy but still orderly. They booed and hissed as the police arrived. This was an unusual protest in that there was no opposing group. Everyone seemed to have the same objective. An hour later, the doors to Davis Hall were opened and three uniformed Seneca policemen were ejected from the building.

I returned to my office and dialed Livvy's number. Ginnie answered.

"Hello, Professor Lowrey. They've taken over the building and kicked the Seneca policemen out. Oh, wait, here's the provost."

"Five, these people have the building. A group of them sneaked in the side door about an hour ago. Now all the entrances are chained and locked. Daddy's about to have a conniption fit," she gasped. "They've sent me to my office with orders to stay there."

"OK, Liv. Benjo's on the phone with Colonel Kinnard. You keep a low profile and…" just then the phone clicked and she was gone.

• • •

Just as darkness was falling, two platoons of soldiers showed up from the Lazarus detachment. Battlefield searchlights were quickly set up and the front of Davis Hall was painted with light. The silhouettes of the soldiers, their weapons at Port Arms, were menacing.

Benjo came running up, out of breath. "Sixteen GIs and a butterbar Louie," he gasped. "That's what Kinnard got us."

"Are they armed?" I asked.

"Locked and loaded," Benjo replied. "Orders to fire only if attacked and on the lieutenant's order. I mean, Five, this is scary shit." He looked at me, then at Agent Morris. "We'd better be ready to haul ass if those GIs put their gas masks on."

The dinner hour did not diminish the size of the crowd as mealtime usually had for other protests. The noise level was down, as the students obviously had yelled themselves out.

"That's Charlie Brown on the bullhorn now," I told Agent Morris. "Real name's Linus Friedman."

"With a name like Linus, I can see where he got his nickname. Friedman's on our watch list but we haven't had anything definite on him," Morris replied. He scanned the crowd with his binoculars. "Still no sign of Mecklin."

• • •

At nine o'clock, a major of the State Police climbed the steps of the library and addressed the crowd with a bullhorn.

"Attention, you people. You have made your point and now it's time for you to go home," he started reasonably. The crowd responded with jeers and boos. The major made another effort. "All right. You are under orders to disperse. You have five minutes to clear this area before we begin to make arrests. This is an illegal gathering."

From Charlie Brown's bullhorn: "Disperse? Disperse, hell! All together now."

And the crowd roared a rehearsed "Fuck You!"

• • •

Our war council gathered in the now-locked Student Center. Chief Stan Butler and Sergeant Glencoe of the Seneca Police. Major Thurmond of the State Police. Lieutenant Agassi of the Army guard detail. Agent Arnold Morris of the FBI. And Benjo and I representing the CIC and the University. I carried my credentials again. The lieutenant passed out walkie-talkie sets.

Benjo had assumed command, I guessed—at least he was talking.

"The important thing is to avoid violence. Lieutenant, please have your men unload their weapons."

"Those aren't my orders, Mr. Kostic," the butterbar replied.

"They are now," Benjo growled. "I'll take full responsibility with Colonel Kinnard and on up the chain. But I will not take responsibility for one of your soldiers killing someone."

He turned to the civil police. "We screwed up by not having all the entries to Davis Hall guarded or locked. And your men," he said to Chief Butler, "did a good job of not reacting when the kids threw them out."

"These aren't kids," Major Thurmond protested, "they're lawbreakers."

"True," Benjo answered, "but they're still students—most of them—on private university property. The buildings are normally locked at night so they technically haven't broken any laws."

"Holding the board of trustees and administration personnel is kidnapping," the major protested.

"We don't really know that anyone is being held," I commented.

In the end, we had the soldiers unload their weapons and everyone stood by with tear gas canisters.

• • •

The Old Main clock chimed twelve and, shortly after, a second-floor window in Davis was opened and a young man appeared. The crowd roared and he motioned for them to be quiet.

"I think that's a student named Kincaid," I commented. "He ran for student body president, got beaten."

"People," Kincaid shouted. "Everyone's in good shape in here but the members of your board of trustees are getting hungry. Could we have some food?"

Major Thurmond instantly responded by bullhorn. "No food until you unlock that building, release everyone, and then surrender."

"Christ, where is that guy coming from?" Benjo muttered.

A few minutes later, the lights in Davis Hall went out.

At three in the morning, the crowd was still present, though many of them were sitting down. The night was chilly but no one showed interest in going home.

Suddenly, a puff of smoke appeared near the steps of Davis Hall and the protesters immediately scattered from it. "Tear gas!" someone shouted.

"Who fired tear gas?" Benjo shouted into the walkie-talkie. Negative replies from the Army, state cops, and local cops.

"The bastards did it themselves," Morris muttered.

Behind us, we could hear the "gas, gas" alarm being passed down the line of soldiers. They immediately donned their gas masks.

"That's smart," I said. "Making 'em wear their gas masks the rest of the night will play hell with morale and nerves."

Beyond shouting and the constant blare of the bullhorn, everything remained calm. Davis Hall stayed dark although an occasional figure would appear in one of the windows. Everyone was exhausted, and as the first light of pre-dawn appeared, many of the demonstrators were seen to be sleeping on the ground.

Throughout the night, Dicky Reb moved through the crowd like a shadow, shooting by the available light of the searchlights.

Suddenly, all hell broke loose. Clouds of tear gas burst among the crowd and tear gas canisters were lobbed toward the lines of troops and police. Benjo had brought a water bucket and soaking towels which we quickly wrapped over our noses.

The demonstrators on the Davis steps seemed to be in a fight of some sort. Signs were swung at other demonstrators. Fistfights broke out among the crowd. Something broke a window on the ground floor of Davis. A group of protesters ran for the perimeter and began rocking a State Police cruiser. In seconds, it was rolled over and flames appeared.

"Sonofabitch," Benjo shouted, "that had to be a Molotov cocktail. It went up too fast."

"These bastards aren't just students," Agent Morris shouted from beneath his wet towel.

From behind the police lines a fire truck immediately began spraying the burning car but not before its gas tank blew with a *whompf*. A couple of demonstrators were on the ground and being handcuffed by state cops.

A thick cloud of gas hovered over Eden Fields. The State Police had waded into the mob and were flailing away with riot sticks. The soldiers held their ground, but lobbed gas canisters on order.

With three quick beeps from an air horn, the whole thing stopped. Protestors sat on the ground and placed their hands on top of their heads. Whistles blew, and slowly the police halted their punishment of the protesters.

The first rays of sunlight cast beams of orange into the mist of tear gas drifting through the dogwood and rhododendron blooms. It was the beginning of Black Wednesday.

— 62 —

Black Wednesday

It took nearly two hours to sort out the demonstration. None of the leaders, including Charlie Brown, were to be found. Not a single non-student could be identified. The few who were really wounded were taken to the infirmary, about a dozen students in all. Police arrested a total of six.

No one appeared inside Davis Hall, but a number of people opened windows to say they were locked in their offices.

I finally gave the order to smash the front door of Davis and watched the cops cut the chain with a bolt cutter. The bolt cutter came in handy, as each office in the building was padlocked with a chain. So, slowly the university leadership was released from imprisonment.

Police clipped the chain locking the board room and we discovered eight of the nine trustees. On the second floor, I found a tearful Ginnie, Liv's secretary, in the outer office of the provost.

"Ohhh, Professor Lowrey, they took the provost," she bawled.

"Who took her, Ginnie?"

"That woman… the dance teacher, McDearmid was her name. And the little fat man, everyone called him Froggy. He was the leader," she said breathlessly.

"When was this?" I asked.

"Froggy brought her out of the board room about two o'clock… last night… er, this morning," she recounted, "and the McDearmid woman came a little later. She didn't look the same, McDearmid, and I wasn't really sure it was her. Her hair was short… she's lost weight… but she had on those blue coveralls I've seen before and of course, the face is hard to miss."

Busby Ferris, chairman of the trustees, walked over to me. He looked near tears.

"Five, they took Livinda. The short fat man with big glasses took her out of the board room, then came back and got me. He said they would release Livinda after I made a full, public disclosure of the Lazarus Project before seven tonight."

"Mr. Ferris, did he give any clue as to where they were taking her?" I asked.

He shook his head and began to sob.

• • •

It took nearly two hours to piece together the story of what had happened in Davis Hall. Everyone estimated that only a dozen protesters held the building, well equipped with padlocks and chains. *Froggy*, obviously Adam Mecklin, was armed with a "tiny machine gun." Two of the other ringleaders were armed with pistols.

The objective sounded twofold. To destroy the records of the university and to force the trustees to reveal the secret Lazarus Project.

413

The paper records from the registrar's office were shredded in the Davis Hall basement, using the machine the university used to destroy old tests and out-of-date records. The university's IBM computer was smashed and sprayed with a fire extinguisher. The protesters, of course, had no idea that all the Seneca records were being recorded on computer tape at UVA.

The dozen protesters left the building sometime after three o'clock, and the intensified demonstration outside was obviously staged as a distraction. They got out of the building through a steam tunnel manhole at the gate of Old Main.

• • •

Benjo and I, Agent Morris, and Lieutenant Agassi met with Bus Ferris. Dicky Reb joined us, a Leica and a Nikon F bouncing on his chest.

"I've scheduled a press conference at six o'clock tonight. That's an hour before their deadline," Ferris said.

"The Bureau has six more agents coming in," Morris added.

A squawk on Agassi's walkie-talkie drew our attention. He stared intently as he listened to the voice in the earpiece.

"I've got orders to get my squad back to the base immediately," he said. "Something's happened there. Sounds like they took some fire."

"Give us a one-minute briefing, Lieutenant Agassi," Benjo said. "I don't know enough about the Lazarus Project. The entrance is hidden on the east side of the highway, right?"

"Yessir. There's a tunnel under the highway, then a camouflaged road up to the staging area," Agassi responded. "The turnoff is about four miles south of town. If you have your lights on, you'll see three green reflectors in the center line of the highway. The turnoff is at the third reflector."

"How many entrances?"

"Just the one at the staging area. That's where our problem is, I guess."

"What about the entrance at the north gate?" I asked.

"That's been sealed off inside the mountain. It's just a facility to distract the curious."

"So there's no other way to get inside? Now describe the inside. I know there are living quarters," Benjo continued.

"There are two chambers with living quarters and records storage. And one chamber which is where they've stored the CBR munitions," Agassi said.

"Are the chambers connected?"

"Only at the staging area entrance, sir. The CBR chamber's blast door isn't completed yet. The blast doors for the other chambers are. Sir? I've really got to get going," the lieutenant said with a wave salute. He left the room.

"What do you think, Five?" Benjo asked.

"I think the cave's the place," I responded. "Agent Morris, when will your team get here?"

"In about two hours," he said. "They're taking a chopper in from Quantico."

"I can't tell you what to do when they get here but I think we may need more firepower and containment at that staging area," Benjo said. "We can show you where the hidden gate is."

"And what are you going to do?" Morris asked.

"We know a very difficult alternate way into the Lazarus Pit. Unless construction has covered it, we could come at them from the inside."

415

"It sounds like these people are pretty well armed," Morris commented.

"We'll be armed too," I added, thinking of my .32 caliber revolver and fancy .22 target pistols.

• • •

Since our first exploration of the Lazarus Pit, I had kept my caving gear in a duffle ready to go. It took me less than 20 minutes to get home, change, grab my weaponry and the caving duffle, and head back to town. At the last minute, I stuffed the .410 sawed-off and all the rock salt rounds in the bag.

Bubby Bristo pulled up in his pickup just as I left the cabin.

"What's happening, Five? I know that demonstration at the University got pretty rough."

Quickly, I outlined the situation and told him about our suspicions of Livvy being held hostage at The Lazarus Pit.

"What can I do?" Bubby asked. "Miss Livvy's like a daughter to us. I have to do something."

I grabbed Bubby's shoulder and said, "Pray."

Benjo was waiting for me on the sidewalk. Beside him was Dicky Reb.

"Can I go, Five?" he pleaded. "Benjo said he doesn't care but I'll be on my own."

"Fine with me, Reb. Don't bring much stuff 'cause it's going to be a tough climb," I said.

"I'm ready to roll. One Leica, one f:1.4 wide angle. *Lots* of film."

• • •

We drove to County Road 28 and started up the mountain. Where brush had once hidden the path to the entrance, the hillside was a mess of broken vegetation and debris. On the right side of the road, brush was broken and tire tracks led over the edge of the bluff. We got out and peered down. A battered red pickup truck lay at the bottom of the gully.

"Doug Kaminsky's, I'd bet," I observed.

"Cyndy's old boyfriend?" Benjo asked.

"Yep. Doper Dong Bong Doug," I cracked, sort of hoping that Doug wasn't more involved than lending his truck.

We made our way up the trail to the base of the big hickory tree.

"Someone has enlarged the entrance. So this is how they came in, I'd bet," I said.

"Look at all the trash," Reb said. Someone had emptied cardboard cartons and left them strewn around the entrance.

"Modeling clay," Benjo read. "I'd like to get a sniff of that modeling clay."

We geared up and lit our headlamps. Reb carried a flashlight and we put him between us. The Mole People, or whoever, had enlarged the first crawlspace with a shovel. We hadn't gone ten yards before I saw my first clue that Liv was with them… a blue heel from a woman's shoe.

With the enlarged crawlspace, it was easier to reach the place where we could walk upright. Benjo and I crabbed down the chimney and Reb lowered our equipment down by line. We illuminated the chimney and he imitated our crab maneuver without a flaw.

At the bottom of the chimney, Livvy's blue pumps, one without a heel, lay in forlorn repose. We scanned the floor of the pit and Benjo turned up another item.

"Look at this," he said. "Here's the goddamn modeling clay. Their bag must've spilled."

He held up a lump of material about the size of a bar of laundry soap. It was wrapped in greasy paper. He put the material to his nose.

"Semtex," he muttered. "I would've bet anything on C4. These motha's are going to blow something up."

"Or down," I added morosely.

• • •

Knowing where we were going made our trip to the edge of the big room easier and faster. Along the way, we found a few items of discarded gear. An empty canteen. A broken flashlight. We inspected a rest stop where someone had recharged a headlamp. The warm carbide ashes made a gray pile on the cave floor.

In two places, I saw a partial footprint... a bare foot painted on the rock in blood.

Out of breath, we finally arrived at the entrance to the big chamber. Peering over the ledge where we'd last seen a frontloader shifting debris, we realized that the floor of the chamber was considerably higher than before. And the string of lightbulbs was reduced to a couple of permanent fixtures near the entrance to the tunnel.

There was no sign of activity. The tracks of our quarry were visible down the slope of smoothed debris, accented by the backlight of the spotlights.

"How many people do you suppose?" Reb asked. "The tracks are kind of messed up but I'd say at least five or six."

"Do we go down here," Benjo mused, "or should we use another part of the slope so our tracks won't show?"

I shrugged. "It's going to be a showdown if we catch up with 'em. Fuck it. Let's go here."

• • •

In the curving exit tunnel, mine lights in wire cages lit the passage every fifty feet or so. Escape niches lined the walls on either side, and a red cross on a doorway indicated rescue equipment.

"It's a lot more finished than last fall," Benjo commented.

"Go on, guys, I'll catch up," Reb called as he squatted to shoot us walking through the tunnel.

Finally, we came to a blast door at the end of the tunnel. It was ajar and its lock was riddled.

"No key, just shot their way in," I observed. "Must have a silencer on that little machine pistol."

"I'll bet it's one of those Israeli Uzis," Benjo said.

One by one, we stepped through the blast door into the first living chamber. As we'd seen before, the long living quarters occupied nearly half the room. What had been an empty side of the chamber was now filled with a structure that resembled a huge garage.

No one was in sight. As we walked between the buildings, our headlamps illuminated tracks in the dusty floor, including spots of blood.

"Someone's bleeding badly," Reb mentioned. "I'll bet it's Livinda. Those bastards made her hike in here barefoot."

I said nothing.

• • •

The second blast buffer was a thick wall, penetrated by a Judas door which led through a switchback passage. This door was unlocked and left ajar. Before we entered, we doused our headlamps.

The next room was practically identical except that the ceiling of the chamber lowered toward the far end, and a low building with long, thin windows sat at the head of the chamber. Faint light glowed from the windows.

The tracks continued through the room toward the low building. Reb ducked into the shadow of the long dormitory and virtually disappeared. I could hear the click of his shutter. Using hand signals, I went to the right while Benjo hugged the dormitory wall. We both had our pistols drawn. In addition, I had the vermin gun tucked into my belt.

As I crept along the wall in deep shadows, I suddenly stumbled over something. Something soft. I shielded my flashlight and revealed a body. Doug Kaminsky was lying face up, a pool of blood haloing his head.

"Sheeit," Benjo whispered, "this isn't some hippie prank. These bastards are serious." We huddled in the doorway of the low building which bore a sign reading *Administration*. Tracks in the floor led past the doorway but a couple led up to the door.

"Someone went in," Reb whispered. "Someone with bloody feet."

"Cover me," I ordered. "I'll go in."

The interior of the administration structure was dark with just faint light coming from a room beyond. I held to the wall with my revolver at the ready. As I inched along the wall, something scuffled in the darkness. I dropped to the floor, pistol aimed toward the noise. Cautiously, I turned my flashlight on and instantly rolled to the left to avoid the inevitable shot. Nothing.

The light revealed a bloody foot and leg, bound with silvery tape to a chair. I grabbed the light and hurried across the room, expecting the worst.

Livvy sat still as death in the chair, her eyes huge above the strips of tape that covered her mouth.

"Liv! It's Five," I hissed. "Don't make any noise."

Gently, I peeled the tape away from her mouth. Mucus was flowing out of her nostrils, tears from her eyes.

"It's OK, darling, I've got you," I whispered as I put my arms around her. "Hold still. I'll cut this tape and you'll be loose."

Livinda Ferris was in bad shape. Both feet were bloody and one leg was scraped up to her hip, exposed by the remains of the skirt she'd worn to work yesterday. Her cashmere sweater was in shreds and her brassiere was filthy. I picked her up and held her in my arms.

"Can you walk, Liv?" I asked gently.

"I got this far, Five. How much farther do I have to go?" she sobbed.

"I don't know. I carried her into the next room and laid her gently on the floor in a corner."

In the dim light, I could see her face was abraded from forehead to jaw on one side.

"Where are the others? How many are there?" I asked.

"Six or seven, I think," she gasped through tears. "The fat guy with glasses is the leader. He's Adam Mecklin. He came and got Gillian and me during the takeover. Gillian told me she was going to rescue me," she sobbed. "She lied."

"Where did they go after they left you here?"

"I don't know, but three of the men have packs with explosives and one guy has a bag of detonators. They made him follow way behind us."

"Were they stringing wire?" I asked.

"No! They'd just push a block of this stuff into a crack and then the detonator guy would stick one of them into the block."

Radio detonators.

The rattle of automatic gunfire interrupted us. I hurriedly reached into my bag and pulled out the Hi-Standard .22 pistol. I handed it to Livvy.

"We've got to find these people, but I'll be back for you. We'll get you out of here." I pulled the slider and cocked a round into the chamber. "For God's sake, don't shoot us when we come for you. But use this on anyone who isn't Benjo, Reb, or me."

I unscrewed the single lightbulb in the room and handed Liv a flashlight.

"I'll be back, Liv. I promise."

Benjo and I broke through the door and went into a crouch in the shadows. The sounds of gunshots echoed through the cave.

"Do you suppose that's the Army? Or the FBI?" I asked.

Quickly, I told Benjo what Liv had told me.

"OK, troops," he muttered, "let's move out toward the sound of battle."

We made our way through a second narrow blast maze and emerged on a platform above the low room I recognized as the chamber next to the entrance. The tunnel we'd used before was to the right but plugged with a solid concrete wall. Below us, five dark figures scurried from one loading dock to another. They moved with military precision toward a big entry at the far end of the room.

Light from outside illuminated the chamber through the entry. Clouds of dust and smoke made the scene one that might've come from Dante.

"I'll bet the entrance is a Z shape," Benjo said. "Whoever's firing isn't getting rounds in here."

"That bastard over there is planting plastique," I said, pointing to a figure stretching to reach a crack in the low ceiling.

"And look at the guy with the pack," Reb said. "He's following the other guy. Planting detonators, I'll bet."

Three of the figures crawled up to the mouth of the entrance. Then, one by one, they ran around the corner, firing pistols and a rapid burst from an automatic weapon. Heavy automatic fire responded, and we heard a scream.

Quickly, two figures ran back around the corner, dragging a companion between them.

"Let's get out of here," someone screamed. "They've broken through."

The explosives guy ran to the center of the room and dropped his pack. The man with the detonators followed him and stuck a detonator into the pack. I could hear the click of Reb's shutter as he recorded the action. Clouds of gas swirled through the entrance door.

"Watch out," Benjo grunted, "they're coming our way."

"I'll bet the radio detonating control won't work through these blast walls," I said. "Or he's using a different frequency for each room."

"You want to take the chance and take 'em on here in this maze?" I asked.

"Let's do it. Reb, get your ass back to Livvy. Be sure to let her know who you are."

"Aw, shit, Five. I'll miss this if I do."

"There won't be anything to shoot if our plan doesn't work."

— 63 —

Showdown

Just inside the second room Benjo and I stood on either side of the Judas door that led from the maze. The maze was just wide enough for one person at a time to move through it. Benjo had his .38 at the ready, while I hefted a four-foot two-by-two chunk of lumber.

We could hear grunting and shuffling as the enemy started through the maze. Suddenly, a figure in a caver's hat *backed* through the door, dragging someone. I immediately swung my club and dropped him on the spot. Benjo dragged him away from the door and I flashed on the body lying in the maze. It was Gillian, her eyes and teeth clenched from the pain of a stomach wound.

I pulled her out of the tunnel and dragged her into the shadows. Quickly I frisked her for a weapon but felt nothing but familiar curves and blood.

The third bomber emerged from the door, and Benjo clubbed him with his pistol. He let out a scream and staggered back, drawing a pistol of his own. Benjo fired, and the guy dropped to the floor of the maze tunnel. Another scream followed and we both leaped back as someone came running through the tunnel behind a burst of automatic fire.

He didn't expect to have his attack countered by a club to the face, which I applied as he ran into the room.

"Grab the weapon," I yelled, and Benjo jerked a small machine gun from his hand.

"Just one more," Benjo grunted. "What if he blows that room before we can get to him?"

A self-answering question. An enormous w*hump* was followed by the terrible roar of rock falling. A cloud of dust was pushed through the maze passage and we could hear debris and random rocks falling from our chamber.

Adam Mecklin came shambling through the cloud of dust, a pistol in one hand and a detonator box in the other. As I raised my pistol, the guy I'd clubbed grabbed at it. I lost my grip, and the .32 went skittering into the dark.

Benjo couldn't fire, for fear of hitting me. I kicked the bastard who'd grabbed at me, and got him in the groin. Then I ducked and grabbed the .410 out of my belt.

"Mecklin!" I screamed, and the round figure before me whirled. I could see his head turn and I let him have a barrel of rock salt right in the face.

As Bubby had predicted, rock salt might not kill anyone but it turned Mecklin's thick glasses into powder. He dropped the detonator and staggered around, one hand to his face and the other firing his pistol into the ceiling. Suddenly, he stumbled over Gillian and, before I could stop him, he lowered the barrel and fired a round into her head.

I fired the other barrel of the .410, and knocked him back. On the ground, he put the barrel of his weapon into his mouth and pulled the trigger.

Click.

• • •

We used duct tape to bind our prisoners' hands behind their backs. Mecklin was crying through the mass of tiny cuts that covered his face except for the strange mask where his glasses had been.

I was surprised to find Charlie Brown, AKA Linus Friedman, was the fourth guy—the second one I had clubbed and who'd attacked me back. He was docile as we stripped him of three Uzi magazines and taped his hands.

Benjo examined the first man through the tunnel. "I'm afraid you did the job on this one, Man," he said. "Simple bastard didn't have his helmet on right when you clubbed him."

Benjo's victim in the tunnel was dead also, as was Gillian.

I cried softly as I examined her once beautiful face, now a smear of blood from a fatal wound just above the ear.

Reb came running back from the admin building.

"Livvy's going into shock, I'm afraid," he told us. "She's cold and wet."

"I'll get this caving suit off of Gillian," I said. I unzipped the suit and peeled it away from her body, clad in her familiar leotard. "Reb, get her socks and boots and bring 'em quickly." I hurried toward the admin block.

• • •

Dressed in Gillian's bloodied caver suit and with thick socks and Gil's boots, Livvy seemed out of danger of shock. She sipped from a canteen and gave me a bloody scowl when I told her I'd forgotten to bring cigarettes.

The four of us discussed what to do with our prisoners.

"Can we get out through the front?" Benjo wondered. "Let's try the blast door."

426

We made our way through two legs of the maze and came upon a massive rock pile closing off the front room.

"So much for that," I muttered. "So we go out the back way."

"How are we going to get a blind fat boy out of here?" Reb asked.

"Frankly, I don't give a flying rat's ass if they don't get out. Livvy's my only concern right now... and us, of course," I growled.

Benjo rigged a double noose with climbing line and tethered the prisoners together. The nooses were attached to my 2x2 and he could tighten them with a jerk on the line.

"Saw this done in 'Nam," he grinned. "We'll put Charlie Brown in the front and let Chubby, here, follow by sound."

We never found the detonating box or my pretty little Lady Smith revolver. Liv still clung to the Hi-Standard until I convinced her it would do me more good. And so we set off.

Reb led the way, his headlamp flickering through the chunks of fallen ceiling in the chamber. From time to time, the big room would echo with the sound of more falling rock.

I followed, carrying Livinda, who clung to my neck. Behind me came the two prisoners. Charlie Brown had his companion's smashed caving helmet on with a headlamp. Benjo brought up the rear, holding his noose club with one hand, the Uzi in the other.

"Well, we did fix you military-industrial fuckers," Mecklin said in a surprisingly high voice. "The whole world should know about your fucking secret cave and your illegal government contracts." He paused, then gave a high squeal.

"You're the only one who's fired this thing," Benjo growled. "How sensitive is the trigger? I could punch a bunch of rounds right into your spine and leave you here to die and rot."

"No, no!" he cried. "Don't leave me here. Let's get going. I'll be quiet."

"Oh, why not? Let's just tie you two to a big rock and let someone topside come down and get you," Benjo said in a teasing voice.

"We've got a half hour to clear out of these rooms," Charlie Brown spoke for the first time. "The charges are set to fire in 30 minutes after the detonator was pushed," he blurted.

Now, that's a bit of information to get one's attention. We hustled through the blast doors, then the curving tunnel, stopping only to grab a stretcher from a rescue niche. Livvy reclined as Reb and I carried her across the last room and up the slope of scree.

The two Weathermen fell behind, despite Benjo's urging and prodding with the Uzi. Mecklin puffed and gasped as the slope got steeper.

Then the second and third rooms exploded. Dust and smoke came through the small blast door and the security lights flickered and dimmed. Mecklin screamed and slipped sideways, dragging Charlie Brown with him. Benjo let go of the club and let the pair slide down the slope.

"Come on, Benjo, haul ass up here," I shouted. Reb and I couldn't lift the stretcher above the ledge.

"Out, Livvy, you've got to climb over the ledge. Hurry!"

Reb tumbled over the ledge and reached for Livvy's hand. Benjo caught up with me and we cleared the ledge together, just as the last detonators went off. The ground shook as the four of us ducked into the passageway. Then an ominous *thump* was followed by a cloud of dust blowing through our tunnel.

428

Down the passage, we could hear individual rocks falling but no major shift. I crawled back to the ledge but it was no longer a ledge, just a wall of stone.

— 64 —

Escape from the Pit

It took nearly an hour for us to labor back down the passage, picking our way around new ceiling falls and dodging the occasional boulder clunking down from other breakdowns.

As the passage narrowed to the bottom of the chimney, I crawled with Livvy clinging to my back like a baby raccoon. She cried softly as she sat on the chimney floor and held up her tattered blue shoes, still there as reminders of her abduction. I crabbed my way up the chimney, holding onto the safety line. When I reached the top, we looped the safety line under Livvy's arms and I hoisted her up the chimney, Reb crabbing directly beneath her to break a possible fall.

Even duck-walking out the enlarged crawlway was a painful experience for Liv and uncomfortable for the rest of us. Halfway, I got back on my hands and knees and Liv climbed aboard again.

Finally, the daylight showed at the end of the passage.

"We're there," I yelled. "We've made it."

Suddenly a large figure loomed into the beam of light.

"Five, it's me. Bubby! Can I help?"

"Bubby, where'd you come from?"

"I followed you guys out. But I didn't bring a light so I just stayed here to cover your backs," he explained.

"Can you take Livvy?" I asked. "She's in pretty bad shape."

Bubby took Livvy's hands and gently pulled them away from around my neck.

"Here, here, Miss Livvy darlin'," he crooned. "Bubby's got you. You're OK now."

But our joy was squashed, as an amplified voice called, "Throw down your weapons. Come out with your hands over your head."

"Sheeit," Benjo growled. "Our rescuers have come just in time."

The amplified voice boomed, "Identify yourself."

"It's me, Arthur Bristo," Bubby yelled back. "I have Miss Livinda here, and Professor Lowrey, and two others are behind me."

I couldn't see anyone, but knew the surrounding woods had to be full of armed and angry FBI agents or soldiers.

When he could stand upright, Bubby picked up Livinda and carried her in his arms out of the cave.

"I'm Special Agent Thomsen Lowrey the Fifth, United States Army Counterintelligence Corps, with Special Agent Josefus Kostic of the CIC and Richard West of *Look* magazine," I called.

— 65 —

After Action Report

Slithering out of a hole in the ground on your stomach with your hands over your head is no easy task. I was surrounded by shooters but, thankfully, I recognized one—FBI Agent Morris.

"At ease, everyone," Morris called. "He's who he says he is, and one of ours." He helped me to my feet.

A pair of soldiers were already bringing a stretcher for Livvy. Dicky Reb emerged from the entrance, his Leica to his eye. Culden screamed from the back of the crowd and ran forward to hug and kiss her husband. He surreptitiously slipped a bag of exposed film into her coat pocket and whispered in her ear.

I walked over to Livvy, who was sitting on the ground in the arms of her father. "I can stand up, Five," she said in a low voice. I tried to help her stand but she pivoted and fainted onto the waiting stretcher.

With Reb shooting away, the group trudged down the hill to a waiting ambulance. Louise Ferris ran forward as Livvy's stretcher reached the bottom of the slope.

Liv's eyes opened and she gave her parents a faint smile. "Hi Mom, Daddy. I'm gonna be OK. Five saved me... Five and his friends." She closed her eyes again as the ambulance technicians loaded her into the vehicle.

"I'm going with her," Louise Ferris announced. Shortly, the ambulance moved out, its siren hooting. Reb grinned as we watched Culden's car in close pursuit.

• • •

"Everyone wants a piece of you guys," Colonel Kinnard told us. "Do any of you need medical attention? Can we have a short debriefing here?"

"Yessir," Benjo answered. "How did it go outside here?"

"Not too good, Mr. Kostic. Four GIs are dead. Three shot down in the cavern, a fourth caught in the flying debris when the cave blew. One dead state policeman. One FBI agent on his way to the hospital in critical condition."

He waited a few seconds. "The good news is that the explosions didn't affect any of the CBR munitions, although the chamber caved in. And of course... that you got out and rescued Miss Ferris."

A squad of soldiers ringed a big olive drab van which we climbed into. Colonel Kinnard, a one-star general with a Stawicki name tag, Morris, Busby Ferris, and a couple of other civilians circled us as we sat in folding chairs.

"Since you didn't bring back prisoners," Agent Morris began, "how many bodies do we have in the cave?"

"Six, I would guess... that we know of," Benjo replied. "Mecklin, Friedman, a woman named McDearmid, a local hippie named Kaminsky, and two unidentifieds. Someone executed Kaminsky before we arrived and we saw Mecklin shoot the McDearmid woman."

"And the others?" Kinnard asked.

433

"I shot one dead in the firefight and Agent Lowrey clubbed one in the head. He, ah, expired. We captured Mecklin and Friedman, and were attempting to bring them out when the final detonation took place. They slid down a slope and were trapped in the roof fall."

"Our major concern was getting Miss Ferris out," I tossed in.

Satisfied with our initial debriefing, Colonel Kinnard and General Stawicki ordered us back to town, the van in convoy with a big armed guard.

"I have lots of comfortable room at my farm," Bus Ferris volunteered. "It's only six miles from the campus and it will be a lot more private. Agent Morris, the general and I have a press conference in a half hour. Why don't you men get cleaned up, a bite to eat and some rest. If no one has any objections, we can resume the debriefing at the farm in the morning."

So we headed out for Braddock Branch Farm.

I talked with Louise Ferris at Petersburg Hospital and she told me Liv was fine and would probably be released tomorrow. The three of us wolfed down some sandwiches and beer, then showered and hit the sack.

• • •

Breakfast the next morning was a celebratory affair on the patio. Bus Ferris joined the three of us as we finished our meal and lit up over coffee. The officers were obviously sleeping late in the guest house.

"Nothing's been said about my photos," Reb said nervously. "I'm sure Culden got yesterday's film on the plane for New York. But what do I do if the Army says this is classified?"

"You've been covering the protests and hippie community," I responded. "No one has said anything about that being classified. Project Lazarus was classified, but you were just one of three fraternity brothers on a rescue mission."

"Do you really think you'll get anything from inside the cave, Reb?" Benjo asked.

"Oh, yeah. Tri-X pushed to 1200 ASA and a 1.4 lens? It'll be grainy as hell but we'll have images. I even got a shot of Five pulling Livvy out of the chimney. Should be a nice shot of her butt," he laughed. "And I changed film just before we left the cave so the daylight stuff is exposed properly."

We watched as Culden pulled up in her red wagon. Little R.T. came running to his daddy.

"I got the film off fine, Reb, and Roger called last night. They want you in New York as soon as possible."

Reb grinned, and hugged his boy. "OK, but take this roll of film and get out of here before the spooks arrive. That way I can honestly say the film's on its way to the magazine."

• • •

When the brass arrived, the atmosphere remained congenial. Neither officer said anything about Reb's photos and after contributing to our narrative, he was given permission to leave for New York. He gave us the ACE secret sign as he dialed Culden to come and get him.

Everyone wanted more detail on the gunfight in the tunnel. The Army officers were fascinated with my use of the vermin gun after my handgun was lost.

"Rock salt! I'll be damned," Colonel Kinnard explained. "You fired right into his face and all it did was pulverize his glasses?"

"Oh, he was hurting, all right," Benjo said. "He was trying to shoot us but was staggering around, firing into the air. I think without his glasses he was blind as a bat. He tripped over Gillian, didn't know who she was, and fired a shot into her head."

"I fired the second barrel," I continued, "knocked him down, and then he tried to kill himself. But he was out of ammunition."

A few minutes later, an ambulance arrived. The attendant helped Louise Ferris and Jake Jericho ease Livvy into a wheelchair. The right side of her face was bright orange and two enormous bandages covered her feet. I ran down and gave her a gentle hug and a kiss on the left side of her mouth.

"Oh Five, you guys are OK? I'm so glad," she exclaimed. "Even though Mom said you were, I was afraid to believe it." She kissed me with swollen lips. "Now... food, coffee, cigarettes. All that damned hospital would give me was ice chips and a broth that tasted like the cave."

Everyone was patient as Liv devoured a plate of bacon and eggs and drank cups of black coffee. Finally, she settled back and I lit a Pall Mall for her.

"I'm just fine," she smiled in answer to Agent Morris' question. "For someone who crawled a half mile or so in her bare feet and totally inappropriate clothing for a cave expedition."

"The doctors said her feet will be fine," Louise contributed. "She should just stay off them for three weeks or so."

As Liv recounted her part of the story, tears came to her eyes.

"Poor Gillian," she said with a choked voice. "What a messed-up person. I honestly can't tell you if she was a part of this plot or not. Five and I both knew she liked the protest world… and she abused alcohol and drugs. But I thought of her as a friend, and that's why I went with her without a fight."

"She did take part in the firefight at the cave entrance," I commented. "Mecklin and Friedman dragged her back after she was shot. She might have bled to death from the wound if Mecklin hadn't shot her."

• • •

Finally, the debriefing was done. Benjo and I were instructed to submit Agent Reports on the incident. The clatter of a helicopter approaching drew our attention.

"That's my ride back to the real world," General Stawicki said. "How would you folks like to take a ride and look at the mountain?"

"Oh, can I come too?" Liv asked.

"Of course, my dear. It's your mountain as much as anyone else's."

As the Huey settled onto the meadow adjacent to the house, I carried Livvy across the lawn. She peppered my cheek and neck with little kisses.

"I've never flown in one of these before," she whispered. "Is it scary?"

"Nope. Like a magic carpet," I answered. "And this one will have seats, since it's a general's private bird."

We strapped into two rows of seats and replied yes when General Stawicki asked if we wanted to leave the doors open. With a roar, the Huey lifted off the ground about ten feet, then tilted its nose down and we accelerated across the meadow, climbing rapidly.

"Damn, but I wish Reb were here with his camera," I shouted. The other two nodded. We leveled off about 200 feet above the mountains and headed south toward a gray-brown cloud.

"That's just dirt and dust," General Stawicki yelled over his shoulder. "We haven't detected any trace of CBR."

The pilot threw the Huey into a tight circle over Skidmore Mountain. A huge crater filled with fallen trees described a *W* in the side of the massive mountain. We stared in awe at the place we'd been less than 24 hours before.

• • •

None of Reb's pictures made the cover of that week's issue of *Look*, but his coverage of the student protests and the Seneca demonstration ran to eight pages as the lead story. We bought every copy we could find in Seneca and Petersburg and examined the black-and-white photos over and over.

"All told, the university didn't come out of this too badly," Bus Ferris observed. "It's a black eye for sure, but the writer doesn't criticize us for our actions."

"Still, we've got to beef up our policies on student organizations and security, Dad. We need a full-time security team, not just one part-time cop," Liv said.

"I agree. But I think you and Five and Agent Kostic did a fine job with the entire episode."

The next week's issue of *Look* was a different story. There on the cover was Benjo's photo of me pulling Livvy out of the chimney. My face was contorted with the effort and my headlamp threw deep shadows, outlining Liv's body as she stretched for the top. The cover tag line read *Daring Rescue from Underground Battle.*

Our social group sat on Liv's terrace, each of us with a copy of *Look*. Reb was ecstatic about the coverage.

"I told you they'd be grainy images… about like Capa's D-Day pictures," he said to Benjo. "But look at that spread!"

The opening spread of the story showed the huge room. Mecklin and Friedman were dragging Gillian back from the entry. The two explosives guys were in the middle of the chamber with their packs. The picture captured the smoke and dust from the firefight.

Another photo showed me on hands and knees, Livinda clinging to my neck as I crawled with her on my back. A close-up of Benjo, his .38 snub-nose at the ready, was made just before the enemy started through the tunnel.

A wonderful blurred chiaroscuro of a figure coming through the tunnel, Benjo aiming his pistol, and me standing over the first guy I hit with the club—Gillian's body on the floor of the tunnel.

It was an incredible feeling to realize these photos were of us, and being seen by people all over the world.

— 66 —

Beginning of the End

Livinda Ferris was an excellent patient. Within a week, her facial scratches had healed to tiny scabs. Every afternoon, I massaged her legs and feet with oil and, usually, these sessions would evolve into a back rub and disrobing and other pleasant activities.

By two weeks, her face was clear of any signs of the cave experience and, against doctor's orders, she was wearing thick socks and outsized après-ski boots and trying to walk. She tooled around Davis Hall in her wheelchair, supervising the installation of the new computer and input terminals.

Benjo and Cyndy were living from day to day, as the protest threat had diminished and he was expecting new orders.

The bombing of Lazarus Pit had put a damper on protest enthusiasm. I drove Blondie home one afternoon and was struck by how much the hippie community had shrunk.

"I'm going to move in with Cyndy when Benjo moves on," she informed me.

We all enjoyed a brief period of local fame, autographing copies of the magazine and answering the same questions over and over. Fortunately, this period ended quickly.

• • •

Our classes wound inexorably toward finals and the end of the school year. I avoided the continued advances of Susan Longmeyer in the classroom. Liv and I were asked to chaperone the Kappa formal, and I managed to avoid dancing with Susan until the end of the evening. With a slow song, she snuggled into my chest in a very uncomfortable way and I was glad when the band swung into *Jeremiah Was a Bullfrog*.

Culden accompanied me to Dean Cruz-Garcia's office, where he made a big deal of presenting me with my next year's teaching contract.

The last finals were held on a Thursday morning and the seniors were invited to a traditional lunch on Eden Fields. Although many underclassmen had left for home, a crowd of more than 500 young people lounged on the warm plaza under a brilliant sky. I wheeled Livvy's chair onto the gallery deck and we watched the scene below.

The first water balloon arced across the plaza and splatted in the middle of a group of girls. Screams and squeals followed.

"This is another tradition," Liv said. "I'm afraid I can claim this one, but it's all in good fun." Water balloons came from all corners of Eden Fields, and soon a fire hose was aimed into the air. The kids danced and cavorted beneath the manmade shower.

"What fun it is to watch these kids throwing water balloons instead of tear gas," Liv exulted.

• • •

I waited with the other Fine Arts faculty at the gate of Old Main. From inside Eden Fields, the band was playing *War March of the Priests* and below us, Ed Gales was leading the academic procession up the steps from the Underhill Campus.

Provost Livinda Ferris sat in her wheelchair, directly in front of me. As Ed Gales approached us, he stopped the procession and brought the mace over to Livvy.

"Will you do the honors this year, Madam Provost?"

She choked back a sob and nodded, then took the mace. Slowly, I pushed the chair into the courtyard in time with the music. Livvy held the mace high as the degree candidates of other schools joined the procession. As we crossed Eden Fields, onlookers applauded.

When we entered the stadium, a packed throng stood and cheered, I think as much for Livvy as for their graduating seniors. I struggled to push the chair up the ramp to the stage, but finally got Livvy in place and locked. Another cheer went up as she presented the mace back to Ed Gales, who placed it in its holder.

The band changed to *Pomp and Circumstance* as the first graduation candidates filed in. Sporadic cheers and shouts erupted as someone's kid was recognized.

Finally, the last graduate was seated. Dean Gerholt delivered the invocation. From my seat in the faculty section below the podium, I was stunned to see Livvy slowly rise from her chair and, with great effort, walk to the lectern.

"Please rise and join me in singing our alma mater, *Morning Mountain Mists,*" she said. Then with a clear voice, she proceeded to sing the beautiful song, swaying behind the lectern.

The ceremony went on with the usual announcements of awards and a stirring commencement address by Lieutenant General Valdemar Stawicki.

To a low roll from a kettledrum, the provost once again rose and hobbled to the lectern.

"President Skinner, Deans, Faculty members, members of the board, and above all, honored parents. It is my pleasure to present to you the candidates for graduation as members of the Class of 1968."

President Skinner brought her wheelchair forward, and Livvy settled into it gratefully. Then she began to read.

"James Graham Alfonso, Bachelor of Liberal Arts..." and on, and on.

• • •

As the mortarboards rained down, I hurried forward to the podium. Livvy was smiling as she shook hands with everyone on the platform. I shook General Stawicki's hand and thanked him for his wonderful address.

At last, the crowd had cleared and I walked forward to Livvy's chair. She raised her head and I kissed her gently on the lips.

"I have never been so proud of anyone as I am of you today," I told her, kneeling before her wheelchair.

"Madam Provost! You are indeed my one true love."

THE END

— Epilogue —

It's a beautiful, crisp September Saturday. An early cold front has begun to turn the leaves. Hints of scarlet and gold border Eden Fields. Culden's scarlet station wagon offers a tailgate of food and drink. Culden, Reb, and R.T., dressed in his miniature Warriors jersey, are excellent hosts.

Paige Duerhoff, experiencing her first Seneca tailgate party, talks with Cyndy and Benjo, who has driven down from his permanent assignment in Pittsburgh.

We all stand and clap as the Fighting Warriors Marching Seventy-Five prance to the center of the plaza and break into the *Warpath March*.

"That's my song," Livvy yells. "Go, Warriors!" Her diamond flashes in the sunlight as she claps wildly. I explain to Paige that Liv composed the fight song.

Paige nods her approval. "Bear likes it. I think it's neat."

Piper Stadium is nearly full as we take our seats below the President's Box. It's the first home game for the unbeaten Warriors and excitement is high. In The Bear's coaching debut, the Warriors put a 48-0 punishment on West Virginia Wesleyan in Buckhannon. And last week, they played Marshall to a 14-14 tie in Huntington.

And now for their first home game, Ohio University's Bobcats are the opponents, thanks to Bear's pulling strings and calling on old friendships.

The Fighting Warriors Marching Band at the end zone and the Mountain Mamas strut onto the field

The crowd cheers mildly as a long row of beautiful girls in skimpy metallic scarlet costumes strut from the tunnel and line up behind the band. Playing *Warpath March,* the band moves down the field and the PA man introduces Lucinda Latimer, our *Golden Girl Of The Glen!* To our relief, Lucy from Big Creek launches her baton into the blue West Virginia sky and *catches it!*

Good-natured boos and hisses greet OU's Bobcats as they jog onto the field. They look huge in their natty white helmets and jerseys and green pants. Culden, Benjo, Paige, and I—loyal alumni all—stand and clap for the visitors.

A mighty cheer rises as the Warriors come out of their tunnel. They wear their gold pants and scarlet jerseys with gold-and-white sleeves, and the smooth gold helmets. But true to Bear's word, the jerseys are faded and patched, the helmets are scuffed, and a few players wear khaki practice pants instead of the gold.

The Warriors are Bear's workaday football team.

Introductions are another eye-opener, with Seneca names like Piotrowski, Strawn, Chimmelwitz, Herb and Henry Stover, Nixon, and, for the first time, Herm Bristo, the first of his clan to ever go to college. All told, The Bear starts nine freshmen.

• • •

OU receives the opening kickoff and their return man roars to the Seneca 29 before he's shoved out of bounds. A tiny whiff of gloom sweeps the stands. But on the next three plays, the Warriors stuff the Bobcats for no gain, then block a field goal attempt.

"Let's go, Warriors, let's go, Warriors," the cheerleaders implore. The crowd joins in.

Liv elbows me in the ribs. "My God, Five, look down there!" She points to the cheerleaders, where a familiar blonde head bounces up and down above a scarlet cheerleader costume.

"Is that Blondie?" Livvy asked incredulously.

"Our little secret," Culden says. "We lost a model and gained a student. She's even shaving her legs."

• • •

Evermont Nixon drives the Warriors for three first downs, and the crowd is delirious until an interception turns the ball over. But Piotrowski and Strawn, Bear's 'bookends from the coalfields,' sack the OU quarterback twice and hold once more, to force the Bobcats to punt.

A decent return by Herb Stover, one of the black running backs from Wheeling, puts Seneca into OU territory for the first time.

Monty Nixon's second pass is a beauty, hitting Herm Bristo on the OU ten. Nixon then rolls out and passes to Culcaine, one of last year's Warriors, for the score. Quickly, the Warriors are up 7-0 over mighty OU.

The excitement is far from over. Nixon passes for two touchdowns and runs for one, to give Seneca a 28-0 lead going into the final quarter. The Bobcats mount a drive but stall on the Seneca 20, and manage a field goal for the final score.

It seems like the beginning of a golden year.

• • •

On the porch of Five's Five, we all sit around sipping Old Bristo and reliving the day's events. Tibby Bristo is excited to see Livvy's engagement ring, and gives each of us a big hug and kiss.

"When's the wedding, Five?" Benjo asks.

Livvy and I smile at each other and embrace.

"Oh, sometime in April," I say evasively. "Livvy wants to serve ramps at the reception."

• • •

This will probably be my last book. After all, nobody wants to read the adventures of an old married couple.

Five Lowrey

James Patterson
Largo, Florida
Wednesday, January 14, 2004

About the Author

James Patterson lived many lives before he passed away May 28, 2004 while photographing Monet's gardens in Giverny, France. He served with the Army's Counterintelligence Corp in the final days of the Cuban Missile Crisis, and on administrative staffs of three universities. Patterson was a 1958 graduate of Ohio University in Athens, Ohio. He drew extensively upon those experiences to create *The Thirteen, Sphinxes*, and *The Lazarus Pit*.

Patterson was a writer, journalist, graphic designer, traveler, and photographer. He won numerous international awards for writing, photography, and design. He was also a freelance travel photojournalist and wrote for computer, photography, and graphic arts magazines. He lived in Largo, Florida, with his wife, Betty.

Printed in the United States
90088LV00001B/8/A